I0772314

A Reckoning of Cinders

Ryan Elledge

For Grayson,
this book, and everything that follows.
It's all for him.

OTHER BOOKS BY RYAN ELLEDGE

A Balance of Shade and Radiance
The Light of Shadows
A Reckoning of Cinders

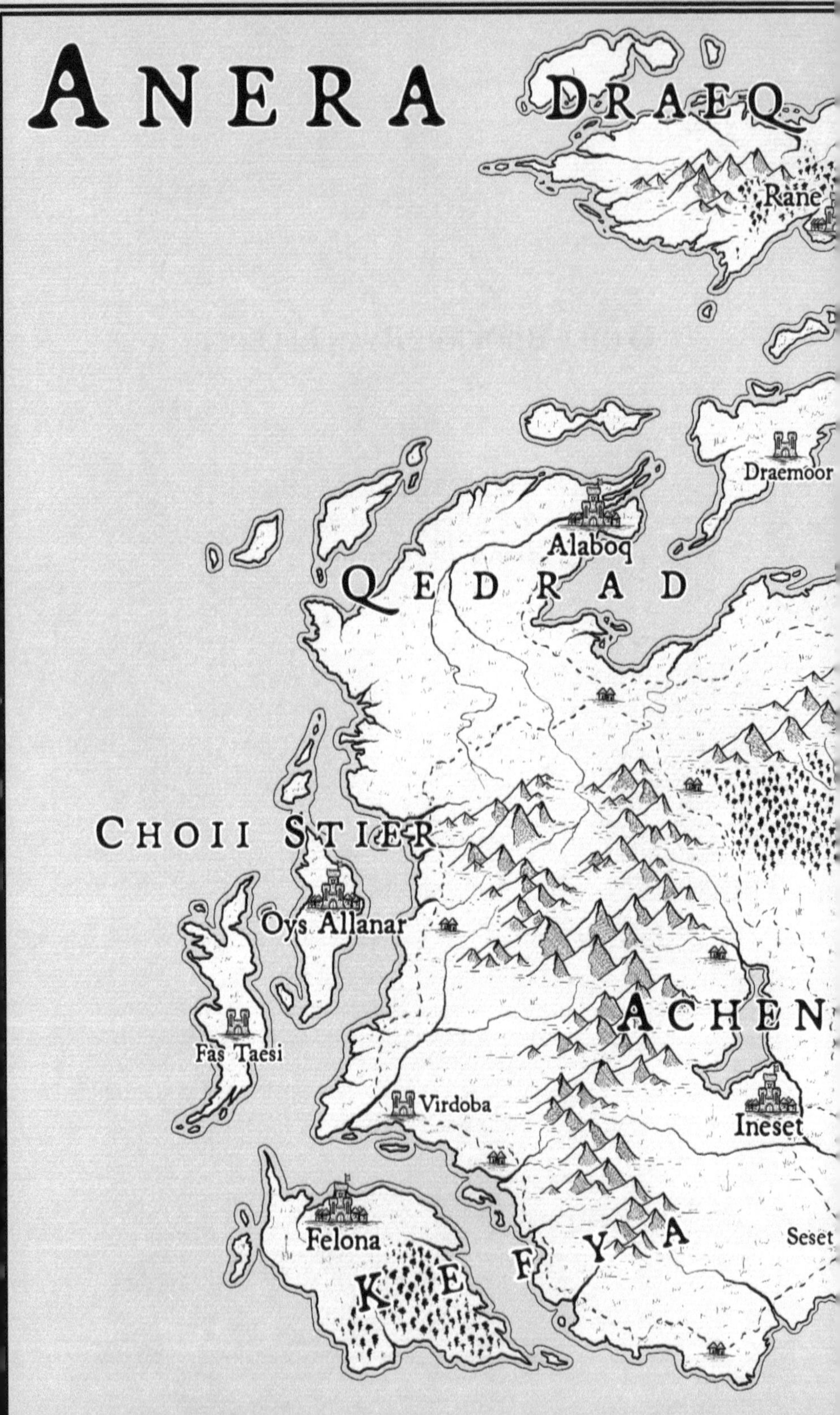

ANERA DRAEQ
Rane
Draemoor
Alaboq
QEDRAD
CHOII STIER
Oys Allanar
Fas Taesi
ACHEN
Virdoba
Ineset
Felona
KEFYA
Seset

Qravburn
Brey
DESTUEQA
Havine
EBKARII
Oretol
Woross

CITY OF
Felona
CYANCAP RIVER
BINDWEED CONSERVATORY
THE TROUGH
SEASPRAY THICKET
LEROS' PATH
THE CREST
THE RELIQUARY
THE TROUGH
THE HORN AND PLANKS
THE TANGLED VINES
N

PROLOGUE

The light patter of blood dripping onto the stone floor was a needle driving into Tetamii's head. It pierced through the pounding of his heart, as if his body could not be bothered to drown out the sounds of what he had done. Tetamii wanted to wrench his eyes shut, but he knew what Vulmar Magzii would do to him if he turned away. The frozen remains of a balding barrister lay discarded at the foot of the stairs, underlining that threat—the consequences of trying to offer payment for a kind gesture at the wrong time. Portions of the man's skin were black and cracked, his eyes brittle and fixed unblinkingly on Tetamii with his icy mouth agape. This was the fate that would await him should he fail.

Even now, Magzii stood behind him, arms crossed against a broad chest as he stared down at Tetamii expectantly. A chill crept down Tetamii's spine, but whether that was a gentle reminder from Magzii to finish what he had started or just the effects of the man's stern glare, Tetamii had no clue.

Either way, he knew his task. He had known it would lead to this from the moment the Clipped Gulls plucked him out of that back alley. Tetamii just hadn't imagined it would be this hard.

Sitting in front of him, slumped over in a chair with only taut coils of rope wrapped around his torso to hold him upright, was a handsome elven man. His once fine emerald coat was now tattered and bloodied. The man coughed and sputtered, sending more blood down onto the gray floor.

A cadre of Gulls surrounded their prisoner, some of them laughing and jostling those around them in anticipation. Others, though, merely trimmed their fingernails with daggers, eyes occasionally landing on the prisoner before sliding away, as if he were no more important than a piece of firewood soon to be split or a chicken about to have its neck snapped. Conversation over the weather dominated the room, and from the top of the stairs, someone hummed a jaunty tune. Tetamii swallowed, his breath coming faster. He was to end a man's life, and those around him were bored.

But that was the whole point of this initiation, wasn't it? *Desensitizing us from society's weaknesses.* That's what Magzii had called it. Maybe that dulling would happen soon, but Tetamii feared it would only come after he had pulled the blade out.

"Well," Magzii said, "we haven't got all day, son. You did a good job getting the fancy man here, and the rest of the family have done their part. He's all trussed up and drugged out of his gourd, so no need to worry about any indoor storms striking you dead where you stand." Tetamii felt the temperature around him plummet, his ragged, quick breaths suddenly visible in the previously humid basement. "No use delaying the inevitable. Are you going to be welcomed into the fold, or did I make a mistake when I pulled you from your filthy hovel?"

Magzii leaned forward, his breath leaving frozen flecks of ice on the side of Tetamii's face that stung like miniature daggers digging into his flesh. "Don't you remember what *respectable* men like this did to your mother and father?"

It was true: men just like this one had come and stolen his father from them one afternoon. Surrounded by a squadron of Felona's finest, men in silk coats and shined leather shoes had burst into Tetamii's small family home and shackled his father right in front of him. Tetamii could remember a clenching in his gut as shouts were levied back and forth about money that was owed to the city, could still vividly recall the vein on his father's temple near to bursting as he pleaded for his freedom. Tetamii had only ever seen that blood vessel when he was being scolded, but now it was tied to panicked commotion and a sudden invasion of his safety. He hadn't understood most of the details; it had all happened several years ago, and Tetamii was only now in his eleventh summer.

But what he could understand were his mom's tears, her fists beating fruitlessly against their breastplates as the soldiers hauled her husband away. He could also understand that with his father locked up, there would be no way for his mother to come up with the interest. Not that it mattered; she died of fisherman's lung the next winter, a week after they learned Tetamii's father had been killed in prison.

He had spent the next few years getting by however he could on food scraps and the occasional kindness of strangers, but that only ever extended to pocket change or the last crumbs of a meal. No, no matter how deep the pockets of these fine coats went, the men wearing them never seemed to be able to reach deep enough into them for his benefit.

But then Magzii and his Clipped Gulls had come along and taught him how to plunge the depths of those pockets himself.

The training was grueling, long hours and the constant threat of a Felonian guardsman's cudgel only rewarded by a cold cot that was somehow both loosely strung and hard as iron. But it was a better sleeping arrangement than curling up under an awning with the rats, and at least Tetamii now had company, people to spend the day with that weren't competing with him for food and drink. Sure, the Gulls might hit a mark before he could, robbing his target blind and leaving him with nothing but a disappointed glance from Magzii for his efforts. Those looks stung worse than the hunger pains—Magzii didn't offer failures their morning or evening portions—but nothing compared to the hard-won pats on the back or invitations to join the veteran Gulls for a round or three of ale. Their leader doled out such praise sparingly. When it came his way, Tetamii knew he had truly earned it.

Magzii's methods were mercurial. Punishment and praise were always around the corner, because Tetamii never knew when he was being watched, when he was being compared to the other desperate initiates, but Tetamii couldn't argue with the results. Magzii was a self-made man, having built a family from the dregs of Felona into one of the city's most potent factions. However unpredictable and harsh the lessons, they taught him that he had to be better than everyone around him to get by in this world of self-absorbed lords and ladies.

But this man had been different. The wounded man before him had shown Tetamii another side of the aristocracy, one that actually tried to live by the example set by Teacher Irasil. Charitable outreach, not out of pity but out of a desire to create a better world for all who shared it with us. Every gift or donation Tetamii had been given since his parents were ripped from him had been offered only with some precondition, some string attached. He had lost count of how many times he had spied on a business rival or roughed up another thieving child just to repay someone for their leftover table scraps. But the man seated before him, the man Tetamii had delivered into this den of vipers himself, had only ever been kind to him. His dagger felt heavy in his hand as he twisted the hilt over and over.

Vulmar Magzii stepped in front of Tetamii and squatted, his silver-ringed irises catching the light from the flickering sconces on the wall. His eyes were striking, and like most of their kind, the man would be judged attractive by most of their human neighbors. He had waves of dark hair cascading down to his shoulders, one of the mandated styles to any member of the Gulls. Clothes that wouldn't pass muster in the Crest or the Bindweed Conservatory diminished his appearance only slightly, though they were certain-ly more clean and well-tailored than any worn by his comrades in the room.

But this close the imperfections that came with a life of merce-nary work were readily apparent. Scars that were just a shade lighter than his alabaster skin decorated his face and neck, and one corner of his mouth no longer rose as high as the other, so his grin was more off-putting than comforting.

"It's all right, son," Magzii said, laying a heavy hand on Tetamii's shoulder. "You've done us a service as it is. This Crester prick was going to turn into a real pain in my ass if the election goes the way everyone is expecting it to." The man turned and laughed at the doubled over elf as he coughed and sputtered more blood onto the floor.

"I have to hand it to the man, he does have a honeyed tongue. Not so much after a sizable helping of the Smuggler's Hood in his tea, but that can't be helped. Left alone, he would've wrapped the whole city around his little finger and brought down the law on all the nooks and crannies I've established for us over the years."

Magzii gave Tetamii's shoulder a pat and sent a bone-chilling jolt into his chest. Tetamii bit down on his cheek to avoid a gasp. Then, the man stood to face their captive. "As it stands, he's already done too much to bring curious eyes our way, and that can't go unpunished."

The temperature in the room dropped further, crimson crys-tals forming in the pool of blood below the bound man as the rivulets running down his face hardened into bloody icicles.

"It is a shame, though," Magzii continued. "I saw a fire in you, boy, more than your connection to the World Shroud. You and I, we could've made something of ourselves; grown this ragtag bunch of cutthroats into a force the Council couldn't reckon with." The man started spasming against his restraints, and Tetamii wondered what it must feel like for all the moisture in his body to slowly freeze. It must be torturous, and whatever his ilk had done to his family, *this* man didn't deserve to die in agony.

"Stop," Tetamii said, instinctively raising the ambient temperature as he pulled taut the smoky wisps of the World Shroud, drawing heat in to combat Magzii's torture technique. Tetamii had always known he had this connection to the Wellspring; when both one's parents were scorchers, it was a foregone conclusion that he would follow suit. But neither had the chance to work with him on using his power, so each time he drew heat from beyond that veil, it was haphazard and reckless. Thankfully, this time he seemed to have reached the desired effect as Magzii turned back to him, face unreadable.

"Did you say something?" Magzii asked, the tiniest of twitches flickering one eyebrow before his stoicism returned.

Tetamii stepped forward, blade heavy in his hand but his strength bolstered with new resolve. "I'll do it," he said, stepping past the leader of the Clipped Gulls while the other thugs in attendance murmured their assent. Everyone was impressed by him, and while the whole situation felt wrong, Tetamii had already seen what awaited him on the other side of his initiation. He had watched other children welcomed as brothers and sisters in this very room, changing immediately from desperate urchins into lifelong, blood-bound family in a round of cheers and bear hugs.

Tetamii's last embrace had been lying next to his mother on her deathbed.

Stopping just before the bound man, Tetamii tightened his grip on the hilt of his dagger and steadied his breath. Another racking cough sent more flecks of blood onto the floor and the top of one of his new boots—the pair this man had purchased for him just days ago. Shakily, the elf lifted his head to look up at Tetamii, his once smooth silky hair now hanging lank and matted in front of his eyes. Blue-ringed irises flashed, and Tetamii almost leaped out of his skin before he remembered the man had been drugged. He wouldn't be raining down lightning any time soon, or ever again.

Instead, this flash was one that he recognized. It was the effortless glance that the man always had at the ready, a twinkle in his eyes that let anyone he was speaking to know that he truly cared about what they had to say. Tetamii's stomach turned.

"Listen," the man said, his voice hoarse but unmistakably powerful. "Whatever these people make you do, whoever they tell you that you are, remember this. You are a good person, Tetamii. No one has to be defined by the worst thing they've done. Not as long as they try to do better." His eyes went wide as a rush of blood spat out over his chin, but he still managed a small smile and nod before Tetamii pulled the blade out of his gut.

Magzii chuckled. "I knew you were special, kid. Welcome to the Clipped Gulls."

PART I

Chapter 1

Off the Western Aneran Coast

"Haven't been on a ship to Felona at this time of year. Cooler than I thought it would be," the gruff voice said, muffled by the oak door that sealed all but the faintest line of light from creeping into his dungeon. Tetamii could not recall how long he had been aboard this vessel; King Berenqar's poisoner had seen to that. Careful dosing of the hidden hand's infused poisons every day kept Tetamii in a gossamer-like consciousness, unable to keep track of how long he spent awake, much less remember how many days—weeks?—he had been at sea.

This lack of self-continuity was a pittance, though, when compared to the torturous deprivation the tinctures of severing were exacting on him.

Since he was a boy, the curling tendrils of the World Shroud danced at his call, the raging inferno contained just beyond that veil always mere moments from summoning forth on a whim. But with each vial of that callous elf's concoction—Smuggler's Hood, as the Clipped Gulls called it—the familiar warmth he had always known was torn away from him. It was as if his captors had rammed hot pokers into his eyes or ripped his tongue from his mouth; one of the fundamental ways Tetamii experienced the world was simply gone.

For now, he struggled to remind himself. But how many times had he reminded himself of that fact? How many times had he been forced to think through his predicament before another wave of sedation pushed him back down below the blackness waiting to embrace him again.

"It can't be a tropical paradise year-round, spongebrain," another voice said, this one feminine. "Winter is winter. Just don't be expecting to make any snowballs, they probably haven't had any snow . . ." The voice began to drift off into infuriating mumbles as unconsciousness beckoned to him. Waves lapping against the side of the ship became a soothing lullaby. Tetamii fought it at first, desperately searching for the wisps in his vision that would allow him to blow this ship to cinders. He would swim to shore if need be. But he had been blinded, and he sank back onto his heels, letting the chains from either wall droop as his arms went slack.

For now . . .

***

The resonant warbles of coastal swallows pierced through the mental fog, and Tetamii forced his eyes open once again. His calves screamed in tingling agony, knees burning as he took in his surroundings. He was seated back on his heels in a dark, barren room. No seating, no wardrobe, not even a simple cot to be found, and he was dressed in his underclothes, though they had not seen soap in some time. He brought his hand down to push himself up, and his wrist snapped back with a metallic *clang*. Handcuffed to the wall, as was his other arm, without enough slack in the chains to stand from this miserable position.

A memory bobbed to the inky surface of his mind. A grand hall after the Qedradan fashion, the floor gleaming with painted geometric lines that he stared down at in this same position, while just yards away a small group of people sat at a long banquet table and decided his fate. A prisoner—that's what he was now. On his way to face justice in Felona for the schemes of other men. That was the trouble with mercenary work; one always made a convenient scapegoat for the person holding the purse strings.

"Is it that time already?" a woman's voice asked from behind the door in front of him. "I guess I shouldn't be questioning it. I'd rather you give him too much of that stuff than not enough."

A heavy latch clicked, and the door swung inward, followed by a sturdy human sailor wearing simple clothing and a tie of fabric holding his unruly hair back into a tail. He acknowledged Tetamii with a sneer, then shifted aside to hold the door open and said, "Yes, Garla. Let's not question the man keeping us from ending up as a drift of soggy ashes along the bottom of the Marrow Strait."

The hallway beyond was lit by evenly spaced lanterns, and just through the threshold stood Garla, an elven woman in similar workman's clothing and wearing a knit cap, who looked as if she could have rowed a ship this size on her own. There weren't many other elves who looked like a physical match for Tetamii, but even he would give pause before trading blows with someone like her.

Her golden-ringed eyes met his with an even expression before she looked up at the elven man next to her. "He's all yours, Lord Tragala."

To her left stood a slightly taller elven man, though his physique was waifish in comparison to hers. He wore a crisp black doublet over matching trousers, each contrasting severely with his pale skin. The light from the lanterns beyond him glinted off his shaved head as he strode into the room, a slight uptick at the side of his mouth the only emotion displayed on his face.

"And how are we this morning, Mr. Fiadar?" the man asked, hands clasped behind his back.

"Fffeh . . ." Tetamii managed before the effort caused his vision to swim. His tongue was thick and heavy, almost rooted to his gums.

The elf tutted, kneeling with spindly legs to look him in the eyes. "Now we've talked about this. Etiquette is always worth the effort, and I've never insisted on titles. The proper response is 'I am well, Ubadrii. And how are you?'"

From behind his back he pulled forth a thin vial, the glowing liquid inside shifting from one hue to the next by the second. "But I suppose your instruction *has* been impaired over this journey. Perhaps I've been a tad heavy with the infusions, but I do so enjoy caressing the World Shroud, teasing out its power into my creations. You understand that, don't you? How easy it is to lose yourself in the sheer immensity of it all?" Ubadrii's smile curled to meet the bald elf's crimson-ringed eyes for the first time. "You haven't already forgotten, have you?"

Translucent whisps flickered in and out of perception throughout the room as Tetamii reached out for them in desperation. But each time he thought he had a hold on one, each time he pictured a searing lance of fire erupting from the air to consume the hidden hand's smug face, the tendril slipped away, disappearing into his drug-induced haze.

Ubadrii pulled open Tetamii's lower jaw and unstoppered the vial with his thumb before pouring the liquid into his mouth. Tetamii didn't struggle; he wouldn't give the man that satisfaction. Its taste shifted as often as its color—charred bitter roots, brackish water, astringent spoiled dairy—nothing pleasant. A fresh wave of numbness to the World Shroud crashed over him with such force that his ears rang and his eyes clouded, the pain in his knees almost vanishing for a moment. A sense had been closed off with such force that his mind scrambled his others.

The hidden hand patted Tetamii's cheek lightly, and he was able to focus his gaze once again on the man's cold smirk. "This isn't a permanent arrangement, assassin. Once the Council in Felona passes judgment on you, you will be placed under their care. I'm certain one of their hidden hands will be able to seal you from your abilities without leaving you hovering above a puddle of your own drool."

Ubadrii stood, stepped back a pace and shrugged. "I know I could, I'm just not inclined to do so. There are consequences for attempts on my sovereign's life, after all."

The sailor holding the door chuckled. "You think he'll still be able to flip on that nobleman? The bastard seems like he may not ever be able to speak again."

Ubadrii patted the man's shoulder as he walked from the room. "He'll find his tongue when I need him to, don't worry. And all this ugly business will be concluded."

Spitting on the floor in front of Tetamii's lap, the sailor swung the door closed. Garla's eyes beyond the threshold stayed locked on his even as Tetamii struggled to keep his eyelids open. By the time the latch clicked shut, his mind had followed suit.

***

Kymil had spent much of the journey along Anera's western coast attempting to entertain himself and others, all the while harboring a festering boredom in his mind that threatened to consume him. He had traveled great distances by boat before, but there had always been distractions aplenty on board the pleasure vessels he usually selected—or he had provided his own. But Captain Tomau ran a tight, boring ship, with the supply of booze dwindling precipitously in the first week of the voyage and not a single crewman seemingly inclined to indulge Kymil's charms.

Matters had not been helped by his uncharacteristically troubled mind. He had taken his recent amputation at the tip of the scorcher's bastard sword in stride, at least outwardly, and he had managed to avoid losing a step in his musical performances despite the loss of his limb. However, there was a part of Kymil that scrutinized his listeners' faces now, searching for signs of pity or—worse—awe. He wanted his audience to come away entertained, but he couldn't stomach being the bard who was "good for playing one-handed."

At times, he saw his father's chiseled face in the crowd of sailors, sneering at the thought of how difficult his son's "flighty and feminine" career would be now that he was down a hand. Kymil had put in too many hours and given up much that was dear to him in an effort to prove that callous man wrong, to show that he could make a life for himself from his passions, regardless of how much it "embarrassed the family." But if his skill was now limited to a side-show act, the pity purses would dry up once the gimmick grew stale, and he shuddered at the notion that he might have to return to Liiashae, dragging his lute through the dirt behind him as he trudged toward the chastisement awaiting him.

So, each evening began with a lively performance for his friends to disrupt the monotony—and prove to himself that his talent was still intact—only for Kymil to find himself back in his quarters, praying to Teachers Faaras and Melan for anything of interest to occur while he tuned out Mareq's nauseous belches from the bunk below.

He would have to have a word with those deities, though, because having their ship broadsided by what was now decidedly *not* another merchant vessel made for poor entertainment.

Another barrage of cannon fire sent wooden and iron shrapnel flying into the air. Kymil could hear screams from below deck as the metal spheres ripped through the hull and into the belly of the ship. Some of his friends were down there, and he felt a pit form in his chest at the thought of a cannonball tearing into Anni-ka—or even Ubadrii—but there was a more immediate concern. Heavy metallic *clunks* sounded along the deck as grappling hooks buried into the gunwale, one directly in front of him.

This time it was Kymil's turn to feel sick to his stomach, but he didn't think the infused herbs in Mareq's pouch would do him much good. There would be no forgetting the coppery smell of blood that splashed across his face as he whipped his stiletto-bladed cloak forward at the sun-worn man scrambling over the railing. Kymil planted a once pristine suede boot into the man's chest and kicked him overboard, still clutching the laceration across his throat.

Kymil didn't want to be in the hero business—that kind of work was far too messy and exhausting—but since he had decided to tag along with this crew, it was as if the Dawn Ones were telling him he was meant to be the subject of legends, not their purveyor. And what choice did he have when raving pirates had boarded their vessel?

Other areas of the ship had not been so capably defended, as a dozen or more bedraggled men and women teemed over the side, with the footsteps of more of their compatriots scaling the hull behind them. Within seconds, several of Tomau's crewman were skewered by cutlasses or dropped by crossbow bolts, and panicked cries consumed the deck. The crew of the *Fortune's Rose* were brawny and efficient to a man, but trained fighters they were not.

"What is happening? Am I clear to make a break for the hold?" Mareq shouted over the scrapes of steel and screams. There was more than a slight tremble in his voice, but not many would see the draqeshi's fear as clearly as Kymil. Short and broad, his friend was huddled down behind the longboat, look-ing like just another piece of heavy equipment on the deck. But there was a whirling torrent of terror behind that solid exterior.

"I suppose clear is relative," Kymil answered, bringing his bladed cloak back around in his left hand, the dozen stiletto daggers hanging from the hem now coated in pirate blood. Not bad for his off-hand. Necessity had been a quick teacher. "But there is a nice trail toward that door between the dead bodies if you can be quick about it."

Mareq darted out from behind the longboat, stepping deftly over dropped weapons and around pooling blood to reach the door into the stairwell, with Kymil right on his heels. All around them Captain Tomau's sailors fought bravely, having rallied at the sight of their leader on the quarterdeck above. The captain lashed out with a rapier that gleamed in the sunlight, no knicks or smudges in the metal to dull the reflection. Surrounded by three angry ravagers, Tomau was holding his own, but Kymil doubted he would for much longer, and his crews' utility knives weren't meant for open conflict against men with more traditional weapons. Still, they had the invaders outnumbered, and Kymil hoped the pirates would have sense enough to fall back in the face of a larger force.

"Aagh," Mareq yelped as he dropped into a slide along the deck. In front of him was a pirate with a long ugly scar tracing down her cheek and through her lips, brandishing a gore-coated cutlass in either hand. His friend's boot caught on a warped plank, sending him into more of a tumble than a slide and spiraling him enough off course that the woman's quick downward stab missed Mareq by a hair. Kymil was on her before she had another opportunity to run Mareq through, but this was a seasoned fighter, and she had been ready for him.

Her second cutlass stabbed forward at Kymil's torso but found only a fold in his cloak as he twisted to the side, her sword passing harmlessly through the space his right arm would've been. For a moment, though, he could feel the honed edge of the blade rip into phantom flesh, feel tendons and muscle sever as they had when the scorcher's blade split his arm in half like kindling. Unfortunately, some parts of his mind had not yet received the message that he was down an appendage.

Completing his turn, Kymil brought his cloak around and forward like a whip, stiletto blades slicing the air so quickly that they whistled. The woman stepped back in time to avoid the worst of the damage, but a few of the daggers dug deep into her forearm as the violet fabric tangled itself around her wrist and the weapon's hilt.

Luminescent tendrils still flitted around his cloak, though not as brightly or energetically as they had before the assault; his luck would not be infinite. It was enough for now, though, as a deft snap of his wrist popped the cutlass out of the pirate's grip. The weapon clattered to the wood below, and Kymil made to sweep it away with his boot before being pulled off balance by the still-bound woman, his years of acrobatic performances the only thing keeping him on his feet.

With a sharp *whoosh* the other cutlass swung up in a wide arc, cleaving the cloak in two and causing Kymil to land hard on his back against a crate of rope. The swirling lights around the fabric dissipated in an instant, his infusion finally running out.

The pirate smiled, her teeth far cleaner than Kymil would've expected from a woman who spent her life at sea. "Nice moves, showman. Pity there won't be an encore." She pulled her other cutlass back to stab at his middle but screamed and toppled forward as Mareq sliced her dropped weapon across the folds of her legs.

The woman fell in a heap on top of Kymil, who wrapped his arm around her neck and squeezed. "Thanks for the compliment," he hissed through gritted teeth. "But I'm starting to think I should learn some new tricks before more parts of me are sliced off."

She kicked and squirmed but couldn't find the leverage with the newly severed tendons in her legs, and eventually her movements slowed before coming to a stop. In time, she would wake—hopefully in the brig—but for now, the immediate threat was ended.

Mareq shifted her unconscious form off Kymil with little effort and offered a hand. "We need to keep moving," he said, pulling Kymil to his feet. "Annika and Ubadrii are still in their quarters, and I doubt they'll fare as well as we have on their own."

"Right," Kymil said as he picked up the tattered remnants of his cloak and opened the door, taking the stairs two at a time. "We've really shown them the error of challenging us. These pirates will surely think twice before attacking the one-armed bard and his lucky friend. Maybe stay behind me from now on, though? At least until I get a chance to infuse your boots again."

Mareq muttered something about Kymil touching his things, but silenced himself as the pair reached the end of the stairwell. Blood soaked the walls and little flames flickered along the corridor, only interrupted by the doors that had been kicked open and wrenched off their hinges. Sounds of heavy furniture scraping against floorboards came from the end of the hall.

"That's Annika's room," Mareq shouted as he bounded ahead of Kymil, who raced after him.

Legs almost as long as his friend was tall couldn't match the draqeshi's burst of speed, though, so Mareq got to the door first and shouldered it open, revealing the struggle within. One of the invaders had made it below deck and now pinned Ubadrii down on top of a large oak table with one forearm over the elf's throat. The hidden hand's feet could still reach the ground, and each kick propelled the table away from his assailant, but the pirate had an iron grip. In the attacker's other hand was a small crossbow, aimed across the room at where Annika sat, unperturbed by the circumstances.

As the door clattered against the inside wall, the man turned and fired a bolt. A human would've been caught directly in the sternum, but the bolt passed harmlessly over Mareq's head and lodged itself in Kymil's left shoulder as he squeezed past his friend.

Seeing an opening, Annika launched a thick leather tome across the room that landed with a *thud* on the pirate's hip. It wasn't much, but the blow had taken the man by enough surprise that Kymil could close the distance and stab at him with one of his stiletto daggers. Swirling a bladed cloak around without luck imbued in the material was a recipe for self-inflicted lacerations, so he would have to settle for the knives' more pedestrian use.

Kymil was never much for one-on-one combat, though, despite his father's best efforts at bare-knuckled discipline, and the pirate sidestepped his strike with ease. Tossing his empty crossbow aside, the man threw an elbow into Kymil's gut, knocking the breath from his lungs. He doubled over, wheezing.

Ubadrii was still pinned to table, his pale face turning blue while Mareq stood defensively in front of Annika. Kymil met Ubadrii's eyes, nearly popping out of the elf's skull with his efforts to inhale. "No . . . breath . . ." the poisoner sputtered as he continued to slam the back of his boot harder and harder on the floor.

Yeah. I understand the predicament.

Kymil wheezed before a wide backhand cracked across his jaw and sent him to the floor. Ubadrii's kicking grew more frantic, and Kymil glanced up just in time to see a portion of the elf's sole dislodge with a spring mechanism, sending a tawny powder spraying out around them.

Oh, "don't breathe," he thought as he rolled away from the pair, fighting the fire in his chest that was screaming at him to gulp in fresh air.

The pirate coughed as he inhaled much of the tan cloud, then staggered back and began to scream. His eyes were wide as he slapped at his arms, chest, and face. He ripped the cloth wrap from his head and tore chunks of hair from his scalp before finally digging fingernails into his skin and gouging out deep furrows of flesh, tearing open his shirt for better access to his torso. Crimson streaks marring much of his body, the pirate ran shrieking from the room and lunged into an open flame, rolling in the cinders as he continued to carve away at himself.

"Phantasmal Infestation," Ubadrii said as he stood, gingerly rubbing his throat. "Such a dramatic result from infusing dried honeycomb, but you never can know when it might be of use."

The screams from the corridor quieted as Ubadrii pulled the bolt from Kymil's arm, using a handkerchief to slow the bleeding. No major vessels seemed to have been hit, but he was tiring of taking damage to the source of his livelihood.

"Perhaps I should've gone off with Ravael and Wymund," he said, wincing as the hidden hand tightened the makeshift tourniquet. "They would be doing a better job of keeping my blood inside where it belongs. Had I known I would be thrust into the hero's role on this voyage, I would've leaped overboard weeks ago."

"I seem to recall those two being present when you lost your arm," Mareq said, helping Annika to her feet. "At least you're still in one piece."

"There's no time for your tittering," Annika said, brushing past the three men and out into the hall. "Didn't you see?"

The woman hobbled over to the body of the man who had held her captive, favoring her left hip; of course, she would've tried to defend herself when he initially broke in. As bullheaded as she claimed Rav to be, Annika could hold her own. Her weathered hand pointed down to the man's ears as she stooped over him, the severed tips of his ears visible despite the flames.

"No," Ubadrii breathed before sprinting out of the room, running headlong up the stairs and back toward the chaos above deck.

Annika had filled them in on the Clipped Gulls and their jobs in Felona. They had integrated themselves into many facets of everyday life in the city, and anything from intimidation to assassination was on the table for the organization. But based on her understanding, the Gulls had more than enough funding. Attacking and looting a merchant vessel made little sense. But maybe that wasn't the goal.

"Stay together and bar the door," Kymil shouted to the two who remained as he chased after Ubadrii. "I'm not in the mood to compose a funeral dirge." Their calls of protestations were quickly subsumed by the din of battle as he emerged from the stairwell.

***

Screams and explosions sounded from the deck above, and outside the walls Tetamii could hear heavy splashes into the sea. But it wasn't the cacophony that brought him back to consciousness, it was something more familiar than that—something that had been missing for an unknowable amount of time.

Fire—he could feel the heat radiating down into the room and from beyond the oak door, smell the dark smoke as it curled below the gap and filled his nostrils. He coughed, weakened abdominal muscles cramping at the sudden effort, but welcomed it just the same. Tetamii thrived in flames. His captors would soon learn just how hot a ship could burn.

Invigorated, Tetamii strained against the manacles holding him in place. The metal was affixed to the walls with four heavy bolts on either side, though, and the restraints did not move an inch. He screamed, yanking the chains harder and harder until his vision began to swim. Too much exertion while under the effects of Ubadrii's concoction—or was it? The room wasn't spinning, nor was he fighting to keep his eyes open. The movement dancing across his vision was not vertigo, but rather the curling tendrils of the World Shroud that he had not witnessed for some time.

Whatever was going on above, it had delayed the hidden hand's dosing schedule.

That did not mean Tetamii felt restored, though. With each attempt to reach out to the veil, the wisps slipped through his grasp. It was as if he was trying to capture a fistful of smoke. He guessed his full strength would return in time, but this may be his only opportunity. Tetamii folded the membrane into a loop at the wall to his right with an agonizing amount of caution; working any faster would only increase the odds that the World Shroud would drift away from him again. But finally he closed the loop and could feel the familiar heat begin to climb within the membranous bubble.

He began to sweat, more from concentration than the temperature. If he lost his hold on the veil now, the pressure within the fold would plummet and there would be no explosion. Each second passed by like an hour until he could feel the bubble tremble against the pressure that had built within, and with a precision he had honed over decades, he punctured the membrane.

The explosion wasn't impressive. In fact, it would have been an embarrassment at any other time. But under the circumstances, Tetamii was filled with pride as he watched a chunk of oak blow away from the wall, allowing the chain to drop loose. He tried to stand but stumbled to his knees as the room did begin to spin in his vision this time; there was no chance he could pull off another maneuver like that and remain conscious.

"What in Melan's dark waters is going on in th—" the male sailor started to shout from beyond the door before he was interrupted by a loud *thud*.

Tetamii held his breath and struggled to his feet, unsteady but prepared as he gripped a loop of the chain dangling off his right hand. A few moments passed before the door swung open and slammed against the wall, propelled forward by the sailor's dead weight, now slumped across the threshold with a fishhook-like sickle rammed up into his back. Garla gingerly stepped over the man, no urgency in her movements despite the sounds of battle raging above and the flames dancing behind her in the hall.

"Oh good, you managed to get one arm free. I really wasn't looking forward to prying both plates off the walls." Garla retrieved the curved blade from the man's back. "We'll have to find a key before we go overboard, though. In your state, I'm not sure you'll make it ashore as it is, but definitely not with those chains dragging you under."

"What . . ." was all Tetamii could manage.

"Shhh. Save your energy for the swim," Garla said as she stuck the tip of her sickle behind the manacle plate and wrenched it free from the wall. "I could probably keep you afloat and backstroke us to land with my other arm, but that just sounds exhausting. Besides," she added, pulling her knit cap off and revealing the severed tips of her ears before her chin-length, golden-brown hair fell into place. "Magzii says you're special. I want to see just how much."

***

Circumstances had not improved in Kymil's time below deck, with much of Tomau's crew now lying dead or wounded on the blood-stained oak. Those who remained upright were either tending to their fallen or pushing the invaders back, though the ground they were gaining seemed to be given rather than earned. The pirates were leaving, heaving sacks of stolen goods over the side and into the boarding vessels waiting below before they followed over the side.

They could've taken the entire ship, but they were never here for that. Spotting Ubadrii across the deck descending another stairwell to the hold, Kymil followed, knowing what they would find.

There had never been any need for a proper brig, but Tetamii's improvised cell had done its job, thanks to full-time monitoring and Ubadrii's infusions. However, as Kymil caught up to the poisoner at the end of a long corridor, heavily shadowed by the dying embers littering the path, he finally saw what was waiting for them.

The bald elf stood over the crumpled corpse of a sailor with a wound in his back, his head hanging low as he rested his face in his palm. There were two holes in the cell's walls where the chains had once been attached, one of which appeared to have been blown open by the scorcher himself.

"I was late with the next dose," Ubadrii muttered as Kymil arrived to stand next to him.

He placed a hand on Ubadrii's shoulder. "It's not as if you weren't otherwise occupied, my friend. They would've gotten their man out with or without his connection restored." But Kymil felt the gnawing pit form in his stomach, too. All these weeks transporting a murderous sociopath back to Felona to face persecution, and they had only managed to reunite him with his allies.

Chapter 2

The Tesigan Peaks

The wind bit through the layers of fur and leather as if they were silk, and Rav's boots had long since given up any ability to retain heat. Sometime around the middle of their second week scaling the mountain range, all the cold weather supplies they had obtained from Ormuq lost their effectiveness. It taught her a valuable lesson: Draqesh temperature thresholds were vastly different from her own. Even Wymund was struggling in his own stoic way, his jaw clenched tighter and tighter with each trudging footfall in the snow.

"Do you think all draqesh winter gear is useless at this altitude?" Rav shouted above the flurry. "Or do you think living so long with a winterborn wife has altered his perception of freezing one's ass off?"

"Ormuq and Tiialya were kind enough to outfit us with these furs," he said through chattering teeth. "We should be grateful for the coin they saved us. Stocking up in Alaboq would've cost us more than our purses combined." He slipped on a patch of ice, dropping to a knee momentarily before righting himself. "Though a warning about air and frost permeability would've been appreciated . . ." It was bad if even Wymund had begun complaining.

Ram's Point rose on the horizon, its crook-shaped peak growing larger at an agonizingly slow rate. But the map Mrs. Luviire provided had been accurate, at least. It had taken them half a week longer than expected to reach this point in the mountain range, but it was exactly where she said it would be. However, that was never really in question. Rav trusted dusty old maps to locate something as massive and fixed as a particular mountain. A few purchase reports and off-handed comments in a decades-old journal that alluded to a hidden school, though? That was a much more dubious proposition.

The Illumined Scale was meant to be a retreat for lightbloods at risk of overdrawing from the World Shroud, a place where they could learn to regulate the electrical energy their bodies siphoned from the Wellspring automatically, without placing their lives in danger to do so. The archives in Vinsart Hold held precious little information about the place, only reports of a man purchasing lumber and other supplies dozens of years before, but Mrs. Luviire and the old woman had thought it was in her best interest to make the journey—to avoid the Illuminated Death that Rav had already flirted with on three separate occasions, twice only surviving due to the intervention of others.

She understood Annika had already lost someone to over-siphoning, but would she feel just as bad if Rav succumbed to the elements on her way to learn how not to die? She chuckled, the air condensing and stinging her face.

That will teach her to keep her nose out of other people's business.

They forced each footfall through the hardening snow, the powder becoming more like ice with each passing step, but that wasn't what was slowing Rav's pace. Ram's Point would be within reach before nightfall, but she had been hesitant about reaching the end of their journey since Wymund had first noticed the hooked cliff a few days prior. Trepidation had taken hold of her heart as much as the bitter cold.

"We should find a spot to set up camp for the night," Rav said. "I don't want you to stumble into a crevice on the final leg because we tried to reach the summit tonight."

Wymund glanced over without slowing his pace, his face mostly obscured by a thick wool scarf, but one eyebrow clearly cocked. "I'm not spending one more night out in this tundra than I have to, Ravael. We're low on food, and I haven't felt my toes since the morning. Your concern for my safety is noted, but I'll be fine. Now keep up, siphon from the Wellspring if you must, but keep your feet moving."

"That's not how it works, and you know it," she replied. "If I could control my connection to the World Shroud, we wouldn't be near death on the side of this Irasil-damned mountain."

"Shall I get behind you and chase you with my short sword, then? Danger gets the electricity flowing."

"Danger would, yes," Rav said. "A shame you're no threat to me even in this frigid state."

Rav heard his laugh over the wind, but after a few minutes more of nothing but the sound of frozen crystals crunching under their boots, she tried again. "I want to stop, Wymund."

Her friend took a few more steps before her earnestness sunk in. Wymund turned and walked back the few steps between them. A part of her was still irked that a human stood a few inches taller than her, but the concern in his eyes snuffed that momentary cinder of jealousy.

"Are you hurt?" he asked, his gaze scanning her for any obvious injuries. "We can make another night out here work if needed. I might be able to find some rabbit, or given the name of the place, perhaps a mountain goat."

Rav smiled wanly. "No, I'm fine. And if one of us is going to be hunting with any hope of success, it would be me. I just . . . I don't belong with these people. Everything I've learned in life I've learned on my own, and not because I had to—my mother tried to enroll me in any institution that would have me. But I don't play well with others, and now the old woman expects me to sit still and listen to some stodgy lightblood explain World Shroud theory to me? I don't see that ending well."

"And you're afraid?" Wymund asked.

"Of hurting someone or killing myself by accident? Sure. You don't know how it feels to have all that energy coursing through—"

"No," he said, waving his hand to cut her off. "Of disappointing Annika." She let his words hang between them for a moment, the howling wind doing nothing to carry away their weight.

It was true. Annika's opinion of her had grown, like a tumor, from mere annoyance to strangely important. The old woman was far too similar to Rav's mother, with all the good and bad that association entailed, so of course some complicated feelings had crept into their relationship. But it wasn't just a fear of letting Annika down that made Rav want to turn on her heels and flee back down the mountain, at least not directly.

Annika's sister, Alauvar, was a witch who had drawn more power from the World Shroud than her body could handle during the Rebellions of the Commons, infusing healing serums for her allies until her last breath. Her fellows had succeeded, fighting back against what they viewed as the tyranny of Kefya's Council and forcing the creation of an elected seat on the governing body. It was a position that could speak for the voiceless citizens of the nation who had been told what to do throughout their history, first by Qedradan rulers, then indirectly by elven expats, their former alliance in the War of Arrival quickly forgotten once Kefyans began to bristle at their new neighbors' elevated noses.

Rav knew that Annika saw Alauvar in her, the woman's apparent recklessness, but also her passion. It was a compliment, to be sure, but the woman had literally changed the world through her sacrifice. How was she supposed to live up to that comparison?

"I'll take the pointed absence of a biting retort as a yes," Wymund said. "Listen, the only way you could fail her would be if you turned away now and ended up dying from your own gifts. This school sounds like your best chance to avoid that fate, since I don't see you giving up your perilous lifestyle."

"And if my more abrasive qualities lead to expulsion and failure anyway?"

"I learned a long time ago that any skill or talent in life is worth working for," Wymund said. "Otherwise, you won't appreciate what you can accomplish."

Rav decided she would allow Wymund to continue believing her anxieties were only about living up to Annika's expectations rather than the standards she had placed on herself. She was more comfortable in a competitive paradigm, where snark and attitude could shoulder past her feelings of inadequacy next to Alauvar's memory. Besides, there was enough truth in his reading of her that she didn't feel like she was deceiving him.

"I don't know," Rav replied, sighing and walking past him. "It feels good to nab a trinket or two from some rich dolt's place, and there's hardly any effort left in that for me. But for *your* sake—not hers—I'll give this 'trying' thing a shot. Maybe there's something to it."

Wymund fell in behind her and said, "When you're finished here and we meet back up with everyone in Felona, you really need to sit down with Annika and your mother to have a chat. There's a confusing tangle of issues there that I'm ill-equipped to unravel."

The next few hours were largely uneventful, though that did not make the trek feel any less arduous. Her emotional load had lightened, even if she was miffed that Wymund had read her like a book. The way she felt about Annika was wrapped up in a lifetime of miscommunications and disappointments with her mother, and it did not help matters that the old woman would be arriving in Felona long before she finished her training here in the Tesigan Peaks.

A horrifying vignette had rooted itself in her mind that she found herself replaying over and over throughout the silent ascent—her mother and Annika sitting across a table and sharing a kettle of tea, planning out the next phase of her life. It would be infuriating if she hadn't recently been taught the value of letting things go, especially when the sources of the frustration were two women who cared about her well-being. As it was, she found the thought only moderately annoying.

As they reached the final leg of their climb, the incline steepened, and their pitons came out. Rav drove the steel spikes into the icy rock, creating handholds where there were none, while Wymund did the same to her left. Her arms burned from exertion, but it did not lighten the load on her legs, as the angle of the slope demanded everything she had left in reserves. Still, though, Rav did not feel the familiar crackling heat course across her skin. For a moment, she considered flipping backward off the cliff face to see if that would force her body to tap into the Wellspring, but she couldn't trust that Wymund would not dive after her. Even with the added boost of energy from the World Shroud, she was not sure if she could catch him and haul his unwieldy form back to safety.

No. Slow, steady, and painful was the only way forward for now.

After a precarious half hour, Rav jammed a piton into the rock above and scrambled over a snow-covered lip, with Wymund following close behind. Darkness settled over the barren expanse as the sun finished its journey along the sky, dipping below the high peaks to the west and scattering deep oranges and purples across the sparkling terrain. But they had made it. The flattened tip of Ram's Point stretched out before them, and the rest of the majestic Tesigan Peaks surrounded them for as far as they could see, piercing the multihued sunset like rocky daggers. As breathtaking as the view might have been, though, Rav was distracted by the empty serenity.

"Where's the Irasil-damned school?" she asked, her footfalls crunching through the snow as she paced forward. "There's nothing up here but more snow and ice. If I'm supposed to learn something from frozen water, I could've done that about a week back!"

Wymund trudged forward to join her, his eyes narrowing as he searched the area. "I don't know, Ravael. It was supposed to be here." He ran a hand along his head, a habit he maintained even with his hair buried under layers of wool. "The records in the archive were old, though. Maybe the school moved or shut down."

"Arghhh," Rav growled, throwing her arms wide and stalking around the ice. "All this time spent scaling a mountain range, probably losing some permanent sensation in our extremities, and nothing to show for it but chapped lips and a sore ass. Meanwhile, Annika and mother are probably sitting out in the orchard, laughing and schem—"

Her rant was cut short as her foot slipped into a narrow crevice that had been obscured by a snow drift, sending half her weight crashing down as her leg dropped between the sheer rocky walls to either side. Wymund shouted, but it sounded muffled and slowed, like a drunken man yelling at a distance. Before her waist fell below the top of the crevice, she felt a surge of liquid fire erupt under her skin. Her muscles roared to life with renewed vigor, trembling to be unleashed, and she found she had drawn a piton and driven it deep into the top of the mountain before Wymund had finished his howl.

"Ravael!" Wymund shouted, racing forward into a slide and grabbing her shoulder. "Are you all right?"

"Fine," she replied, kicking off the crevice wall and joining her friend. She grimaced as a muscle at the base of her skull twinged, an early warning of what would come if her body drew too much energy from the Wellspring. "In fact, I'm great. There may as well be a giant crack up here to complete this fruitless effort. Why shouldn't the destination be as miserable as the journey?"

"Hold back that fire for a moment," he said as he gripped the piton she had driven into the ground. "This might not have been as fruitless an endeavor as we thought."

He shifted the steel spike back and forth with some effort, and Rav peered over his shoulder to see that the piton had not been jammed into rock or ice, but rather a bronze plate. Wymund pulled the climbing implement free and wiped a gloved hand over the metal, clearing the snow away to reveal a thin sheet of bronze, close to a foot square, with an etched scale on its surface. The weight pans on each side of the scale's pillar were perfectly aligned, despite one bearing three upward slashes and the other a lone line that twisted around itself. Even more strangely, the second weight pan was not depicted as connected to the scale at all, but instead was floating at the same level as its more loaded counterpart.

"One would think such a learned instructor could find a more conspicuous location to mark an entrance," Rav said.

"Perhaps locating the school is part of the lesson," Wymund said. "Like an entrance exam of sorts."

Rav sniffed. "Sounds like the place is run by a pretentious git. I thought teachers were all about educating the masses?"

Wymund laughed. "Stop stalling. You already passed the first test. Annika would be proud."

She took the piton back and swung a leg over into the crevice, purposefully this time. "Women like Annika and my mother don't feel pride. It's not compatible with their constitutions."

Rav tapped the bronze plate. "It's not lit," Rav said. "Does that mean they aren't home?"

"Illumined can also mean enlightened," Wymund said as he secured a rope to the piton while Rav cinched the other end around her waist.

"I'm not a dolt, Wymund," Rav said with a sigh.

He blinked. "You made a pun. This is worse than I feared. You must truly be on edge about this place."

Rav tested the knots on herself before reaching over to help secure Wymund. The crevice was narrow, but he had found a portion that looked wide enough to accommodate his frame. "And unless you promise never to tell anyone, I'll cut your line my-self."

CHAPTER 3

THE TESIGAN PEAKS

It soon became obvious that finding the entrance to the Illumined Scale was only the first entrance exam—avoiding a quick plummet to the bottom was the next. There was little room between the craggy walls, and Wymund had to hold in his stomach to squeeze through many sections, but it was not so tight that they couldn't fall at any moment, and she wasn't ready to trust their rope tethers entirely. Handholds were visible, spaced unevenly along the walls, and without the pitons Rav thought the descent would be impossible. It was apparent the handholds had been placed in each spot with purpose, though. They were too perfect to be naturally occurring imprints.

"Are we cheating?" Rav asked, keeping her voice barely above a whisper. It was nice to no longer shout over the whipping gales above, but inside the crevice her voice carried, bouncing off the walls and down to whatever mysteries awaited them below. "By the spacing of these hand and footholds, they seem to only want initiates with a gymnastic or criminal background."

"I don't think they're looking to test your dexterity here," Wymund said, grunting as he reached down to ram another piton into the rock near his waist. Before entering the crevice, Wymund had lit a lantern that was now dangling from his belt, casting a soft orange glow. "Even with your innumerable talents in that area, this climb would be impossible without you siphoning power."

"So, it's a test of my connection to the World Shroud, the very thing I'm here to improve." Rav laughed. "This is why schools and I never mixed. They expect you to know things before they explain them to you."

"Are you sure you were listening to the instructor the first few times the topics were explained?" Wymund asked.

Rav yanked a piton free and dropped several feet. Wymund gasped and reached out a hand, but Rav caught the handhold she had aimed for and smirked up at him. "I wasn't being paid to learn. They were being paid to teach. Perhaps they should've been more effective if they wanted to maintain my family's patronage."

Spike after spike was driven into the walls of the crevice as Rav and Wymund descended farther into Ram's Point. It was not long before they had reached the end of their ropes and were forced to untie themselves, an act the pair did without question, but she could feel the weight of that decision linger in the space between them. It felt much like the pull of gravity on their untethered bodies as they clung desperately to the icy walls.

Though they were free of the shearing wind, the temperature continued to drop, and Rav found herself pausing more often to flex her stiffening fingers. Wymund was struggling too—his mass was beginning to catch up to him, and she was slowing her pace so she could keep an eye on her friend. He was stopping every few yards or so to catch his breath and shake out his arms, and Rav was worried that if he did fall, he would not have the strength left to regain his hold on the cliff.

But after what felt like an eternity, the bottomless shadows below the edges of their lantern light began to dissipate, revealing the icy surface of a cavern. It was surprisingly even, with no large rocks or icy mounds obstructing the space. Someone had cleared the area for entry.

"Only about twenty more feet to the bottom," Rav called up to Wymund.

He glanced down, but as he shifted his weight, his boot slipped out of the foothold, and Wymund was suddenly supported by a lone piton in his left hand. He scrambled with his other to find purchase, his legs kicking wildly at the wall as he tried to find another small ledge, but all Rav could see was the spiderweb-like cracks forming in the ice layer around his spike.

Rav scampered up the wall to reach him, recklessly driving pitons into the wall at the top of each leap. She wasn't siphoning energy from the Wellspring. There were no arcing tingles or crushing pains in her neck. But her mind had clicked into a familiar mode, a sort of flow state that she had spent so much time in during her jaunts across the rooftops of Felona. The handholds could not have been more apparent in her vision if they were gilded and illuminated from within the ice, and where they were out of reach, she knew which spot on the opposing wall to springboard off.

Within seconds, she found herself at Wymund's ankles but without any remaining pitons. During their careful descent, she had pulled each free as she passed by, but in her mad effort to reach her friend, Rav had driven her entire supply into the walls. She unsheathed one of her twin daggers and began chipping away at the ice before her, hoping to create a place for Wymund to set his boot, but she was too late. The ice around his piton gave way, and her friend began to drop. With a final scream, Rav drove her dagger into the wall and flipped around, catching Wymund's outstretched hand in her own.

"Drop me," Wymund said, with wide eyes that belied his otherwise calm features. "You'll only hurt yourself."

"Oh, stop being dramatic," Rav said as her muscles began to quake, pulling deeply from beyond the veil. It would seem the added weight on an improvised piton was cause enough for her body to tap into the Wellspring. "Give me a momen—"

The blade snapped free from the hilt, and the pair began to drop the remaining thirty feet to the rocky ice floor. Fueled by electrical energy, Rav was able to catch herself between the two walls before it opened into the larger cavern. She stretched out and dug her heels into the ice on one side of the crevice and caught a final handhold on the other.

Wymund was not so lucky. He landed with a heavy thud on his left shoulder, unable to roll with the straight drop. He bellowed in pain but was already moving to stand as soon as he impacted. The fall would cause more than a bruise, but Rav hoped the heavy winter layers on top of his leather armor had provided some cushion.

A slight whistling to her left caught her attention, and Rav shot a hand out to catch the free blade of her dagger between her fingers as it spun down in a straight path toward Wymund's skull. He looked up at her, rolling his shoulder and taking a quick step to the side before nodding his appreciation. Rav let the blade clatter to the ground and held onto the lip with both hands, allowing her legs to drop before releasing. The five-foot drop was jarring but nothing she was unaccustomed to, and she stood from her crouch to check on him.

"As I was saying," Rav said. "Give me a moment and I'll have us both down on solid ground once again."

Wymund's shoulder caught mid-roll, and he winced. It might not be out of its socket, but something was out of place. "I would've waited longer than a moment if the resulting plan was less expedient."

"I've seen less graceful attempts," a voice called from across the cavern. They glanced over to see an elven man with wavy auburn hair that fell around his ears, both of which extended through his mane farther than Rav's own. He wore a wool-lined gray tunic with matching trousers and heavy boots and a polite smile that didn't reach his eyes, barely disturbing unblemished skin that was a shade or so lighter than hers. He looked like so many of the boys she had grown up around in Felona, entitled and sure of themselves beyond their ability.

"But not many that were more humorous," he added.

To his left stood a titanic woman with even fairer skin, also in the same gray outfit but with a look of unease. She stood taller than her partner despite ears that marked her as only partly elven, clearly visible with her sandy hair pulled back into a tight braid. The rest of her form was stacked with layers of muscle that could only come from a draqesh lineage, making Wymund appear scrawny by comparison.

"I'm pleased we could provide some entertainment," Rav said, taking a step further into the cavern. The lantern had detached from Wymund's belt on the fall but did not break, and had rolled to the midpoint of the chamber. Behind the two figures, hanging lanterns illuminated a passage deeper into the mountain. "Are you the school's headmaster? You look the type."

The man's smile ticked up further. "And what type is that?"

"The type that's bought so much into their own work that they exude smugness like body odor."

Wymund sighed. "What she means to say is—"

"What she means to say," the elven man interrupted, "is that she's so very sorry for attempting to break into a place of learning, and that you will both submit to the judgment of Master Zylnala for your disturbance." His words were like honey, flowing melodically from one syllable to the next. She recognized a Choii Stieren accent when she heard one.

Rav laughed. "It would seem we're not the only entertainment on the bill tonight. Come on, Wymund, these two will show us to the actual person in charge."

The elven man's hand dropped to the hilt of a rapier at his side, but his partner placed her hand on his arm. "They obviously aren't invaders, Adiin. We can just bring them to Master Zylnala as they are, then he can decide what to do with them."

"She's correct," Wymund said, joining Rav's side. "My friend is here to learn, as I assume the two of you are, as well."

Adiin took his hand off the hilt and instead unbuckled the scabbard, allowing it to drop to the ground. "Fair enough, not invaders then, Riqu. But I also haven't seen any evidence that the woman's a lightblood, and we can't have any old trash wandering through here."

He slid something over his leather gloves that looked like two small plates of metal connected by straps, one covering his palms and the other the backs of his hands. "Maybe she'll demonstrate more aptitude in combat than she did scaling our wall."

Rav had been willing to work with Wymund on de-escalating the situation if it had come to blades. She was here to learn restraint, after all. But a less lethal confrontation? She relished the thought of putting this arrogant prick in his place.

"You just let me know when I've proven myself enough for your standards," Rav said, dropping her remaining dagger on the ground. "I would hate for you to introduce me to the headmaster looking too disheveled."

"This is really unnecessary," Wymund said, but Rav had already darted forward. This man might have been studying in this place for some time, but she could guess how much comfort he had grown up in. She had been surrounded by it too, but she had chosen to live a life with more excitement. He would see how much more could be gleaned from real-life experience than lessons taught in a chilly lecture hall.

She leaped into the air and flipped over his head. A quick grapple behind his back and they could be on their way. A lesson learned with no punch thrown. Not that his face didn't look punchable—it most certainly did. But shame would sting worse.

However, she felt a sharp tug at her waist mid-flip, and she looked down to see the elf had placed the metal plate on the back of his glove against her belt buckle. That was all she could register before the sudden loss of momentum sent her crashing down onto her back. But she was already rolling back onto her feet and lunging at him before she caught her breath.

Adiin batted her hands away as he sidestepped her charge, and Rav stumbled into the middle of the cavern. She spun back and saw that he remained unruffled, and she felt herself flush. He was faster than her—much faster, as if he could anticipate her movements before she made them. This must have been what it was like for people that Rav had fought while drawing energy from the Wellspring, and it was infuriating. If this man's skill was any indication, perhaps there was more to gain from this school than simply learning how to remain alive.

She spared a thought for how impressive it was that Tetamii had managed to keep up with her assault in King Berenqar's chambers, but that gave her an idea. If she couldn't match the pace of an activated lightblood, she would have to rely on splitting the threat.

Rav picked up Wymund's dropped lantern and threw it at the wall behind Adiin. It shattered, spilling the flaming oil across the wall and floor of the tunnel entrance. Riqu jumped and began stomping on the flames, while her partner turned his attention away from his contest to distance himself from the flames. But Rav was already moving.

She slid across the ice behind him, raising one leg up in front of his waist while the other found the bend in his knees, then she drove her legs in opposite directions. Adiin's legs buckled as he was forced down to the frozen ground, now held between Rav's own. She reached with her right arm and grabbed his wrist, pinning it back at an awkward angle as she tightened the hold on his lower body.

"Entertained yet?" she asked as he tried to writhe out of her hold, but the icy ground provided no traction. His face turned red as his smile finally dropped, replaced with the indignant rage of a spoiled brat losing at a game.

"Hardly," he muttered before he extended his free arm toward the broken lantern pieces. Rav watched as a flaming metal shard that had been several inches out of his grasp slid toward the plate on his palm, which Adiin then brought up to hold against her thigh. Rav screamed at the intense heat, then released her grip and tumbled backward, reaching for her discarded blade. It was just like a petulant rich boy to change the rules when he was losing, but she was happy to oblige.

As if he sensed the shifting battle dynamics, Adiin dove away as well, scrambling toward his rapier.

"Enough!" Riqu roared, catching Adiin at the waist and lifting him off the ground and away from his blade. Rav's fingertips brushed the hilt of her dagger before she felt Wymund's boot kicking her weapon away. She made to dive after it, but he caught her by the collar.

"She's right, Ravael," Wymund said. "That's enough."

Rav stood, the spot on her thigh stinging from the flames, but her pants had not burned through. Her leg would not have been too damaged then, though it would require some attention.

Across the room, Adiin struggled against Riqu's grip, but there would be no escaping her massive arms. "Unhand me!" he shouted. "That wretch has defiled Mater Zylnala's school and will not be allowed to take one step further."

"She defiled nothing," Riqu said as she placed the elf's feet back on the ground, though without releasing him. "The ice that melted will freeze again, and if he wants it reshaped, we can take care of that as part of our morning duties."

Adiin huffed. "I will do no such thing. But these intruders might be allowed to repair this damage as penance before they are dismissed."

"We will be happy to repair any damages," Wymund said, releasing Rav's collar. "Please, just allow us to speak with this Master Zylnala. We can explain our presence here, and then, we hope, Ravael can begin her studies."

Riqu and Adiin glanced at one another, the woman's entreating gaze appearing to relax Adiin as his shoulders dropped. "Very well," Adiin said. "But we do not make a habit of allowing rabid animals to traipse through our home without proper precautions. Her daggers remain behind." Rav opened her mouth, but Wymund squeezed her shoulder.

"And your blade, as well," Adiin added, nodding to the short sword at Wymund's side. "You've demonstrated restraint, but I can't trust that she won't pull it free from your scabbard in a fit of rage."

Wymund complied, removing his sword belt and leaning the scabbard against the wall. Rav gestured toward Adiin's rapier on the ground. "And your weapon? Are we to trust that your wounded pride won't spur an opportune backstab?"

"I have no reason to be asha—" Riqu placed a heavy hand on his chest, blocking him mid-stride. She bent down to pick up his sword.

"I'll hold on to it for now," she said, before swinging her arm wide into the tunnel. "Welcome to the Illumined Scale."

CHAPTER 4

THE ILLUMINED SCALE

The trek deeper into the mountain was much less taxing thanks to the excavated, well-trodden path, but each step brought Wymund another wave of sharp pain just the same. He could move his arm, so it had not been dislocated in the fall, but every time he swung it he felt a pop in his shoulder, as if a band was shifting back and forth over bone. He carried on, though, keeping an eye on Rav next to him and praying to whichever Dawn One he thought might listen that there would be some form of healer in the school ahead.

Rav walked forward with an intensity that had not diminished since her fight with the elf, and he feared that her demeanor would have a similar effect on the headmaster. The last thing they needed after the weeks they had spent reaching this place was to end up right back out on the peak. Wymund assumed an educator would at least care enough to restock their supplies before sending them packing, but he had seen Rav's "charms" at work many times before, so that assumption would not be a safe bet.

Lanterns had been strung down the entire length of the tunnel, and the farther they walked, the more he was impressed by the craftsmanship of the passage. Support beams were spaced evenly along the path to reinforce the excavation, and there were even small branches off each side of the main walkway that ended in large supply rooms, each one hewn into perfectly circular spaces. Contained within were crates and barrels, most sealed but a few left open as their contents blossomed over the rims, leather scroll tubes and stacks of bound books being the most common sight.

Decorating the walls within were etched figures representing the Dawn Ones, all of them by Wymund's count, which was strange given the regional variance in worship. Stranger still were the brass rings at the tops of the circular rooms where pairs of round emeralds had been set, running in sets of two jewels around the circumference. They brought to mind the verdant-eyed Witnesses that were so frequently depicted alongside their deities, though the placement of the gems above the Dawn Ones ruled out that explanation—the Witnesses would only be shown in a place of deference to the gods. Still, confusing symbolism aside, the amount of work and laborers it must have taken to accomplish such a clean design was staggering.

He knew the dedication that was required to execute an artistic vision, and the dull ache that formed in the pit of his stomach when practicality pulled his further away from it. Whoever had overseen this project persevered, which was more than he could say for himself. For now, though, the stabbing pain in his joint took precedence over the ache of his abandoned dreams.

"We're approaching the Gem Hall," Riqu said. "Walk to the center when we arrive and wait. Adiin and I will go fetch Master Zylnala." Wymund glanced back at the woman, who was keeping a wary eye on Rav. "Keep out of Sloam and Myrii's way. And please, don't cause Luviila any trouble. She works so hard to keep this place running."

"You don't have to worry about us," Wymund said. "We can mind ourselves."

Adiin huffed as he pushed past them, rounding a corner and disappearing. "I'll let her know to steer clear of these two for now. I wouldn't want her to accidentally flash any valuables and send our guest into a thieving fury."

Wymund reached out reflexively to grab Rav's arm but found that she had not taken the bait. She continued her casual walk next to him, but he could see the muscles in her jaw working. If he couldn't expect her to let statements like that roll off her back, he would settle for this demonstration of restraint. Of course, repressing a retort now might only lead to a misplaced barb at the headmaster when he appeared.

One at a time. He and Rav followed the elf around the turn.

A massive cavern opened before them, the walls an even mixture of ice and rock, and the ceiling reaching up at least five stories. Lines of lanterns were strung in a swirling pattern all the way to the top, their flickering lights creating a mesmerizing glare off the icy surfaces behind them. The space was circular, though not perfectly so as the storage rooms had been. Instead, it appeared to have naturally formed inside the mountain, and a number of tunnel exits pierced the walls at various points around the chamber.

Man-made structures of wood and stone had been built along the walls on the ground level as well as farther up, spaced around frozen ledges that dotted the sides of the space almost to the highest point. Wymund recognized the style from his recent journey through the Qedradan countryside—these buildings were constructed like many of the farmhouses he had passed on his way north from Virdoba. The ledges were connected to each other by rope ladders and bridges, and the cords looked thick enough that Wymund would have no worries crossing any of them.

A human man and woman were positioned outside one of the buildings at the base of the western wall. He was portly, and his belly stretched against the confines of his gray tunic as he leaned forward on his stool, peeling a potato that would soon join the pile of raw vegetables in the crate beside him. By contrast, the woman was lithe and energetic as she shuffled around boxes of unpeeled tubers to the man's right. They each eyed the newcomers with bemused but not-unwelcoming expressions.

The room's most prominent feature was at the center, though: a large wooden platform about fifty feet in diameter with emeralds inlaid around the circumference, once again in sets of two, and a single, massive icy stalactite descending toward it. The frozen pillar stopped about fifteen feet above the stage and was capped by a brass plate, in which had been set two of the largest gems Wymund had ever seen. Each emerald must have been five feet across and reflected the lantern light without a hint of impurity in the facets.

Riqu stood at the center of the round wooden platform and pointed at her feet. "Wait here," she said, before striding toward one of the larger structures at the back of cavern. She passed through a set of heavy oak doors and disappeared inside.

Wymund and Rav took their places beneath the enormous gemstones. "How much do you think those are worth?" she asked, eyes wide as she stared up into the deep green jewels.

"As good as you are, I don't think there's any chance of you making it out of here with those emeralds unnoticed," Wymund said.

"Doubting me only makes the challenge more interesting," she replied as a pair of soft footsteps announced the arrival of another person to the platform.

They peeled their eyes away from the gems to find a middle-aged human woman had joined them. She wore an outfit much like Adiin and Riqu, though hers had been dyed green and had a fluffy white fur trim where theirs had wool. Thin and short with graying chestnut hair pulled into a bun, she looked to Wymund like many of the Qedradan women he had seen in his travels, with the wiry arms of someone who was accustomed to handling tasks on their own. Behind her, Adiin walked at a hurried pace toward the building Riqu had entered.

"Blinded Miabalar tells me that I am to be careful around the two of you," the woman said with a stern face. "Though I assured him that the decades I have spent in this place have left me hardened to any threats you might pose."

She appeared at first like a farmhand, but the way she spoke could only come from a formal education. "We are no threat to you, I promise" Wymund said. "Riqu mentioned someone named Luviila who was responsible for the school's upkeep. Might I presume that is you?"

"Blinded Perris's assessment of my role here is too kind," Luviila said, her expression softening. "The girl does have a tendency to build others up, no matter how many times we direct her not to belittle her own contributions."

"What's with this 'blinded' talk?" Rav asked. "Does Master Zylnala have such a high opinion of his teachings that everyone still learning must be blind by comparison?"

The heavy doors behind her swung wide to reveal a half-elven man dressed in a matching green tunic and trousers moving toward them, trailed by Adiin and Riqu. His skin was of a shade with Adiin's, a bit lighter than Wymund's and Rav's, and his head was covered in a short but dense tangle of bright white curls. Despite the color, Wymund could not place his age. Even with only partial elven blood to slow the signs of physical aging, the man could have been any age from his early forties to his late sixties.

"I'll allow him to speak for himself," Luviila said. "If you are welcomed into the school."

In contrast to the woman's stern demeanor, the headmaster had an easygoing way about him as he joined the trio on the wooden platform, flanked by his two pupils. He sported a mischievous grin that was devoid of any ill-intent—it was more like the man had a joke he wanted to tell and was waiting for the perfect opportunity.

"Visitors," he announced, silver-ringed irises flashing. "It has been far too long since we've had anyone grace our school with their presence. Though I've heard two substantially different accounts of your purpose here." Behind him, Riqu glanced down at her feet while Adiin continued to stare daggers at Rav. "I've never been one for second-hand accounts, however. So, let's get to know one another and see if we can clear up all this confusion.

"My name is Latheril Zylnala, headmaster of the Illumined Scale." The man strode across the platform and took Rav's hand, shaking it as his smile widened. "And you must be our prospective lightblood. While impressive in most regards, your handsome friend over there does have rather drab eyes." Wymund flushed, but Rav smirked. Zylnala's talent for disarming others rivaled Kymil's.

"Rav Trisarin," she said, then tilted her head to the left, adding, "And my plain-eyed friend is Wymund Sylnorin. We might have made a more respectable introduction if we hadn't been accosted by your rabid dog of a student on our way in."

Adiin's jaw clenched, but he was otherwise still as Zylnala threw his head back laughing. "Blinded Miabalar is protective of this place, I will grant you that. We'll see if his assumptions about you were correct once your testing begins. I like to see potential before I pass judgment on who gains admittance to my school."

Zylnala walked over to shake Wymund's hand. "As for you, I typically do not allow non-lightbloods in our midst. Unless, of course, they're working for me." He tilted his head toward Luviila and the two humans across the cavern. "Though I must admit, it's impressive that you managed to make it down the crevice without a connection to the World Shroud to rely on."

"Thank you, headmaster," Wymund said. "I would not have without Rav's assistance, and for that among many other reasons, I know you will be pleased with her as a pupil." Rav rolled her eyes but didn't turn her head fast enough to hide her smile. "As for the presence of unconnected individuals, I see you've made an exception for a select few. Perhaps you could extend me the same courtesy. I'm happy to work for my room and board."

Zylnala glanced back to Luviila and chuckled. "She provides the school with much needed servicing, not the least of which is emotional support for the headmaster. But if what Blinded Perris has told me is accurate, you might serve a similar purpose for your partner." He slapped Wymund's shoulder and turned to walk back toward the building. "Arrangements can be made. Now come, both of you. Testing will begin in a few days after you've had a chance to recover."

Falling in line behind him, Rav muttered, "I could use a month."

Chapter 5

— · —

Ineset

The fumes brought tears to Nasargiel's eyes, carrying a stench that was noxious and unfamiliar even with his many years of life. But he smiled nonetheless—the people of Slaeth were industrious folk, none more so than the humans and draqesh living here on the Aneran continent. Although his kin had departed this plane long ago, it always pleased and surprised him how technology and science continued to advance in their absence. Still, it wouldn't hurt for them to add a dash of cardamom or lavender to their concoctions. This world was spoiled for pleasant smells, and he saw no need for all their reagents to be so malodorous.

But a quick reminder of their progress was enough, and Nasargiel expanded his awareness to the World Shroud surrounding him and all things. Much like the din of a crowded street or the scent of one's home, the veil faded into the background of conscious thought when not attended to. Focusing his attention could bring all the wonders crashing over him, though. When one could tap into the power of multiple Wellsprings, concentrating on the World Shroud could be almost overwhelming.

Smoke-like wisps danced in his periphery, roiling with the heat they held back from this dimension. Other veilmarks appeared more like luminescent, snaking vines along the ground and up the sides of the clay-bricked buildings, while still more could only be described as translucent crashing waves, distorting his visual perception of the world if he focused on them too long.

But instead, Nasargiel reached out to the swirling, near invisible veilmarks that lazily drifted in front of him, spreading them taut below his nose before carefully puncturing a few pinpoint holes in the veil. A gentle breeze carrying fresh air flowed from under his nostrils into a trail behind him. He hoped the Achen workers he left in his wake appreciated the Udynn Wellspring's crisp air.

"Good harvest, heatless," a passerby said as he stepped out of Nasargiel's path. Nasargiel gave the man a polite tilt of his head in return, still feeling foolish at having neglected to return to this plane in a more appropriate form.

He still wore the loose blond curls that draped over each side of his thin face and had kept the same lanky body upon stepping out of the golden flames that supplied his ability to travel. If he was going to begin playing a more direct role in the affairs of Slaeth, he would need to remember that the people here placed significance on trivial matters like pigmentation and hair color. There was nothing he could do about his bright verdant eyes, a constant no matter what form he assumed, but regional variations in appearances would need to be a factor going forward. Walking inconspicuously with a human's skeletal structure was already difficult enough.

Ineset's Tower Lizard district was true to its name. The massive red clay slabs forming the buildings here rose higher than anywhere else in Achen's capital city. The alchemical stench that wafted down many of the neighborhood's cramped streets was accompanied by heavy metallic clangs, smoking hisses, and grinding of wheels—the latter from the newly constructed rail carts that ran on two lines through the district, one north to south and the other east to west. The Granish guild-family had built an operational steam engine for these carts and had yet to share it with any other family, but Nasargiel wouldn't be shocked if a ruling guild-family in one of Ineset's other districts soon had their own.

What the others could not compete with, however, was the craftsman guild-family's independent police force. The Granish's had simply become far too wealthy relative to their contemporaries, having built their mercantile empire around exciting innovations, as well as staples like woodworking and metallurgy, and therefore could afford to retain a larger percentage of Achen's military for their own bidding. This was all an unofficial practice, of course—Achen's standing army served at the pleasure of the nation's elected triumvirate, the chancellor responsible for directing their movements. It certainly did not hurt that Aewin Granish currently held that title, though.

It was this private army that Nasargiel was racing, and it seemed they had finally outdone him from sheer numbers. A patrol of seven Achen soldiers and their commanding blade serpent was nearing the final house on his list, the leader of the squad resting one hand on the hilt of his coiled, linked blade. He had not had the misfortune of seeing a blade serpent unleash one of their weapons, but he had heard enough of them that he wanted it to remain coiled at the man's side. He had no doubt he would survive the encounter, but Wellspring connections or no, Nasargiel had no desire to feel the piercing *crack* of that snaking blade bite into his flesh.

Nasargiel had noticed that at least one of these elite soldiers typically accompanied the more everyman mercenaries, and for good reason. Since arriving in Achen, he had witnessed the tactical brilliance of the blade serpents' command, keeping their grunts in line and harrying his own quest through the city. There had been a few near misses. He had managed to stay one step ahead of them all week, rummaging through the abandoned homes, storage buildings, and laboratories without being seen. His luck had apparently run out, but he was not without options.

Expanding his senses once more, he took notice of the gossamer sheen that permeated the life around him, from the teeming crowds of laborers and couriers to the small animals keeping to the shadows and out from underfoot. Even the dry shrubs and gnarled short trees gave off that distinctive glow, infused with life energy from the Taisos Wellspring despite the arid climate. Importantly, there was no detectable life inside the small fletcher shop several buildings down from his goal, and there was a lone dune palm growing out of the cracked earth beside it.

The luminescent snaking vines he had noted earlier twirled up the length of the ash-white trunk, pulsing at Nasargiel's touch. He concentrated on those veilmarks as they plunged into the clay, feeling where they mingled with tree's root structure, and began to shift the roots into looser soil.

"I'm sorry, ancient one," Nasargiel muttered, knowing how long and how hard the plant must have fought to reach such a height in a place like this. "Your struggle is at an end."

A horrible creaking sounded from down the street as the palm toppled onto the stone roof of the fletcher shop, sending a cloud of powdered red clay into the air as larger chunks of stone slid down onto the street. Pedestrians scattered away from the rubble, and Nasargiel stepped to the side as a donkey cart barreled away from the scene, the animal's eyes rolling in terror.

"Back away from the damage," shouted the blade serpent, his clipped Achen accent landing harder on the vowels. Nasargiel filed that detail away as well. "Let us clear the area before anyone is foolish enough to get hurt."

He and his patrol hustled down from their position to assess the damage, helping up a number of people who had fallen but were thankfully unharmed. Sighing with relief, Nasargiel slipped into the space between the abandoned home and the adjacent structure and found his way in: a boarded up window that was easily pried open. He had bought himself some time, but soon the soldiers would secure the site and resume their search.

Nasargiel stepped over a dusty workbench that was below the window and onto the floor of the single-roomed structure. The building was dark with every window sealed shut, but he was used to this in Nyavelle—no star could illuminate much of the depths in which his people chose to swim. Scattered oak tables covered with a smattering of glass vials and tubes filled most of the room, and the floor was covered with loose papers. Someone had left in a hurry.

He crept forward. The smell was somehow worse inside this structure than it had been outside, but Nasargiel could not place the scent. There was an element of the chemical odor that permeated the rest of the district, but there was something else. Something putrid. Perhaps the Achen soldiers had heard correctly when they were tipped off that someone had been robbing fresh graves. He briefly considered resuming his siphoning of fresh air, but thought better of it. It was best not to have any of his senses distracted when he should be on alert.

Nasargiel knelt, shuffling around the discarded notes and lab reports but finding nothing of substance. This was the right house; he was sure of it now. While the writing was in a form of short-hand, there were enough anatomical diagrams and seeming references to the World Shroud to tell him that this place had been used by the man he was searching for—the alchemist-surgeon who believed he was capable of gifting humans a connection to a Wellspring.

The thought made Nasargiel feel cold. If these connections could be grafted on to people for unsavory purposes, the ensuing race for power would almost certainly lead to a second Rupturing. The man's studies had to be stopped, regardless of what the Assembly believed. He would have his day before the Assembly of Archives Lost when his task was done, and hopefully they would come to see that his meddling in Slaeth was for the greater good. Until then, Nasargiel was just thankful that the surgeon was not as far along as he had feared.

Several months ago, Nasargiel had rescued a young woman from drowning whom he initially believed to be the first recipient of this graft. She had turned out to be partially elven, though, and had come by her abilities honestly. So, while uniquely gifted—enough to send noticeable ripples across the World Shroud—she had not been of help to his investigation. But for now, at least, his worries of successful experiments were unfounded. The surgeon was getting close, though, and he had to be found.

However, the Achen soldier's investigation must have been too public, and fearing being charged with the crimes of removing and mishandling people's remains, the surgeon had disappeared. Satisfied that neither he nor the patrol would be catching their quarry here today, Nasargiel turned to leave, but his eye caught something out of place across the room: a pallid arm, hanging limply from under a dingy white sheet on a table in the corner of the room.

The smell was now obvious—decaying flesh. Nasargiel gently lifted the sheet off the corpse with a simple puncturing of the veil, and watched it flutter away on a light breeze, revealing the body of an older elven man. The body was slack-jawed, his muscles having wasted away since the time of his death, and his head was tilted such that his glassy eyes were staring directly at him.

Nasargiel hurried over to the corpse, noting no visible incisions or biopsy sites. He swallowed hard, fearing what he would find as he gently turned the elf's head away from him. On the man's neck, at the base of his skull, was a three-inch incision that had been retracted and held open by a series of clips. The cut was deep, through the deep layers of skin and muscle, and down to the exposed bone of the spinal column. There, nestled among the upper vertebrae and adhered to the brainstem was a chestnut-sized black sac that confirmed his sense of dread.

Any being with a connection to the World Shroud possessed this organ. Every elf, dragon, or sylid who had ever drawn power from a Wellspring shared this biological sensory tissue. The connections were just another sense, after all. Sight required eyes, taste required tongues, and siphoning from beyond the veil required the tap. It was what showed that every intelligent species on Slaeth was connected biologically at some point in the past, even if the humans and draqesh had lost the feature from the elven line after years of geographical separation. But no one on this plane had known about this structure for millennia. Not since shortly after the Dawn One's departure.

The organ was sensitive to its environment and didn't last long when exposed to air. In fact, it generally liquefied with the merest exposure, allowing its existence to remain hidden during even the most careful autopsies. But this alchemist-surgeon must have stabilized it somehow, developed some concoction that preserved the tissue in this state.

As his mind reeled, Nasargiel heard the heavy footfalls of the Achen soldier outside the boarded front door. He grabbed the corpse under the arms and began to heft it off the table, but dropped it as soon as the first thundering blow to the door partially knocked it ajar. They would be inside in moments, too quickly for him to heft the body out of the window he had entered through.

"Hey!" shouted the blade serpent from earlier, his angular, mustached face looking in through opening one of his soldiers had created. "Don't move, vermin!"

He darted for his exit, pulling the wisp-like veilmarks taut behind him until he could feel the heat aching to be loosed. With a loud creak, the boards holding the door in place ripped free and a stream of Achen mercenaries began to file into the room. Nasargiel mounted the workbench and dove out the window just as an ear-piercing crack sounded in the air behind him, followed immediately by the *thud* of the blade serpent's linked blade embedding itself in the windowsill.

Nasargiel saw the man yank the sharp point of his whip free and wind back for another strike, but he would not be waiting around for another near miss. He tore a jagged orange line in the air above the corpse and unleashed a torrent of flames to consume the remains. Cries of surprise rang out from the window—they had not been expecting a scorcher but as the next snaking whip strike pierced through the conflagration, Nasargiel knew the blade serpent would not be stilled by the display. It was time to disappear.

To his knowledge, elves were not typically cremated, but he was willing to break tradition if it meant preserving the Physicarium. He had a feeling he would be asked to do much more in the days to come.

Chapter 6

— · —

Felona

"Just a little farther," Garla said, keeping Tetamii upright as he struggled to plant one foot in front of the other. "That hidden hand really got you good, didn't he? Don't fret, Magzii's brought on a new herb nurse while you were away who'll have you back in shape in no time." She looked up at him and chuckled. "Though it might come with one bastard of a head rush. Their infusions are what you might call the 'recreational' variety."

Tetamii hardly acknowledged her, focusing on keeping his eyes open and pointed straight ahead. There had been several instances on their trek into the city where the world slipped into double vision, nearly causing him to faceplant over an errant crate or curious dog. Ubadrii's poison coupled with a choppy trip ashore did not leave him in any state to climb Felona's steep hills, but he had no other choice. The Clipped Gulls were based out of the Trough, centrally located for their convenience. He guessed Magzii had never considered the possibility of a drugged and exhausted hike back to headquarters.

Above them, the island peaked into a roughly triangular shape, with manses and villas dotting the cliff face all the way up, the fluted spires on their roofs glittering for everyone below them to see. The architecture was meant to emulate the style the elves had brought from their own land across the sea, to bring some beauty to an island paradise that hardly needed it. All it really did was build resentment in the hearts of those who could not afford a life on the Crest. But while everyone else in the city felt bitterness at being lorded over, the Gulls simply appreciated the shade.

"And here we are," Garla said, letting him lean against a wall as she opened the door to the BUTTONED-UP LAD. It was one of the nicer tailor shops in the Trough, a place where laborers could come if they wanted to look decent but weren't too choosey about the materials. The place didn't measure up to any of the clothiers at higher altitudes in the city, but it was respectable all the same. It was also a front for a Clipped Gulls saferoom.

Inside, a man and his wife were sifting through a rack of neckties before starting at the sudden appearance of the two haggard figures in the doorway. The midday sun had done solid work during their walk through the city, but they still had the appearance and smell of being recently dunked in the ocean.

"Don't mind us," Garla said, waving cheerily at the two shoppers. "My brother here had a few too many and took a topple into the Strait. I fished him out, but we're just gonna have a lie down in the back."

As they passed, Garla reached out and grabbed a honey-colored necktie, then placed it on the man's chest. "This one looks good on you. Matches your wife's eyes."

They left the pair muttering under their breath and approached the door to the backroom but were blocked as a human man stepped defiantly in their path. He crossed a pair of heavy arms across his chest, and a series of scars on his face amplified his deep frown. Tetamii recognized his face but wasn't able to break a name through the fog.

Garla sighed. "We're really gonna do this? You know us, Evin."

"I know people who look like you," Evin said, his bushy eyebrows drawing down over a steely gaze. "But there's all kinds of wonders in this world. How am I supposed to know if some of you magic types can change the way you look?"

"First," Garla said, holding a finger impressively close to the brutish man's face. "Changing appearances went away with the Dawn Ones, so that's a trough of bilgewater. Second, what are you going to do if someone with powers is determined to get through you and the door? Stare at them with menace as you crumple to the ground?"

Evin smiled, his stained teeth ruining the impression of a well-dressed proprietor. "Anyone who ain't supposed to be back here wouldn't hurt an innocent store clerk. And the people who do belong have the password."

"It's a waste of everyone's time and our payroll, if you ask me," Garla said. "But fine: Quick hands, quick deeds."

"A crown does not make a king," Evin replied, stepping aside and pushing the door ajar. As they passed, he leaned back into the room and asked, "What happened to him anyway? He looks and smells like a drowned rat."

Garla cocked an eyebrow and glanced at Tetamii. "He's had a real go of it the last few weeks. And you better hope he doesn't remember you said that."

Evin grumbled something under his breath, but even in Tetamii's drugged state, he could swear the man's jaw tightened.

Once the door shut behind them, Tetamii slumped down into a seat as Garla shifted a shelf full of fabric bolts aside, revealing a door that had been obscured behind it. Behind it was a staircase leading down into a basement safehouse that had been forever burned into Tetamii's mind.

For most of his life, his feelings about this place had been locked away, just as he had been taught to do, only to be dragged out when needed for a convincing deception. But not this time. Suddenly, he felt like a child again, uncertain and terrified, weighed down by a bloodied dagger in his hand.

A deep ache in his lower back throbbed, right where a different blade had sunk, and as Garla opened the basement door, there stood the lightblood that had nearly killed him. She was waiting for him, black hair hanging lank with sweat and blood around her face and the rest of her body covered in scorched flesh from their encounter. She smirked, tossing her dagger in the air. He blinked and jumped from his seat, but the figure was gone.

"Woah, easy," Garla said, hustling back over to his side and wrapping one of his arms around her shoulders. "I know you're in a hurry to get your mind right, but those stimulus powders aren't going anywhere."

"No more drugs," Tetamii said with a thick tongue that seemed to resist movement. "Sleep."

"To each their own, I guess," she said, carefully helping him place one foot down the first step. "But we'll see just how fast Magzii wants you up and at it again."

As the pair reached the bottom of the stairwell, Tetamii was surprised to find the safehouse was busier than usual. Typically, no more than two or three Gulls were present at any given time, but now there were a half dozen members of the group milling about the room. Gatherings were kept to a minimum to avoid suspicion, only allowed for special occasions like initiations. Therefore, it wasn't surprising that he hardly remembered any of the faces in this room—he may not have even met a few of them. He certainly had never known Garla before his rescue.

But Vulmar Magzii was unmistakable. He had already been well into his fifth decade when Tetamii had first met him, but now close to twenty years later, the leader of the Clipped Gulls was only beginning to show his age. Once-dark waves of hair had thinned and lightened, and fine wrinkles disguised many of the pale scars that lined his face. But his silver-ringed eyes still shone with the same intensity over his lopsided smile, a remnant of another wound that sagging skin couldn't hide.

Uncharacteristically, Magzii appeared to have traded in his typical dark, almost threadbare tunic and trousers for a newer set of deep violet, embroidered with an intricate silver pattern on the vest. Tetamii had never known the man to care much for how society viewed him—that had always been *his* thing since obtaining his long, white coat years ago. In fact, the man had always taken it as a point of pride that he didn't look like those "puff pastry-filled lords in their frilly smocks." But now Magzii had clearly put more effort into his appearance. Things had changed in his absence.

"It's good to see you, lad," Magzii said with a swooping gesture toward a table in the center of the room. "We all breathed a sigh of relief when we heard that the Qedradan ship had been ransacked out on the Strait. Not our usual style, mind you, but then again, we aren't used to operating with near bottomless pockets. Paying off a band of pirates for a little mayhem so Garla could slip out proved to be an effective strategy."

Tetamii staggered over to a seat at the table, where he was joined by Magzii. Garla took a spot against the wall with the other onlookers. Everyone appeared at ease, so an execution for his failure seemed unlikely. Though that wouldn't be unheard of. Tetamii never quite knew which Magzii he would get—growing up, the man had been as likely to pat his face with pride as backhand it. Tetamii dug his fingernails into his leg, hoping to regain as much mental clarity as possible should it be needed.

"Pleased you thought of me," Tetamii said. His mouth continued to feel as if it were stuffed with marbles, but he was improving. "Thought I might not be worth the expense."

Magzii frowned. "Don't think so lowly of yourself. Mr. Thymes has been quite happy with your work thus far, and once I assured him that he would continue to need the services of my best man, he was ready to pay whatever was needed."

Magzii's words dripped like honey, almost cloying. He felt his shoulders tense and gooseflesh erupt down the length of his arms. This level of praise from the leader of the Clipped Gulls was usually made in jest, a sarcastic display to shame the failure before they were drugged and spent the night in a closet, the bare skin of their backs frozen to a wall such that their toes barely scraped the ground.

True praise had been few and far between, but that had made it all the sweeter once earned.

"Happy?" Tetamii asked.

"Of course!" Magzii laughed. "He understands that centuries of political ties cannot be undone in a matter of weeks. You didn't urge King Berenqar into a full war with Kefya, sure, but that was always a long shot. However, you did deepen the fervor building in Virdoba, heightening the tensions between the elves and humans there.

"The more unstable we make that powder keg, the more likely it will be to blow on its own," Magzii continued, his voice taking on a steel edge. "And wouldn't an organic conflict be preferable to an artificial one? It would certainly be less traceable."

Wispy tendrils writhed in his periphery in concert with Tetamii's anger. "I don't enjoy being uninformed about the actual objective of my missions."

Magzii's smile never faltered, but something in his eyes shifted, like a light being snuffed. Tetamii felt an icy shiver travel down his spine, and he hated that he wasn't sure if it was from Magzii's abilities or a childish ingrained fear response.

"As always, my Gulls are told what the patron wishes them to be told," Magzii said. "Historically, our benefactors have been loathe to spread their personal details among our ranks for fear that word could get out to their rivals. But now, circumstances have changed.

"Mr. Thymes has opted to have our organization on retainer as our sole patron," Magzii said. He paused to smooth down the silk of his violet vest with an absent smile. The man was actually *preening.* "With no other ears around to pick up on things they shouldn't, my most trusted associates are allowed to know more than they would otherwise."

"Sole patron?" Tetamii asked. The Magzii he had known for years would never be bound to the fate of one individual. He had always stressed the importance of diversifying income channels, building ties not only to the docks but throughout every facet of Felona. At one point, there wasn't even a single High Scholar's coffer the Gulls didn't have at least a pinky in, and those priests were notoriously stingy. Tetamii had missed a major shift during his time off the island.

"We've gone legit," Garla said from the side of the room. "As long as you think taking orders from a councilman is legit."

Magzii gave her a blank stare, but the woman just winked at them. These newer recruits hadn't been around long enough to appreciate the threat behind that cold glance.

"Garla's misguided interpretation aside, she's hit on a bit of truth," Magzii said. "All these years we've spent breaking thumbs and twisting wrists to seize control of the imports and exports of the city have made us a dominant force in the workings of Felona. Nothing gets in or out without the Clipped Gulls taking a cut, and that's funded more of our . . . lucrative and unsavory contracts. But we've made enemies of the merchants, and if they could ever get over their squabbling to organize against us, well, it might not be pretty for us. Not to mention the riot this city will devolve into once cries of war start raining down from the Crest.

"Working exclusively for Elikar Thymes offers us a shield for when the actual battles begin. People in our way of life have a tendency of being thrown to the sharks as a layer of chum, first in line for death in front of the soldiers with names and titles. We deserve better, if you ask me, so I secured that for us."

"Along with a place in Thymes's good graces, I'm sure," Tetamii said, flicking his eyes over the man's new attire.

This time, Tetamii was sure of the source when the moisture in his mouth crystallized, sealing his lips shut and adhering his tongue to the bottom of his mouth. He tried to cough, but the droplets turned to shards of ice that peppered the roof of his mouth.

"Everything I do is for the benefit of our family," Magzii said, his mouth finally evening out as his lopsided smile faded. "I understand how you must feel, spending all that time in captivity after failing at your goals. But that doesn't excuse a sharp tongue."

Tetamii thinned the World Shroud membrane inside his mouth, defrosting his tongue. "Apologies, Magzii. You aren't the source of my animosity."

"Thank you. Maybe it's time you fill us all in on who is, then." Magzii snapped and a wrinkled, spry man scampered over with a leather-bound journal in one hand and a quill in the other. He was short, even for one with only partial elven blood, but age wreaked havoc on a straight spine.

"We know a little of what transpired," Magzii continued. "Otherwise, we wouldn't have been able to target the correct ship. But the details will be helpful for planning what comes next."

Tetamii spent the next hour describing the team that had captured him. The city guard who launched into battle against an opponent who would've sent seasoned warriors running. The old Felonian aristocrat whose ties to King Berenqar's family had weakened Tetamii's arguments. The elven showman, who Tetamii now suspected was a fatestitcher. Berenqar's hidden hand, who had made his transport across the sea a docile, humiliating affair.

But he saved the lightblood for last. His greatest mistake had been not ensuring her death in Virdoba, but in his experience with her, Tetamii thought she might have found a way back from death to stop him anyway. Out of the corner of his eye, he saw glass shards and a thin pool of blood forming around a pair of feminine feet. Tetamii flicked his eyes up, catching the lightblood's indignant face before he blinked, and she was gone once again.

"Well, I can see what has you so on edge," Magzii said. "Bested by an untrained girl who could've as soon been consumed by her own power than fight back? I would be embarrassed, too."

But Tetamii wasn't embarrassed—it had been a learning experience. The young woman possessed things he never had: a reason to fight beyond survival or coin, and allies that seemed to have bolstered that in her. Those elements gave her restraint, keeping her from spilling over into the Illuminated Death and leading to his defeat.

Magzii's plots and his decentralized compatriots had granted them small wins here and there, either satisfying a need for riches or personal vendettas, but as Tetamii emerged from his poisoned fugue, he began to wonder what might have been possible without all the infighting and competition Magzii engendered within his "family."

"But you'll have your chance at revenge, lad," Magzii said, rising from his chair. "Rest up, and once you're feeling yourself again, Thymes wants you out searching for the party that tried to bring you here in chains. When you find them, he wants them silenced."

The gang leader patted Garla on the shoulder on his way toward the stairwell. "Garla is at your disposal, as is everyone else in this room. Don't want to leave any chances at failure this time, do we?"

Tetamii rose, finding himself sturdier on his feet than he had felt in weeks, but the call for a bed was unrelenting. Garla walked over and gestured toward a cot that had been set up in a side room. "No stimulus drugs, huh? The man must really like you."

He didn't respond as he slipped onto the bed, but the answer was there at the forefront of his mind. Tetamii was liked by the man, but he could never be sure if it was as a son or simply a favorite pawn.

Chapter 7

Felona

Mareq strained over the balustrade. The ship's dimensions had not been made with draqesh proportions in mind, and even up on his toes, the dense cluster of mastheads filling the sky in the harbor occluded much of Felona's docks. Captain Tomau had called it the Seaspray Thicket, and with good reason. In his admittedly short time traveling, Mareq had not seen another concentration of wood that better owned the term.

Despite the density of other vessels, though, the captain navigated through with a steady hand and keen eyes that could only come from experience. He had made this run down to Felona many times before, as Mareq had been reminded repeatedly, over his concerns about the ship's condition. Sure enough, Tomau handled his craft with ease.

Sailors still aboard the other docked ships stopped mid-task, holding crates aloft or pausing with sails partially cinched as they gawked at the marred hull of the *Fortune's Rose*, her once-gleaming façade now pockmarked and scorched. But their stares wouldn't faze Tomau, who kept his eyes defiantly set on their destination.

"It's all about projection, Greenboots," Tomau said, turning to face him. Mareq had been unable to shake the nickname given to him by his former captain, no matter his much less frequent his bouts of seasickness were during this voyage.

"How a man carries himself will outweigh the rags he's draped himself in or the rickety transport on which he travels," he continued. "All these wide-eyed and curious onlookers will remember in a week's time is how distinguished the fearsome Captain Tomau looked as he sailed through the Thicket."

"That's not the impression I'm getting from them," Mareq replied, but the captain just laughed. It was a mirthless laugh, though. The man had sunken eyes that hadn't crinkled from the slightest smile since the deaths of his crew. Mareq had noted a bitter sadness in the captain after the boarding attack, but there was something else—a wariness that seemed to stem from more than shock. It was as if Tomau couldn't believe he had survived when he had lost so many, and now the man feared monsters around every corner.

"You'll see. People will believe what you want them to believe. You just have to convince yourself first."

Over the next few minutes, the ship maneuvered through the cluster of vessels until it reached a suitable spot for mooring. Now with his view of the island unobstructed, Mareq could see the sheer cliff face on which Felona was built rising straight into the sky, like a limestone wall erected out of the Marrow Strait. It was capped with a copse of thin, gray-barked trees blooming with vibrant teal flowers. These were seafoam bindweed trees, and even from this distance Mareq saw shadowy, four-legged forms stalking along the cliff edge and the wooded perimeter. They reminded him of the wolves that used to hound his family's farm back in Brey, and he felt his whole body clench. Predators looming in the trees was a primal source of unease.

A narrow and snaking path had been carved into the rock, ascending with a slight incline back and forth all the way to the top, with merchant stalls of all varieties jammed against the wall in a brightly colored zigzag. This left little room for foot traffic between them and the edge of the path, but that did not stop the bustling crowd of shoppers from hunting for the newest arrivals. There were even a few brave souls who deftly stepped outside the wooden fences lining the road and shimmied along it to bypass blockages.

Mareq heard his father's voice in his mind: *Never follow a southman's lead. Their brains are sun-stewed.* Maybe there was something to that old northman's adage.

Teacher Leros's likeness had been chiseled from the base of the great stone wall, standing at least three stories high and still not reaching halfway up the cliff. The Accountant had one hand outstretched, palm upward, toward the arriving vessels, with the other hand raised in greeting. A pleasant gesture in expectation of a fair trade, just as he had always been depicted, but around his feet were wreathes of green and yellow flowers. Most had been scattered, as if ripped apart, but there were a handful of the bright bulbs that had been draped higher up on the carving's body.

□"I see some of Virdoba's prejudices have followed us to the island," Kymil said, meeting Mareq next to the ramp as it was lowered down to meet the pier. "Say what you will for the Kefyans—they're nothing if not consistent."

"What do you mean?" Mareq asked.

Kymil pointed toward the destroyed flower arrangements around the Dawn One's feet. "Rings of Irasil. It's a Liiashan tradition that the elves brought over when they settled on Choii Stier, a symbol of friendly outreach to outsiders. Sadly, it would seem that most have been met with the typical Kefyan hospitality."

"Maybe people just don't like their gods covered in bush clippings," Tomau said as he began to walk down the ramp, followed by a handful of his men. He paused and turned back, plastering a less-than-convincing grin back on his face before adding, "I know I hate it when this lot leaves their trash all over the deck." His entourage chuckled as they continued past him.

Mareq tried to imagine what would happen to a wandering elf who placed a wreath at one of Teacher Dynnir's altars in Destueqa. The flowers would not be the only things dashed on the ground. Not that his homeland was more bigoted than Kefya—far from it—but the Archer did not espouse anything more than self-reliance, and some Destueqans might take the symbol of outreach as an affront.

"Anyway, I have business in the city," Tomau said. "I'll try to catch up with you all again before we head back out. Good luck with your presentation to the Council. Don't hesitate to call me in if I can help with the prosecution. I've been known to spin a convincing yarn from time to time, and without that brute to flip on his bosses, you might need all the assistance you can get."

As he mentioned the scorcher, Tomau's eyes narrowed and flitted about the docks. Mareq couldn't help but do the same. Did the captain really think the assassin would be waiting for them out in the open like this? Before he could ask about the man's suspicions, more footfalls behind them interrupted his paranoia.

"Somehow we'll manage," Annika said, walking up to stand beside Mareq and Kymil, with Ubadrii following close behind. The hidden hand carried his dark leather bag in one hand, the slight clinking of glass vials inside reminding everyone of the power contained within.

"You forget, captain. Despite how long I've been away, Felona is still my city," she continued. "The Council will listen to a favored daughter if she speaks logically."

"And with the backing of a monarch's word," Ubadrii stated, reaching into his coat pocket, and pulling out a sealed letter, bearing the crests for both Qedrad and the king's house.

Tomau gave a slight bow at the waist, then raised his head and winked at them. "And who could argue with that. You've certainly convinced me, so I think I'll be on my way. Good day, everyone." As he stepped off onto the pier, he paused, once again scanning the bustling crowd. Tomau pulled the brim of his hat lower over his eyes, then called out over his shoulder, "Keep a wary eye out for the cats, Greenboots. You might be just the right size for a snack."

Kymil gave Mareq a pat on the back and started down the ramp himself. "Don't worry. You would be far too dry for them. Too much time in the salty air."

It was easy for Mareq to step through the masses, picking his route from his vantage point waist high to most others in the crowd. His frame was wider, sure, but that only added heft to his nudges as he slipped by dockhands and merchants alike. Still, when he approached the cliff face, Mareq looked longingly at the massive elevator rigs that had been constructed on either side of Leros's Path. The winding route by foot would be long, regardless of its gentle incline, and he considered for a moment tucking himself into a crate so he could be carried to the top with the rest of the incoming cargo. But he would never hear the end of it from Kymil, and he shuddered at the thought of the story ever reaching Tomau's ears.

"Is there no passage designated for visiting representatives?" Ubadrii asked, eyeing the soaring limestone wall before them. "A more direct route, perhaps? There is an escaped, regicidal assassin loose in the city, and we have great need to be seen by the Council straight away."

"I'm afraid not," Annika answered with a wry grin. "Unless you have a formal invitation from the Council that you've kept secret from us. In that case, we should send for your palanquin with great haste."

The elf grumbled but said nothing. There had been some disagreement between the two since the group had departed Alaboq, with Annika not understanding why more official arrangements hadn't been made between Qedrad's royal house and the Kefyan Council. She knew how byzantine the process of meeting with the country's rulers could be, particularly after an attempt on the life of another nation's leader became known. However, Ubadrii had agreed with his king—traveling fast and keeping the news under wraps would afford them the best chance of successfully accusing Elikar Thymes.

Though, Mareq had to wonder just how successful their attempts at suppression had been. Everywhere he looked, at the end of each pier and even at regular intervals up the incline, stood a pair or more of city guards, their teal coats reminiscent of the one he had seen Wymund wear. The men and women all sported longswords and dour looks as they rummaged through crates and baskets before waving people along. He had never visited Felona before, but he had to imagine this level of security presence was not the norm.

Mareq followed Annika as she walked onto the mercantile road. She paused at a shellfish stall and breathed deeply through her nose, the playful smile on her face melting into one of earnest contentment. While he wasn't ready for it yet, Mareq imagined that once he had been away from Brey as long as Annika had from Felona, he might feel the same stepping into his family's dairy barn and catching a whiff of his history. Still, he didn't miss her eyes lingering on the guards stationed at the first crook of the path. Not all was as she had expected in her homecoming.

As they climbed, Mareq noted how many elves lived in this city. Alaboq had been a metropolis compared to his own home, with people from across the continent bringing various aspects of their cultures for everyone to either enjoy or bicker over. There had been more draqesh in Alaboq than he had seen so far on the island. Given how few dockhands shared his heritage, where their strength would be put to its best use, he suspected there might not be many like him here at all. But that had not contributed much to the diversity of Qedrad's capital. Humans and draqesh were Aneran siblings, two shoots off the same branch of life. Elves, on the other hand, were another tree entirely.

He had spent a great deal of time with elves since leaving Brey, first with Tiialya aboard the *Fortune's Rose*, then with Rav and Kymil shortly after. But the two women were only of partial elven descent, with neither hailing from Liiashae itself, and while Kymil was born across the sea, the bard was always playing a role of sorts. Felona would be Mareq's first experience with such a distant culture, and if their presence on Leros's Path was any indication, he would be mesmerized.

"Don't forget to blink," Kymil said. "It will all still be here once your lids flutter back open."

"It's just . . ." Mareq started, but paused as an elven man with a brilliant flowering bulb attached to his lapel slid past, each petal giving off a bright amber glow. "Do all the elves here flaunt their abilities so flagrantly? It doesn't seem like a good idea with the way things are brewing across the Strait."

"Not all elves have connections to the World Shroud," Annika said. "Despite what you may have heard."

Ubadrii eyed the glowing boutonnière and grunted. "That was little more than a simple parlor trick, my friend. No siphoning from the veil needed when you have the crests to pay for the right luminescent dyes."

"Besides," Kymil said. "You won't see the truly wonderous sights until we reach the top. Liiashan artwork scrawled across buildings, the outdoor bathing fountains, and, of course, the predatory cats large enough for a draqesh to ride into battle."

"All right, all right," Mareq said. "I'll keep my jaw from dropping and embarrassing the lot of you. No need to make things up for the uncultured hick."

Kymil placed a hand over his chest in mock offense. "I do not make things up. I reveal truths to the world though my work. How could my reputation ever recover if I was found to be a liar?" He then stooped down to Mareq's height, adding, "I have been known to embellish on occasion, however."

"So how big are the cats then?" Mareq asked.

Kymil smiled wide. "I only exaggerated the fountains. They are actually pools, so all the good bits are hidden below the surface to protect you Anerans' sense of modesty."

Mareq swallowed hard, thinking back to the forms he had seen on the cliff's edge. "The cats are a real thing?"

"They are indeed a real thing," Annika said, already turning around a bend in the path and moving up to the next level of carts. A heavy splash in the distance drew their attention, followed by another four-legged shadow leaping from the seafoam bindweed copse above and into the waters north of the docks. Annika looked back at him and shrugged. "Best not to dawdle."

After fending off several insistent coffee and tea vendors who had set up shop near the top of the path, each of whom claimed to have brewed their drinks from the freshest ingredients and nearly came to blows to settle the dispute, Mareq and the others finally arrived at the top of the cliff. And Kymil had been right—Felona proper was unlike anything Mareq had ever seen.

While their first steps took them into a district that looked much like any other working-class neighborhood, with men, women, and children scurrying about their tasks in every direction, a quick scan of his surroundings brought some of the city's quirks into view. To the left, row after row of buildings painted with vibrant murals of plant life, sea creatures, and even scantily clad dancers extended for at least half a mile. Some of the structures were constructed with half-domed ceilings, projecting multiple styles of music out into the city, mingling in a not unpleasant way despite the differing compositions. In one alley, costumed performers practiced stage fighting with such skill that Mareq thought Wymund would have been impressed.

In the distance, a wedge-shaped cliff rose from the center of the city, with massive homes perched at all heights and patches of more bindweed trees providing pops of cerulean around the limestone. At the top of the bluff, more impressive structures had been constructed, some of which had the Choii Stieren fluted spires twisting up from their roofs.

But all these buildings were dwarfed by another, an umbral amphitheater with yet more spires shooting into the sky even higher from within its misshapen walls. The black stone reflected branching lines of sunlight from gilded veins that had somehow been worked into its surface. This was the Hall of Merchants, the largest Dawn One ruin still standing on the Aneran continent, and its spectacle had not been overstated.

A deep warble snapped Mareq's attention to the right, and there he saw a creature that his mind initially refused to register staring at him from a dense tree line. It stood nearly four feet tall from paw to shoulder, and the length of its body was coated in a short layer of navy fur, oily in appearance like an otter's pelt. The features were feline for the most part, though with smaller ears that were pressed flush against the animal's skull, and long flowing whiskers that appeared to be moving with some imagined current. With a huff, it turned and stalked back into the trees, revealing a wide, flat tail that was decidedly not catlike. Fearing that the beast had his scent, Mareq hurried to catch up with the group that had left him staring at the city in awe.

"So, what will be our new approach?" Ubadrii asked as Mareq reached his companions. "Surely you have new tactics in mind now that the Gull has escaped our custody. The captain was correct; it will be much more difficult to convince the Council that the blame for these horrible events stems from one of their own."

"I have been weighing our options," Annika replied. "Though given our sudden lack of corroboration, I believe taking some time to get a feel for the political currents among the councilmembers would be wise."

"You've lost faith in my ability to persuade these people on my own?" Kymil asked. "You have seen me at work, and I doubt any infusions would be necessary. My oratory talents are up to the task regardless of any stored insurance."

Annika rolled her eyes but smirked all the same. "You might find that when money is being passed under the table and behind closed doors, all the flowery arguments in the world could be broken wind for the outcomes you would find."

Kymil himself didn't seem persuaded, but he nodded anyway. Ever since losing his arm in the fight against Tetamii, the bard's need to have the last word had diminished. Mareq had even caught him staring off the deck at night, face like stone, on numerous occasions. He was still able to put on a boisterous façade, but it was starting to show cracks.

"We don't know what other members of the Council have aligned themselves with Elikar Thymes, or whether they are also involved in his plots," Annika continued. "Give me some time to arrange individual meetings, and perhaps we can determine where everyone stands. It would be good to know a friendly face from an unfriendly one when we are standing before the Council on official matters."

"We're finding an inn, then?" Mareq asked. "As long as they don't serve hard tack or rock back and forth while I'm trying to eat, I'll be overjoyed. That district with all the music and performers ought to have good food, or up near the Hall of Merchants if Qedrad's national banks are willing to cover the expense." Ubadrii shot a glance his way but said nothing.

"No, we're going to being staying somewhere a bit more domestic than a tavern," Annika said, turning right onto a street that ended with a ten-foot-tall iron gate, behind which was a large glade within the seafoam bindweed wooded area. Another neighborhood had been constructed within it, composed of manor-like houses with expansive lawns.

And no cat deterrents in sight.

"The Iatorii family home?" Ubadrii asked. "Qedrad appreciates the hospitality."

Kymil's grin returned. "Please tell me there will be childhood portraits. Or were we still painting on cavern walls back then?"

Annika sighed. "I'm afraid a tour of the Iatorii vineyard will have to wait for another time. The amount of land my family needed to grow our grapes required an estate outside the city. Luckily for us, we have a connection with a woman living on an orchard beyond that gate. Once we introduce ourselves, I believe she will be thrilled to welcome us into her home."

Kymil laughed and pulled the lute from his back, playing an energetic tune in the one-handed fashion he had mastered in no time at all. "Oh, this is going to be a delight."

Chapter 8

Felona

It had been decades since Annika set foot in the Bindweed Conservatory, but it was as if the neighborhood had been frozen in time ever since. Each manse they passed brought back a memory of some gala or banquet her family had attended, many of which she recalled fondly. Annika had shared her first kiss with the son of an elven glass magnate who lived in the large family home nestled on the edge of the glade, its honey-colored bricks gleaming as they had all those years ago. That boy had lived a full life since that time, and likely still lived there with his own family—real estate didn't often fall out of familial hands in these districts. But as fun as it might be to surprise him with a social call, they had another destination in mind, one whose inhabitant she could be confident would not be allied with Elikar Thymes.

"How do you know Ms. Trisarin still lives here?" Mareq asked, his eyes never venturing far from the tree line as he glued himself to Kymil's side. She would tell him the urlyri panthers were aquatic hunters, and that the ones here were trained to keep sharks and other sea beasts away from the docks—eventually.

"As long as she hasn't passed on, she will have stayed in her family home," Annika said. "We know her heir is waist deep in snow and ice at the moment, so she hasn't bestowed the house just yet."

"And if her disposition matches her daughter's?" Ubadrii asked.

Annika laughed. "Then we should all be quite practiced in handling her rougher edges."

"You mean you've never met the woman?" Kymil asked, continuing to happily pluck at his instrument. "I was led to believe that the entire social universe of Felona revolved around you and your house."

"Hardly," Annika said. "But we certainly had ties with most of the upper crust. People tend to seek out relationships with the best damn winemakers in the hemisphere. However, everyone knew her husband, at least by reputation."

Kymil's tune slowed down, his fingers finding more melancholic notes. "Rav shared with me what little she remembered of the man. It sounded like he was absent for most of her life before he was killed."

"Rav's father was murdered?" Mareq asked, finally able to pull his attention from the hidden felines stalking the woods. Even Ubadrii's eyebrow cocked.

"Yes, by a member of the Clipped Gulls, if you can believe it," Annika said. "Ilphas Trisarin was a popular figure in the city, particularly with the workers in the Trough. Many believed he would be a powerful advocate for change should he be elected to the Council—a reformer who would work to make life more equitable in Felona." Her face darkened. "That was until he was found dead in an alley, a knife wound in his gut and disposed of like an animal."

"Fathers grasping for power and finding only violent ends," Kymil muttered.

Annika knew enough of Kymil's story to understand that there was no love lost between him and his father, though he was uncharacteristically tight-lipped about that aspect of his life. Ilphas Trisarin was no abuser, but Kymil had struck upon an interesting parallel: those wishing to control or influence others often found themselves with the largest targets on their backs. She patted his shoulder, and his morose tune skipped as he instinctually pulled away from her, though he recovered smoothly, offering her a small, warm smile in return.

"I wonder who paid that tab with the Gulls?" Mareq asked sardonically, kicking at a loose cobblestone, and sending it skittering down the path.

Annika sighed. "Money has always been more important than blood to those who have more of the former. Our current troubles are not new."

The group caught more than a few glances from passersby out on a stroll, though Kymil's performance put them at ease. Of course, Annika and Ubadrii looked right at home in such a district, so she had been right to assume they would not encounter any resistance. But that did not mean that there weren't private guards stationed at each estate, funded solely by the families themselves and responsible only for their safety, so Annika made sure no one strayed too far off the main road. The last thing they needed now was for one of their party to end up in a brawl for trespassing.

Finally, she spotted the twin tart orchard she had been searching for, the distinctive orange-yellow berries hanging heavily from the branches. The citrus fruit grew in pairs from each bulb, and had become popular since the seeds had been brought over to Aneran soil centuries ago. The bright flavor profile had become a dominant staple of Felonian pastries, and no one had been quite as prodigious at growing them as the Trisarins—so much so that some in the city even whispered that the family were seeders. But Rav was a lightblood, which meant Ilphas was a stormforger, and any talent in the garden was technical rather than magical.

The manor itself was only two stories tall, half as high as most others in the Conservatory, but it made up for its stature with wings branching forward from the main house, leaving the home an unfinished square. Dozens of rows of twin tart trees had been planted in the plot between the parallel wings and ran all the way to the road. Unlike most of the other properties they had passed, this was a place to live and work, and among the trees were a handful of workers plucking the fruit pairs as they passed. Also notable was the lack of hired protectors at the edge of the grounds.

Annika walked down the central path, the rows here spaced a bit wider than the others to accommodate delivery carts, with the rest of her company following behind. Her eyes were set on the polished double doors to the home, so she was surprised when one of the harvesters called out to her.

"You are a bit early, I'm afraid," the woman said. "We have another week with these harvesters before their contract is up. You're welcome to inquire after work sometime early next week, if you so desire."

Her skin was olive-toned, and she looked to be of a similar age to Annika, past her prime physically but with a keenness to her eyes that was unmistakable. Another similarity was her wardrobe, consisting of practical clothing that someone with an eye for detail could notice was tailored and crafted to the woman's specifications. No flash, but costly just the same. Over the top of it all, the woman wore a cream-colored cloth sack draped over one shoulder, into which she was depositing her collected berries.

Though the human imperfections were evident—a too-round-tipped nose and ears slightly misaligned—the woman was without a doubt Rav's mother. Same glowing skin, same silky black hair, even the same almond-shaped eyes. The girl's perfect angles had come from her father's blood, but even carrying the weight of decades, Annika knew Niri Trisarin had turned many heads in her life.

"Actually," Annika said, "we were hoping to acquire room and board. Your daughter made your home sound so beautiful and accommodating, but I can see now her words did not do your lands justice."

Niri's face drew tight. "You must have met with someone else's daughter, because those words do not sound like the Ravael I know. Perhaps a scholar's child, who had been steeped in the knowledge of right and wrong day in and day out. You might have better luck finding such a home in the Reliquary."

Despite the callous tone, Annika caught the slight choke in Niri's throat as she finished. Not anger, then; at least, not entirely. Concern for her absent daughter was as potent within her as bitterness.

"Oh, you just have to know how to listen between all the scoffs and acerbic quips," Kymil said with a laugh. "She's really quite lovely, if you can ignore everything she says or does."

The bard threw back his violet cloak, its new rosy seam more a distinguishing detail than a mark of the garment's recent damage, and bowed. He then took Niri's hand as he rose to face her. "My name is Kymil Adii—poet, scribe, and puckish nomad. These are my attendants, Annika Iatorii, Mareq Iq'Urlset, and Ubadrii Tragala. It is a true pleasure to have met you in your picturesque orchard."

Niri smiled at him, giving a slight tilt of her head, but flicked her eyes to Annika. "Iatorii? Of the vineyard?" she asked. "I was under the impression that Kiif was managing the work out there now, and there have been no marriage announcements . . ."

"My cousin is indeed in control of the family estate since I decided to leave the island," Annika replied. "I found that while I had the head for it, there was no resuscitating the passion after the Rebellion of the Commons." An expression that Annika hadn't seen in many years crossed Niri's face, one of recognizable pity. It was the reason she had fled Felona after her sister's death—it took the entire width of the Marrow Strait to escape the public knowledge of her loss.

"My apologies," Niri said. "It's been so long. I had forgotten the Iatorii's adopted a daughter as well."

"That lapse in memory was intentional on my part," Annika said, now fighting her own tightening throat. "But unfortunate business has drawn me back to the island, and we were hoping you might be able to help."

"Unfortunate business is the only type Ravael likes to deal in." Niri sighed. "What has she done this time?"

"Prevented a war," Mareq said.

"Delayed one would perhaps be more apt," Ubadrii added, stepping forward to take Niri's hand. "Though the nation of Qedrad is in your family's debt, nonetheless."

Niri stood speechless for a time, mouthing words that wouldn't come. Finally, she said, "That child was always getting into more than she could handle."

Annika leaned forward, close enough that no hired harvesters would overhear. "You would be surprised how much a lightblood can handle if taught the proper restraint."

The color drained from Niri's face as her eyes darted back and forth, lingering on each nearby worker plucking the yellow citrus fruits on the adjacent rows. She cleared her throat and stood an inch taller, then turned and began walking toward her home.

"I believe my crew will be sufficient to finish today's haul. It's best if we continue this conversation inside. Follow me."

Niri led Annika and the others up the central row of twin tart trees, the acidic fragrance building with each step. Annika's mouth began to water—she had forgotten how much more sour a freshly picked twin tart was compared to what she could buy in Virdoba. But before she gave in to the urge to pluck one of the sunburst-hued orbs from a dangling branch, she found herself climbing the steps to the massive cherrywood doors of the Trisarin estate.

At Niri's first footfall on the deck, one of the polished doors swung inward, revealing a thin human man dressed in a formal dark suit, of an age with both Annika and Niri, and with more hair on his brows than remained on his head. Behind him, a grand foyer opened into a sitting room decorated in an understated style, though a few elements revealed that an elf had once lived here as well.

Ornate crystalline timepieces sat atop multiple surfaces in the room, the intricate gears within visible except for the distortions caused by the twisting of the clocks' glassy surfaces. Though much of the colors were subdued, Annika recognized vibrant green and blue accents in the décor that were popular among the elven immigrants to Anera. Most telling, however, was the family portrait over the mantle, featuring an attractive elven man in a clay-colored coat, one arm wrapped around a young Niri Trisarin and his other hand resting on a little elven girl of four or five. The artist had managed to capture a mischievous twinkle in her eye.

Before Annika could comment on Rav's unchanged disposition over two decades later, a loud click from either end of the foyer summoned her attention. Behind the group, the elderly man had his hand on a candelabra jutting off the wall at an odd angle, while Niri had done the same at the entrance to the main chamber. With only a second's pause, two iron gates dropped from the ceiling and latched into hidden plates on the floor, caging them in the estate.

The man who had opened the door calmly pulled a hand crossbow from a wooden locker against the wall, then pointed it at the group without a hint of emotion. Niri shuffled her foot onto a spot on the floor that depressed under her weight, and three panels in the ceiling opened to reveal large paper satchels suspended above.

"Frosted scat!" Mareq cursed, taking a step behind Kymil, who kept his warm grin in place despite gripping the hem of his cloak.

"Over twenty years, is it?" Niri asked. "And you Gulls have decided it's time to rob the world of another beautiful and gifted individual because, what? She declined an invitation to join your little club? Are your egos truly so fragile that you can't accept not everyone wants to be your friend?"

Ubadrii cleared his throat and gestured to his ears. "Do these look maimed to you, madam?"

"I have no way of knowing how the membership dues have changed," Niri said, then pointed at the dangling parcels. "But I do know the shelf-life of infused flayer's powder, and several pounds of a fresh batch is mere feet above you, held in place only by my continued pressure on this plate." She twisted her foot on the floor, and the bags quivered.

"One would think that having your internal membranes slough off into their respective cavities would be a horrible way to leave this world, so I would think twice about trying to harm me or Regi." The man with the crossbow tilted his head at them. "Now, speak plainly about your true motivations here."

"Twin tarts of the same bulb, it would seem," Annika said. Rav may have inherited her talents from Ilphas, but her fire was a maternal gift. "I haven't spoken a dishonest word, Niri. I am Annika Iatorii, and everyone else here is as introduced. But I can see now why Ravael was so surprised by her identity. You were trying to keep her safe."

Niri's face twitched, but her foot held steadfast. "Speak. Plainly."

"Despite your best efforts at hiding her, even from herself, a member of the Clipped Gulls named Tetamii Fiadar found your daughter after she publicly manifested her abilities in Virdoba." Annika paused as Niri winced at the targeted words, but quickly added, "Ravael is fine, rest assured. Neither the Illuminated Death nor this mercenary claimed her. She is with a friend learning how to remain safe in her own body, but I'm afraid we are here with unfinished business.

"The man who attempted to kill Ravael has escaped," Annika continued, "and with him our best bet at preventing the war Mareq mentioned outside." Mareq summoned the courage to step out from around Kymil's leg, lending a pair of pleading eyes to Annika's words. "Our aim in presenting ourselves to you was first, to bring you word of your daughter's safety, and second, to find an ally who has a vested interest in our success as well as more up-to-date knowledge of the city."

Niri disengaged the switch, sending the gate back up to the ceiling as she shifted her foot off the plate. Annika and the others flinched, but saw that the panels in the ceiling had once again covered the deadly infusion. With a flick of her wrist, Niri signaled across the foyer and Regi followed suit, calmly replacing the crossbow in its place.

"Put on a kettle for our guests, Regi," Niri said. "I always knew that girl would bring trouble to my door." The butler gave a slight nod of his head, then exited the room. Niri led the others to the sitting room, where Annika took a seat on a richly upholstered couch across from her.

"We're hoping to keep the trouble away from your doorstep," Annika said. "I plan to meet with a few members of the Council individually, ones who would be more open to the idea that one of their own is shifting the continent toward ruin. Do you have any leads on who would make strong allies before we meet with the Council as a whole to present our evidence?"

Niri sighed and shook her head. "You've been away a long time, Annika. Much has changed. When is your meeting with the Council?"

Annika sent a side-eyed glare at Ubadrii. "We don't have a standing appointment, unfortunately. Though my family name should still carry enough weight to grant us an audience."

"Not anymore," Niri said. "After the attempt on Berenqar's life—and by this man's presence in my home I'm assuming Ravael played some role in that event—Elikar Thymes tightened security in the city, particularly on people moving in and out of the council hall. No new meetings are scheduled without a thorough vetting, a process I'm told takes months.

"And if Elikar is the one you aim to accuse, which seems evident by your tense jaws and just the fact that the man is known horse's ass, I don't think you'll be passing the inspection any time soon. If he has any hint that you might know compromising information about him, you might find yourself in prison before long. Elikar is a powerful man, and despite being a prick, he does have a wealth of support in the city. Many of his trade decisions have improved the general quality of life in Felona. He is not an enemy to make lightly."

Annika's mind spun. Their plan was unraveling before they had even begun. Without the mercenary to flip on Elikar, and now no chance for a meeting with the Council, what hope did they have of stopping a rebirth of the War of Arrival?

The piercing sound of a boiling kettle pulled her out of her spiral. She glanced up to see Niri eyeing her with concern.

"But if you're sure," Niri said after a moment's hesitation, "I can get you in. The Bindweed Conservatory sends a representative to meet with the Council every quarter to discuss the district's needs. I can take my turn at the job—Irasil knows I've dodged it the last few times anyway."

"It sounds like my king was wise in not announcing our arrival, then," Ubadrii said as an aside to Annika. The man had a childish streak behind that serious façade. "It would only have allowed Councilman Thymes to be prepared for us, but now we can catch him by surprise. When is this meeting, Ms. Trisarin?"

"Tomorrow," she replied, with a half-smirk that made Annika feel as if Rav had suddenly joined them. A taste for chaos ran deep in this family.

CHAPTER 9

FELONA

Elikar Thymes's office was a thing of beauty, with polished leather seating and lacquered wood surfaces, but this was not always the case. The role of the Kefyan Port Admiral was an important member of the Council, but the person sitting in the seat often cared more for nautical themes in their décor. As such, when he had assumed the position, he found himself discarding garish mounted marlins and decorative netting as his first order of business, followed soon after by more than a few bottled ship replicas.

It wasn't the gaudy bits and bobbles that he found most offensive—though they certainly were. No, it was the hypocrisy of it all. His posh predecessors wanted the appearance of being salty sea dogs, but they stirred their tea with the same silver spoons he always had. Elikar much preferred people to own their station in life. It helped those beneath him to remember where they stood.

A knock came at the door, and Elikar answered, "Come."

His secretary, a pudgy man with tight dark curls on his head, pushed open the door and stepped into the office. "Councilman Thymes, your associates have arrived."

"Thank you, Grively," Elikar said, not bothering to adjust his relaxed posture in his chair. Not for these two. "Walk them back, would you?"

"Certainly, sir. Right away." Grively stepped back out, softly shutting the door behind him.

Elikar had been eagerly anticipating this meeting since learning of the Clipped Gulls' successful extraction days earlier. His incriminating loose end was now back in safe hands, but he would have answers as to how Magzii's "best man" was captured in the first place.

More pressing, however, were the captors themselves, now apparently at large in his city. Without their captive, this group's case before the Council would be their word against his—an eventuality he was comfortable he could overcome. Still, it would be unfortunate to call in favors or have his name associated with dark rumors when he was on the cusp of his greatest achievement. His reputation needed to remain spotless, so these pawns needed to be taken off the board.

A moment later there was another brief knock at the door before it swung inward once more. Grively stepped through carrying a bottle of dark rum in one hand, then shifted aside to reveal the two men he had been expecting.

Vulmar Magzii was perhaps the roughest-looking individual who had ever set foot in council chambers without being in chains, and that was considering all the elven aesthetic advantages with which he had been born. One long scar dominated much of his face, though other smaller ones competed for attention, and his silver-ringed irises almost sent a chill up Elikar's spine without the man even having to tickle the World Shroud. He had heard the rumors about the gang leader's abilities—there was not much that went on in Felona to which Elikar was not privy—but there would be no icy assaults this night. Regardless of Magzii's veil connection, the man had to know where the real power sat in this room. Moreover, there was a boyish, almost cocky smile on Magzii's face, so he trusted the leader of the Gulls had come with good news.

His compatriot, however, was a bundle of nerves. Soren Tomau followed the Clipped Gull into the office, tricorn hat in hand and held in front of his waist as his eyes anxiously studied the gleaming floorboards. Elikar was not concerned about the captain's anxiety, though. The man had played his part well enough.

"Councilman Thymes," Magzii said, striding across the floor and shaking Elikar's hand. "We've got some news that I'm sure will set a grin on that stony face of yours. But I had your man fetch a bottle of the barrel-aged stuff so we can loosen up the good captain."

From the doorway, Grively presented the bottle with both hands. Elikar nodded and gestured with a wrist toward a silver bowl of twin tarts at the side of the room. After a slight tilt of the head, his secretary walked over to the cabinet and pulled out glasses.

Elikar turned his gaze to Tomau but said nothing. The only way to get the truth out of a scared man was to let them talk until it all came spilling out.

"Councilman Thymes," Tomau said, shaking Elikar's hand with much less confidence and much more sweat. "Thank you for granting us this audience to explain what happened aboard my ship."

A stretch of silence followed, only broken by the clink of ice in glasses across the room, as Elikar continued his stare. Tomau cleared his throat.

"You see, I was prepared for the Gulls to board us, but I had not been warned about the day or time," Tomau said. "Had I known it would be that far out from the harbor, I would have worked to keep your man's captors occupied so your crew could . . . you know, handle things." The captain's eyes once again shot down at that.

Grively walked over to the three men seated around Elikar's desk, handing an amber-colored drink to each before stepping back out of the room. The tang of the fresh twin tart juice was mellowed by the rum's molasses notes, and as Elikar took a sip from the Felonian sour, he decided it was time to let Tomau off the hook.

"Everything went as planned, captain," Elikar said. "Collect yourself. Have a drink."

Tomau exhaled and settled back into his chair before taking a solid gulp of the cocktail. Magzii laughed and slapped a hand on the man's shoulder.

"We never planned on killing those other folks on the ship," Magzii said. "How would that have looked? Only the newcomers killed while the rest of your crew was left unharmed?" The captain's eyes narrowed at that, but he wisely kept his mouth shut. Magzii wouldn't hurt Tomau in this office, but if the captain complained about his maimed crew, there was no assurance he wouldn't be gutted the second they made it off council grounds.

"No," Magzii continued, "we would've had to kill everyone on board and sink the ship for good measure if we wanted to keep rumors from flying."

"Ah," Tomau said. "You wanted the people who interfered with your plans in Alaboq to dock here safely?"

"I have more resources at my disposal at home to clean up the mess they are trying to make than I would attempting to silence them at a distance," Elikar said.

"And on that note," Magzii said, holding up a finger as he drank from his glass. He grimaced. "A bit too much honey for my taste. But I guess you fancy types like your drinks a little smoother than us down in the Trough."

Elikar's silent gaze turned toward Magzii now, taking in the brute's feigned opulence. Magzii had taken to wearing tailored clothing, though the stitching revealed its humble origins to anyone with an eye for fashion, and had even adopted Elikar's relaxed posture in his seat. He was growing too comfortable, reaching beyond his station. But his desperation for acceptance in the higher strata of Felonian life made him controllable, so Elikar opted to enjoy the farcical attempt rather than take offense.

Under Elikar's scrutiny, however, for once Magzii's cocksure grin faltered. "Ahem, as I was saying. The Clipped Gulls have already taken the initiative on that front, and I've tasked my best man with rooting those troublemakers out. Soon enough, you'll have no one to speak out against you. Then, you can get right back on track toward lining your pockets with all that blood money."

"This wouldn't happen to be your 'best man' who they captured in the first place, would it?" Elikar asked.

"Tetamii can get a little sure of himself," Magzii said, and Elikar struggled to keep his eyes from rolling out of his head at the irony. "But after his embarrassing display up north, he'll make better choices this time around. Plus, he has the rest of the organization at his disposal now that he's back home with us."

"And the girl isn't here, either," Tomau said. The man still refused to make eye contact with anything other than what was directly below his nose. Elikar would have to have a talk with him about the dangers of a conscience when money has already changed hands. "From what I hear, the rest of the group won't stand much of a chance against him without the lightblood."

Elikar nearly choked on his drink, but took a moment to recover before he spoke. "Lightblood?" Why wasn't I informed of this? A trained lightblood would be able to run circles around even the best scorcher, and your agent never thought to send word about this pest?"

Magzii grinned wide. "Like I said, my boy Tetamii can get a bit cocky. It won't happen again."

"And for what it's worth, I don't think she was trained," Tomau said. "That's why she and her friend didn't come aboard with the rest of them. They were talking about going off to find some school where she could learn how to control her abilities."

The elf laughed, leaning back and crossing his leg nonchalantly. "See what I mean? The rest of us won't let him hear the end of it, and that will be sure to fix his judgment. He deserves all the ribbing he gets if Tetamii couldn't stop a little girl who was just as likely to fry her brain as land a punch."

Magzii drained his glass and smiled, then tilted the glass toward Elikar. "This is growing on me, by the way. The honey coats the throat, and you can really taste the oak notes."

Elikar ignored him and the fact that the rum had been aged in a heartfir barrel, instead turning back to Tomau. "Where is the school?"

"Oh," Tomau said, swirling the remaining ice in his glass. "Somewhere up north, I think. It's hard to say, really. If you ask me about any spot along the coast, I can describe it to you so that you feel like you're standing right there in the shallows, but anywhere on the map that's not touching the sea might as well be a blob of shi—"

"Captain," Elikar interrupted. Tomau's eyes pulled away from his drink to meet his own. "Where?"

Tomau swallowed. "The Tesigan Peaks. Somewhere in the northern stretch of that mountain range. I swear, I don't know anything more specific than that."

Elikar sipped from his glass. The northern portion of the Tesigan Peaks was in Qedrad, too far to send another local agent that way. He couldn't risk the girl leaving before one of the Gulls managed to find their way to the school. Plus, Magzii's crew were island dwellers. They were apt to get lost in the first snow drift they came across.

"All right then," Magzii said as he stood up and strode over to the side table, then began helping himself to more rum. The simpleton added more than triple the amount of honey than was called for, and Elikar grinded his teeth. "Once Tetamii is finished with the easier targets here in Felona, I'll send him back up north.

In the meantime, I can have some of my other guys scout the location out an—"

"No," Elikar said, setting down his glass and pulling on a wire next to his desk. A bell chimed outside his door, and within seconds Grively popped his head back into the room.

"Yes sir?" he asked.

"Gather the names of my connections in Achen, specifically the Granish guild-family," Elikar said. "It is my understanding that they control the largest portion of their country's military through their own private funding, and I want to call in a favor or two."

"Will you be inquiring after their more efficient officers?" Grively asked. "If so, I can collate the contacts in order of those with the highest concentration under their control."

Elikar appreciated his penchant for keeping information vague in mixed company, but in this instance, there was no need for subtlety. Tomau would faint if the idea of betrayal even crossed his mind, and Magzii wouldn't dare bite the hand that fed him. The leader of the Clipped Gulls was no longer a scrappy street hound. Elikar had made him a lapdog.

"Yes," Elikar replied. "If this lightblood put a scorcher out of commission, I want any contingent I send after her to have more than a few blade serpents among their number. She might be fast, but her body has its limits. She can't outpace a whipcrack, much less a dozen."

"Right away, sir," Grively said, stepping out just as quickly as he had arrived.

"That's really not necessary, councilman," Magzii said. One of his eyebrows twitched at the reminder of his man's failure. He took a drink from his overly sweet concoction and grimaced. "The Clipped Gulls have everything under control."

"No, Magzii," Elikar said. "I have everything under control. Remember that."

INTERLUDE

BEFORE

The older boy's fist slammed into Tetamii's stomach for the second time, and still he felt as if he wasn't getting his money's worth. The jeers from the crowd of street kids that surrounded them were convincing enough, but he was concerned that an adult would not be so easily fooled. Tetamii feigned doubling over in pain, keeping his back to most of the gathering as he looked up to make eye contact with his attacker. He gave the boy a quick head tilt, trying to hide a message in the face of someone who had just had the wind knocked out of him.

His attacker cocked an eyebrow that accompanied a nervous smile, but when Tetamii gave him another nod, the other boy just shrugged. Money was money, and Tetamii had paid him enough libers to do just about anything. Not that it had been much—a few silver libers the Clipped Gulls had placed in his hands the day prior—but to children accustomed to living on the streets of the Trough, that was a small fortune. More than sufficient to punch a crazy kid as hard as he wanted to be hit.

Another blow landed, this one across Tetamii's jaw, and he tasted blood. *Finally*, he thought, suppressing a smile. *Now keep it up, you oaf.*

Before he regained solid footing, a knee rammed into Tetamii's side, sending him stumbling into the wall of children.

"Get back out there, dagger-head," one of the boys sneered as he caught him, then gave him a shove back out into the center of the impromptu fighting ring. Tetamii fell flat on his face, skidding to a stop a few feet from the lanky adolescent's scuffed boots. It seemed the other boy's partial elven blood had made him the crowd favorite against Tetamii's undeniable heritage.

"Careful you don't get those ears stuck in the mud," shouted a black-toothed girl from the other side, getting a round of laughter from everyone looking on.

Suddenly, Tetamii's vision erupted with violent translucent wisps, and he grasped at them, feeling the heat behind the veil rising on pace with the heat in his cheeks. He pulled and flattened the tendrils, each one trembling and ready to tear at the slightest effort. Tetamii pictured flames raining down on the ring of spectators, roasting every one of the dirty urchins who dared to mock him.

But somewhere nearby, down the street, or in a window above, or any other nook Tetamii had not thought of, Vulmar Magzii was watching. This wasn't only a test of his deceptive skills, after all. Tetamii was also being observed for his ability to maintain his composure, particularly his restraint when provoked. He wouldn't miss out on this chance to escape the dredges of society because some bigoted children made a comment about his ears.

With a deep breath, Tetamii released his grip on the World Shroud, and the ambient temperature of the alley dropped the dozen or so degrees it had climbed in those few seconds. He pushed himself back to his feet and set his fists. He needed to lose this fight to remain sympathetic to his target, but that didn't mean he couldn't get in a few good hits.

"He's still got some fight in 'em," his opponent said with a quizzical glance, then gave a slow spin to share in a laugh with the crowd. But by the time he completed his circle, Tetamii was landing three quick jabs into his scrawny belly. His knuckles burned and crunched with the impact, as Tetamii's thin elven arms struggled against the older boy's sheer mass. However, the attack had been enough of a shock to send the teen back on his heels, and Tetamii pressed on.

He leaped at his face, swinging an elbow down so it crushed the boy's nose. Blood sprayed out across each of their filthy tunics as the pair landed on the ground, locked in a rolling grapple. Tetamii clawed at the boy's shoulders, but in seconds the boy had knocked Tetamii's arms aside and flipped over on top of him. Now, Tetamii was flat and defenseless on his back, his arms pinned to his side under his opponent's knees. A trickle of blood continued to drop out of the boy's nose and splash into Tetamii's eyes and mouth as he struggled to squirm out of this position.

"This isn't what we talked about," the older boy whispered, then spat a glob of bloody saliva beside Tetamii's face. "So the price just went up. If you can't pay it, I'll just have to amuse myself this way."

Fist after fist pummeled Tetamii's face, and his vision began to blur. He could feel the flesh around his eyes tightening as it swelled, but it was more than that. His body was screaming out for the World Shroud, and the smoke-like curls were responding in kind, flooding his senses more than he had ever experienced. One little tear in the veil, and this brute would see what true power was. Tetamii took hold of a wisp that swam around his opponent's head and pulled, feeling the fire beyond it fueling his rage.

"What's all this?" a voice called from down the street, sending much of the gathered children scrambling in the opposite direction. The man's accent had a musical lilt, one Tetamii believed his mother shared, though he was beginning to forget the sound of her voice, and that snapped him out of his fugue state. His target had taken the bait.

As the crowd cleared, three city guards were revealed, each of them leaning against the wall without a care in the world. One was even halfway through a massive turkey leg and had grease smeared across his smiling face. But when they turned to see the new-comer, they stood a bit straighter, the one on lunch tucking his remaining food behind his back.

Through his remaining open eye, Tetamii saw the man he had been expecting: a tall, raven-haired elf dressed respectably for the Trough but not ostentatiously. He was clean and pressed, two words not often ascribed to the wardrobes found in this neighborhood, with a matching set of dark green woolen coat and trousers. His shoulder-length straight hair was pulled back into a tail, and its dark color popped all the more due to his sandy skin tone. His physical traits were a bit rarer in Kefya, but Ilphas Trisarin was a native of Liiashae, so Tetamii shouldn't have been too surprised.

"Are we just standing around and watching children beat each other senseless these days?" Ilphas asked the guards. None offered much more than a half-hearted shrug or embarrassed grin. "I'll have to have a word with Guard Captain Vyrew the next time I'm visiting the Council's chambers. This is a distressing change of policy, and one which I'm sure the councilmembers will line up against once it has been brought to light."

"No sir, Mr. Trisarin," the greasy-faced one offered, finally remembering to wipe his mouth on the back of his sleeve. It was impressive how much respect this man commanded, and he hadn't even been elected yet. "But you know how kids are. Sometimes they just have to knock some sense into themselves, learn about life's ins and outs."

Ilphas stepped forward and brushed aside the single cerulean knot attached to the guard's collar, the lack of any companion knots denoting his low rank. "Do you have children, private?"

"No, sir. Not yet."

"I hope that by the time you do, you'll have a different philosophy on their education." Ilphas turned to regard Tetamii and the other boy, who was attempting to stop the hemorrhage in his nose by stuffing it with a dropped handkerchief. "Now, which of you two wants to tell me what the commotion was about?"

"He shtarthed ith," the boy said with his head tilted back.

As Ilphas's gaze turned toward him, Tetamii wiped the blood from his mouth and said, "He's right, sir. I did." He stared down at his feet, which he shuffled about nervously. Tetamii thought it was a good affectation for his performance, particularly because it mirrored how he was feeling.

Ilphas frowned. "Care to tell me why?"

Tetamii shot a brief glance at the older boy. "All the bigger kids get to work, so they have more money to spend on food while the rest of us have to riffle through the garbage or live off crumbs until we can scrape together enough for a meal." He paused, looking up at his target and letting free the tears he had been holding back since his beating had begun.

"Today, I just decided that it wasn't fair anymore. I took some of Atusiin's lunch and gave it to a few of the other boys, and he got mad at that. But he's forgotten what it feels like to go to sleep hungry since he started apprenticing at the tannery."

"That nod wha—" Atusiin started.

"Tears don't excuse theft, boy," one of the guards said as he took a step forward to stand next to Ilphas. "Should I take these two criminals to the pen for a night or two, sir? We both want to save the councilmembers the trouble, right?"

Ilphas shook his head. "No, private. You can't correct survivalist behaviors by locking someone up. Besides, these are children. They need to be in schools during the day where they can be provided a substantive meal."

"I don't think the Cresters will take kindly to kids in rags joining their precious little ones in class," said another guard from behind them.

"They shouldn't have to," Ilphas snapped. "There's no reason all of Felona's schools should be bound to the Crest and Reliquary neighborhoods. But that will be one of many reforms coming our way after the election.

"Until then," Ilphas said, looking back to the two children, "escort the older one back to the tannery where he apprentices. I would like to have a few words with the instigator myself."

With a few curt nods, the three guards helped the larger boy to his feet and began walking him away. But before they cleared the alley, Ilphas called out to them. "I will be checking in with him and the tanner later. I want to give the Council a report of your courteous and prompt service to the city, so do give me something positive to say." Mumbled agreements were the only response. Then they disappeared out into the busy street.

Tetamii sniffed. "Please, sir. I won't do anything like that again. We can keep picking through the discards for a few more years." He raised a hand to his face and gingerly touched the flesh around his eye. "It's not worth the bruising."

Ilphas knelt to meet him, a sad grin gracing his face. Tetamii had to admit, the man was good for someone who was just another smile in a suit. The way all the downtrodden of Felona hung from his every word was testament to his skill, and from what Tetamii had heard, Ilphas's speeches rivaled the stage presence of most traveling bards. Perhaps he had another calling as an entertainer, but the man was smarter than that.

Why perform for a pittance when you could perform for power?

"Your health and well-being are worth a lot more than a black eye or a bloody nose," Ilphas said. "I'm sorry that the state of this city has told you that this was your only recourse to fill your belly. But if I have my way, that won't be the case for long. Big changes are coming to Felona—ones that will let boys like you have every opportunity to live the lives they deserve."

"I don't think there will ever be a place for me out there, sir," Tetamii said, gesturing out beyond the city's walls where wealthy families had established vineyards and orchards over the rest of the fertile island soil. "Unless you mean you could get me a spot as an aphid. The word of a man dressed like you would probably go a long way."

Tetamii hoped his enthusiasm at the possibility of working as one of the hired farm laborers in the Tangled Vines would drive home the guilt trip. Instead, Ilphas' mouth split into a knowing grin before the man let out a chuckle. Perhaps Tetamii needed to work on subtlety when trying to manipulate someone who wasn't just another street child.

"Does that mean you enjoy working with plants?" Ilphas asked. "I know you don't want to spend all day running back and forth along those dizzying paths."

"Oh, of course," Tetamii lied, the tension in his chest un-clenching as he realized he was not going to be called on his attempts to maneuver into Ilphas' orbit. "Who wouldn't? You get to help something grow and grow until it can start feeding people around it."

Ilphas laughed and stood, taking a moment to wipe the alley dust from his knee.

A man must have his priorities, Tetamii thought. *Can't have the public see him parading down the street with grime on his pants.*

After a moment glancing Tetamii up and down, Ilphas nod-ded. "You're a bit young yet, but I could use an apprentice myself at my orchard. How would you feel about coming to work for me? You'll be paid fairly, of course, and there may even be some extra twin tarts for you to spread around to your friends."

Tetamii let his tears flow more freely, squeezing out past his swollen eyes so that they stung all the cuts on his face until they reached the edges of his widened grin. He hoped Magzii could see this performance—it might even rival his target's own. If Tetamii had the stomach for screwing over people for personal gain, he thought he could even have a go at this politician thing with some success.

It's a shame I'm a better person than that.

PART II

Chapter 10

The Illumined Scale

The sound of iron scraping against iron had become less grating than infuriating over the last few days. Since Rav had begun what Master Zylnala referred to as training—but in reality must have been some obscure form of Qedradan torture—she had spent day after day waiting for that soul-crushing sound to come and announce her latest failure.

She held her right arm in front of her, palm flat and wearing a metal-plated glove like the one Adiin had worn during their introductory sparring session. It was pressed hard against a heavy iron disc, at least two feet in diameter and weighing close to thirty pounds, which in turn she had pinned in place against a larger iron slab affixed to the cavern wall. The task was simple, in theory if not execution: keep the disc against the slab for eight hours, with the caveat being she was only allowed to touch the plate with the flat of her palm.

After days of this, her arms had bypassed soreness and entered a state of numb acquiescence. With her experiences on the less trustworthy sides of life, Rav initially thought there must be some trick involved; some loophole in the instructions that would make the job simple, if only she could figure it out. But then she witnessed both Adiin and Riqu hold their plates against their slabs for half the required time without breaking a sweat or making so much as a strained expression. All while her plate clattered to the floor repeatedly.

Another such crash was blocked out by Rav's scream of frustration. She bent and gripped the disc with both hands, then tossed it off to the right before stepping up to stand inches from the iron slab. There had to be something she was missing, and not for the first time, Rav pulled off her gloves and began running her fingers over the wall plate. A notch, a depressible section—there would be something there, if only she could find it.

"Have you tried smelling it?" Adiin asked. The elf had walked into the chamber silently, as was his habit, and was leaning against the back wall with a smirk that would shame even the smarmiest conman. "Or perhaps tasting it would be best. Either way, your investigations with touch and sight are clearly coming up empty."

"Maybe I could slam your head against it to check the resonance," Rav said, slinking over to retrieve her disc with slumped shoulders.

Adiin laughed in his haughty way. "Kudos on the creativity, but might I recommend your own skull? I have a feeling the internal acoustics would be superior."

Rav felt her hackles rise, but instead of unloading the full force of her fury on the prick, she took a breath and returned to her spot in front of the slab. No matter how irritating Adiin's barbs were, he was right. She had spent hours already looking for some cheat that would allow her to pass Zylnala's test, but that wouldn't be the point of his exercise. The purpose of the Illumined Scale was teaching lightbloods to control their own power, and that couldn't be done with a shortcut.

"Did you need something?" Rav asked as she put her gloves back on, feeling the weight of the small iron squares on either side of her hands. "Or are you here to practice your powers of annoyance? You're already quite talented in the area. It might be a better use of your time to work on another social skill, like not being a complete ass."

Rav watched his smug grin fall from his face and couldn't stop her own from blossoming. She raised the plate back up to the wall, placing her left palm against it this time—her right could hardly be lifted more than a few inches from her body after the last effort—and already she could feel the disc starting to slide.

Adiin tutted. "That's it. Put your whole shoulder into it. I wonder, will your stubborn misplaced pride give out first, or your tendons?"

She tried to block him out. Anger wasn't going to be the key to solving this problem. If it were, she would've passed this trial days ago. The only thing that had unlocked her powers before was mortal danger, and that was obviously not needed for either Adiin or Riqu. But if it wasn't peril or fury that was opening those two up to the Wellspring, what else could be forming that connection?

"My crests are on the tendons," Adiin said as he walked into her peripheral vision. "Someone as mule-headed as you could drive your body into the ground before you realized it was time to give in."

He was right about one thing. Rav wasn't about to give up on the first task the school placed in front of her. Not only did she refuse to let a man-child like Adiin to get the best of her, but she wouldn't slink back to Felona with her head low and listen to the disappointment dripping from the mouths of both her mother and Annika. Not to mention the memory of Alauvar's sacrifice, a mantle that she felt had been unjustly draped across her shoulders, but one she found herself wanting to live up to nonetheless. Annika was using her as a chance at redemption, which was both unfair and understandable, and Rav was compelled to provide that for her.

She denied the possibility of failure as an outcome, even if it meant she would spend the next few years of her life here, in this spot, holding a metal disc against a metal wall.

Suddenly, she felt a tickle on the nape of her neck. If she hadn't seen Adiin standing several feet to her right, she would've thought he had crept up behind her. But the tickle quickly spread, racing over every inch of her flesh until she felt the coursing energy of the Wellspring build into a thrumming pulse.

The weight of the disc had not lessened, but her muscles were being replenished as they drank deeply from beyond the World Shroud. What once had been a task she could manage for minutes at a time, she now felt as if she could do all day. Without muscle fatigue, pinning the iron disc to the wall was merely an exercise in will, and though she would never admit it to her audience, Rav's stubbornness could be the stuff of legend.

Adiin took a step closer, shifting so that he could see more of her face. "Impossible," he breathed. "You've been at this for less than a week. Where were you trained before coming here?"

Rav's face was stone, her eyes never flickering away from the disc. It and the wall might as well be the same hunk of iron for as little as she was allowing it to move. Bright lights were beginning to pop throughout her vision, which was not unexpected as her body siphoned more and more energy, but it had never started this quickly before. If the past was any indication, she would have to drop the disc long before the required time or risk pulling too much electricity through.

Adiin paced forward. "Master Zylnala will not stand for this misuse of his time and resources. The Illumined Scale is a place for lightbloods who need help mastering their abilities, not arrogant girls looking to show off—" He stopped, then took another step closer so that his face was less than a foot from hers.

"Oh, I see," he said, all the venom now absent from his tone.

The lights were blinding now, consuming every corner of her vision as the muscles in her arm began to spasm. The base of her neck felt as if one of her pitons was slowly being driven through her skin. This wasn't right. She had run through entire cities, even fought a scorcher at the height of his powers, all without drawing so much energy so quickly.

"You have to stop," Adiin said. Was that concern in his voice, or more mockery for an initiate he believed to be beneath him?

Metal scraped against metal as the disc began to slide, but Rav leaned into her hold. She could no longer see the wall or even her hand, but she didn't need to. The disc would stay in place—nothing was going to change that.

"Seriously," Adiin said. "Stop now. You're going to kill yourself."

But of course he would say that, when she was so close to besting him. The Wellspring would fuel her through this, and she would prove to everyone in this damn school what she could accomplish.

A hand landed across her head, fingers gripping into her forehead, and her vision blurred. Then, she heard the disc clatter to the ground once again before she lost consciousness.

***

She awoke sometime later, though she guessed it could not have been long. If she had been out for an extended period of time, Rav thought she would've been moved to her quarters, and Wymund would've been pacing at the foot of her bed.

Instead, she was at the opposite end of the chamber, across from the three iron wall plates, and propped up against the rocky wall. Adiin was nowhere in sight, but seated beside her was Master

Zylnala, his legs bent in front of him as he stared forward with a serene expression.

"How are you feeling?" he asked without shifting his eyes toward her.

"Like I just survived another fight I didn't have any right surviving," she said. Rav reached up to massage the base of her skull, no longer spasming but sore deep into the tissue. Her arm fought her the whole way up, achingly moving through its own fatigued state. "What did Adiin do to me?"

"You know," Zylnala said, finally turning toward her. "Despite his best efforts, not everything stems from his actions."

"So you're saying he didn't grab my head?" Rav asked. "I know I can't really trust my body when I get into that state, but I've never hallucinated another person touching me."

"Oh, I didn't say no one grabbed your skull," Zylnala said, holding up his hand in a jaunty wave. "It just wasn't Adiin."

Rav raised an eyebrow. "No 'Blinded Miabalar?'"

"I don't get the sense you are one for standing on ceremony," Zylnala said with a wink. "Besides, you will soon learn that I enjoy keeping my initiates guessing."

Rav sighed. "And I've heard it's difficult getting information out of *me*. Well, whatever you did to me, I suppose I should be thanking you for saving my life. Did you just tilt my head back to pour a potion down my throat? That's been the trick to pulling me away from death's grasp in the past."

"It was nothing so exorbitant as dosing you with a witch's serum," Zylnala said. "Those are expensive and far too difficult to get up here in the mountains. You haven't even passed the entrance trial yet, and therefore haven't shown yourself to be worth that sort of investment." The elf stood, then offered Rav a hand up.

"No," Zylnala said. "I simply forced your mind to take a little nap for a bit. Much more cost effective, if you ask me."

Rav remembered a time not that long ago, after her first encounter with Tetamii and second brush with the Illuminated Death, when another man had touched her head and made her fall asleep. He had also spoken with a serenity that was reminiscent of Zylnala's way of speaking, but that was where the similarities ended. The master of the school didn't have the same striking emerald eyes or practiced physical grace that the blond-haired stranger possessed.

But that man wasn't elven, she thought. *He couldn't have been a lightblood, too.*

"Nice trick," Rav said. "I've seen it done better, though."

Zylnala sighed playfully. "Ah well, I never claimed to be the pinnacle of lightblood technique. Only a purveyor of safe practices." He turned to walk over to the iron walls, gesturing for Rav to follow. "To that point, why don't you tell me what happened today?"

"I don't really know," Rav said. "Adiin was trying to break my concentration, which is nothing new. Only this time, I realized that anger had never worked as a key to my abilities, so I tried to block him out."

"Anger is antithetical to a lightblood mastering her powers," Zylnala agreed. "However, something you did opened the veil, and you appeared to let it course through you unchecked."

Rav walked over to the spot where she had been practicing, then bent over to retrieve the disc. It was still heavy even with both hands supporting the weight—a reminder that she was nowhere close to the level of control that was needed to pass Zylnala's trial.

"I think I just . . . decided I was done failing," she said. "After seeing Adiin and Riqu keep their discs in place for hours every day, feeling his mocking sneers and her sympathetic glances creep up my spine, I was done not meeting that standard." She placed the disc back on the ground and turned to look back at Zylnala, whose smile was now accompanied by a surprised cocked brow.

"And that was when the floodgates burst open," she said. "I've never felt the energy from the Wellspring consume me so quickly."

"Determination is an important component of what we do," Zylnala said. "But it is only one side of the scale. If that's all you use to tap into your power, the balance is lost, and you will draw too much. Without the counterweight, you become a conduit for the World Shroud to siphon through, and our mortal bodies were not built for that."

"I don't get the feeling you're going to tell me what sits on the other side of the scale," Rav said with a sigh.

Zylnala laughed. "And deprive you of the joy found in learning? What kind of teacher would that make me?" When Rav grumbled, he added, "But I also understand the importance of decompressing. Take the rest of the day to recover and resume your trial tomorrow. We're in no hurry to boot you or your friend from our halls."

"Wymund will appreciate you letting him to stay," Rav said. "Put him to work if you have to. He likes feeling useful."

"I have the man doing more than he knows," Zylnala said, then left Rav to gather her things and return to her bed for a more natural slumber.

Chapter 11

The Illumined Scale

Wymund dodged left, then right, avoiding Riqu's lumbering blows with ease. She was tiring, but that was only exacerbating the problem she had since the start of their sparring match. Despite the woman's ability to siphon electrical energy like Rav, the size of her body—particularly her limbs—was preventing her from maximizing on the speed it granted her. The partial draqesh blood that flowed through her veins would make any successful punch land like hammer strike, if only she could make contact.

When Wymund struck back at her, though, Riqu's defensive talent shone. She knew how to twist her body to minimize the damage, reducing most of Wymund's strikes to glancing blows, or positioning herself so that he could only land punches on less vulnerable spots. A fist he had aimed for her open abdomen suddenly became a raised thigh as she turned her hip to intercept the attack. She was able to capitalize on her enhanced speed for these smaller protective movements, just not for any larger assaults.

Riqu's left jab passed harmlessly by his head as Wymund sidestepped it once again, and this time he hooked a leg behind hers and pulled. Her knees buckled and she toppled to the ground, catching herself before her face landed flat on the wooden platform.

"Aargh," she screamed, slapping an open palm on the planks. Wymund braced himself for a tirade or a brash attempt to lunge at him, but instead, Riqu closed her eyes and took a deep, slow breath. When she flicked her eyes open, she stood and adjusted her tunic. There was an odd look of acceptance on her face rather than the defiance he had expected.

I suppose not all lightbloods have a quick fuse.

"Frustration is understandable," Wymund said. "But that's only because you're trying to force your body into a fighting style it's not fit to use. Fast jabs and kicks may work well for people like Rav and Adiin, but you'll want to bring people in closer. Grapple and pin your opponents how you want them, and then push your advantage."

"I see why Master Zylnala wanted you to work with me," Riqu said. "Before I came to the school, I didn't have much martial training. Clearly, there is a lack of fundamentals holding me back."

Wymund shrugged. "I honestly believed Zylnala was hoping to keep me occupied. He didn't know what to do with a non-lightblood here, so he decided to take advantage of the one skillset I have to offer."

Markis and Fulja, the husband and wife they had seen preparing vegetables upon entering the Illumined Scale, had obviously been hired and kept on for their culinary prowess. Markis had kept their bellies happy and full since their arrival—a welcome change of pace from their mountain trekking meals—and Fulja had a knack for pastries that would put the greatest bakers in Kefya to shame. And while Master Zylnala was technically in charge of the school, it was clear just how lost he would be without Luviila's administrative skills. She kept the place running.

If Wymund possessed a marketable skill beyond fighting, he might've been put to work doing something else, but he supposed he should just be grateful that he had been allowed to stay. He had no passion for combat, but he did enjoy building others up, and he thought he could add some benefit to Riqu's training.

"Don't diminish the task he's given you," Riqu replied. "Developing a martial technique is an important part of the master's training regimen."

"Is he attempting to build up a legion of lightblood warriors?" Wymund asked, shuddering at the idea of a contingent of Ravs let loose on a battlefield.

"Nothing so ominous," Riqu said with a laugh. "It's more to do with the nature of our connection to the Wellspring. The power that flows through us uses us, rather than the other way around. We don't have the benefit of creating external entryways into our world for the energy like direct siphoners do. When a stormforger calls lightning, it can come from the sky or anywhere else they desire. For us, our bodies are the only gates."

"And to sustain that, your body needs to be as strong as possible," Wymund said. "It makes sense, though with your heritage, I'm not sure how much more strength you can expect to gain."

Riqu's face turned sullen. "If only it were that easy." She turned away from him, taking a seat on the edge of the platform that faced the network of buildings Zylnala had constructed within this icy cavern.

"Besides," she added, turning back to him with a half-hearted smile. "It's not so much about raw strength as it is physical discipline. In order to control the flow of energy through us, we have to master both our bodies and minds. The sparring practice is just one part of it."

Wymund walked over to join her, taking care to walk around the spot underneath the massive emeralds in their brass fixture. He was sure that the Gem Hall had been constructed well enough, but Wymund couldn't trust ice to be a permanent building material when supporting gemstones the size of barrels.

"You show more promise than you give yourself credit for," Wymund said as he settled in next to her. "I've been in this line of work for quite some time. You shouldn't feel ashamed that you couldn't best me in only a few hours."

Riqu looked at him, and Wymund recognized something in her eyes—he had seen it in the mirror for much of his life. It was the look of a person who felt unrealized, and from his own experience, he knew this was not only the result of losing a practice bout.

"I don't mind not being a natural warrior," she said. "I spent most of my life in a small town south of Qravburn, where most of my neighbors were just other members of my family. We rough-housed, sure, but my self-worth was never tied up in winning those scrapes."

"Then what was it tied up in?" Wymund asked.

Whether the task was to master a combat technique or excel in mental focus, she would need confidence to do it. He had worked with many recruits in his time with the Virdoban Guard on just that—finding the root of their self-doubt and helping them break free of it. Wymund had lost count of the pep talks he had given over the years, ranging from encouraging someone to pursue a romantic interest or resist the downward pull of a toxic familial relationship. In the end, it was all the same. Negativity in a part of one's life dragged down performance in any other aspect.

"I'll let you know when I find out," she said with a wan grin.

"A good misery wallow can feel like a warm, cozy bath until someone points out we're drowning in it," Wymund said. "Trust me, I've felt the pull of those waters before. But I've also helped others navigate them. I need a bit more insight than you're offering, though."

The pair sat in silence, each staring forward at the icy outpost Zylnala had constructed. They could see Luviila through one of the windows of the main building, tidying their quarters with an eye for detail that would put most of the inspectors Wymund knew to shame. Elsewhere in the cavern system, Rav and Adiin were practicing, though he was noticing fewer metallic thuds than he had previously. Perhaps she was improving, or he had simply tuned out her repeated failures.

Finally, Riqu spoke. "I didn't care about winning those fights with my cousins because I always won. It's hard not to when you're the size of an ox and everyone else is a slight thing by comparison."

Wymund cocked an eyebrow. "If you didn't care about winning, why continue wrestling with them then? Were you bullying them?"

Riqu's eyes narrowed as she tore them away from the chamber to focus on him, watering a bit at the edges. "I wasn't the one picking those fights. It was a game to them. 'How many slaps can you land on the bear' or 'pull the mule's braid and run.' As you might expect, in an elven family with stormforger and lightblood roots, being fleet of foot is a point of pride."

She sighed. "I was a convenient target, plodding and close to home."

"But you must have had others with draqesh blood around you," Wymund said.

"Just my mom," Riqu said. "But no one would dare mess with her. She could send my cousins scampering away to hide under their mothers' skirts with the briefest of scowls." There was a momentary look of pride on her face that disappeared just as quickly. "She didn't pass that gift on to me though. Only her body mass, which apparently was an insufficient deterrent when paired with a quiet soul."

"I'm sorry, Riqu," Wymund said. "It must have been an alienating way to grow up. Being made to feel like an outsider by your own family . . . I can only guess how you've borne those scars over the years."

Her soft smile returned, this time with sincerity. "It's nothing I can't handle."

"I meant what I said, though," Wymund continued. "I know what it's like to not belong. Like you're living a life that was thrust upon you by forces outside your control."

Riqu laughed. "I'm a lightblood. I don't have much choice when it comes to mastering the flow of energy from the Wellspring, unless I decide to welcome an untimely death. The others in my family realized I couldn't learn in the same way they had, so I ended up here. I think I'm making the most of it."

"Making the most of it isn't the same as realizing who you were meant to be," Wymund said. "You deserve to be accepted by your family the way you are, on your terms. Growth takes work—anything worth having does—but I hope whenever you leave here and return home, you'll show them the strength of your mind outweighs the power they already know you wield. Command their respect, and they'll have to give it."

She nodded silently, her eyes searching deep into his. "And what is it you deserve?"

The question caught him off guard, but not because he didn't know the answer. Much like her, he had "made the most" of what life had allowed him, finding employment that offered him financial stability and a degree of autonomy. Wymund had even excelled in the field, but rising through the ranks of the Virdoban guard had never sated that part of him that necessity had buried—the same part that his father had allowed to bury him.

"I came to peace with my identity crisis a long time ago," Wymund said. "Those echoes of opportunity still sting, from time to time. I think they always will. But they don't hold me back anymore, professionally or personally."

She turned toward him, folding one leg in front of her and smiled wide. "Who's light on the offered insight now?"

Wymund felt his face flush, but he had steered the conversation in this direction. It was only right to share in the vulnerability.

"Fair enough," Wymund said. "My father was a painter, by passion and eventually by trade. It was a love we shared, and it was through his eyes that I saw the beauty of the world, all the vibrant colors and perfect imperfections." He paused, remembering the mural his father had scrawled across his childhood bedroom, depicting the Virdoban coastline in an almost dreamlike quality, some mineral in the paint glinting when the sun had hit it just right.

"But a life in the arts is often a hard one to subsist on," he continued, "more so when you have another mouth to feed. He eventually had to choose between the canvas and my well-being, and so he ended up painting walls for uninspired lords and ladies on their fourth homes."

Wymund sighed. "When the time came for me to make my own way in the world, I decided to forgo any attempt at painting professionally. Seeing how hard it was on my father to let go of something he loved after failing to make a name for himself, I thought it best to keep my passion as a project, separate from any burden of financial hardship that could taint it."

"You mean hidden from anyone but yourself?" Riqu asked.

Wymund cleared his throat. "I suppose that would be one way of looking at it. But it was valuable seeing how much that loss impacted him. Impacted his ability to thrive in another line of work."

Wymund stood and drew his sword from the scabbard he had left to the side of the platform, then arced his blade through the air in a series of masterful patterns. "I protected myself from that, and while I do miss those nights I spent as a child turning the blank canvas into any fantastical scene I could see in my mind, it hasn't impaired my focus and drive to be the best I can be in my new field."

"But is that what you want?" she asked, standing to join him.

"Isn't that the point of all this?" Wymund asked, raising his hands to gesture at the icy cavern. "Mastering the elements of your mind and body that are holding you back from your full potential?"

Riqu stooped and retrieved the empty scabbard, then walked over to hand it to him. "I thought the point was putting in the work to get the growth you see for yourself. Didn't someone just tell me how much that was worth?" Wymund kept his eyes trained on sheathing his sword, so she continued. "To me, it sounds like you quit before you even began."

"Are we all calling it a day then?" Rav asked, appearing suddenly at the side of the wooden platform. She looked exhausted, with hair hanging limply around her face and a shaky smirk, but her silent footpad tendencies must have been effortless and second nature. "I didn't realize Zylnala ran such a loose ship."

"Master Zylnala wasn't the one who ended this lesson early," Riqu said as she turned to walk toward the steps. "Maybe all our instructors are having an off day."

Rav joined Wymund on the platform as Riqu disappeared into the main structure. "What was that about?" she asked.

"You know how it is," Wymund said. "Fighting can open up old wounds and memories that are better left in the past." Rav shrugged and began to lead them back to their quarters, but Wymund wasn't sure he believed that himself anymore.

Chapter 12

INESET

Nasargiel spent the next week in and around the flaming husk that once was the alchemist-surgeon's lab, keeping a watchful eye on anyone who tried to poke around in the charred building's remains. He had to be sure his quarry had truly moved on from the area rather than hiding out until the blade serpent and his patrol lost interest. If the man was smart—an undeniable fact at this point—he would have fled Ineset and never returned, but Nasargiel was nothing if not thorough.

His intuition had proven correct. The only interested parties in the rubble were Granish employed investigators—and nosy children, most of whom were quickly shooed away by the former. After days of breathing in the putrid fumes of the Tower Lizard district and observing nothing of interest, Nasargiel was ready to move on. The only trouble was that he had no further leads on the surgeon's location.

However, he had his theories. Now that he knew the man had discovered the World Shroud-sensitive organ, Nasargiel believed the man would look for a new base with more readily available specimens. Achen was a largely human nation, as was Ebkarii to the east, and Destueqa was an equal split of human and draqeshi. Choii Stier would be a bounty of riches for a man searching to study elven biology, but he would also be surrounded by the people he hoped to use as subjects, and who may not take kindly to that designation.

Kefya, then, was the obvious choice. Of the Aneran nations, it had the next densest elven population, and as Nasargiel knew from his recent travels, there was no love lost between the humans and elves sharing the land. He could imagine an unsavory human making deals with the surgeon to pass along living samples without much arm twisting. But an entire country was a massive area to search, even if he started with the largest population clusters. There was no guarantee he would pick up the trail again.

"—crazy amount of gold," a soldier said as he hustled by the bench where Nasargiel sat. The soldier was young and wore leather armor that bore no cracks or scuffs, but the Granish guild-family insignia on his left pauldron spoke to its quality. New recruit or not, they only paid for the best.

The man he was speaking to loped ahead of him, moving with a steely-eyed purpose. He was older, his face pockmarked and scarred from a lifetime of duty, and his voice was gruff when he called back to the novice trailing him. "The foreign contracts usually are. Blade serpents are good, but their reputation outside of Achen borders on mythical. Some even believe they pull from the damn World Shroud! It really drives up the prices for one of our units."

"Shouldn't those heatless in Virdoba know better though?" asked the younger man. "They're bound to have seen one or two of them in their lives. They're just on the other side of the mountains."

At the mention of a Kefyan city, Nasargiel stood and fell in behind them. Any significant events in the bordering nation might concern his interests.

The veteran laughed but projected his voice low such that Nasargiel had to strain to hear. "Those pompous limpswords will take any chance they get to talk about their skills. The more those

Kefyans and their waterlogged ears heard about the blade serpents' exploits, the more the legend grew."

Nasargiel followed the pair as they made their way through the district, stepping around oily pools that leaked out of alchemists' workshops and dodging a lumber-toting steam cart that careened down the tracks. The invention was still new to the city, and pedestrians stepped across the tracks with abandon—whoever set the limit on the cart's speed would need to make an adjustment before someone paid the price.

Before long, though, Nasargiel found himself on the outskirts of Tower Lizard territory, where it began to meld into the neighboring Twilight Petals neighborhood. He hadn't spent much time in the arts district since arriving in Ineset, but understood from several passing conversations that this was the place one could find the best food and drink Achen had to offer. The Three Heats were not just an Achen philosophy paying lip service to cooking; it was an artform the city respected like any other.

The duo pushed into a tavern that had earned its spot here in the blurred space between the districts. The clay slabs that formed its structure were perfectly hewn, with no errant chisel marks or mineral deformities noted on a cursory glance. Further into the Twilight Petals, the building aesthetics were more vibrant and filled with flourishes, but so close to the city's manufacturing center, this establishment wanted to demonstrate pure craftsmanship over flashy designs.

Inside, a boisterous crowd was shouting over one another for refills of spiced ale or *blide*, a drink made from the fermented sap of the desert lace succulent common in the lands around Ineset. Most of the patrons were wearing similar uniforms as the men he had followed into the bar, but there were a number of other stragglers hugging the walls. If he played the part well enough, Nasargiel should be able to blend in.

"A blide over here," he shouted as he snapped a minuscule tear in the World Shroud, creating a momentary flash of flame no larger than a candle's several feet above his head. The light was gone by the time the barkeep's eyes flitted over to it, but her attention had been successfully drawn to the lanky foreigner with blond curls near the entrance with his hand raised.

She unstoppered a tan clay bottle and poured a viscous straw-colored liquid into a mug, then slid her way through the crowd toward him. Nasargiel guessed that she must have been attractive given all the attempts by the soldiers to grab at her wrist or other parts of her body, but he had never been the best judge at what passed for human beauty. They had too much hair on their bodies to see each other properly anyway.

"You know what you're in for, heatless?" she asked as she plopped the mug onto his table. "You look like you could be from as far away as Qravburn with that complexion. Blide isn't something to try without a proper warning. It has what some folks call an acquired taste."

"How does one acquire it?" he asked.

She blinked a few times, and Nasargiel knew he had misspoken. The languages on Slaeth were less straightforward than the ones his kind now spoke, and often found his way into awkward exchanges due to idioms and slang. Thankfully, this situation appeared to only be a little odd rather than horribly offensive.

"Um, I guess you're right," she said. "Only way is to try it for yourself. Let me know if I can get you something else."

As she returned to her place behind the bar, Nasargiel raised the mug to his nose and scanned the room. It was pungent, but not necessarily off-putting. He took a sip, and locating the men he had tracked sitting at a nearby booth, he settled into his stool. The drink was sour and reminiscent of the scent of rising bread, with a light frothy head that gave way to a syrupy body. He was thankful that this form he chose had apparently acquired this taste, because there was nothing like it in the waters of Nyavelle. His original, salt-water accustomed tongue might have been repulsed.

"Keep your voice down, Coril," the older soldier said as he sent a furtive glance around the tavern. The novice snapped his jaw shut and settled back into the booth, where four other Granish-funded soldiers sat with them. "You never know what other guild-families have ears in this bar."

"Oh, everyone here is one of us," another soldier said, waving a tankard of ale in the older man's face. "Leave the kid be and just tell us about the job."

The veteran grumbled, but after a swallow from his own tankard, he said, "There's whispers of some mercenary work, hiring out of Felona. It sounds too good to be true, if you ask me. But if it pans out, it might be worth cashing in our leave chips for."

"I wouldn't mind a trip to the island," a female soldier said. "Fight whoever needs fighting, then find one of those pretty elven men to shack up with for a night or two. Count me in."

The others at the table laughed, but the veteran shook his head. "You'll have to find your elven bedmate another time, Ylora. The contract is from Felona, but the work is sending us north."

"This have to do with that attack in Alaboq?" a large stone-faced soldier asked. "I don't care how much coin is on offer, I'm not attacking a royal. If someone wants to kill a king, they should have the stones to do it themselves."

The older soldier frowned. "I don't think it's connected. As far as I know, we're just meant to head up into the mountains to find a couple of people. A Virdoban guard and some half-elf lightblood."

Nasargiel nearly choked on his blide. Lightbloods were not common on Slaeth. Could they mean the same woman he had rescued in Virdoba? She was indeed powerful, if more than a bit raw, but how had she found herself with so many enemies?

"A lightblood?" Coril asked, looking for the first time as if something might be more important than the contract's payout.

"That could be a problem even if we brought a blade serpent with us, right?"

"And how are we meant to find two people in all the Tesigan Peaks?" Ylora asked. "Might as well be asking us to find a specific snowflake while we're up there."

The older soldier held his hands up to quiet them. "It might be a problem for a single blade serpent, but with the small horde this contract promises, an entire regimen is likely to sign on to the job. Not to mention the rest of us there as support. One lightblood and her bodyguard shouldn't be much of a problem against those odds."

Turning to Ylora, he added, "We've been given a general location. It will still be difficult to find them, but there can't be many fissures in peaks that lead down to an underground school for lightbloods."

"So now there's more than one lightblood?" the large one asked, his face growing more skeptical by the second. "And from what I heard, a lightblood was mixed up in that attack on King Berenqar. Stopped a scorcher from offing the bastard. The odds are sounding less favorable, Nimus."

Nimus sighed. "Word is it's just a lonely old man teaching baby lightbloods how to control themselves. Should be pretty deserted by the sounds of it, being up in the mountains and all. And if we're fast enough, the girl won't have much time to learn anything, will she?"

A hermitic man trying to assert control over the flows of the World Shroud? There were differences, sure, but without any other leads, the similarities were too much for Nasargiel to ignore. A mountain range on the outskirts of Kefya might be a brilliant place for the surgeon to set up shop.

Plus, if this was the same lightblood he had met in Virdoba, Nasargiel felt compelled to get involved. He had rather liked that girl. With her potential—and the fact that she seemed to be opposed to attempted regicide—she might make a powerful ally in the future. As long as she can maintain a grasp on her abilities and not contribute to the Rupturing.

"It warms my heart to see the grunts taking such an interest in Granish affairs," a new man said as he strode over to the table. He carried a mug of blide in one hand while his other rested on the pommel of a coiled metallic weapon, and though his tone was friendly, his eyes were those of a shark. Slicked-back dark hair and a steel scale-layered cuirass only enhanced his predatory appearance.

"But I'm afraid all your little plans were for naught. This contract pays well enough that the guild wants to ensure their cut. They're only accepting leave chips from a hand-picked patrol of blade serpents, and with most of us out of the city, they'll need you lot around to protect their assets."

Nimus turned to face him, standing nearly as tall as the blade serpent but revealing with a dimness in his eyes that he knew where he really stood. The old soldier's mouth twitched, and then he nodded.

"We'll keep the flames stoked and the irons hot while you boys are gone, Shilik," Nimus said. "The guild-family comes first, after all."

Shilik smiled, baring his teeth as he cupped Nimus's face in what was more of a slap. "That it does. There's a good man." The blade serpent then rapped his fist on their table a few times and said, "Now finish up here and report back to your posts. Can't have you foot soldiers nodding off from too much drink. You'll ruin our sterling reputation."

The blade serpent drained his mug and set it on the table upside down so that the remnants of the blide seeped out and dripped onto the floor. Then he left to join another table full of soldiers dressed more like him. Nasargiel was beginning to study the blade serpents' mannerisms, how they spoke and carried themselves, when hushed muttering drew his attention back to the booth with the regular infantry.

"We'll be going up there ourselves," Nimus said. "Don't you worry about that. Old Aewin will want to make sure his family has claim to the money tied up in this job, so he'll be sending any available bodies."

Nasargiel sighed and returned to enjoying his drink, thankful that he would have the cover of insignificance when choosing his next form. Trying to pass as a specialized warrior within a smaller class of soldiers would've been far more trouble.

Chapter 13

Felona

"You would think that they would at least offer us some water," Kymil said as he sat in the padded armchair, its dull and faded purple upholstery a testament to the drab décor throughout the rest of the holding room. "Not that it will impair an experienced orator such as myself, but I'm sure most of the dignitaries who visit the Council would prefer not to launch into their presentations with a dry mouth."

Annika and Ubadrii sat in two other armchairs across the room, each one the same shade of dusty plum that could inspire no one toward an impressive performance before the Council. Both had adopted prim postures that befitted their stations, sitting with straight backs and waiting patiently for the agent of the Council to arrive and usher them into the larger hall. By contrast, Kymil had draped a knee over the arm of his seat—something had to liven the place up, and it might as well be him. It usually was, anyway.

Mareq was pacing, his heavy footfalls being absorbed by the dense velvet carpet. This, at least, was a royal hue of purple, but the silver patterns worked into the flooring were fraying and in a style that hadn't been popular in decades. Between this dull room and the lack of interest in slaking their thirsts, Kymil might have taken offense at their treatment, if he wasn't just thankful that an assassin hadn't been waiting for their arrival.

Niri turned away from the window, and for a moment her smirk made her almost indistinguishable from Rav. "As I warned you all before we arrived, I wouldn't drink anything they offered anyway. If Elikar's man made it back to him after he escaped your ship, your identities could be compromised. We'll be safe surrounded by the other members of the Council, but do not forget that Elikar will also be sitting in attendance."

Kymil stood and walked over to join Niri by the window, beyond which was a garden that must have taken all the Council's color expenditures for the year. Every shade imaginable was painted across the flowers and trees that spiraled out and around the council building, running down in rows over the gentle slope of the Crest.

A little to the east, the Hall of Merchants jutted out from the side of the hill and rose to share the skyline with the Felonian Council Hall. It's gold-veined dark marble towered over the rest of the city, with four fluted spires the size of a ship's mast piercing the sky at each corner of the structure. Long ago, part of the ceiling had caved in and crumbled onto half of the sloped seating, but within the hall, hundreds of marble seats and a raised central dais remained immaculately preserved, seemingly immune to the notorious island rains. Despite the ravages of time, the Dawn Ones' ruin was still more impressive than what the people of Felona had constructed for their governmental seat.

"And if the rest of the Council has decided to march arm in arm with Elikar on his path toward fortune and anonymous saber rattling?" Kymil asked.

Niri stared at him evenly, but it was Annika who spoke. "As believable as it is that Elikar either strong armed or paid off the other councilmembers to fall in line, the man's arrogance might be our salvation in this case. Why would he spend money on silence or split any potential war profits if he can avoid it?"

"She's right," Ubadrii said. "I've worked alongside those in power most of my life, and even with the more thoughtful and decent ones, there's an element of ego that needs to be fed. Sometimes even more than the desire for greater wealth or control."

"Forgive me if betting on the integrity of Elikar's self-importance isn't exactly reassuring," Mareq said, finally stopping his nervous path he had tread into the carpet. "Tell me again what our plan is once we're inside?"

Kymil had come to view Mareq as a younger brother in the short few weeks since they met, partially because the draqeshi was more genuine and open than most of the scamps and scoundrels in his typical acquaintance. Not to mention the emotionally stunted and conniving members of Kymil's actual family. A father who only knew how to express emotions through his fists and a mother too demure to intervene had left him with scars both physical and emotional. By contrast, a naïve and decent presence like Mareq was a comfort, more than the draqeshi knew. It was refreshing to speak with someone who held no hidden motives or caged inner demons.

But in this instance, moments away from testifying before the avatars of law and authority in Kefya, wearing one's emotions on their sleeves might prove a fatal mistake—however charming it might be.

"Take my seat and get comfortable," Kymil said, gesturing to the banal armchair. "You don't have to join us in there, Mareq. With my gifted tongue and the lofty reputations of my retinue, your account would be a superfluous addition. Let's leave a little suspense in their ruling so when I recount it later to my adoring public, they will be hanging on my every word."

"Dramatic tension isn't our aim here," Annika said, her sharp tongue as honed as ever. "We'll need to overwhelm them with evidence if they're to believe our story."

Her tone softened as she turned to Mareq, who had traipsed by her, shoulders slumped, to sit in the empty chair. "I'm sorry, son. But you'll need to stifle those jittery nerves of yours. The same skills and societal standings Kymil speaks of can also be read as a practiced and plotted grab for power. We need someone like you who exudes earnestness from every pore if we hope to keep suspicions at bay."

Mareq nodded, his face contorted into a facsimile of resolution despite the continual bouncing of his legs—all the more pronounced in a chair sized for humans and elves. The draqeshi glanced at Ubadrii. "You wouldn't happen to have any concoctions to help with that, would you?"

The hidden hand shook his head. "None that made it through the search when we arrived," Ubadrii said. "Only a select few infusions remain on my person, and while initially calming, they tend to have effects you might find adverse in the long run. That is if you enjoy sensing things around you, or breathing."

"I have grown quite fond of those things," Mareq said with a sigh. He closed his eyes for a moment and stilled his legs, then opened them once more. "I can do this. We'll be fine."

Kymil smiled at him. "Yes, we will. Stand next to me and perhaps my stage presence will bleed into yours."

A knock at the door announced the arrival of the Council's agent, and it swung open before anyone in the room could answer. A woman entered wearing gray and blue livery, and with her short brown hair swept neatly to one side. Her smile was perfunctory, just another element of her uniform, but her voice was pleasant enough as she beckoned them all out into the hall.

Ubadrii and Niri led the way, followed by Mareq, but Kymil caught Annika's arm on the way out. He pulled the folded document from his breast pocket, trails of luminescence drifting off it as he passed it to her.

"Were you able to draw enough?" she asked. She couldn't see that the paper was brimming with the energy he had infused into it.

"Fatestitchers never reveal the extent of their works," Kymil said with a wink. "It spoils the air of mystery we work so hard to maintain. We can't have people believing we are devoid of any natural talent."

Annika rolled her eyes. "Certainly not. People would cry out in the streets and the structures of the world would crumble if that secret were revealed."

The group made their way through the byzantine layout of larger walkways and side passages that formed the Felonian Council Hall. Without a guide, they might never have found the location of their meeting, as there was no signage to speak of, nor many attendants that appeared in the least bit helpful. Aides scurried about their menial tasks with a single-minded focus that left little time to point guests in the right direction. It appeared that if one was in this building, it was assumed they would know where to be and how to get there. Kymil briefly gave the Council credit for the security feature before deciding it was more likely a deterrent, preventing more work from finding its way to their desks.

No, the actual security measure was imposed by a pair of guards posted at nearly every branch point, each standing at attention with a polearm in one hand while the other rested on the pommel of a longsword. Each duo they passed eyed the group like trained hunting dogs, only held at bay by the absence of the signal that would unleash their drive to kill. Kymil thought the sheer number of guards was stifling, but Annika had mentioned that the martial presence in Felona had been bolstered significantly since her last trip home. That was to be expected, Kymil supposed—when someone came for one leader's neck, others must begin to think that theirs is too exposed, as well.

Finally, after passing through hall after hall of off-white walls and a few still-life paintings of hackneyed subjects like a robe resting over a chair or a front door hanging ajar—as if the building's designers found the possibility of thought-provoking art offensive—the group arrived in front of a single, unassuming light birch door. Kymil had passed through the grand entranceways of palaces, so to find the rulers of a nation waiting behind this thin sheet of wood was at first surprising. Even some particularly nice taverns had lacquered double doors. But on second thought, it matched the rest of the place's drab aesthetic, and he took comfort in that consistency.

After a quick knock, the door opened inward, revealing a pair of attendants dressed in identical blue and gray livery, each with a blade at their hips. Two more guards stood just beyond them, gripping their polearms in both hands and with expressions that dared any uninvited guest to pass over the threshold. When they saw the group, they parted, standing at attention to allow Kymil and the others to enter the massive chamber.

Modeled after the Dawn Ones's amphitheater just across the hilltop, this central hall was lined with row after row of ascending seats for much of the perimeter. They rose at least twenty feet, stopping just below a wide paneled window that covered the length of the wall behind them. Every one of the audience seats was empty, causing their footsteps to echo loudly off the polished granite tiles below. Even the black iron chandelier was strikingly lackluster—not one of the candles adorning its many arms was lit—though it did cast an ominous shadow over them as they passed.

The only signs of life waited on the far side of the room, where a long, raised table was positioned to allow those seated there to watch anyone who approached. Seven seats had been placed behind the table, each supporting one of Kefya's councilmembers wearing expressions that ranged from hostile to bored. Kymil smiled. He did enjoy a challenge.

"Ladies Trisarin and Iatorii, Ubadrii Tragala, Qedrad's royal representative," the attendant said with a bow, then added, "and associates." Mareq shuffled his feet, his face blossoming into a brilliant shade of red, but Kymil took the dismissal in stride, returning a grander bow.

"In attendance today is the Kefyan Council in its entirety," the aide continued. He gestured to the left end of the table. "Tano Scrin, Voice of the Many." A man early into his fourth decade with short-cropped dark hair and the early stages of a beard nodded, a polite smile gracing his face that marked him as the friendliest person seated before them.

"Churi Bleone, Voice of the Dawn," the attendant announced, and a graying woman with deep forehead creases nodded from the opposite end of the table. She wore High Scholar vestments of Teacher Melan, the subdued oranges and purples of the robes meant to represent the horizon of the setting sun. The Ambassador espoused the virtues of travel and exploration in her teachings, but Kymil never could figure out what she had against sunrises.

This went on until the attendant had introduced every member of the Council. Garend Hull and Livella Riber, first secretaries of defense and home, respectively. Each appeared mildly interested in the proceedings at best. Relus Vunii might have caught Kymil's eye for a number of reasons if the circumstances were any less dire. He had always found the fiery spirits of half-elves intoxicating, and Relus was handsome besides. The fact that he was the first secretary of culture was only an added bonus.

At the center of the table sat Chief Magistrate Brosh Thalin, a wall of a man who appeared to be able to emote as much as one. The scant hair on his head rested in a tightly moussed horseshoe pattern, as if the rest had fled in preparation for his total transformation to stone.

But it was the man seated to his left that held the eyes of his group. Elikar Thymes, Kefya's port admiral and the only other councilmember to offer a smile, though its intent was projected with enough force that even a blind man might have called it a snarl. He was dressed in a fathomless black waistcoat, trimmed with gold and white accents, and his brown hair was swept to the right, with a stark gray streak at the front. Though he was not at the center of the table, it was Elikar who addressed them first.

"It is a pleasure to welcome one of Felona's own back to her shores, Ms. Iatorii," Elikar said. "And in such esteemed company. I had always heard your family made every effort to form close bonds with King Berenqar, sending any visiting Qedradan dignitary home with a case of your finest vintage. I'm glad to see those ties still hold after all these years."

Annika ground her teeth, loudly enough for Kymil to hear. The rest of the Council might not be aware of the nature of this accusation, but Elikar knew what was coming, and he had planned accordingly. Insinuating a relationship between the Iatoriis and another nation's royal family wouldn't help their case, particularly with Annika's decades spent out of Felona.

"And Niri," he continued, "how long has it been? You've become so reclusive since Ilphas's tragic passing. It fills me with joy that you are taking part in managing your district's needs. Though with such strange company, I have to wonder if our attendants were correct in informing us that today's agenda has taken an unfortunate turn."

"I never quite got a taste for high society functions, Elikar," Niri answered with a glare that could set a person ablaze. "I much prefer the company of my trees. I know they have a solid foundation."

Elikar laughed quietly, but gestured that he was done with introductions. Magistrate Thalin nodded, oblivious to the bubbling hostility in the chamber.

"Well, now that all the niceties are out of the way and we're all caught up," Thalin said, "why don't we get started. I'm told we have grave business to discuss on a day I believed we would be discussing crop yields and neighborhood pests. As Kefya's chief magistrate, I will hear your accusation and deliberate with my fellow councilmembers on its veracity and, if warranted, pursue further investigation."

His brow creased as he studied their group. "Now, who will be speaking on your behalf? Without knowing the nature of this presentation, I assume the presence of King Berenqar's emissary indicates he is to speak, but either of our own esteemed ladies is welcome to state their case as well."

"If I may," Kymil said, stepping forward, his head tilted down just enough to indicate deference without hiding any of his charms. "I have been elected to present our findings, but we will all add to this insidious tapestry as it unfurls." Kymil felt Garend Hull's eyes roll from close to twenty feet away, but the tiniest of grins crept onto Relus's face—having read some of the plays written by the culture secretary's mother, Kymil had known the man would appreciate verbal flourishes.

"And who might you be?" Livella Riber asked. She had a fragile, almost avian frame with accompanying birdlike features, her sharp eyes peering down on him over a hooked nose. But there was also an elegance about her, present in the way she was dressed and sat, that softened the severity of those characteristics.

"Pardon my disrespect," Kymil said. He walked over to Mareq and placed his hand on his friend's shoulder. "Our introductions must have been lost before your man brought us before you." Kymil flashed a smile at the attendant, who appeared to be testing the strength of his jaw as he stared down at the floor.

"My name is Kymil Adii, and this is our companion, Mareq Iq'Urlset. As you'll see, the five of us have uncovered the threads of a plot that would threaten the stability of Anera, if not the continent's relationship with Liiashae, as well. These strands have been woven into a web so sinister that began righ—"

"If the matter is so monumental," Garend interrupted, "why don't we move this along? I would hate for this web to ensnare something precious while we're all sat here listening." The defense secretary's eyes were set deep within their sockets, partially obscured by the graying curls that draped over his forehead. It brought to mind the conservatory cats that had watched their arrival to the city through the trees.

Tano Scrin leaned forward to glare at his colleague, which Garend only dignified with a huff. "The Council will gladly sit here for weeks if it means the safety and comfort of our nation's citizens," Tano said. Then, adopting a softer tone, he turned to look down at Kymil. "Please, continue."

"Annika," Kymil said with a wave toward the Council's attendant. "If you don't mind."

The old woman grinned with a ferocity that rivaled Elikar's. "Gladly," she said, before pulling out the infused document.

The aid took it without question and walked it over to the Council's table, where it was handed to High Scholar Bleone. The Voice of the Dawn unfurled the paper, setting aside a smaller, wax-sealed note that had been rolled within, then set her beady eyes to scanning its contents. Kymil concealed his joy as he watched his luminous wisps drift from the papers to snake around the seven councilmembers.

"We present to the Council a document containing the forged signatures of three of your members. Namely, Port Admiral Thymes and Secretaries Hull and Riber," Kymil said. The three mentioned raised interested eyebrows, and even Elikar's feigned shock was convincing. "It weaves a narrative of elven terroristic assaults across Kefya, and issues a warning to King Berenqar that these foreign threats from Choii Stier were moving north to continue their grievous campaign.

"Of course, we all know this to be a fabrication," Kymil continued. "The firebombings in Virdoba were the result of the dispossessed laborers in that city, gaslit into believing the elves were the root of their woes, and intending to demonstrate to those around them how dangerous these immigrants could be."

"This is a troubling find," Livella Riber said as the parchment was passed to her. "Our names should not have been attached to such lies, nor signed without our permission. I presume the fact that you're here before us means that you know who forged this document."

"Indeed we do," Kymil said, meeting Elikar's eyes and finding the man's demeanor had remained cool and unflappable. "The smaller, folded document was delivered surreptitiously to one of King Berenqar's advisors, Sylicera Hadac, who was later revealed to be a traitor to her nation and sent to work off the damage she had caused.

"It refers to an 'emissary' we discovered to be a Clipped Gull assassin named Tetamii Fiadar," Kymil continued, "hired from here in Felona and posing as a representative of this council. It was he who forged the larger document in an attempt to sway Qedrad from forming deeper economic ties with the elves of Choii Stier.

"Furthermore, physical characteristics of the note also reveal this plot originated from within these halls," Kymil said as the smaller note made its way down the table. "You'll see the Kefyan crest pressed into the wax seal, and find that it is indistinguishable from your own official stamps. No forger could have reproduced the exact mane of the stallion, down to the strand, or the same break pattern in the bit that the horse is snapping through.

"This is an authentic wax pressing, and the 'E.T.' signed at the bottom of the message reveals the culprit." Each other member of the Council turned to face Elikar, whose smirk had only grown over the course of Kymil's presentation. Kymil was unperturbed—it was not often a bard dealt in strictly fact, and having the truth on his side bolstered his already overflowing confidence.

"Elikar Thymes hired Tetamii Fiadar for this task," Kymil concluded, "knowing he would stand to lose influence over trade deals if Qedradan and Choii Stieren ships began to bypass Kefyan ports."

A suffocating silence filled the expansive chamber. It was not the reaction Kymil was used to, but one he found satisfying all the same—until Elikar stood and began to clap, breaking into a booming laugh. The note reached him as he rose, and the trailing luminescent swirls surrounding it began to disperse, violently ripped asunder by some unseen force until they were no more.

"Annika and Niri, this has truly been an exceptional gift. We don't often get surprise visits from such a talented performer, and to incorporate me into the script was a stroke of genius. It really drew me into the drama of it all." As the man finished, the last of Kymil's glowing strands were shredded to tatters, falling limply to the table.

A hexant? Kymil's eyes darted about the room, as if to catch someone in the act of disrupting his infusions, though the act wasn't warranted. The fatestitcher's opposite would have needed to infuse an object ahead of time to counteract his work, which meant that his powers of influence were anticipated and prepared for. Fortunately, Kymil was not without less fantastical talents.

"Now hold on, Elikar," Tano Scrin said from his end of the table, the Voice of the Many craning his neck to see him. "This was brought before us by two respected members of our city and an advisor to a ruler of an allied state. You can't expect to play this off as a practical joke." The man glanced down to the group. "Where is this Tetamii Fiadar? I would be interested to hear his testimony."

"In a coincidence that should surprise no one," Annika said, "the assassin was liberated from our ship as soon as we entered Felona's waters."

"You're right, Ms. Iatorii," Garend Hull said. "It is not surprising that the Clipped Gulls would take the chance to free one of their own. Particularly one they were confident enough to send across the continent on their own criminal designs. I would've liked to have faced the man that sought to implicate me in one of their schemes, but you have failed to grant me that gift."

"It was not the Clipped Gulls on their own," Kymil interjected, fearing a retort from Annika would further sour the proceedings. "They have no motive to interfere in international affairs. Remember the use of the seal, and Port Admiral Thymes's position with Kefya's ports. He hired the group for his own ends."

"Unfortunately, we don't know the full extent of the Clipped Gulls' reach, nor their aspirations for more power," Brosh Thalin said.

Relus frowned, keeping a wary eye on Elikar before eventually sighing. "And I'm afraid the seals are not as exclusive to the people in this room, as you seem to believe. Our aides frequently use them as well, and while we aim to hire only the most respectable candidates, it is possible one might have slipped out at some point."

Kymil's mind raced to catch up with the rapid failure this presentation had become. Perhaps some concession could still be salvaged. "Chief Magistrate, if an organization like the Clipped Gulls can operate with such precision in and around your city, perhaps Felona is overdue for a deeper inspection of the group. It would only serve the public's interest to know how integrated these criminals are into their everyday lives."

Thalin pursed his lips and tilted his head, but before he could respond, Elikar returned to his seat, a believable facsimile of bewilderment painted on for all to see. "So this is a real accusation then? Where did you come by this sealed note with my initials?"

Mareq stepped forward, the quiver in his voice apparent as soon as he opened his mouth. "I . . . I found it, sir. I found where Ias's Ghosts stashed their messages before delivering them."

"What is your role in all of this?" Relus asked. "Are you a member of the king's guard in Alaboq, an investigator?"

"I'm, uh . . . I deliver the fruit." Kymil's stomach sank alongside his friend's eyeline.

"Mareq has proved himself a friend of the crown," Ubadrii said, the bald elf's face as stony as ever despite the utter catastrophe taking place. "He has earned my king's trust through his great service to our nation. If you dismiss him out of hand, you are doing the same to King Berenqar."

"We do not mean any offense," High Scholar Bleone said. "But in Kefya we rule by council, not monarchical fiat. We need evidence to make any decision, especially one that asserts a member of this body is treasonous.

"In fact," she continued, "if any offense should be felt, it should be by us. For a neighboring nation to ambush us in our chambers with such a haphazard delegation makes me wonder if perhaps we *should* be rethinking our economic ties to Qedrad."

Ubadrii bristled. "I would take this opportunity to apologize on behalf of my king. Had we known we would be forced to obtain this meeting through subterfuge, I'm certain other arrangements would have been made.

"As for the evidence, I will see to it that Sylicera Hadac is brought before this council," Ubadrii said. "Give us a few weeks for her travel here, and we can resume this session."

Kymil's insides unclenched. Nothing was ideal about this testimony, but Ubadrii's plan could rescue it. Sylicera's account would work just as well as Tetamii's if they could get her to cooperate.

"Sylicera Hadac is dead," Elikar said, and just like that the vise that was Kymil's insides returned. All their circumstantial evidence had been summarily dismissed, aided by some hexant meddling, and without a person like Tetamii or Sylicera ready to turn coat, they had nothing—nothing but a dangling accusation against one of the most powerful men in the world.

"We received word of her demise before word reached us of her banishment," Elikar continued. "This council had already sent our condolences to King Berenqar for their nation's loss, which was an embarrassment when we learned of her treachery later, but that is unimportant. What matters is the woman is dead, and this poor attempt at a ruse has gone on long enough." He snapped, and the two attendants at the back of the room began to march forward, flanked by their guard counterparts.

Niri stared up at him through narrow slits. "How did the woman die, Elikar?"

The port admiral shrugged. "Random band of thieves, or so we heard. It's a shame, but when you live in a nation where the very government doesn't give its people a voice, what else can you expect but a little rebellion on occasion."

"Please see this group back to their holding chamber to gather their things," Brosh Thalin said as the two attendants reached them. "While I'm not sure I agree with my colleague that this was all some juvenile prank, it's apparent that there has been a case of mistaken identity, and worse, an attempt at placing blame on a member of this council for an international incident. We will discuss this matter further and reach out to you if we need anything else, but rest assured, the Council will look into the matter."

After a pause, Thalin's eyes met Kymil's. "And we will also launch a new investigation into the Clipped Gulls. Perhaps you are right, Mr. Adii. It has been so long since we have tried to root out the organization that many in the city have simply taken them as a fact of life, another spoke in the wheel of Felona's operations. But complacency can endanger lives, and it can go on no longer."

Kymil nodded before being led out of the chamber. Despite this modest win, for the first time in his life Kymil was speechless. Not only had he failed in his argument, but his infusions had been negated by some outside force. Elikar had been prepared for his abilities, which meant that Tetamii had indeed made it to shore safely. The knowledge that the scorcher was free and in close proximity somehow only left him feeling cold.

CHAPTER 14

THE ILLUMINED SCALE

If Rav had perfected one technique since arriving at the Illumined Scale, it was learning how to cut off an overwhelming flow of Wellspring energy. After weeks in the same icy chamber with the same iron disc, she was now able to tap into that flow of electrical power at will and pull back when she felt herself drawing nearer to that final threshold. But her growth had been limited to the determination side of the equation, tilting Zylnala's scale too far to one side and causing the force from beyond the veil to move through her with reckless abandon.

Unfortunately, staring at the scale was proving to be as ineffective as day after day of repetitive *clangs* and sore shoulders. As had become her habit, Rav was sitting with her legs crossed in front of a mural of the scale that someone had painted on a dry stretch of cavern wall—she guessed it had been Zylnala; Luviila didn't seem the artistic type, and while Markis and Fulja could create impressive culinary works from meager ingredients, Rav couldn't picture them painting the side of a passage. Its brass weight pans were in perfect alignment, one bearing three straight lines angled upward and the other holding a single stroke, twisting and looping around on itself to form a ribbon.

Her assignment was to discover what balanced the raw desire to accomplish a task, but so far, the answer had eluded her.

"You know there are other drawings back in our quarters," Riqu said as she stepped out of the training chamber. Despite the ever-present chill of their surroundings, the woman wiped her sweat-drenched brow on a towel, freeing the little hairs that had matted down during her training. Like Rav, Riqu frequently stayed later than was asked of her, though Riqu seemed to be driven by something other than one-upping Adiin or a fear of failure.

"Honestly," Riqu said, "I'm surprised the image hasn't imprinted itself in your vision at this point. What do you expect to learn by staring at this every night?"

Rav bit her tongue. Riqu was a kind person and didn't deserve a frustrated retort—she would save those for Adiin. She inhaled deeply through her nose, then stood with an exasperated sigh.

"I never was much good at studying," Rav said. "Hands- and boots-on learning were always more my speed. But as you can tell by the many dents and chips on the ground in there, my usual tactic of running headlong into something and figuring it out as I go isn't working this time."

Riqu laughed. "I'm sure Wymund loves that learning habit."

"Oh, yeah," Rav said, a wry smile breaking through her gloom. "Mr. Planned Precision is a big fan of my improvisational tendencies. Your dogged work ethic must be a real drain on him in your sparring sessions."

The towering woman glanced away as she shifted her weight to her other foot and crossed her arms. Something had pricked her defenses, but before Rav could probe, Riqu asked, "How did you learn to survive your abilities before you got here? I've heard all that you went through. Any novice lightblood should've been consumed by the Illuminated Death on more than one of those occasions."

"In an unlucky turn of events for me," Rav said, "the only thing that seems to impress knowledge into my skull besides practical experience is the badgering of a stubborn old woman. The more like my mother, the more effectively their shrill harping bores its way inside my skull."

Riqu pursed her lips and cocked her head, then reached forward to pat a meaty palm on Rav's shoulder. "Maybe that's your answer," she said with a wink, then began to walk back toward the main cavern chamber.

Shaking her head, Rav slid her back down along the wall and resumed her seated studies, the minutes trickling by as her mind kept returning to Riqu's words. Annika wasn't here, and the thought of sending her a letter asking for help made Rav's stomach do flips. Plus, if the old woman had located Rav's mother and then *she* found out about the request, there would be another layer to the dysfunction whenever Rav did make her way back to Felona.

However long it took, Rav would rather spend the days here pulling her hair out in frustration than beg for help. Not to mention the fact that if Annika could have offered more information about her abilities, why hadn't she said anything after seeing Rav through two near-Illuminated Death experiences? More insight would have been appreciated before staring down that reptilian behemoth in Qedrad and their face-off with Tetamii in Vinsart Hold.

"She doesn't know what she's talking about," Rav muttered as she picked up a small stone and tossed it down the path after Riqu. The rock skidded and bounced around the corner before it hit something softer with a *thump*.

"Would that be me or Blinded Perris who you find lacking?" Luviila said as she stepped into view. She had never ventured this way into the icy complex that Rav had seen, typically keeping herself busy running everything else in the school so that the students could focus on their assignments. Rav doubted the woman had run out of administrative and domestic tasks, then decided to take a stroll. Riqu had sent her this way, and while a few decades shy of Annika, she supposed Luviila could fit a similar description.

"Not you, Luviila," Rav said as she stood to greet her. "Though Riqu must not be too blinded if she found you so quickly to lecture me on Zylnala's musings. What's with the 'blinded' title anyway? No one likes to simply explain things around here."

The woman sighed, then chuckled as she cocked an eyebrow up at the mural. "Do you not feel blind right now, or have your eyes simply gone crossed from staring at this piece?"

"As much as I've stared at his painting, I could stick hot pokers in my eye and still see every vivid detail in all its glory."

"I appreciate the compliment," Luviila said, smiling at Rav's puzzled expression. "I painted the representations of Master Zylnala's theories. I found them to be too vague to be of much use to any prospective students, so I decided to give his words a visual interpretation."

Rav laughed. "Well, I stand by my comment on its quality, but I'm afraid it hasn't done much to keep my iron disc from nearly crushing my toes every day."

The two women stared at the painting for a moment, before Luviila said, "Zylnala chose the word blinded as a literal moniker, referring to the state of your vision as you lightbloods draw more electrical energy than you can handle. But I prefer a more abstract explanation.

"When you come to us, students are blinded by a false end goal: control. It's what you all think that you're here for, seeming to forget the well-established law that passive siphoners cannot consciously direct their flow from a Wellspring. If that is your aim, you will burn yourself out," Luviila said. "Literally or figuratively."

"Well, enlighten me then," Rav said, feeling the heat rise in her face, steaming the chilled mists that drifted throughout this network of caverns. "That's the purpose of a school, isn't it? Obviously, I'm not picking up on the inscrutable teachings through either of your methods, and I'm not inclined to spend the rest of my youth freezing my ass off down here until I do."

"You grew up on an orchard, yes?" Luviila asked.

Rav was taken aback by the non sequitur, but only for a moment. "If this is about to turn into a lecture about the values of patience as it pertains to growing fruit, I'm going to bed."

Luviila shook her head with a small, quiet laugh. "Not exactly, but I would ask for a little patience right now to perhaps make a connection for you." Rav grunted her acquiescence as she settled back against the wall.

"Wymund mentioned to me that you were raised in a family that grows twin tart berries. I'm not from a region with a climate suitable for those trees, but I hear they can be finnicky."

"They're bastards, is what they are," Rav said. "Everyone makes a fuss about nature's harmonious rhythms, but those trees compete with one another like starving stepsiblings. I can't tell you the number of mornings I spent out there cutting back roots that were venturing too close to a neighboring tree's. Or worse, scaling the tallest ones to remove some branches so that it wouldn't hog all the sunlight."

"And on those mornings," Luviila said, her eyes studying Rav's, "what was on your mind? The health of the orchard as a whole? The acidity of the berries?"

Rav snickered. "I cared less about those things then than I do now. Waking up early enough to catch Teacher Melan's first piss with the rising sun, all I wanted was to clip those damn trees back far enough for me to catch a few more minutes of sleep."

"So not the ultimate purpose of the task, but rather the task itself?" Luviila said.

"You're saying that I've been trying so hard to wrestle control of my power, when really all I needed to care about was keeping the disc against the wall?" Rav hung her head. "And here I thought I was onto something when Zylnala spoke with me about determination."

Luviila stepped in front of her, giving a small gesture of her hand so that Rav would meet her gaze. "You were. As you discovered, determination is the key to tapping into your Wellspring Flow." The woman turned to point toward the left side of the scale and the three slanted lines. "It's one half of the equation, but determination is all about momentum, and without something to balance the scale," she said, shifting her finger over to the looped line, "it will drive that power through you until there's nothing left for it to consume."

Rav stepped around the woman and walked toward the mural. "So if those three lines represent unchecked siphoning, then the continuous line on the other side of the scale must represent somehow redirecting the energy. But I thought indirect siphoners couldn't manipulate Wellspring energy like that?"

"It's not about redirecting, Rav," Luviila said. "It's about containing and using the energy that has already filled you. When you were pruning the trees, you weren't controlling them, but you were limiting them, and they were forced to make do with the resources they had been allowed."

The woman traced a finger through the looping shape. "Focus. Keep training your mind on the task in front of you, and your body won't call for ever more power to accomplish an end goal you can never reach."

"You make it sound so easy," Rav said.

"It's nothing of the kind," Luviila said, turning to leave. "But you might be surprised with how much can change with a new perspective."

As she disappeared back into the frigid corridors, Rav felt a renewed sense of hope blossoming in her chest. After so much time living through failure after failure, watching her fellow "blinded" students make strides where she couldn't, she had almost forgotten what it felt like to believe she could pull out of a cycle of defeat. Despite the hour—though day and night had ceased to have much meaning within a mountain—Rav would capitalize on this feeling while she could, without the burden of an audience to distract her.

She returned to her well-worn patch of chipped ice and rock, then took her place in front of the iron plate that had begun to haunt her dreams. She slid on her metal-plated gloves and bent down to retrieve the disc. It felt lighter in her arms. Whether that was from weeks of holding it against the wall or her burgeoning optimism, she took it as a positive sign.

She tapped into the Wellspring, something that by now had become second nature, and felt the familiar prickling sensation on her neck as the energy fueled her. The disc could have been half its weight as she pinned it to the plate with her palm, then a quarter of its weight as the arcing energy raced down her arms.

This was nothing new, however. It was what would happen after five minutes, or even ten on her best trials, that determined how successful this new insight could be. The power coursing across her skin stung, and the muscles at the base of her skull quivered with the threat of total spasm looming.

It wasn't working. The flow that connected her body to the Wellspring was widening with her efforts, and it would only be a matter of time before the dreaded echo of her failure resonated around the cavern once again. It was foolhardy to think that after a short conversation she would be able to make a noticeable advancement. As her arm began to shudder, she leaned her weight through her shoulder, control over her abilities still frustratingly out of focus.

Focus.

Rav took a breath, realizing she had fallen into her old pattern once the siphoning had begun. The goal was not directing the flow—that was impossible. No, the goal now was keeping the disc on the iron wall. Nothing more, nothing less.

With the mental shift came a physical one, the pulsing waves of energy no longer racing along every inch of flesh, and instead settling into a constant thrum. There was no more unbridled cascade of electricity racing through her, only a slow current that she could feel looping back and forth from her shoulder to her palm. The dull ache in her neck remained but did not feel as if it was building to a decapitating crescendo.

Distracted as she was by the new sensation, it wasn't until the next breath that Rav noticed the weightlessness of the disc against the wall. Carefully, she shifted her weight back and let her joyous laughter reverberate through the space in the place of a metallic clang—until that familiar sound followed moments later. But it rang sweeter this time, more like bells than a clattering pan, and she returned to her quarters sporting a grin that not even Adiin could chase away.

CHAPTER 15

FELONA

"You're sure these people will be willing to help us?" Annika asked in a whisper, leaning her face closer to Niri's so that the vacant-stared clerk wouldn't be jolted out of her menial task at the desk and become interested in their plans. It was already bad enough that the Council had been prepared for their arrival—the last thing Annika wanted was a nosy assistant warning her bosses of their intentions, possibly tipping off someone on Elikar's payroll.

"As sure as I can be," Niri replied. "Those on the Crest can espouse ideals until they are blue in the face, but we all know that at the end of the day, they only answer to the loudest and heaviest purse." She pointed to the door over the clerk's shoulder. "But the lower magistrates, well, they haven't climbed that ladder yet. Haven't sold themselves off to the highest bidders.

"The people working down here are still true believers in the law," she continued. "If we want to make sure Thalin follows through on his promise of investigating the Clipped Gulls, who better to ask then the people who would be responsible for carrying out that plan?"

Annika glanced over to Kymil for his opinion. He was sitting to Annika's other side, but she had thought he would have been eavesdropping. Instead, the bard was sitting silently, biting the corner of his lip as he stared absently at the back wall. She had known something was off with him when they left the council hall, but when he hadn't returned to Niri's home with Ubadrii and opted to stay with her instead, Annika thought whatever cloud had settled over the man after their defeat was starting to dissipate.

Now, though, it seemed to have only darkened.

Must I always be responsible for the emotional states of these young people who flock to me like coastal swallows? Annika smiled softly. *Then again, I'm the old fool who keeps feeding them bread.*

"This isn't over, Kymil," she whispered, his name finally snapping him out of his reverie. "This process won't be as easy as we had hoped, but since when has anything been easy for us in this business of stopping wars?"

Kymil inhaled slowly, some of his posture returning with the in-breath as one corner of his mouth ticked up. "You know, for once I would like it to be, though. I tire of putting in effort. I don't know if you've noticed, but most things usually break my way."

Annika studied him for a moment, then said, "Don't do that. You aren't putting on a show. You don't need to keep the story moving with a song and a smile just because the audience noticed a hitch in the performance. If something is troubling you, you should talk to me about it. I've accumulated a lot of wisdom along with stiff joints and gray hairs over my years. The least you could do is allow me to use it."

His smile drooped, not disappearing but morphing into one brimming with sadness. Kymil's eyes flicked down to his amputated limb for a split second before returning to meet Annika's gaze. "Beaten by a hexant and no ability to sway an audience on my own merits anymore. Apparently, a smile is all I've got left."

His confidence had taken a hit, there was no doubt about that. But it seemed to be more than a simple outmaneuvering by the Council. The bard was experiencing a crisis of identity, something about which Annika knew all too well. She had lost her sense of purpose for years after the Rebellion of the Commons and

Alauvar's death, and she had chosen the absolute worst path to navigate the turmoil: isolation. They didn't have time for Kymil to indulge in a similar tactic. As alluring as that option was for someone who felt unmoored, Annika had learned purpose is best found in community, and Kymil would have to learn to open himself to that sooner rather than later.

She settled back in her chair, turning her eyes forward as he did the same. She hoped the loss of eye contact would allow the bard to lower his walls—for one so in tune with the emotions and motivations of others, Kymil tended to keep people at arm's length. But she needed him to hear her now.

"A smile's worth is measured by its capacity to be shared with others," she said. "Before you give up on yourself entirely, might I suggest checking in with those of us who care about you? We apparently see aspects of your value to which you've been blinded."

She received no response other than a shifting of weight in his seat, but sometimes no response could speak volumes.

The door behind the clerk swung open, nearly knocking her and the stack of papers she was riffling through aside. Another clerk, a young man dressed in a navy vest and matching trousers, stepped into the room. "The magistrates are ready for you, Ms. Trisarin."

Niri stood to lead the others back into the offices, then leaned closer to them so that only Annika and Kymil could hear. "We aren't dealing with an immediately hostile audience this time, but they can still be uptight. Be deferential, but firm."

Annika nodded, and even Kymil muttered an agreement. Normally Annika would be concerned about the elf coming off as flippant or making an inappropriate comment, but now, at least, she figured his introspective mood might work in their favor.

The trio followed the clerk down a long hallway that buzzed with activity, as if this hive of legal clerks were doing their best to compete with the work ethic of an actual bee colony. Despite the pomp and importance demonstrated at the council hall, with all the liveried aides and plush décor, Annika knew this was where all the vital work for the city was done. Approvals and citations were signed, then passed along to either messengers or patrolling guards depending on the necessary tasks for their function. These were the city's drones, but without them, Felona would collapse under its own weight.

At the end of the long hall, the group was filed into a small room with a desk and three chairs arranged in front of it, one of which was already occupied by a balding, stout man who wore his years on his face well. There were lines, to be sure, but they only served to harden his already prominent jawline rather than result in any sagginess. He stood and nodded at Niri as she entered, then offered a slightly diminished tilt of his head to the others.

Behind the desk sat a woman at least twenty years his junior, with her auburn hair pulled back and out of her face. She looked frazzled as she shifted documents around on her desk, then rolled her neck and let out a sigh before sitting back into her chair. She gestured toward the remaining two seats, and Kymil opted to stand behind them while the two women sat.

"Please tell me this isn't about garbage blowing into the Conservatory again," the woman behind the desk said. "We're well aware that the Trough has a litter problem, but we'll get to that as soon as we figure out how to keep neighbors from bickering over property lines and enterprising restaurateurs from selling unregulated mystery meat from their carts."

"As I told you, Jebune," the older man said, "Niri wouldn't be wasting our time with that nonsense. She would be more likely to chase down the litterers herself with a pair of shears than come complaining to us about something so trivial."

"Thank you, Magistrate Irbon," Niri replied, "but I like to think I would be sensible enough to use a blunt instrument instead. Shears would only create more of a mess."

Irbon let out a gruff chuckle, but Jebune's exasperation was unfazed. "So what is this about then? I've been told that Irbon handled your family's case in the past when he was an inspector, and I am truly sorry about your loss, but unless you were suddenly able to find decades-old evidence, I don't see how we would be able to make an arrest for your husband's murderer."

The woman's bluntness sucked the air out of the room. A suffocating silence hung in the air for a moment as Niri stared daggers at the magistrate, but just as Annika was about to speak up, Kymil cleared his throat.

"No new evidence on that front, I'm afraid, though from what little I've heard of that incident, perhaps a related investigation needs to be launched." Kymil's words were flowing through him again with confidence, but he still lacked that characteristic twinkle in his eye. Some of her pep talk must have broken through, but part of his mind was still elsewhere.

"The Clipped Gulls appear to have been given free rein in this city," he continued, "operating unperturbed for decades and integrating themselves into Felona's economic interests with little resistance. Isn't it time their little club feels the weight of the law across their backs?"

Annika bit the inside of her cheek. He had chosen a fine time to snap himself out of his pity party. *Perhaps deferential doesn't have the same meaning on Liiashae's shores.*

Jebune's face reddened to match her hair, but Irbon raised a hand. "No need to take offense, Jebune. This man is right, and sometimes it takes a frank discussion to get the message across."

"Look," Jebune said, "I'm no fan of those dogs myself, but we don't have free rein to send patrols out through the city kicking in doors and busting heads. A citywide investigation like that involves approval from the Council, and I don't see that—"

"Chief Magistrate Thalin just ordered a thorough investigation of the Clipped Gulls in our audience with the Council,"

Annika interjected, and she noted Irbon's gaze sharpened. "Niri simply wanted to check in with some of the Lower Magistrates because she knows where the real business of the city's management occurs."

Jebune's face softened, her complexion returning to its normal shade. "While I appreciate the compliment, we'll have to coordinate with aides working in the council hall to ensure that this is legitimate."

"But in the meantime," Irbon said, crooking a finger at a messenger and two guards who had been stationed out in the hallway, "I see no reason not to get a head start. I've still got an ear to the ground—the investigator life never really leaves you—and there are a few hotspots around the city I've been itching to look into. This seems like the perfect opportunity."

He scrawled a few notes down on several scraps of paper, then handed them to the messenger. "Disperse these to a few of our available patrol units. Hit the SPOILED PUDDING first; I hear they have a rough clientele—out of the ordinary for an arts district." The messenger offered a quick bow of the head and departed, followed swiftly by two flanking guards.

"Thank you, Irbon," Niri said, dropping his appellation. "You never were one to let things go easily."

The magistrate crossed the few feet between them and knelt to her eye level. "Only when I'm forced to, Niri. When the leads started to run dry, I was stonewalled by my bosses. No one was motivated to look into the death of the man who wanted to shake up the city's power structure that was already benefiting them.

"But I'm in their seat now, and I've been hoping for an excuse to take these bastards out since I was a recruit. Let's flush out these rats."

CHAPTER 16

FELONA

"Will my services be required again?" the gaunt elf asked, his sunken eyes and hollowed cheeks combating his people's tendency toward natural beauty. His eyes shifted furtively, lingering on every other Clipped Gull in the room who were keeping to themselves but well within earshot. "I understand that the impetus for my involvement is still on the board."

"There's no need to speak in code," Garla said, combing a flop of golden-brown hair out of her eyes with her hand as she sat propped on a stack of crates, a game of cards meant for one person spread out in front of her. "Everyone here knows what you did, and who you did it for."

The hexant licked his lips and turned his gaze back to Tetamii, who nodded. "Well, the terms of my infusion didn't specify who knew the details." He pulled a gray handkerchief from inside his dark coat, then dabbed at the beads of sweat that had started to form on his forehead. "I've found in my line of work, it pays to be overly cautious.

"However, it seems I may speak plainly," he continued. "The fatestitcher is alive and well, and likely planning another attempt at bringing our benefactor low. Will he be needing another infusion prepared to counteract the bard's manipulations? If you could provide me with his jacket again, or another personal ite—"

"We'll be in touch should the need arise, Habrum," Tetamii said, passing over a fat leather pouch full of silver libers. The man was nervous and twitchy, not surprising given that he was in a den of vipers, but Tetamii wanted him out of their safehouse as much as the hexant wished to leave. He was reluctant to stay in the presence of another man who could twist fortune around his little finger. The scar on his back from a lucky blade was reminder enough for a lifetime to deal as little as possible with these individuals.

He would keep Habrum's talents in the back of his mind, though. With the bard still in play, Tetamii might need to call on him once again before this matter was settled.

Habrum bowed slightly at the waist. "Of course, Mr. Fiadar. Please don't hesitate to call on me in the future."

And with that, the spindly elf half-ran up the steps toward the BUTTONED-UP LAD, where he would look less out of place in his tailored clothes but be less welcome. Evin was already uncomfortable with siphoners, but having a man like that in his shop for long might send him over the edge. No one wanted to risk stubbing their toe on every cobblestone on their way home, and that was only if the hexant was in a good mood.

"You all right, Scorchy?" Garla asked as she swung her legs off the side of her perch and slipped down to the floor. Despite having fully recovered from his poisoned state, she continued to watch him like a mother hen. "He didn't curse your belt to unfasten at the worst possible time, did he?"

"Let's hope not," Atusiin said. The half-elf sat at a small table near the stairs with his legs propped up, where he was gliding the tip of a pocketknife under his fingernails to clean them. "Fiadar's already shown enough of his ass as it is."

A round of snickers circled the room, bolstering the smirk on the man's face. He had not even deigned to look away from his task before slinging the insult. But that had always been Atusiin's way, more comfortable with a whispered word and stabbed back than any real confrontation—even their fake childhood scrap to lure in Ilphas Trisarin had to be weighted in his favor for Atusiin to agree to participate. It was the central reason that despite their coming into the Gulls around the same time, Magzii had favored Tetamii. But Atusiin was scrappy. If he smelled Tetamii's blood in the water, he would not hesitate to strike.

"Habrum wouldn't dare so much as infuse an eyelash on anyone in this room," Tetamii said. Garla nodded with her typical childlike grin, but the way she eyed him told Tetamii that she wasn't so sure he even believed it himself. Garla had only just met him, and in a pathetic state no less. She hadn't yet learned that other than Magzii, when Tetamii spoke, people listened. Still, she wasn't the one he needed to remind of their place.

"And on the topic of asses," Tetamii continued, turning to face Atusiin, who was now standing and clapping the backs of a few of his fellow revelers. "Have we forgotten the number of times I've planted you on yours over the years?"

"No one needs to remind us of the passage of time, friend," Atusiin said. "The weight of the years has landed heavily on your shoulders if we're to believe what we've heard about your exploits up north. It's a good thing Magzii has people like me around who have proven more resistant. But I guess that's to be expected when one of us has to hone their craft instead of falling back on your little magical gifts." His eyes narrowed. "You've grown lazy. Soft."

Atusiin would have been nothing but a sooty stain on the stone floor if Magzii's rules hadn't been in place: No Gull strikes another, lest the flock devours its own. But he also encouraged a pecking order among his crew, and Tetamii would see it enforced.

Tetamii crossed the room to meet him, and the three Gulls that had gathered around Atusiin returned to their seats, their eyes trained on their boots as they went. But their abandonment didn't seem to faze him, who stared upward at Tetamii, defiant in the face of a figure twice his size. Atusiin never could pack on the muscle that Magzii requested of his elven recruits, but to his credit, he had funneled that shortcoming into an unparalleled mastery of stealth and traversal.

"The only thing you've honed is your mouth, Atusiin," Tetamii said, "which explains this preoccupation with backsides. Has Magzii's grown tiresome and stale after having your face planted there for so long?" Tetamii tutted. "And with nothing to show for your efforts."

Finally, the half-elf's cool snapped, his eyes flaring to a fiery life like they had so many times during their upbringing in the Gulls. Each patted head or extra sweetbread that was granted to Tetamii instead of him had resulted in that same watery-eyed glare and ruddy complexion. Atusiin's hand reached down to a dagger at his belt, and Tetamii watched the smoky wisps dance with anticipation in his vision. Magzii had no rule against self-preservation.

But before Atusiin could pull the blade from its sheath, Garla was there, placing one hand on his chest and the other on Tetamii's. Her affable expression was all the more impressive in its resilience to the charged atmosphere permeating the basement like the air before a storm.

"We're all very impressed by your verbal barbs," she said, "and I certainly don't doubt either of you could put up a fight that would leave the rest of us standing in puddles of our own urine. Maybe we keep on the boss's good side for now." When Atusiin's lip turned up in a snarl, Garla was quick to add, "No need to have the boss lose trust in us."

Atusiin stood a bit taller with a huff, failing to reach much higher than Tetamii. "Magzii knows what I'm capable of, but if Tet has forgotten, I'm happy to oblige."

Both men had been raised on the streets of the Trough, and particularly with Magzii's parental philosophy of pitting his initiates against one another, that background did not teach one to back down from a threat. Each man had their way of handling such situations, with Tetamii favoring more direct resolutions and Atusiin tending toward subtle yet decisive—methods of taking out the person who had threatened him. The half-elf had even managed to one up Tetamii a handful of times over the years. He was crafty and quick, often snagging a goal set for Tetamii before he had a chance to reach it, but here in this room, the rat had nowhere to run.

However, before Tetamii could remind Atusiin of his place in the organization yet again, the door at the top of the stairs snapped open. Hurried footsteps announced the arrival of a man drenched in sweat, his coat unbuttoned and flapping wildly behind him. His look of panic was the only thing that saved his life, as blades were drawn and bolts were leveled in crossbows at his chest as soon as he came into view. It had not been the wisest decision to arrive wearing the colors of the magistrates, but the man was clearly distraught rather than leading a charge.

"The lower magistrates are sending a squad after Magzii," the man said between heaving gulps of air. "They're on their way to his club now."

Tetamii knew Magzii had runners working in the magistrate offices, keeping him apprised of any ordinances that might impact his bottom line or crack down on the Gulls' activities in the city, but that had always been secondary to this eventuality: when the law decided to come directly for Magzii's head, he had wanted a warning.

"To the Spoiled Pudding, then?" Tetamii asked, already smelling the dank musk of Magzii's favorite nightclub. A golden opportunity to regain status with Magzii and crush Atusiin had fallen into his lap, and he wouldn't have to leave a scorch on the man. "I trust one of us will be able to handle a squad of city guards. Feel free to watch from the shadows where you're comfortable watching real Gulls do their work."

The half-elf clasped a hand on Tetamii's arm. "I'll have a bowl of the rotten stuff waiting for you when you finally get there," he said, before spinning Tetamii aside and launching himself toward the stairwell. Atusiin flew up the flight, taking three steps at a time and shoving the runner down the rest of the way, reaching the top faster than Tetamii could reach the banister.

"You're going to have to move quicker than that, Scorchy," Garla said, dipping her hand in his coat pocket before he started up after the half-elf.

Tetamii made a note to stop the use of that nickname before it spread through the ranks, but the weight of what she deposited on him was distracting enough for now. Whatever it was felt round and soft as it bounced off his thigh with each step, with enough heft to be noticed but not enough to be coins or a weapon of any kind. She meant for him to know it was there, so when he burst out into the tailor shop above and saw the front door already swinging closed in Atusiin's wake, Tetamii chanced a peek.

From out of his pocket, he pulled a bundled hemp sack, tied tight with a thin strip of rope. He could feel the crinkle of ground plant matter inside, accompanied by a powerful aroma that smelled of licorice and burned meat. He rolled his eyes and slipped the pouch back inside his coat. No matter Garla's insistence that Tetamii try the new herb nurse's infusions, this was not the time to partake in that man's experiments. Magzii only recruited the best talent, but that did not always mean the most stable.

Evin stood behind the counter, one bushy eyebrow cocked as he tilted his head toward the door. A pair of young women examining spools of fabric in the corner were whispering to each other worriedly—although the store was a front, Evin didn't want the façade broken for his customers. A failed business meant Magzii had no reason to keep him around. With a curt nod, Tetamii slipped out the door to find more of the mayhem Atusiin had left in his wake.

An overturned cart rested on one side several paces from the door, its driver and passengers spilled out onto the dusty street. A few passersby had stopped to help them, though between the cursing and moaning, Tetamii wasn't sure anyone had been able to glean the extent of their injuries yet. Most of the others lining the road, however, had their necks craned toward the rooftops, where the disappearing silhouette of a thin half-elf could be seen leaping away toward the Horns and Planks district.

Tetamii pushed his way through the gathered crowd until he could move more freely, then dashed down the street, scanning for his own more discreet way up to the skyline. He had held his own against the lightblood girl's speed in Virdoba for a time, and that had involved a far less dense cluster of buildings and greater leaps between them. Atusiin was cocky, but Tetamii believed he could match the non-enhanced man once they were on a level playing field.

Finally, he spotted an iron trellis that a launderer was using to air-dry a small family's worth of clothes, complete with undergarments flapping in the dusty breeze. No one would accuse the Trough residents of having an eye for aesthetics. But beautiful architecture or no, the structure supported Tetamii's weight as he scaled the side of the squat building and pulled himself onto the roof.

Atusiin's figure had grown even smaller, unhindered as he was by the pedestrians below, but Tetamii began the chase anew. He had not allowed his reliance on his Wellspring connection to weaken him physically, and Atusiin would learn that soon enough.

Magzii's usual haunt was nestled deep within the Horns and Planks neighborhood, or as its denizens preferred to call it, Ias's Bosom. After all, it was where the arts district shifted from music halls and stage plays to a more colorful mélange of dives, dens, and bordellos. The fact that the Dawn One of thievery and deception had been invoked in the sobriquet had not proven to be a deterrent to travelers, as the borough was frequently the first stop for any out-of-towner. Of course, it helped that the neighborhood was so close to Leros's Path, beckoning fresh arrivals into said bosom with the sights and sounds of revelry. From Tetamii's position, though, the path to the SPOILED PUDDING was obscured by a mountain.

The Trough completely encircled the Crest, like a ring around the base of the mountain that served as the literal and metaphorical center of Felona, so a direct route to the club was out of the question. They would both have to run around the peak's circumference, and Tetamii felt good. After existing in a drugged stupor for so long, then enduring the lingering stares of both pity and hunger from his fellow Gulls, powering through his legs to scale the rooftop chasms was exhilarating. His heart pounded in his chest, each beat a drum that drove him forward.

One ramshackle roof led to another, and while Tetamii was keeping pace with his opponent, it became apparent that it would be impossible to catch up. His relative success with the girl in Virdoba likely came down to her blind rage and lack of discipline—the lightblood had been faster than him, but he had been in control of their route. Atusiin was another story, and his slight edge in speed combined with the familiarity of Felona's skyline meant Tetamii would gain no ground.

To their left, the glade of the Bindweed Conservatory was already beginning to transition into the exit from Leros's Path, with the nightlife district just minutes away. Marching down the center of the street, shifting pedestrians aside with gentle nudges, was a squad of orange-coated guards with polearms and longswords gleaming in the sunlight.

Soon, Atusiin would be arcing his path around the Crest and would exit into the more decorative buildings of the Horns and

Planks, where he would have the distractions of noise and color on his side to pick off the guards before they reached the club. Tetamii had seen the man work in his element, and despite his taunts to the contrary, he believed Atusiin was capable of eliminating this cadre of guards if they were caught unaware. The chase would end in defeat.

Tetamii felt the weight of Garla's gift bounce off his thigh with each leap and remembered her suggestion that he move quicker as she slipped it to him. Since returning home and seeing all the infighting within the Gulls, the competitive animosity to curry favor with Magzii and advance within the ranks, Tetamii had already realized how that mentality led to an untrained lightblood besting him. If he learned anything from that failure, it was that trusting in an alliance might actually lend strength instead of opening up a vulnerability.

Tetamii skidded to a stop and pulled the pouch free once more, unfurling the rope that held it closed to reveal broken bits of brown, striated leaves. He pinched some between his fingers and shoved it into his mouth, nearly vomiting as the combination of char and fennel flavors turned his stomach.

Garla is eating the rest of this bag if I lose this challenge.

As he resumed his race, Tetamii chewed the shredded vegetation until it was an aromatic paste, the odor enveloping his sinuses from within. But he noted no boost in speed, no quickening footfalls or extended leaps. He had expected something from Garla's gift, but perhaps he had been a fool. An herb nurse could only do so much—mend bones and break fevers, sure, but not grant lightblood abilities. Garla should've known better than to take an infusion from a crackpot and pass it off to him like some boon. Tetamii cursed under his breath. *He* should've known better than to trust her with this.

That was when he noticed the radiant fissures cracking through the craggy mountain surface to his right. Tetamii tucked and rolled into a crouch behind a soot-covered chimney, fearing some sort of quake inside the peak was causing it to rupture, but after several seconds of calm, he chanced another glance. The glowing jagged lines seemed to move of their own accord, slithering along the rock's surface without any disruption caused by the changing topography. Whatever this was, it was not a geological phenomenon. Tetamii had never seen anything like it—other than the wisps of the veil he could grab to pull forth flames.

Without pausing to think how, he acted on pure instinct, just as he had his whole life when siphoning heat from the Wellspring. Tetamii leaped toward the mountain as he pulled apart the edges of a fissure with his mind and gasped as he plunged into a newly formed crevice instead of faceplanting into the stone. More luminous cracks flared to life in this short tunnel, not providing light for his vision but simply revealing their presence to a connected individual. Tetamii broke into a run, pulling apart the mountain in front of him to create a tunnel that would serve as a direct line to Magzii's club. He lit his path with simultaneous microtears from the more familiar smoky tendrils, allowing a soft orange-red glow into the otherwise pitch-black mountain interior.

Along with the tightening at the base of his skull, Tetamii could feel the stone tremble under his feet, and he wondered if this was how orecallers felt when they pulled from the veil. The sheer power of the ground itself vibrating in concert with Tetamii's will was intoxicating, unlike anything he had ever felt siphoning fire. This gift Garla had given him was not just a simple way to win this race. She had also proven the lesson he had gleaned from the lightblood: there was power to be gained from trust. Following Magzii alone had stifled him, but now Tetamii knew he had the potential to be even greater.

In a time that would've been impossible for even a lightblood at the height of their power, Tetamii found himself leaping out of the mountain and onto a rooftop in a section of the Trough that overlooked Ias's Bosom. However, the expected sounds of drunken debauchery were drowned out by the growing roar of earth behind him. He turned to see the fissures spasming and sputtering, the mountain groaning in protest to the damage he had done by traveling through it. Realizing his recklessness, Tetamii reached out to knit together the vein he had opened within the stone, but suddenly his neck relaxed, and the jagged lines of the veil blinked out of sight.

It was temporary, Tetamii thought as his heart skipped a beat. He had gotten lost in the immensity of the power granted to him by the infusion, but of course it wouldn't be permanent—that was the nature of infusions, after all.

He staggered away from the cliff face and knelt to grab hold of a beam, stabilizing himself as a portion of the mountain the size of a large house tumbled free. The chunk of stone cast a looming shadow over a part of the Trough that Tetamii had bypassed, all to prove his superiority to a man he already knew was his lesser. His whole body shook as the massive stone rumbled and tumbled down, crushing a number of buildings that had been built against the cliff, before rolling to a stop that was punctuated by a momentary deafening silence.

Shouts soon followed, though, accompanied by the dust climbing into the air from the rubble. Near the stone's resting point, Tetamii could make out scattered polearms and streaks of blood, while a few onlookers tried fruitlessly to tug an orange-sleeved arm free from the wreckage. Others jumped into the smashed business and homes that the piece of mountain had leveled on its slide, shouting names through panicked cries.

Through the rising dust cloud, Tetamii saw a thin form sliding to a stop on a rooftop on the other side of the damage. Tetamii had won; he had cut off Atusiin's path to Magzii and decimated the guards who the magistrates had dared to send after the Gulls. His legend would be rekindled among his brothers and sisters. All it had cost was the lives of people living in the same slum that had birthed him. Tetamii closed his eyes and took a slow breath, burying whatever emotion his mind threatened to throw at him into a mental chest.

There's a good lad, he could hear Magzii say, just as he had so many times over the years. Perhaps he couldn't toss out those lessons entirely in favor of the strength to be found in an alliance. There was indeed something to gain from trusting a friend, but there was also so much to lose. When that happened, Tetamii had the lessons of a cold mentor to keep him standing.

Chapter 17

Felona

Mareq busied himself with pouring coffee into the ceramic cups Niri had left out for them, adding more than a few spoonfuls of sugar to his own mug before picking up the tray. The dark liquid this island tried to pass off as coffee was far too acidic for his tastes—the roasts back home in Destueqa tended toward a nuttier profile—and he couldn't be grimacing for their entire meeting with Tano Scrin. The man had already looked haggard and emotionally drained when he arrived, and Mareq didn't want to annoy him further.

He pushed through the door and moved into the sitting room, which he continued to find excessively opulent despite Annika's declarations that the design was understated. But as well traveled as the old woman was, she had never seen a dairy farm in Brey. Mareq's family home had been understated; to his eye, Niri's estate was the epitome of luxury.

One of four teal velvet sofas in the room was occupied by their guest, the Voice of the Many having come to call on Niri about a half hour too late. She and Annika had left to meet with other councilmembers, expressing their desire to attempt a more subtle persuasion after Kymil's failed performance. But even with Mareq explaining their absence, Scrin had insisted that he speak with the rest of them anyway.

"Is it typical for heads of state to make house calls in this country?" Ubadrii asked as he accepted a cup from Mareq. The bald elf brought the coffee to his face, the slightest smile forming on his lips. Qedradan coffee was even worse than Kefyan in Mareq's estimation—bitter to the point of tasting charred—so he supposed this tart roast would still be an improvement for the hidden hand.

"Not typical, no," Tano said, rubbing his fingers over the dark stubble on his face. "But it's also not typical to have another member of our council accused of treason by a group I find to be a reputable source."

"Have I truly fallen so low as to become 'reputable'?" Kymil asked with a playful grin. "I've spent too long with you lot and away from my people. Mareq," he said as he picked a cup from the tray. "You and I are going out tonight. Everyone should feel the warm embrace of Ias's Bosom once in their life."

Mareq felt his face flush, though whether it was the casual heresy, or the implication of a night spent at Kymil's direction, he didn't mind. He was more pleasantly surprised that his friend was seeming more himself than he had in the few days since their dismal performance before the Council. Mareq could tell Kymil had taken the loss hard, but he was coming around—at least outwardly. The man had a frustrating penchant for putting on a show even while off the stage. He would have to check in with him and pry the man's emotions into the light when he had the chance.

"I'm afraid that neighborhood won't be much fun for a while," Tano said with a wan grin. "With all the damage the rockslide caused in that section of the Trough, some of the families have moved into any available rooms for rent throughout the other districts in the city. Even the more . . . flesh-baring establishments have opened their doors to the displaced, so your return to self-indulgence might have to wait."

"That was so horrible," Mareq said, taking a seat on another sofa facing the councilman. They had felt the foundation of Niri's house shake when that portion of the mountain fell. Thankfully, they learned most of that area had been empty as a tanner's workshop was being renovated after a spill of his liming agent. The surrounding shops had closed up as well until the overpowering earthy odor dissipated, but the unfortunate cleaning crew had been caught in the devastation, along with a few guards. Annika and Niri had grown suspicious at their deaths, but Mareq was not convinced. He believed political animals like them saw conspiracy around every corner. Sometimes, harvests spoiled. Nature had a way of not caring about mortal plans, but it didn't point to subterfuge.

"I've read that islands tend to be more unstable than the mainland," Mareq said. "Has something like that happened before?"

Tano shook his head. "There's never been any volcanic or quake activity here in Felona. Some of our inspectors are looking into the possibility of an orecaller or a venter looking to cause havoc, but I can only put credence in one conspiracy theory at a time. For now, I'm just inspired by how our people have risen to the occasion and helped their neighbors. It drives me to continue to honor their trust in me."

"It need not be a separate conspiracy," Kymil said, voicing Annika and Niri's suspicions. "Elikar and the Gulls have demonstrated a willingness to send a siphoner abroad to unleash their power. Why not bring that action home if he's feeling threatened?"

"It would be a great distraction," Mareq said with a resigned sigh.

"It would, if it didn't also lighten Elikar's purse, and there's nothing he cares about more than the heft of that bag." Tano sighed. "If the damage had been located in the Reliquary, maybe I could be persuaded to believe you. Elikar never turned a profit from the High Scholars and their proselytizing. But right in the heart of the Trough? No. His labor force could've been crippled, and he can't have full ships left docked in the port."

"The implication of your distinction being that you do believe us about Elikar, then?" Ubadrii asked, face and tone unmoved by the loss of life. Mareq knew the man was an ally and cared about justice, but at times Ubadrii's calculating dispassion sent a chill down his spine. Though it was likely the very trait that made him such an effective hidden hand for King Berenqar—compassion wasn't a value one looked for in their royal information gatherers.

Tano tilted his head slightly, chewing the inside of his lip. "I would say I'm open to hearing more. Going any further than that would prohibit the continued functioning of the Council, as it would require emergency investigations and a cessation of all our legislative duties."

"That sounds appropriate," Kymil said as he tapped a jaunty beat on his mug with a nail. Performance was a compulsion for him, lute in hand or no. "The snake shouldn't be allowed to push through any other dangerous elements of his agenda while the rest of you deliberate on tweaking tax structures."

"They need to be able to help out with the damage in the Trough," Mareq said. Kymil rolled his eyes, but Mareq received an appreciative nod from Tano.

"I can't speak for the motives of my fellow councilmembers, but I do want to do what I can for those who were hurt or unhoused by the rockslide," Tano said. "I can't do that if I formally side with Elikar's accusers. The investigations alone would take months, requiring us to be separated from one another and leaving all city matters in gridlock."

"Were we not told the matter would be looked into during our hearing?" Ubadrii asked.

Tano chuckled mirthlessly. "That was said, and perhaps Chief Magistrate Thalin actually meant it. I'll let you know when we get to that action item in a decade or two."

The Voice of the Many stared deeply into his cup for a moment, his eyes revealing an inner struggle that was plain to even a farm boy like Mareq. Finally, he brought his gaze back to the three of them.

"All I'll say for now is that Elikar Thymes is the single most ambitious individual I've ever met, a quality common to those of us who find their way to a seat of power. But while most people have some ethical mooring that we can either look to for guidance or, at worst, feel bound to, my impression of our port admiral is that his only allegiance is to himself—whatever the cost.

"You alerted my suspicions," Tano continued. "If I can help you discreetly, by setting up a meeting or making an opportune introduction, let me know. I was elected to my seat to serve in Felona's best interests, and I intend to see them done."

***

Annika tried to ignore the sense of eyes boring holes in the back of her skull as she walked with Niri across the mustard yellow tiles of Teacher Melan's college. Swooping purple tapestries ran in inverted arcs between the ceiling beams, extending the entire monumental length of the cavernous building and looming over her stroll like a hovering parent. The sensation was residual, a lingering echo of her time spent in these halls as a child, when the judgmental gazes of the acolytes fell on the adopted human charity case.

The Iatorii's were well-known parishioners of this college, even respected by each side of the racial schism—the Melan Humanists went so far as to keep the family's name on their roster for celebratory invites—but no one knew how to process their newest addition. The sigh of relief was deafening when she had shown little interest in taking part in the Dawn One's study. A human aligning with the elven theory of Melan's origins out of familial loyalty might have cleaved the college in two.

Still, she straightened her spine and brushed her unruly silver waves down self-consciously. Even after decades away from these hallowed halls, she felt out of place. Thankfully, Niri carried no such baggage, so when the pair they were meeting stepped out of a side chamber, the woman was ready to claim the advantage.

"While we appreciate the meeting," Niri said, coming to a stop before Relus Vunii and Churi Bleone, "it might have been more considerate to offer a place more centrally located. Ever since the landslide, getting out of the southern portion of the Trough has been almost more trouble than it's worth."

Browbeating two councilmembers on something as superfluous as decorum was not the tactic Annika would've opted for, especially considering the secrecy with which this meeting had been arranged. As far as she was aware, only the four involved and the two guards stationed at the office door had any knowledge of the gathering. The two owed Annika and Niri nothing more after hearing them out in an official capacity, and the last thing they needed was to have this favor rescinded before it even began. But when Vunii's face flushed and Bleone drew her lips into a tight line, Annika guessed there were other effective strategies for diplomacy. The Trisarin's seemed to possess a heritable knack for setting their opponents on their back feet.

"While we can understand your frustrations, was it not your request to keep this encounter inconspicuous?" Bleone asked, her dark beady eyes refusing to flinch from the reproach. The sunburst colors of her High Scholar vestments clashed with her dour countenance, all the rich golds, purples, and reds of a setting sun stifled by the storm cloud the woman wore for a face. "What would be less noticeable than the Voice of the Dawn staying put on her own grounds?"

"Still, Churi," Vunii said, verdant ringed irises sparkling as he scanned the grand hall behind them furtively. "It might have been wise to avoid having these two make such a long trek to the Reliquary. It offers too many opportunities for wandering eyes to notice them and report on their comings and goings." He reached a long, thin arm around Annika and Niri and ushered them forward into the room. "Come, let's at least get them out of view."

"Oh, we weren't followed," Niri barked. "Is it so out of character for a couple of lonely women to be out on a stroll among the Dawn Ones' colleges? It's where we're meant to find meaning in our lives, is it not?"

"More importantly," Annika said, suddenly feeling the muscles in her back unclench now that she had moved out of the echoing hall, and away from the Melan iconography of ships at sea and wayfinders with their mariner astrolabes. "Why are you so concerned about being seen with us? I thought we offered little more than a curious story, not damning evidence about the activities of a colleague."

"Do not read so much into Relus's anxieties," Bleone said, shuffling over to her seat behind a cream-colored palm wood desk. The chair was lined with indigo stained velvet, and stitched into the headrest was the visage of Teacher Melan, her hair blowing back to reveal round-tipped ears. It would have been a scandalous depiction of the Dawn One in Annika's youth, but times had changed, and the Melan Humanist sitting in the seat must have felt comfortable with the changing tides.

"He cares deeply about the public's perception of him," the High Scholar continued. "Enough that it sends his mind into somersaults. It's a sickness, I think. One borne of his mother's incessant need for attention and adoration, though at least she had the stage to validate her work." She sent a sidelong glance toward the half-elf, who was finally getting around to shutting the door after peering through the crack.

"My mother did indeed curse me with a drive to be liked and respected," Vunii said as he walked around the desk and leaned against a bookshelf behind Bleone. "It must be freeing to be granted such things by virtue of those silly robes you wear. Not even in Myrii's books would we be able to find how someone such as yourself could acquire them by merit."

There's no love lost between these two, Annika thought, impressed that the previously nervous culture secretary had uttered the Analyst's name inside Melan's college.

Much like with Teacher Irasil, humans tended to bristle at the mention of the definitively elven Dawn One of knowledge and science, believing her favor to be a central source of the Liiashan's air of superiority. But Annika didn't need these two to be dear friends—she simply needed them to have open ears.

"I don't buy it," Niri said, taking one of the empty seats in front of the desk. It was also made of palm wood and had crashing waves carved into the ends of the armrests. "Hiding us away to maintain your social standing? No. Regardless of our fruitless argument before the Council, any one of you councilmembers would be lucky to have people with our names and resources in your pocket."

Annika sat next to her. "Which means you want this encounter under wraps as much as we do," she said. When neither answered, Annika added, "You believe us, and you don't want Elikar catching on to that fact."

Bleone laughed. "Don't be ridiculous. Your story was, and remains, full of holes and gaps in logic that I wouldn't have been able to leap even in my youth. Unless something has changed in the days since we last spoke?"

"Well then why did you accept our request for a second meeting?" Annika asked. If these two had agreed to see them simply for another opportunity to insult them, she would pull every last string she could to see them fall from grace alongside Elikar. They may not be treasonous warmongers, but she did loathe bullies.

"Because while we don't believe your story," Vunii said with a sigh, "we can't deny it has a certain verisimilitude. The man is not above such tactics if it means personal gain."

"Then you mean to help us?" Niri asked, her tone more disbelief than optimism.

Bleone shook her head. "We only mean to offer you a channel to report any future discoveries. Should anything materialize, bring it to me or Relus first, and we can see that it is properly handled."

"We would hate for word to reach Elikar before you had the chance to unveil his treachery," Vunii said, then held up a hand. "Should that be the case, of course. He may shut down any further communication between you and the Council."

"Or worse," Bleone added. "Who knows what else Elikar could be capable of if this turns out to be true."

Annika studied the two leaders' faces, recognizing the careful masks of civility that all good Felonian upper-crusters employed to hide their true feelings. She had been known to don it herself like it was second nature a lifetime ago.

But that was before Alauvar's sacrifice. When one lost a sister based on loyalty to her own convictions, particularly ones that were antithetical to the self-serving attitudes expected of them, disguising emotions could feel like a shameful act. Needless to say, these two seemed unperturbed, but Annika had already sussed out what they were hiding.

"This is about perception, after all," Annika said. "Not about how you're seen with us, though. You just want to be seen on the right side of how this plays out. If you continue to find us lacking, you can join Elikar in shutting us down, likely in the public eye if I have you two pinned correctly." Vunii and Bleone each grimaced, the half-elf's expression tinged with a modicum of shame, but growing up as the child of one of Kefya's finest playwrights, he might have picked up a trick or two.

"And if we end up with irrefutable evidence," Annika continued, "you can take the credit for striking the corrupt, evil influence from the council chambers. One can only imagine what that sort of goodwill would bring your way."

"You believe us to be so conniving?" Bleone asked with a scowl.

"I do," Annika said. "Luckily for us and the rest of Anera, we don't need the recognition. So we will take your offer, and you can parade around like the pompous jackals you are while you bring Elikar to heel. But do remember to take note of how far he falls—grow too selfish, and you may chart the same path."

Vunii and Bleone shared a look, and when she nodded, the half-elf shrugged, then gestured toward the door. "Well then, ladies. Do be in touch. We look forward to hearing from you."

"Likewise," Niri said as they stood. "I can't wait to see how each of you feign indignation at a colleague's betrayal. Start working on it now so it might be more convincing than this charade."

CHAPTER 18

INESET

Nasargiel stoked the flames of the campfire one last time, taking a final look at the slumbering forms that had gathered in his circle for the night. Most were undecorated Achen soldiers, having learned early that the quiet new recruit was particularly adept at building fires during the breaks between marches. But word had spread, and a few blade serpents now regularly posted themselves near his cluster each night. It wasn't ideal—an officer was more likely to pose him a question about Achen culture or military structure that Nasargiel had yet to glean—but so far, they had been satisfied with the guarantee of a warm bedroll.

A company of twenty-five Achen soldiers, exclusively those funded by the Granish guild-family, had set forth from Ineset on a path north toward the Tesigan Peaks. Despite the arrogant blade serpent's assessment in the bar, the force was evenly split between the elite warriors and common soldiers, and Nasargiel had fallen in with Nimus's bunch rather easily.

However, every night when they settled down to rest, there was a chance someone would decide to pry into the new guy's life, and the pit in his stomach would form anew. He had hoped to learn a more specific location for this lightblood by now and travel there directly, but there was a long road ahead. He still had time to determine where the girl would be and keep her away from these mercenaries.

Nasargiel tilted his neck to stretch, feeling his heavy dark braids shift along with the movement. Although he had been in this new form for days now, the differences in hair styles and textures still managed to surprise him. The former blond locks he had sported were much lighter, but there was something to be said for the heft created by these braids. Nasargiel found them comforting, and the way they moved with him reminded him of the waters back home, always tracing across his skin as he moved through them.

It had been some time since he had traveled home to Nyavelle. Despite the importance of his work on Slaeth, Nasargiel did miss it. Not that the rest of his people would be accommodating of a nostalgic trip. He would likely be subject to months' worth of admonishing conversations and strong encouragement to study the Archives once more—no matter that he had studied them as much or more than the Assembly, and would not suddenly reach their desired conclusion.

No, seeing home again would have to wait until he was sure the Rupturing had been prevented.

A *crack* sounded off to his left behind the tree line, like a small twig that might have been snapped by any manner of creature, from rodent to mountain lion. No one stirred from their sleep, and a quick glance toward the north of the camp showed that one of the company's posted night watchmen had already dismissed the noise as he resumed fussing with the fit of his belt.

Nasargiel closed his eyes, tuning into the thrumming veilmark chords that vibrated everywhere life was found, their luminescence pulsating in the rhythm of a heartbeat. With his vision cut off, it was easier to separate the billowing golden silhouettes of individual creatures where the veilmarks reverberated against them. The rest of the mercenaries were accounted for, their glowing yellow forms resting within the confines of their camp, and outside the perimeter were untold numbers of animals: insects buzzing toward the light of the fires, owls holding vigil from the highest branches, a small family of foxes nosing through the underbrush. Even the flora gave off a distinctive light, though the roiling energy was more subdued in them, as if the veilmarks were less interested in interacting with stationary life.

A surprise was also loitering within the copse of trees. There was another figure, humanoid and standing perfectly still as it stared back at him. As unexpected as that was, it was the shape's proportions that made Nasargiel rise silently to his feet. A curious hunter out on the trail or a greedy highwayman could have been ignored, or their presence made known to the soldier on watch. But not this watcher. The sloped shoulders leading to arms longer than the torso, as well as the avian-like legs with inverted joints, told Nasargiel that this visitor was here to speak with him.

Normally, Nasargiel would slip off unnoticed by distracting the soldier on watch. A perpetual breeze passing by the man's ear or a flickering flame off in the distance would have done the trick. But knowing what was waiting for him, he felt any drain on his concentration might lead to an unfortunate end. The old-fashioned approach would be required.

"Hey," Nasargiel said, pitching his whisper so that the watchman would hear him. "I'm off to take a leak." He had heard his fellow travelers use the phrase numerous times so far and had a fairly strong grasp on its meaning. There was still more to learn though—leaks implied accidents, and in his experience in human form, that particular act was rarely accidental.

The soldier grunted. "Careful you don't step in badger scat. I don't want you dragging that back into the camp."

Nasargiel grunted his understanding, then picked his way through the shrubs and out into the thicket of trees lining the road. Unlike other regions of Slaeth he had visited, the trees north of Ineset were dry, their bark gray and brittle. But they appeared sturdy enough despite the relatively arid conditions, and though their leaves were small and barbed, they held a certain beauty. Any vegetation that found its niche was always a sight to behold.

Plucking lightly on the rootlike veilmarks in his path, Nasargiel coerced the trees to shift their barbs out of his way, and he eventually found himself in a clearing not more than fifty feet into the copse without a scratch on him or a tear in his clothes. As he had expected, a visitor was waiting for him there, though his physical form looked much different from the life echo he had clocked from camp.

An imp of a man stood with his arms crossed in the middle of the glade, standing about half as high as his whirling golden silhouette. His limbs were all in proportion, and he was so slight that if it weren't for the week's worth of ginger stubble gracing his jaw, he might have passed for a teenager. Strawberry blond hair fell down to either shoulder from a part in the middle, revealing a long, mischievous face punctuated by a pair of emerald green eyes.

"How nice of you to come to me, Nasargiel," the man said, ticking one corner of his grin even higher. "It's always unpleasant when we must clean up after your mistakes. Extermination is messy business. But depending on how careless you've been interacting with these walking hairballs, I suppose I might still have to get my hands dirty."

Nasargiel had hoped the Assembly would send Yofie once again. They had their disagreements, and had rehashed them countless times, but she could be reasoned with when it came to the lives of these people. When he had returned the dead chegatha to Tellahhr, after the lightblood and her friends had slain the disoriented reptile, Yofie had not expressed any need to chase after the group and eliminate them simply for interacting with life from another plane.

Unfortunately, the red-headed man was not Yofie in a new form—this was Opysis, one of the more callous agents of the

Assembly, and someone who would use the literal translations of the Archive to justify whatever cruel whim crossed his mind.

"These are soldiers, Opysis. Not scholars," Nasargiel said. "Even if they were suspicious of a new member in their ranks, not one of them would expect an extraplanar visitor. There will be no need for your brand of tidying today."

Opysis stuck out his bottom lip. "You cause so much anguish for the Assembly and now you would deny me my simple pleasures?" Veilmarks began to roil and writhe around him—the smoky tendrils of Tellahhr's Wellspring most of all, but Nasargiel could see nearly every variety accounted for. Opysis was preparing for war.

"Fine," he continued. "It holds with the teachings of the Archives Lost to avoid interference with the denizens of Slaeth anyway. Not that our texts hold much sway over you and your schemes."

"I have no schemes," Nasargiel said. "Everything I have done, everything I will do, has been explained to the Assembly, along with a plea for their support. But everyone seems content to bury their heads in the muck while the Physicarium drives ever closer to a second Rupturing. The results of the last one are still being felt in some planes. The wounds on our universe have not yet healed. Further damage might not be conducive to continued life."

The short man yawned, though he maintained his grip on the World Shroud. "We've heard your squealing before, Nas. The issue is it's just not true. If anyone is pulling us all toward devastation, it's you and your meddling. The more you engage with these naïve ants, the more likely you slip up and reveal something they shouldn't know."

"They've discovered the veiltap, Opysis," Nasargiel said, and watched with a measure of pride as the man's eyes flared for the briefest of moments. The organ at the base of any connected individual's skull had remained a secret from anyone on Slaeth for millennia, and many sylidae had become convinced that it would always be the case. But even a bloodthirsty psychopath like Opysis would have to see the danger in the people of Slaeth possessing this knowledge.

"I believe a brilliant man is close to learning how to transplant the organ from deceased siphoners to non-siphoners. Think of the implications, of the strain this could place on the World Shroud! Then there's always the dragons. What happens when they decide to stop bickering—"

"Nothing has changed!" Opysis seethed, causing every blade of grass and shrub to shudder away from his outburst. His grip on veilmarks had always been volatile. When Nasargiel didn't match his display of power, Opysis craned his neck and took a heavy breath. "Nothing has changed for thousands of years, and it's long past time for you to return home. There will be no second Rupturing with you safe back in our waters, away from any accidental damage you might cause."

"You speak of my safety?" Nasargiel scoffed. "Somehow I don't expect I'll be received with a celebratory procession."

"Once I bring you back, I can guarantee your safety. You'll be quite well protected in a cell," Opysis said, with a smile that didn't touch his eyes. "Prior to that door locking behind you, though, no promises."

The confrontation was heading in a direction that Nasargiel had hoped to avoid—any other representative the Assembly sent could have been reasoned with. But Opysis didn't respect him, seeing him as a fool at best and a dangerous traitor at worst. Any opinion Nasargiel raised, no matter how solid his evidence, would fall on deaf ears. As far as Opysis was concerned, the Assembly had ruled: No sylid interference on any plane, in accordance with the text of the Archives Lost. But if their attack dog truly was loyal to those teachings, perhaps he would listen to a doctrinal argument.

"This doesn't have to escalate further, Opysis," Nasargiel said. Tempted as he was to grasp veilmarks of his own, he kept himself disconnected from the World Shroud. An offensive posture would only whet the man's appetite for violence. "I will make you a deal, one that will allow you to drag me before the Assembly like a long-awaited prize. If we come to blows, there's an even chance you walk away with nothing."

It was now Opysis's turn to scoff, but the narrowing of his eyes revealed the truth. While Nasargiel had a reputation for diplomacy, his siphoning skills had not been forgotten in his time away from home.

"What's this deal, then?" Opysis asked. "It had better be damned impressive if you're hoping to avoid what's coming to you. Chasing you all across this plane has left me hungry to blow off some steam." He punctuated his point by tearing a pinprick in the veil and flaring a white-hot flame beneath the underbrush, sublimating the dead leaves into a dark vapor.

"Come with us," Nasargiel said, gesturing back to the Achen soldiers back at the camp. "Travel ahead to the next town and pose as a mercenary looking for work. A few of the blade serpents have been on edge about facing a hive of lightbloods, so they should be willing to part with some coin in order to have another body to soften up their quarry.

"Be sure to take a less conspicuous form, though," Nasargiel added. He looked down at his arm's almond shade. "I made the same mistake upon arriving in this country. It's odd, but having a rarer skin tone than the general population draws more attention than we typically want." Pulling himself out of the puzzle that was Slaeth's cultural dynamics, Nasargiel turned his attention back to the short man across from him. "How does that sound?"

Opysis tilted his head but did not lessen his hold on the veil-marks teeming around him. "I'm waiting on the part that makes you think I would want to do this."

Nasargiel smiled in a way he hoped would pass for modest piety. "This could be your chance to return to the Assembly with a siphoner of immense natural talent, one who seems to have a stronger connection to her Wellspring than many who have dedicated their lives to forging that link." He had no true intention of letting Opysis abscond with the lightblood—or himself for that matter—but it could buy Nasargiel more time to convince the man of his claims.

"You know as well as I what is written in the Archives Lost about such individuals," Nasargiel continued. "Think about what it would mean to come home with such an important find."

"How exactly do you know you are heading for this person? You've met her?"

"She survived an encounter with a trained scorcher assassin without any knowledge of her own abilities," Nasargiel said. "Then, she took down a lost beast from Tellahhr who had been driven feral from fright at its new surroundings. This lightblood might be one of the Vanguard."

"Bah," Opysis said. "Now we're back to your fixation on a falsehood. The Vanguard appear at times of great need in the Physicarium, to herald events that threaten the integrity of the planes. But you're only seeing what you want to see. There is no second Rupturing, so there are no signs to be found."

A powerful gust of wind tore through the glade, whipping Nasargiel's braids about as Opysis siphoned the gale through the World Shroud. "The time for talk is long past, Nasargiel," he said. "Are you returning with me of your own accord, or are you going to make this interesting?

"I know which choice I prefer," Opysis snarled. "And perhaps I'll pay a visit to this pet lightblood of yours regardless. Such a powerful connection recklessly endangers the veil, wouldn't you say?"

Nasargiel felt his blood boil, and faster than Opysis could recognize, he unleashed a gale of his own, propelling himself forward to grapple with the brute. It was an unorthodox tactic—not many talented siphoners would close the gap on a threat when attacking at range was an option—but Nasargiel needed to create a more important distance: away from the camp.

White-gold flames consumed them, devouring their bodies until only their consciousnesses remained. Through the torrent of radiant fire, Nasargiel felt Opysis's mind rage. While it was normally a pleasant experience, it was never easy to force another to travel against their will. Surprise had given him an edge, though, and Nasargiel did not intend to travel far. It was enough to relocate their conflict out of the camp's earshot, so when Opysis finally wrangled himself free of their mind tangle and reconstituted his human form, Nasargiel was happy to do the same. They were deposited deeper into the woods, the life echoes of the Achen mercenaries mere specks in the distance.

Opysis screamed. "You're soft, Nas. You wanted to protect them so much that you dare to force another sylid to face the flames unwillingly. Know that you've just ensured their deaths."

Nasargiel took a deep breath before buckling the earth beneath Opysis's feet. Surprise had worked before—he might as well press that advantage. A crater as wide as a wagon wheel plummeted into the ground as Nasargiel wrenched apart two adjacent veilmarks, this pair a set of rigid, geometric lines that represented the mountainous power they contained.

Opysis attempted to take flight, leaping away from the sinkhole with an impressive reaction time, but Nasargiel was ready for the maneuver. Before the mighty wind could lift the man to safety, he grasped onto the root matrix of another Wellspring Flow's veilmarks and tore a hole in the veil, which unleashed three thorny vines from beneath the crater that wrapped themselves around Opysis's legs and one arm. The barbs pierced the smaller man's flesh before the vines snapped him back down to the ground with a heavy thud.

"This doesn't have to happen," Nasargiel said, but a sweet, metallic scent announced Opysis's intentions, allowing just enough time for Nasargiel to erupt a sheet of stone from the ground to intercept the bolt of electrified plasma tearing through the air. The odor only intensified as the lightning sizzled, cooking the air around them and scorching the impromptu shield. It wouldn't hold forever, but Nasargiel didn't need it to—the rock only needed to provide cover long enough for the necrotizing to begin.

The pulsating golden veilmarks of life had shadows that clung to their paths, lines of dark purples and blues that quivered and jerked at random, more akin to death throes than any regular heartbeat. It was these that Nasargiel clung to behind his stone wall, pulling them taut over the puncture wounds his vines had created in Opysis's limbs and releasing a trickle from the Gesh Wellspring into them. Nasargiel could feel the margins of the bloody holes began to blacken and fester, and he began to feel ill himself.

Sure, it was a dirty tactic, typically reserved for the vilest of opponents, and the guilt he felt over using it against another sylid contributed to his nausea. But there was also something about simply touching this Wellspring that left one feeling as if they had one foot in the grave. Nasargiel could not risk being subdued, though, and they were too evenly matched. If he let this battle go on long enough, he was certain Opysis wouldn't feel any qualms about using this connection himself—he had just beat him to it.

"Aagh!" Opysis screamed as the flesh around his wounds blistered with pustules. Through gritted teeth, frothing with spittle, he said, "None of us thought you were this deranged, Nas. The Assembly will not be so lenient as to send one scout from now on. You've signed your own death warrant."

Unearned self-righteousness aside, Opysis was right. Resorting to the powers of death and decay was offensive enough, even if the target could heal just as readily with pure life energy, but coupling that with an extensive history of rejecting Assembly orders and 'meddling' in the affairs of another plane? Nasargiel had likely skipped right over excommunication and landed squarely on grounds for execution. He had done so knowingly, however, and would do so again.

What was the alternative, after all, if not the death of every living thing in the Physicarium?

While Opysis writhed on the ground, struggling to break free from the vines that grasped him, Nasargiel sent even more of the tendrils to wrap around him. Pinned as he was, growing weaker by the second, Opysis limply tugged on the glowing yellow veilmarks that could release the power needed to revert the necrosis. But that would take time, as Nasargiel had been aggressive with the application of Gesh's rotting influence—it was in Opysis's bloodstream now, and dulling his ability to siphon. He would heal, in time, and break free of the thorny vines that bound him. The band of Achen soldiers would be long gone by then, and Nasargiel even farther besides.

He took a few slow steps toward his prone opponent, stopping so that he would be in clear view of Opysis's gaze, which had been jerked to one side by a thick vegetal band across his head. Despite the fact that the soldiers Nasargiel had traveled with meant harm to the lightblood girl, and therefore also ran the risk of ushering another Rupturing along even faster, he did not want to see them face the unbridled wrath of a shamed Opysis. Most of them were solid men and women, doing the work expected of them by their guild-family so they could provide for their own families, and they didn't deserve to be scorched or ground to dust simply by associating with him.

"I truly didn't want this to happen," Nasargiel said. Opysis hacked a cough that sent globs of red-tinged saliva out onto the ground. The rot had reached his lungs—it would take days for him to be capable of traveling.

"You want only for your name to be inscribed alongside the foolish Dawn Ones the people of this plane so adore," Opysis sputtered. "We should have seen your pride sooner, stopped you before your arrogance grew to the point of believing one person can shape a world."

Nasargiel smiled wanly. If after all these years, the rest of the sylidae did not believe the sincerity of his beliefs, but instead thought him a megalomaniac reaching for glory, they would never understand him or his mission. He had thought Yofie might come to stand in his corner, eventually, but that would no longer be possible. Nasargiel was now as good as dead, but he would see the planes saved before that fate came for him.

He wreathed himself in the familiar white-golden flames, experiencing their comfortable warmth as his body began to dissemble, burning away so that it could reform at his destination. Nasargiel watched the light reflect off Opysis's wide eyes, then turned his head to the north, ensuring that the man knew he would no longer be traveling with the Achen soldiers. Before he was whisked away in the traveling fires, he pulled a slab of earth over the crater that held his opponent—it would not do to have one of his former companions discovering a bound stranger in the woods should they decide to investigate his absence.

His vision turning white, Nasargiel's body was finally consumed. He would reconstitute in the Tesigan Peaks, closer to the girl geographically, if not effectively. The mountain range was long and wide, and while he might have a short cut to the region, it would still require a thorough search and a bit of luck to find her.

INTERLUDE

BEFORE

Tetamii hurried to keep stride with Ilphas as they hasted through the streets of the Trough, a heavy parchment pad slapping against his leg with each shifting step. It had been half a year since he had started working in the man's service at one of his family orchards, out past the Tangled Vines and nestled in a serene expanse of the island that contrasted sharply with the daily bustle of Felona. While Tetamii had done a lot of growing in that time, Ilphas still towered over him and could practically walk faster than Tetamii could jog. Mercifully, the merchants, tradesmen, and those out of work all seemed keen to slow the man down on their way to the Crest. Everyone wanted to bend the ear of the soon-to-be councilman.

"And you'll speak up about the butcher's tax, then?" another man said, his nose so wide on his face that it nearly lined up with the outer corners of his eyes. He wore a long apron that had likely been white at some distant point in the past, but had been so stained with blood and other nondescript fluids that it had taken on a blotched, ruddy hue.

"No one sitting up on that mountain cares about getting quality beef and lamb for a fair price," the man continued. "And why would they? They can all reach deep into their pockets for the best cuts of meat, no matter how those of us doing the cutting feel about it. My daddy didn't get into this line of work to only put food on their fine plates, while the rest of us have to pick at the scraps." The butcher shook his head, taking a moment to wipe away a bead of sweat on his brow with his dirty apron. "All so they can raise a few libers and build a new wing for their buildings."

Ilphas patted the man on his shoulder, not minding the fact that he had soaked through his shirt, and flashed him a smile that most would find suspicious on a politician but somehow, he made charming. "I'll have them eating their fair share of skuttle bait at the next gala, just you wait."

The thought of anyone on the Council dining on that bottom-feeding fish made Tetamii grin, however unlikely he thought it to be. Then again, Ilphas had a magnetism about him that made him effective, gave him a certain heft when he made demands on which everyone knew he could deliver, particularly with the people of Felona literally backing him up.

There would be no threat of violence against the Council, of course¬—the scars left by the Rebellion of the Commons a few decades ago still lingered over the city—but the decision-makers understood that with a word Ilphas could grind the inner workings of Felona to a halt. No one's livelihood would escape that type of economic downturn unscathed.

He's a new breed, that one, Magzii's voice echoed in his head. *All smiles and sincerity up front while he's forging the largest damned knife to stab right into the small of our backs. After he's done using our shoulders to climb to the top of the hill, that is.*

Tetamii's grin faded. It was easy to get lost in the optimism and earnestness of a man like Ilphas, but he had to remember that an empty promise was an empty promise, whether it was made from a dais or in a more personal style. Everyone who sought this sort of power over people's lives was the same: ambitious to a fault, making sacrifices and cutting deals that always landed them with the upper hand, and with someone else left holding the bag.

No one with any authority had truly offered to help him after he was orphaned by a councilmember's carelessness. They had arrested his father in a case of mistaken identity, not bothering with activities as frivolous as questioning or collecting evidence, because it would put *them* at risk to alert a pair of scorchers of their suspicions. And after the true tax dodgers were eventually found and dealt with, Tetamii had not received so much as an apology. The only attention he had received from the upper crust was when they needed a pocket picked or an urchin bruised.

"We're going to be late, sir," Tetamii said as he tapped Ilphas on the elbow.

Ilphas smirked and playfully rolled his eyes. "Oh, how the world would end if the Council were made to wait for once. Come then, we can't have their tea getting cold."

They were all the same, and Tetamii knew where this assignment was heading, but Teacher Irasil himself would think this man was convincing.

The pair hustled through the last few streets of the workman neighborhood until they reached the path that ascended to the Crest. Tetamii had already been up this way a handful of times with Ilphas during his short time working with the man, having impressed him quickly on the orchard. It had been difficult work, long days leading to a sore back, but it wouldn't have done to be separated from his target all day, picking twin tarts while Ilphas was galivanting around Felona shaking hands and amassing support. So Tetamii had excelled, stayed later than the other pickers, organized the day's haul by color and ripeness after learning that different merchants preferred certain varieties. It wasn't long before Ilphas asked Tetamii to join him on his jaunts through the city, acting as his scribe and taking notes of all the promises he had made.

The ambient smells of the Trough, at times pleasant and others not depending on the block—bakeries around the corner from the sweaty work of a masonry yard was a particular shock—transitioned into the crisp, clean sea air found in the higher altitudes of the city. There were no trades being practiced once one started the incline, with the exception of barristers or clergy, and they rarely produced an odor to pollute the air, except metaphorically.

But it was always the striking cerulean sky that offered the starkest contrast with Tetamii's life below. Down there, something always obscured his vision, be it a clothesline, a wafting trail of forge smoke, or the inescapable throngs of taller people not bothering to step out of the way of a street kid. It was beautiful, and enough to make him understand why so many strove to escape the slog that life became when one didn't have means.

That didn't excuse Ilphas's actions though. Tetamii would not use the good intentions of others to make his way in the world. He would come by his successes more honestly. Say what you will about the Clipped Gulls, but their targets always knew where they stood with them. In a certain light, an assassin's blade was indeed more trustworthy than a politician's promise. There was no need for guessing at hidden motives.

"It's breathtaking, isn't it?" Ilphas asked. Tetamii pulled his eyes away from the sky to see that the man had noticed his longing gaze. Ilphas nodded politely at a young couple who passed by them, each dressed exorbitantly, as if they wished to parade their wealth around for people who would have to save for several years just to purchase the man's coat, then joined Tetamii in looking out at the blue expanse.

"This is what I'm working so hard for," he continued. "The world can be such a beautiful place when you don't feel burdened to keep your head down and work every minute of your life. Part of me thinks that it's not simply money and authority the people of this district want to keep out of the rest of the city's hands, but rather this." Ilphas gestured out around them. At this height the alabaster limestone cliffs surrounding Virdoba could be seen gleaming across the Marrow Strait.

"Knowing this splendor is out there, to be enjoyed by anyone with the leisure time to view it, is a secret I suspect they want withheld. As long as they keep the masses focused on a desire for wealth and power, they can keep them working—after all, plying their trade is how people are told they can climb the gilded ladder themselves. But if they knew they could find peace and satisfaction by taking a break, pausing to spend time in nature with their loved ones, suddenly Felona's illustrious industry leaders become much less productive."

Tetamii nodded, continuing to be impressed at how altruistic this man could make his political bluster sound. "So if you are elected to hold the Voice of the Many, you plan to do what? Enforce mandatory vacations?"

Ilphas laughed. "It sounds so simple and ridiculous when you say it, but yes, among many other things. If coin is the central value in everyone's life, it becomes the focal point of everything: materialism trounces internal satisfaction, productivity surpasses personal fulfillment. I want to share with others the opportunities that I've had from a life not spent chasing down every last liber, and that starts with shifting the values of our society toward the people and not precious metals."

As they neared the top of the mountain path, the sparse rock began to liven up with cultivated hanging gardens draped over the wrought iron fence posts of mountainside estates, constructed such that the buildings jutted out over the edge of the cliff face, literally looking down on the people living below. The vibrant hues of the plant life grown here rivaled the Bindweed Conservatory's forested neighborhood that Ilphas called home, a far cry from the drab architecture found in Tetamii's portion of the city, where soot-stained walls were more likely to be encountered than a pop of color.

Ilphas cocked an eyebrow as he looked down at him. "Hopefully in your time with me I've shown you some of what I mean.

You're such a bright kid, but life has dealt you blow after blow through no fault of your own, and the city would have kept you there because everyone feels as if it's where you belong. All you needed was a chance to prove yourself, and you've excelled beyond what I expected when I put a stop to that scrape I found you in."

Tetamii tried to look ashamed, casting his eyes at his feet, but really he was proud of that performance. Magzii had called him a natural after it, and even encouraged him to keep building his deceptive skills if he wanted to make a name for himself as a Gull.

Maybe I can excel at whatever I choose to do, Tetamii thought, suppressing a smirk. *All of my mentors seem to think I'm a singular talent.*

"I want everyone to have a chance like that, but I can't hire everyone in the city myself," he said with a smile. "So I have to do some work at the top, give the whole system a rattle, and maybe we'll start to see some change."

The top of the Crest was all manicured hedges and flowering trees acting as a decorative spread between the Felonian Council Hall and the ruins of the Hall of Merchants. The latter was as ominous as it was inspiring, reminding Tetamii that even something created by gods was capable of decay. As much of a choke-hold as the Felonian elite had on the lower crust, the Council were no gods—any work of theirs would be able to crumble in a more dramatic fashion than a collapsed roof. Whether the power remained with the current aloof fools or this new breed like Ilphas, nothing they did to him would be potent enough that it couldn't be undone. Not now that he had been empowered.

After striding around the outskirts of the grand gardens, the pair finally reached an unoccupied gate outside the governmental building. There was a small room built into the wall, likely a guard's station, but it too was empty, leaving an entrance to the council hall unprotected by anything more than a padlock.

"This is a new tactic," Ilphas said, lifting the iron lock and giving it a tug. It didn't budge.

"What do you mean?" Tetamii asked, looking around. "Are the guards posted somewhere nearby and out of sight?"

"No," Ilphas said with a sigh. "The Council has pulled them away from this entrance."

"Isn't that risky? Any thief with a hairpin could be through that simple lock in under a minute."

"Not up here, especially in the middle of the day," Ilphas said. "The council building is protected enough by their location and reputation. Besides that, it's likely only temporary. A gambit to delay my entrance and cancel our meeting, citing my tardiness. If the guards were here, they believe—rightfully—the gate would've been opened for me, regardless of their orders."

"Excuse me," a familiar voice called from down the path, and Tetamii felt the hairs on the back of his neck rise. He turned to see Atusiin standing just beyond the corner of a hedge wall, beckoning them toward him. "I saw the lady put that lock on the gate. The guards weren't happy about it, but she said they had to keep you out. But I know another way in."

Tetamii knew the boy likely had a knife waiting for Ilphas as soon as the man rounded the corner. Atusiin had been salivating for months over the chance to steal this task from Tetamii, muttering that Magzii was being too patient with his slow burn of a plan, and that he could get the job done quickly and quietly.

Ilphas's face turned to stone, and Tetamii's stomach flipped. Atusiin making the kill wasn't the only way he could ruin everything Tetamii had worked for. If Ilphas recognized him as the boy that he had been fighting in the alley, he might suppose they were working another angle on him again, and then kick Tetamii out on his ass. Tetamii ground his teeth, watching the whisps dance angrily around Atusiin, yearning for the flames they contained to be unleashed.

"You again?" Ilphas asked. The man's brow furrowed, pulling Tetamii's attention from his fiery designs. In his experience, Ilphas was typically unflappable—this was a new side of the man.

"I checked in with a few of the tanneries in the Trough," Ilphas continued. "None of them had heard of a new apprentice."

"Oh," Atusiin said, his eyes widening as he stood a bit straighter. "That's because, you know, I work up in the Reliqu—"

"Enough!" Ilphas shouted. "I've already given you one chance by not sending the guards after you once I revealed your lie. I suggest you don't dig yourself in deeper. Now get out of here before the next watch makes their rounds. I'm not feeling in a protective mood."

Atusiin turned and scrambled away, which normally would have given Tetamii a good belly laugh, if only his stomach wasn't still clenched tighter than a vise. Ilphas turned his gaze down to meet Tetamii's, scrutinizing him like so many adults had done since his parents were yanked from his life. Sweat began to bead on his neck, and he used every ounce of willpower he possessed to keep his breathing level. Finally, Ilphas raised his hand to his forehead and began to rub it, releasing a sigh.

"I'm sorry," Ilphas said. "I shouldn't have behaved that way. I know he's struggling. Like you were; like so many others continue to. I just . . ." He paused, looking out over the Trough and toward the forested neighborhood he called home. "I give up so much every day to make a difference for this city, and it's upsetting when my investment is tossed aside."

"You gave him money?" Tetamii asked.

Ilphas shook his head and offered a soft, sad chuckle. "Not monetary investment, Tetamii. Time. Days and weeks I'll never get back. You'll understand one day, when you have children of your own. I'm doing all of this for her, to make the city she grows into a more welcoming one, but every night I wonder if she'll see it that way, or if she'll just remember all the birthdays and holidays that I missed along the way."

Tetamii didn't know what to say. If this was another performance, it was a convincing one. But Magzii had warned him that there was nothing and no one a man like Ilphas wouldn't use to gather more power. Why not bring one's child into things if it garnered sympathy. Eventually, he settled on, "I'm sure your daughter will appreciate all your work, Mr. Trisarin."

The man turned the lock over in his hand, glancing around the path behind them with a wary eye. He shot Tetamii a wink. "Then let's get back to it."

Suddenly a crackling bolt of blue-white energy the size of his little finger ripped through the air, slamming into the back of the lock. Within seconds, the electricity had bored a hole in the iron, and the lock popped open.

"Fortunately for us," Ilphas said as he gave the gate a push, which swung inward easily. "I have other connections besides friendly guards."

Tetamii's mouth fell open for several seconds before he snapped it shut, plastering on a false grin as he followed Ilphas onto the council hall grounds. The man was a stormforger. This would change everything.

As far as he knew, Magzii was unaware of Ilphas's abilities. His plan for taking out the noble would have to be reworked, and Tetamii would likely be pulled from the task. There was no way the Clipped Gulls would risk their reputation on an untrained, untested scorcher against a grown man in full control of his own connection. Tetamii could feel his hopes of belonging to a family again burn away in the light of that tiny, sizzling bolt.

A stone tile walkway cut across the pristine lawn that led up to the building's entrance, and by the time they reached the small set of steps at the front, a pair of wide mahogany doors swung open to reveal a long hallway that fed into a larger common area. A guard in simple but well-fitting leathers stepped out of their way, casting his eyes down as he welcomed them inside with a mumble—he had not agreed with his orders to delay their welcome.

Across the wide room was a large desk, behind which sat a pretty elven woman who always smiled fawningly over both Ilphas and Tetamii, though that might have simply been a job requirement for the Council's public intermediary. Behind her were two limestone staircases that spiraled up to a second-floor promenade, where nondescript office doors could be seen through the banisters.

Tetamii had only visited this vestibule a handful of times with Ilphas, never venturing up to the higher offices, but today would be different. Provided the Council didn't find some other excuse to cancel their meeting. He hoped he would have the opportunity to see the leaders in their natural state, unfiltered in their deliberations with a political rival. Scribes were rarely seen, his parchment pad acting more as a smokescreen than a disguise, and one never knew what useful information they might let slip when attentive ears were present. He would need every bit he could gather to convince Magzii that he was still capable of following through with his initiation.

The woman behind the desk stood quickly as she noticed them, then hurried around it, typical endearing smile marred by the strain around her eyes. Unlike the guard posted at the door, she wasn't ashamed at the Council's ploy to keep them out, but she was afraid of the aftermath now that they had arrived.

"Mr. Trisarin," she said, clasping her hands down in front of her flowing silk skirt. "We—I wasn't expecting you so soon. There was a delayed rotation of the guards, so we had to just leave the south gate locked, and it slipped my mind that you might be coming from that direction, but by then it was too late to change the stations. I assumed you would have to travel all the way arou—"

Ilphas held up a hand, his grin dripping with both patience and an understanding that she wasn't at fault. "We all make our little mistakes, Jumina. I know there was no harm intended, and fortunately none was imparted. There was a bit of rust damage on the back of the lock, and quick strike with a rock was able to let us at the mechanism."

The woman blinked, admirably keeping most of the puzzlement from her face. Tetamii was willing to bet she had placed the pristine lock herself.

"Of course, I do accept full responsibility for the damaged council property," Ilphas said. "I'll be happy to cover the cost of its replacement."

"I'm sure that won't be necessary," Jumina stammered. She shot a furtive glance up the stairs behind her, toward a wide hallway that looked important enough that it must lead to the Council's meeting rooms. "But all the same," she continued, beckoning toward the guard at the door, who looked to be trying his best to stare a hole into his boots. "If you'll fill out an incident report with Bygor here, we can make sure no one is blamed who shouldn't be."

Jumina snapped three times in quick succession to catch his attention, and Bygor hustled over. "Yes, ma'am," he said, then finally looked at Ilphas. "I can, uh, get your statement for the Council's records, sir." He had one hand clasped over his leather vambrace, wringing the hide intently with nervous energy. Then he suddenly stopped, his mouth relaxing into a wide grin.

"But I'm afraid you two will have to follow me up the stairs to one of our holding rooms," Bygor said. "It's where we keep the formal stationary for such matters."

"Now hold on," Jumina said, moving to step in the guard's path. "I have plenty of parchment behind the desk that will suff—"

"Protocol is protocol, ma'am." Bygor said, gently but definitively shifting her out of the way. Holding her back with one arm, he tilted his head toward the stairs. "This way, sirs."

The pair of them walked by Jumina, leaving the woman in a huff as they ascended the stairs. Despite the importance of the building, Tetamii was struck by the relative lack of noise, the clicking of their boots echoing around the space with each step, but he supposed he shouldn't be surprised. Everyone always spoke about how little the Council did for the lives of Felonians. It turns out doing little makes little sound.

When they reached the next floor and began their trek down the hallway, Bygor turned and said, "I'll take care of that paperwork for you, sir. No need for you to be held up any longer."

"I appreciate the extrication tactic, but I don't want anyone facing repercussions on my account," Ilphas said. "After I speak with Council, I'll stop by and complete those forms with you. And try not to let this strain your working relationship with Jumina. She was only worried about her job and acting accordingly. All of you need to continue forging ties that can overwhelm the Council's aura of authority. Don't let them pit you against each other."

Bygor stopped and planted a fist to his chest. "Yes, sir. I'll keep that in mind. The Council's receiving hall is just around the corner." He paused, and with a hint of a smile he added, "I wish I could say they are expecting you, but I think they're too proud of their scheme to anticipate it falling through."

Ilphas thanked the man and lead Tetamii to a single, unassuming light birch door, which he stepped through without a thought to what protection might be waiting just behind it. Though now that Tetamii had learned the man was a stormforger, his sense of confidence was more understandable. All wealthy men carried themselves as if they belonged wherever they happened to be, but to walk into a room with world leaders, likely accompanied by an armed detail, took a little more bravado than a full purse could provide.

Three guards, all resting with their backs against the adjacent wall, jumped to attention the moment the door swung open, each of their hands dropping to the hilt of a shortsword at their waists. The blades were drawn halfway from their hilts before recognition dawned on their faces, and Tetamii had to clench his teeth to keep from falling slack-jawed again as they slid their swords back into their sheaths.

"Good to see you again, gentleman," Tetamii said to the trio. "How's the ankle, Gullian? Did my witch friend fix you up?"

One of the guards smiled, tilting his head in a respectful nod. "Yes sir, Mr. Trisarin. Thank you again for connecting us. That's the last time I practice fencing with my boy. He's too quick!"

Magzii was right—Ilphas was too powerful. A man who could put armed guards at ease with small talk could certainly rally them to a cause, particularly if he cared enough to learn their names and family lives. And once he had a hold on the city's law enforcement, Ilphas was not the type to let an organization like the Clipped Gulls go unpunished.

It wasn't simply about fighting for a place at the table anymore; if Ilphas continued his ascent to power, Tetamii's very way of life would be threatened. Everything he knew how to do, how to pilfer and punish anyone who tried to take what was his, would disappear, leaving him with nothing. Who was he if not a street kid? His life before had been taken from him, and now this crusader would take all he had left.

Unlike their guards, the seven members of Kefya's Council did anything but relax at the sudden intrusion. The most admirable attempt was a broad pillar of a woman who was already seated, her face betraying no emotion as she flicked her sandy blond braid behind her head. Her spine had stiffened, though, and Tetamii thought she might have even been holding her breath. It must take a lot to break through the stony disposition of the first secretary of defense.

The other six members, who had previously been milling about behind their chairs, either gasped or clutched onto their seatbacks at the intrusion.

"Ah, I'm glad to see everyone is already gathered," Ilphas said, striding further into the room. Tetamii followed at his heel, though once Ilphas passed the center of the chamber and continued on to the dais where the Council's table sat, he began to let his feet drag a bit. Ilphas was powerful, but even he might not be able to control their reactions to the indignity of an assertive scribe.

"For a moment I was concerned that we all might have run into a snag on our way to the room, but it seems we've all prioritized each other's time," Ilphas said, resting his hands on the Council's table.

Ilphas had stopped directly in front of a younger man with red, frizzy hair hanging loosely around a bony face, who had taken his seat at the center of the long table. His face flushed, surprisingly visible through his trimmed ginger beard, but when he spoke it held a measure of calm that could only come from years behind a judicial bench.

"Ilphas," he said. "It's a pleasure, as always, to have you in our chambers."

"Likewise, Tubrin," Ilphas replied, his smile somehow still genuine in a way that surprised Tetamii—anyone else would've felt justified to adopt a smugger demeanor. Meanwhile, Tubrin ground his teeth, presumably at his missing epithet.

"But I must insist we push forward without delay," Ilphas continued. "I have quite the list of topics I wish to cover today, one that will fill this cavernous chamber with your groans and grumbles, I'm sure. Yet those sounds have practically been the parlance of the Trough for years. It's time for these walls to hear them for a change."

"Before you launch into another of your diatribes, allow me to present you with an opportunity I feel will be of great interest to you." The woman spoke from the left end of the table, where she still stood, her flowing silk dress a glamorous addition to the otherwise subdued space. She had short gray hair that fell just below her ears, and a set of hazel eyes that reminded Tetamii of a hawk's in the way that she studied both of them.

"We've recently entertained a delegation from Woross," she continued as she walked around the table, tracing her fingertips along its surface. "Their premier is keen on exporting larger quantities of their nightbark lumber, but as you might know, the wood is difficult to work with—too difficult to shape or keep hydrated unless treated in the perfect conditions. Who can argue with the results, though?"

The woman tapped the tabletop, and Tetamii stood on his toes to see the beautiful indigo wood that had been inlaid through the center of a more traditional dark rosewood. "Still, regardless of the quality, we simply couldn't justify increasing our expense on the import," she said, finally coming to a stop in front Ilphas. Her grandmotherly face softened. "You know as well as I do that this city deserves better than seeing its government spend more on luxury items that most people never have a hope of obtaining."

"Then what is this opportunity, Moru," Ilphas said, demonstrating a level of patience Tetamii had thought impossible.

"The Ebkariins have offered our nation first claim at a settlement north of Woross," Moru said. "It is a small, remote outpost for now, closer to the desert than the coastline, but with a little care and attention, it could be built into a major trade nexus with Achen by capitalizing on the bordering river."

"And Ebkarii is ceding control of a place with such potential to another nation for what purpose?" Ilphas asked. "If they're looking for more coin, I would think investing in a riverside village would yield greater amounts than what they would get from our wood purchases."

"Ebkarii doesn't operate like any other nation on the continent," Tubrin said. "There is no centralized government, only independent cities with their own priorities. Woross is the largest, and typically deals the most in international interests, but if they are seen to be expanding their reach to another free city, it would violate the charter they have with their neighbors. No city can exert control over another without signaling a desire for open conflict."

"But if Woross were to establish a Kefyan embassy on land that happens to be near this outpost," Moru said, "then perhaps the influence of Kefya's wealth and culture could absorb the town in short order." She patted Ilphas gently on the arm. "We would like you to serve as our ambassador so that everyone prospers. Kefya gains control over a valuable trading location, Woross benefits from the expansion of the outpost thanks to our alliance, and you get the opportunity to turn a town of simple, hardworking folk into a major force in the world."

"And Wesmae gets to keep his seat," Ilphas said with a nonchalance that belied the flare of tension in the room. Near the opposite end of the table, a gargoyle of a man sat hunched forward, listening intently to the conversation. He cocked one eyebrow over a cloudy blue eye, creating even more grooves in an already craggy face—the Voice of the Many's best years were long behind him, but he didn't appear willing to lose an election to an elven upstart.

"Do not insult this council by implying—" Wesmae started, his voice still carrying despite his years. But Ilphas slammed a fist on the table, and Wesmae's voice hitched into a cough.

"I will not be bought," Ilphas said, his soft tone somehow louder in the still silence of the chamber. "You may appoint Wesmae there after the election, if you feel so inclined. He won't have my vote, but if you're fast enough about it, you might be able to slip that by before I get my governing legs beneath me. Let him continue to enjoy the life of a spoiled bureaucrat while someone who actually desires to serve as the city's representative sits in his seat."

The councilmembers looked to one another, seeming to have entire conversations in their glares alone, but before anyone could find another reason to object, Ilphas continued. "Now, we can begin with the butcher's tax."

Tetamii began to furiously scribble onto his parchment pad, keeping pace with the nonverbal tics of each councilmember as Ilphas spoke about each point, but his mind spun at everything he had witnessed today. The man—his target—was a stormforger, information that might cause Magzii to pull him from this task given the higher risks involved. But he might also be rewarded for discovering this information, ingratiating himself further into the Clipped Gulls.

Perhaps he had not lost his chance at a family after all.

His pen caught on the pad as he felt a flutter in his stomach. Every time he had previously thought of being welcomed into Magzii's crew, he had felt a warmth within, a sense of belonging that had been absent for so many years. Now, though, as he watched Ilphas turn down a chance to be a ruler of his own little fiefdom, opting to serve instead as the least respected member of a seven-person Council, he had to wonder if Magzii was wrong about the man. Could he actually want better for the people of Felona as its own end, rather than as a means for personal power?

Tetamii resumed his writing, chewing on the inside of his cheek as he tried to chase down the rampant trails of thought that threatened to pull him apart.

PART III

CHAPTER 19

THE ILLUMINED SCALE

Rav had remained cold since venturing down into the school, her joints becoming accustomed to an unfamiliar stiffness. There were sconces and firepits built into the stone in places, complete with small flues tunneled into the wall to allow smoke to vent, but there was no way to feel truly warm in an icy fortress. However, over the weeks she had spent within the belly of the mountain, her memory of the temperature on the peak had dulled. Cold was her new reality, and that would be the same above or below the school.

It didn't take long for the stinging wind, like tiny wasps pricking her face, to disabuse her of that belief. She had been up on Ram's Point now for half an hour, and no amount of exertion or siphoning distracted her from the constant barrage of icy daggers whipping against her cheeks. In fact, a part of her was considering opening the Wellspring tap wide, letting the electricity course through her in the way she had been instructed to avoid. At least then her skin would be numb to the elements.

"Come on," Adiin said, the bottom half of his face obscured by a heavy woolen scarf. "The faster we get through this exercise, the sooner we can go back down."

Riqu tucked a mallet into the back of her belt, then gave a tug to the last flat-ended piton she had hammered into the side of the cliff. Similar metal plates dotted the mountain's rocky face all the way up the crooked peak, the spikes behind them driven so far into the stone that no handholds were left as insurance. Riqu untied herself from the climbing rope she had looped around her waist, then tossed it to Rav, who had been manning the tethered end.

"Rav was otherwise occupied, but if another of my classmates had been inclined to help me set up the course, we might have already been halfway through it," Riqu said, squeezing her large hands into her dual-plated gloves. Adiin grumbled, donning his own pair as he stalked by her to approach the curving metal-specked wall. Riqu smirked as she caught Rav's gaze, then rolled her eyes.

Rav wasn't sure when she had bonded with the other woman, but it was nice to have someone to sympathize with over Adiin's general disposition. Wymund always gave people the benefit of the doubt—almost to a fault—so he never sympathized with Rav's rants about the elf. She wasn't ready to call Riqu a friend, but no one else understood the man's insufferable nature quite like she did, and an alliance had been formed in those trenches.

"Adiin is only inclined to flatter his own ego," Rav said, joining the other two students near the first set of iron plates. "In fact, we may be at a disadvantage here, Riqu. His inflated head may give him added lift between the pitons."

"This isn't meant to be a race, Ravael," Adiin said as he scanned the mosaic of metal dotting the cliff, his eyes flicking along a path he was devising. "But if you insist, I'll be happy to prove, yet again, how much of a novice you still are."

"I'll see you at the top," she said as she tightened the last fastening strap over her gloves. Adiin frowned. It was a less inflammatory retort than he was used to getting from her, but Rav was done being goaded by him. Something about this new form of directed siphoning was meditative, and the more she had succeeded in the training chamber, the more her hackles seemed to relax. She still had a drive to knock him down a peg, but it was no longer all consuming—a warm, refreshing campfire rather than a raging conflagration.

"Wymund didn't want to come watch the spectacle?" Riqu asked. "I thought he might want to cheer on his lady."

Rav cocked an eyebrow, fighting hard not to laugh in the woman's face. "I'm no one's lady. Wymund is a good friend who's helped me out of more scrapes than one person should ever find themselves in, but apparently not so much of a friend to come up top and weather this skin-splitting cold once more."

Riqu beamed. "Good to know."

"Can we cut the incessant chatter?" Adiin barked, though Rav noted a smile peeling up from one corner of his mouth. "Or does Ravael need more time to acclimate to the cold? I wouldn't want her complaining that she lost because she felt a little chilly."

Riqu muscled herself in between the two, her broad frame enough to block each of their views of the other. "I think I'll act as a buffer. Master Zylnala wouldn't want his star pupils sabotaging each other's climb."

"You think he considers her my equal?" Adiin said. Although she could no longer see his face, she could hear the incredulity in his voice. "Did you knock your head on a rock on the way dow—"

"Go," Rav shouted before planting a boot into a crevice in the wall and springing up to the nearest iron plate. Adiin would be close behind. At least some of his ego was well-earned—he could enter into the continuous looping flow state faster than either of them. But while he was busy trying to denigrate her, Rav had been drawing from the World Shroud, letting the electrical energy course through her arms and down to her hands before curving back around, eventually settling into a reciprocal current that looped continuously over the length of her limbs. It was unsporting, sure, but not devastatingly so.

More importantly, hearing his boots scrape against the snow below was fun.

Her hand slammed against the piton's flat end, and she felt the now familiar tug of her glove as it latched onto the plate. Days ago, having her weight completely supported by the magnetic attraction of her siphoned energy would have been impressive enough, particularly after the arduous series of failures she had endured thanks to Zylnala's vague instruction. But she was ready for more of a challenge, eager to prove to her two classmates and herself that she had grown in her time at the Illumined Scale, so she swung her other arm up and latched it in place on the next panel.

She continued her ascent, aided by metal caps on the toes of her boots, and was urged forward by the rapid clanking that announced the approach of Riqu and Adiin. Luckily for her, she had grown accustomed to forming the thrumming circuits down her legs and into her feet faster than the other two, and had taken pride in watching Adiin stomp away from his iron disc in frustration each afternoon. Luviila thought Rav's aptitude for holding so many looping flows—or polarity folds, as she had called them—was due to her experiences riding the edge of the Illuminated Death, her body already familiar with containing so much power from the Wellspring. Whatever the case, the advantage she had from her extra connections to the mountain aided her scramble and maintained her lead.

Her classmates were not without their own talents, however. Riqu was able to propel herself higher through raw power alone, and the few times Rav chanced a look behind her, she could see the woman's shoulder and arm muscles threatening to rip through the fabric of her tunic. There were larger gaps between the resounding clangs of her connections, as Riqu frequently threw herself up from each plate to link with one several spots higher. Still, as remarkable as they were, her muscles would fatigue faster than Rav's containment of energy, especially as the larger woman's feet struggled to find purchase on the cliff face.

Adiin's technique was less obvious, though he was gaining on her just the same. He had struggled with maintaining four polarity folds for a while, but it seemed he had grasped the concept since the last time Rav had witnessed him fail—he was now also able to make a four-point connection to the course. He should have been far slower than Rav, though, having not spent the time she had leaping rooftops and escaping authorities. And in fact, it was plain that he was moving slower, more deliberately than Rav. But still he gained on her. She could only assume that he had picked out a more optimized path of pitons, but unfortunately for him, that wouldn't be enough to match her agility.

She was more than halfway through the ascent now, and the sounds of Riqu's more sporadic connections were growing distant, replaced by the woman's grunts of exertion. The end was in sight, and the crooked tip of the peak would require a near horizontal climb—not so much of an issue for Rav with her feet also acting as anchors, but Riqu's legs would be dangling below her by the time she reached that portion of the course. The woman's fuel reserves simply wouldn't allow her to conquer that with any speed, and Rav thought Adiin wouldn't fare much better.

That was until a loud metallic snap to her left drew her attention, where she turned to find a startled Adiin, his eyes wide as he first stared at the hand that had just linked to a nearby piton, then shifted to gawk at Rav. To her surprise, the brat actually smiled, big and broad like a child before a holiday feast, then cackled.

"Even with your cheap trick, you're still going to lose," he said when he finally stopped laughing.

Adiin tucked his legs onto the mountain, then pushed off to the right, and Rav gasped as the elf lost all contact with the surface. He flung himself into the open air with no tether, and Rav was already searching for a piton she could latch onto after she dove off to save him from his pathetic gambit. But before she did, she watched as his trajectory lurched, and his outstretched hand moved directly toward a plate several feet away.

Rav was stunned. Adiin had somehow pulled himself toward the mountain. She knew their ability to link to the iron plates was due to a magnetic force they created by looping the Wellspring current through their limbs—or something like that, Zylnala was characteristically vague on the details. But the attraction had never been powerful enough to be felt over more than a few inches. Adiin had managed to amplify the power somehow, enough to draw the weight of his whole body out of free fall.

As he settled himself ahead of her on the course, he looked back with the same cocksure grin that seemed to be his resting expression. Only this time, there was a distinct glint in his eyes, one with which Rav was all too familiar.

"You're going to burn yourself out," Rav shouted over the buffeting wind. "You can't stand the idea of losing to me that badly?"

"If you could survive repeated trips to the brink of the Illuminated Death, I thought I could manage siphoning a bit more power at once," Adiin said. "It turns out it's not so bad. Your inexperience must have been the issue." With that, he threw himself to the side again, launching off the mountain before pulling back toward a distant plate.

The pride she had felt at restraining her desire to destroy him only minutes ago was starting to strain. It was true, the new focused view of tapping into the Wellspring had unlocked more control than she thought was possible for a passive siphoner. Breaking down her needs into smaller, immediate tasks had allowed her to quiet the storm of energy that threatened to consume her any time she opened herself to it, and had even had the knock-on effect of stilling some of her less desirable emotional triggers—prodding annoyances like Adiin could be tuned out when she had her mind trained to achievable goals.

But up here, away from the perfect conditions of their training grounds and the approving eye of Wymund, who could not help but be a little smug about his friend learning to regulate her outbursts, Rav was finding it difficult to remember why she cared about those changes at all. She had learned a long time ago that anyone can behave themselves with the proper motivations. The fancy schools she had been forced into thrived on rewarding what they deemed to be correct etiquette, and she had even gone along with their guidelines when it suited her.

Now though, her only motivations were the loosely defined notions of self-improvement and self-preservation. As far as she could tell, her improvement had stalled and was being surpassed by someone breaking the rules, and she had survived much worse than siphoning enough energy to blow past this lapdog of a lightblood.

"Inexperience?" she muttered as she furiously scurried from piton to piton. "Only one of us has experience going off the leash, you bastard. You're about to see what it's like outside of the kennels."

The speed of the unbridled energy arcing over her was surprising, nearly taking her breath away as she opened herself back up to the Wellspring fully, no longer caring about the next piton but rather about beating Adiin to the finish. Something about already containing some amount of the electricity within her must have made the current able to encompass her near instantaneously. But she was used to this feeling, and as the flaring bursts of lights started to pop in her periphery, she only picked up speed, barely linking with each plate before she was on to the next

Rav didn't know how Adiin was expanding his magnetic pull—and was not fool enough to figure it out dozens of feet in the air—but she did know how to propel herself forward at a pace others would think impossible. By the look on his face as he glanced back to boast, Adiin certainly couldn't believe it.

Thankfully, Rav kept the presence of mind to maintain the four polarity folds in her limbs, otherwise she would have found herself clinging to the cliff horizontally by her fingertips and toes. It was harder to keep the looping currents steady with the torrent of extra energy flooding through her, though, and there were more than a few harrowing moments where a plate connection was more tenuous than she was expecting. There was a reason Zylnala thought these two forms of siphoning were incompatible, but judging by the fact that she hadn't plummeted to her death, maybe the line between the two wasn't as stark as the man believed.

It wasn't long before her sideways spider-climb along the crooked peak caught up to Adiin's lurching pulls. As she raced past him, she yelled, "Pace yourself, Adiin. Don't let the weight of all that experience tire you out."

The curved end of the course bent again, but rather than righting herself and descending feet first to reach the rocky tip, Rav continued without breaking stride. Her hair dangled straight down before being blown into a blinding tangle, though her vision was already impaired by the sparking lights anyway. But the race did not last long enough for either to present much of an issue, as Rav found herself planting a hand on the last iron plate, next to which Riqu had embedded a short rod topped with a bright green triangular flag. Rav yanked it free, then looked up in time to see Adiin rocketing toward a nearby piton.

His hand clanked in place, the link between his glove and the plate somehow not nearly as solid as the scowl he wore. "Have you learned nothing, Ravael? Do you have a death wish?"

"If either of us was courting death today, it was you," she said. "You forget, I've done this before. I know what it feels like to drift too close to that edge. In a fight for my life, where my drive for survival is going to make me unconsciously pull more than I can withstand from the World Shroud, then I would be putting myself at risk."

As Rav spoke, she felt the racing arcs of electricity calm. The lights in her eyes faded, and she craned her neck, releasing the tension that she hadn't noticed was forming at the base of her skull. A sudden jolt of pain shot down her shoulders and through her arms, as if she had been struck by a bolt of lightning, but then her polarity folds snapped back into their gentle thrumming loops. In that split second, Rav thought she might have felt a loosening connection to the iron plates.

Maybe Zylnala was right about open siphoning not working so well with polarity folds after all.

"But I knew that what I needed to beat you wouldn't push me that hard," she continued through her grimace. "And now that I know how to turn off the tap, who knows what I'm capable of?" As she finished, Rav wished she felt more sure of that than she had sounded.

Adiin's face contorted, taking on more of a frown than the fury it had just held. "It was still reckless," he muttered. "You shouldn't be so cavalier with your life. It's . . . inconsiderate."

Rav laughed. "Inconsiderate? Of what?"

"You have people who care about you," he said. Adiin looked away as he began the slow descent back to the beginning of the course. "What would Wymund think if he had witnessed that display?"

Before she could express her incredulity, a powerful gust of wind forced her eyes shut, and by the time she could see again, Adiin had climbed out of earshot. It wasn't like him to give a second thought to the feelings of others, particularly a commoner like Wymund.

Why is everyone suddenly so interested in Wymund?

No, unlike Riqu's curiosity—an interesting development in its own right—Adiin didn't care about her friend. Whatever his issue was with her behavior, it had to do with his own emotional baggage. Spoiled brats like Adiin didn't think much beyond what affected them personally. But she would have to think on crushes and hidden motives another time, because as she carefully picked her way down the crooked peak, she was already mulling over the consequences of her actions. Whatever reaction she had just felt from her World Shroud manipulation, she wasn't keen on experiencing it again.

Chapter 20

The Illumined Scale

Wymund hopped down from a shelf of rock onto the floor of the Gem Hall, the bag of strange, flat-ended pitons clanging at his side. Zylnala had recruited him to hammer the spikes throughout the cavern, with clear instructions to space the plates far enough apart that not even the most skilled climbers would be able to make use of them. He had spent the morning working at the task, hauling ladders up and down to the different levels of the cave so he could reach the higher portions of the walls, and had only managed to cover about a fifth of the perimeter.

He had not balked when Zylnala asked him to work with Riqu one on one, and in fact, Wymund had grown to enjoy his time sparring with her. It reminded him of the training he had done with the new guard recruits in Virdoba, the satisfaction he derived from whipping those tenderfoots into shape, but she was also more pleasant to be around than any of those initiates. They had seen him as their training officer and had kept a distance accordingly, but Riqu was a welcoming presence in this frozen hollow. Wymund was thankful Zylnala had thought to pair him up with her—maybe the instructor saw the benefit they could have on each other's lives. But as he stretched the fatigued muscles in his upper back, he could not bring himself to feel the same for his current assignment.

At the center of the space, Zylnala sat on the massive platform with his legs out in front of him, staring at one of the piton-free walls. If it weren't for the serene smile on his face, Wymund might have thought the man was disappointed in his progress, but the teacher often got like this, adopting a distant gaze while he was deep in thought. Wymund shrugged the heavy bag higher on his shoulder and began to make his way toward the man. If Zylnala had thoughts on plate placements, he would rather hear them now than after the fact. Besides, Wymund wouldn't feel bad about interrupting his reverie—a brief disruption was more than fair trade for the aching back he would have tomorrow.

He climbed the steps, the fronts of which were inlaid with glittering pairs of emeralds like the rest of the platform's circumference, until he found himself standing below the massive brass fixture and the cart-sized emeralds set within. Wymund had crossed underneath the hanging gems numerous times now and had finally rid himself of the intrusive images they brought to mind. Until the image of being buried beneath their weight in a collapse formed in his head as he approached, and he still found himself swallowing hard before he spoke.

"Master Zylnala," he said. "Did you want me to tackle that wall next?"

"Hmm?" Zylnala answered, his short mop of snowy curls bouncing as he turned his head the smallest amount. "Oh, no, Wymund. Well, yes, if you prefer, I meant to say. But in truth my mind was elsewhere." Spinning on his seat to face him, Zylnala's silver-ringed eyes sparkled in a way that rivaled the green gems surrounding them. "By now I've grown to trust your judgment. Finish setting up how you see fit."

Wymund nodded. "Pardon the intrusion, then. I'll get back to it."

"Has she always been so puzzling?" Zylnala said, remaining in his cross-legged position and craning his neck to stare at Wymund.

"Riqu?" Wymund replied. "How do you mean?"

Zylnala laughed. "No, not Blinded Perris. Though it pleases me to know she's on your mind even outside your training sessions." Wymund's face flushed, but thankfully the half-elf continued without poking further.

"She truly has blossomed since your arrival," Zylnala said. "As a fighter, sure, but more importantly as a person. Blinded Perris has demonstrated more self-confidence and simple joy in these weeks than I dared dream possible. When one spends a childhood otherized, it's hard to shake that image of oneself, even as an adult. It can become second nature to defer to those who own their sense of belonging.

"But she no longer takes a second position to Adiin, instead shining in her own right during their exercises. I feel much of that progress is owed to you. You might be a fine warrior, but I think your future lies in leadership, a position where you can focus on bringing out the best in others."

"I can't take credit for her progress," Wymund said, smiling despite himself. "She's earned all that confidence through discipline and hard work. But I agree, she is no one's second."

Zylnala patted the ground next to him. "Have a seat. There will be time yet to complete this course for the next phase of their training—if they don't compete each other to death, that is."

Wymund joined him on the platform, sending a wary eye up to the glistening facets hanging above him like a precariously perched boulder on a cliffside. Walking underneath the enormous gems was one thing, but sitting in this spot made his scalp itch.

"I was actually asking about Ravael," Zylnala said. "I'm having a difficult time pinning her down."

"I get the feeling that you aren't used to having a hard time reading your pupils," Wymund said.

"Understanding my students' motivations and goals helps me better instruct them," Zylnala said with a wry grin, "and I've become quite adept at picking up on those details in my time at the Illumined Scale. But your friend is more akin to a force of nature than unmolded clay for me to shape. It seems at best I can hope to direct her raw power, like a town might divert a river, but she's going to flow forward at her own pace regardless of my intervention."

"Adiin seems driven to the same degree," Wymund said. "Do you not have the same trouble with him?"

"Blinded Miabalar is an open book to someone who has lived even half as long as I have," Zylnala said. With his white hair and crow's feet, the man looked to be in his sixth decade by most standards, but his partial elven heritage meant he was likely much older. One elven parent didn't buy a doubled human lifespan like a full elf enjoyed, but it did tend to tack on a handful of youthful decades in the middle.

"A child born to aristocracy, thinking he was born with a birthright to anything he sets his mind to, including mastering his nature as a lightblood. That level of bullheaded stubbornness does lend itself to a powerful force of will, and consequently a focus on advancing his skill. But Ravael is different."

"Maybe not as much as you think," Wymund said.

Zylnala blinked. "Oh, I can tell she has similar roots. She speaks with an irreverence toward authority that only comes from knowing how toothless those in power often are. I would guess Rav was raised around wealthy socialites and knows full well their words are backed more by hot air than any semblance of potency.

"When I say she's different, I simply mean I don't see a simple motivation in her work ethic that would describe her behavior. Riqu wants to belong, and she has found her people here with us. Adiin seeks to conquer this challenge posed by his bloodline, and thereby prove himself worthy of it. But Rav's actions are often mercurial, and she frequently goes extended periods with no progress until a breakthrough causes a sudden advancement beyond anything I could've expected.

"Any chance you might hold the key to helping me with another of my pupils?" Zylnala asked.

Wymund laughed. "Asking me to explain Ravael is like asking me to interpret the Dawn Ones' scripture. I could get some of it right, but the High Scholar might swat the back of my head and scold me for daring to speak on their behalf."

He paused, trying to get inside her head. Wymund didn't like speaking out of turn, but he did care about Rav's safety, and any insight he could give Zylnala might make her training more effective. As well as he knew her, there was a high chance—practically a guarantee—that she would push herself toward the Illuminated Death again. Wymund wanted to ensure she had the best chance of survival.

"If you were to force an answer out of her," Wymund said, "she would likely give you some line about 'not dying' as her primary motivation. But you and I both know that doesn't fit. A person who was driven by safety wouldn't have spent years leaping from rooftop to rooftop or tempting the blades of city guards."

Zylnala smiled in his mischievous manner, and Wymund thought in another life he might have been locking this man in the cells of the Iron Spiral.

"I believe she's also wanting to prove herself," Wymund continued, "but not in the way Adiin is. He is trying to live up to a name, but Ravael is trying to make one of her own—a difficult enough task on its own, but more so when one doesn't yet know what that identity is meant to be. She bristles at being told what to do and how to act, but at the same time craves the approval of the people whose advice she shuns." Wymund thought of the many arguments he had endured between Rav and Annika, and could only imagine what had transpired between her and her mother in Felona.

"If her progress seems sporadic and sudden to you, I think it might be because she doesn't know what she's chasing," Wymund said. "But she does know that she likes to run."

Zylnala nodded, then tilted his head back, turning his attention up to the giant emeralds set above them. "Thank you for that. It gives me something to build on."

Wymund's eyes followed his gaze, and he shuddered. How this man could bask under their immensity was unfathomable, but perhaps Zylnala had not recently been buried in the ruins of a building by a giant reptile. Wymund hadn't realized it, but he might have developed a phobia in that encounter.

Since beginning his journeys with Rav, Wymund had been batted aside by a creature three times the size of a warhorse, nearly crushed by toppling rubble, and come face to face with a scorcher assassin who could have snuffed him out at any moment. He had faced down his fair share of cutpurses and subdued untold numbers of belligerent drunks during his patrols in Virdoba, but in those instances, he had always felt in control. He trusted in his training, and knew that he would be able to handle whatever darkness that city threw at him.

But what he had experienced in the last few months had been different. By all rights, he should be dead, and in this vast, empty chamber with no true danger to trigger his primal drive for self-preservation, that reality crashed over him like a tumultuous sea. He could feel the weight of those gems bearing down on him, and his chest tightened, his breath restricting along with it.

"Can I ask you something now, Master Zylnala?" Wymund asked, adjusting his seat to face the man, a move which coincidentally shifted him closer to the edge of the platform—and away from the impact zone should the gems fall out of their sockets.

"Of course," he replied.

"What is the significance of the emeralds?" Wymund asked. "You have storage rooms lined with them and decorated with etchings of all the Dawn Ones. I initially thought it strange upon my arrival, and it has only become more so after learning you are not exactly a religious man. At least not a zealous one, anyway, as you haven't brought them up once in my time here.

"And in here," Wymund continued, "the emeralds are featured even more prominently, and there's not a single reference to a Dawn One in sight. So, I'm comfortable ruling out religious fervor, but you also don't live extravagantly. Why not simply sell the gems and fund your work here in perpetuity? You couldn't have built and kept up this place with just yourself and Luviila. Workers must've been hired at some point."

Wymund gestured with his thumb back toward the main house, where the married couple's bickering could be overheard through the kitchen window. "And I can't see Markis and Fulja hefting these emeralds into place. They've worked culinary wonders considering their limited resources, but I don't believe that would extend to other types of miracles."

"Oh, forming the interior of the space is easy when you're in love with an orecaller who would do anything to see your dreams come true," Zylnala said. "Trimon worked tirelessly, pushing crust and shifting mantle so that I could have my private lair in a place that would also be tectonically sound. And we erected the buildings together. As you might expect, I have quite a bit of stamina when I need, and lumber isn't so heavy when it can be lifted into place by the very earth beneath it."

Zylnala's smile faded just a little, before wistfully adding, "He's passed on now. About fifteen years ago."

Rather than succumbing to the memory, he turned his attention back to the verdant boulders precariously fixed above their heads. "As far as the emeralds, like we just discussed, much of what I do involves guiding others based on their unique needs, which I learn through observation. You're right to assume my lack of religiosity—I'm not one for deference to others, particularly those

I can't prove have earned it. One of many reasons I've set up this place for myself away from the morass of imposed rule.

"But I do respect the value of considered guidance," Zylnala continued, "offered without expectation or conditions, for the betterment of the world. That is why I choose to surround myself with iconography of the Witnesses, to keep that inclination forefront in my mind."

"Witnesses?" Wymund asked.

Zylnala chuckled. "You're not one for frequent worship or study yourself, are you?"

"I try to hold to Teacher Melan's teachings on being open to our neighbors," Wymund said. "And living in Kefya my whole life, I've been exposed to the Liiashans' appreciation of Teacher Irasil. We can all benefit from his expectation of charity. But no, my daily life has been dominated with practical, worldly concerns. I haven't had the luxury of sitting down with a High Scholar for a deep reading of their texts."

"Well, you aren't missing much, if you ask me," Zylnala said with a sigh. "Besides, you would be hard pressed to find a High Scholar who would acknowledge the Witnesses as anything other than worshippers who benefited from the Dawn Ones' grace. But that's not how I view the green-eyed mystery figures."

Wymund had seen them before, the men and women often depicted interacting with the Dawn Ones in various paintings and tapestries. None of these pieces of art dated back to their time, of course—the only remains of their civilization were the marble structures tucked in certain corners of Anera and Liiashae—but the artistic interpretation of the Witnesses was based on the few portrayals that had stood the test of time. One such remnant Wymund had seen himself was the platform in Qedrad's Verdant Statuary, where four green-eyed people in long robes are shown speaking with Teacher Melan.

"And how do you view them?" Wymund asked. "Green eyes notwithstanding, I always thought their otherwise nondescript appearance was meant to separate them from the Dawn Ones. To imply with a lack of specificity that these people in the presence of gods are inferior, and weren't worthy of the extra paint."

Zylnala smirked. "A leader or an artist, then. You contain multitudes, young man." He stood, arching his neck to stare right into the gems' facets. "The Dawn Ones had great power, and if there's one thing I've learned in my years instructing brash, novice lightbloods, it's that power needs a check if it's to sustain itself. Something or someone to keep their hands productive rather than at each other's throats.

"I don't believe it's a coincidence that the later scenes from the Dawn Ones' stories do not show them in counsel with the Witnesses. They disappeared, and then the Dawn Ones did as well. I keep their eyes around us here in the Illumined Scale so that we don't vanish like the Dawn Ones did before us." Zylnala chuckled. "As proud as I am of this place I've built, I don't think it will last thousands of years without any upkeep."

Wymund had never heard anyone describe the Dawn Ones' Departure from their world as anything other than a noble sacrifice. They cleansed the world of dragons and the threat they imposed, then left to allow the mortals to flourish. Hearing their absence described as a consequence of their own reckless behaviors was a new one. For the first time, Wymund thought he could see how societal isolation had weighed on the man. Still, the sentiment rang true, if nothing else, and wasn't that the most important part of a fable?

Wymund stood and stepped down from the platform. "While I might not want to sit directly beneath them, I can understand the benefit of their gaze. We can all use a watchful eye and a steady hand to keep us moving in the right direction."

"Rav's been lucky to have you," Zylnala said, then walked past him, leaving Wymund to feel a new form of imposing pressure from the immense jewels.

Chapter 21

Felona

Ubadrii was accustomed to sparse décor. Working within Vinsart Hold for so long, one grew used to uninspired architecture. Sure, the carpeting was lush and the sconces polished, but at the end of the day the building was essentially a giant sandstone block. For an elf who had grown up being taught to appreciate the delicate craftsmanship of Liiashan construction, the home of Qedrad's king was certainly drab in comparison.

However, the council hall was somehow worse, depressing even. The walls were plain, the floor tiles unoffensive, and the ceilings felt lower than he knew they were. Ubadrii thought the design was perfunctory, an insult to the elven influence the rest of Felona enjoyed. But perhaps that was the point—not many of his kind had risen to sit in one of the seven seats that might have a say in renovating the governmental seat.

One of those individuals was sitting across from him now, Livella Riber, having graciously offered to meet with him in her chambers. The walk to her offices had been an exercise in monotony, made even more so by the fact that Ubadrii believed he had been led through nondescript, low trafficked back passages to avoid wandering eyes. At least the woman had decorated her space with interesting odds and ends. As the first secretary of the home, Riber was responsible for maintaining Kefya's relationships with other nations, and the spoils of her travels and summits were evident across the room.

A beautifully carved Ebkarish shifting staff was propped in the corner of the room, the deep purple wood a testament to its value, and shelves were lined with metal worked trinkets from Achen and exquisite leather-bound books that, if he wasn't mistaken, hailed from Destueqan binderies. The difference was so stark from the barren halls outside her door that it was as if he had stepped into a whole other world—the whole world, in fact, complete with representations from every country.

"Thank you for seeing me, Secretary Riber," Ubadrii said. "I know our first encounter was not a pleasant one, for all involved, and the fact that your name had been forged on the document must have been a shock. Let me stress that no one was implicating you in our charges against Port Admiral Thymes."

The woman waved her hand dismissively, smiling in a way that only made her sharp features more angled. "It caused some momentary distress, but thankfully the Council has moved on from that fiasco. However untrue, nobody enjoys having their name dragged through the muds of treason and conspiracy."

Ubadrii clenched his jaw at the thought of the leaders dropping their promised investigation as soon as the door had shut on their meeting, but he had expected as much after hearing about Annika and Niri's chat with two other councilmembers. It was fortunate the women and Kymil had pulled some strings with the lower magistrates to get at least some investigation started. Beyond that, Tano Scrin was still open to their accusation, but one ally and the work of patrolmen would not be sufficient to topple a man like Elikar Thymes. They needed more support.

"Besides," Livella continued, "I could hardly deny the request of King Berenqar's trusted advisor." The woman's eyes sparkled as she thought of his king. "He has been so kind to me over the years in my position, introducing me to other Aneran leaders with such confidence that I felt like I belonged at the adult's table immediately. Not bad for a merchant's daughter, right?"

It hardly seemed appropriate to label the owner of the largest international salt shipping organization simply as a "merchant," but Ubadrii thought better of correcting her. Between her delusions of self-starting and her obvious interest in Berenqar, he had better pathways through this delicate conversation.

"King Berenqar always spoke of your visits fondly," Ubadrii said. Flattery was not his natural currency, not when the authority that came with being a royal hidden hand demanded results, and failing that, infusions that could force said results. But anyone in the service of a ruler learned the importance of speaking with a honeyed tongue, so he could call upon the skill when needed.

"He'll be delighted to know you treated one of his advisors with such magnanimity," Ubadrii continued. "I'll be sure to inform him of your willingness to work with Qedrad's interests, now and in any future endeavors."

"Of course," Livella said, tucking a strand of straw blond hair behind her right ear. "And if young Cailynne is ever seeking womanly advice, please tell her I would love to hear from her."

Livella was attractive enough, by human standards, if a bit on the thin side. But what did Ubadrii know about Berenqar's tastes? His late wife had been shorter and more full-figured than Livella, but maybe there was a future for these two. He had never had much interest in other people himself, romantically or otherwise, so he wouldn't be the best judge of compatibility. Best to keep things vague rather than overpromise his king's affections.

"Speaking of Lady Cailynne," Ubadrii said, "she handled herself well in the face of that scorcher assassin and the betrayal of Sylicera. She was nowhere near the assault on the king's chambers, thankfully, but she stared each of them down as her father doled out their punishments. I believe she may have the backbone statecraft requires, if King Berenqar would ever let her exercise it."

"He's not preparing his daughter for rule?" Livella asked. "I understand your government won't simply pass his seat on to her, but he must suspect Cailynne would be well positioned to be selected for the role."

"I didn't mean to suggest he was slacking in his fatherly duties," Ubadrii replied. "Quite the contrary, in fact. At times I find the king to be a bit overprotective of his daughter, though after the passing of his wife, who could blame him?"

Livella nodded solemnly before beckoning through the door behind him, ushering in an attendant carrying two porcelain cups of tea on a tray. The elven man was older than one might expect for the role and had sunken cheeks that highlighted his dour countenance, but Ubadrii supposed serving someone so entitled all day would put a frown on most faces. The attendant placed one cup in front of each of them, then gave a curt bow and walked out.

Ubadrii picked up the cup, inhaling the aroma as he held it to his lips out of instinct before daring to take a sip. He had no reason to suspect the secretary wanted to have him killed, but if one had the nose for poisons, it never hurt to use it. He swallowed the tangy beverage, hiding his grimace with a napkin dab.

Must everything be citrusy with these islanders.

"She wanted to join me on this trip, you know," Ubadrii continued. "The king wouldn't hear of it, despite my attempts to bolster her case." A lie, of course, but one an aspiring stepmother would like to hear. "I believe she could've learned much interacting with the Council and honestly would've been a force in her own right. She's been known to be quite convincing when she has a mind to be."

Livella pursed her lips. "So, both the king and Cailynne have bought in to this . . . story completely?"

"Very much so," Ubadrii replied. "I wasn't sent here to speak with you and your fellow councilmembers on the off chance this accusation of warmongering was true. King Berenqar believed it was of the utmost importance that your government be informed of these deeds so that an appropriate response could be initiated."

"If he believes one of Kefya's leadership to be so compromised, why has he continued to conduct business between our nations without incident?" Livella asked, holding her cup near her mouth but not drinking, as if she was already trying to swallow more than enough. "One would think that an assassination attempt and a planned international conflict would be enough to disrupt a trade or two."

Ubadrii could only guess at his king's motivations. As much as he was relying on his role as one of Berenqar's advisors in this matter, the truth was he was simply carrying out instructions. The king had not sat him down for a long discussion prior to his departure from Qedrad, nor had he asked for Ubadrii's opinion. Had he done so, the king might have learned that maintaining relations would send the opposite signal he was hoping to convey, and that a sharp swat of the Council's nose could demonstrate how grave he believed this threat to be.

But Berenqar was a sentimental man—he had come by his moniker, the People's King, honestly—and he would have dismissed Ubadrii's counsel. Ubadrii believed the king valued having someone like him around as a logical sounding board, someone who could rein in his empathetic excesses if he was blinded to some potential harm. But in this, Ubadrii believed there would have been no swaying him. Too many Qedradans owed their livelihoods to trade with Kefya, and the nations were too intertwined to suddenly sever that bond, so he would have wanted to settle this dispute in a fashion that did not create hardship for his citizens.

"King Berenqar would not threaten the lives of his people, or Kefyans, by upending the economies of two closely tied countries," Ubadrii said. "Unlike some heads of state, he considers his role to be a caretaker rather than a profiteer."

The woman finally took a drink from her cup, and revealed a warm smile as she sat the tea back on the desk. "It's rare indeed to have a man in such authority lead with his heart and not other parts of his anatomy. Qedrad is fortunate to have him, and when Cailynne is elected as his successor—if she is as formidable as you say—then perhaps he could spend some time here in Felona and show us how it's done."

Ubadrii bit his tongue regarding the certainty of succession. He had his own designs on claiming the throne in Vinsart Hold. While he agreed Cailynne would make for a strong ruler, likely firmer than her father but able to maintain his ideals, Ubadrii couldn't continue to ignore the waste and inefficiencies he had become privy to in his tenure as a royal advisor. They itched at his skin like a rash, even kept him up some nights as he devised plans that would maximize benefit to his countrymen while using the fewest resources possible. Poison-making was an exercise in precision—more so through infusions—and he knew he could apply those skills to shaping his home into the dominant power it once was.

"I'm sure he would be delighted at your invitation," Ubadrii said. "Though in order for him to feel secure spending time on your island, he would have to know this attempt on his life was thoroughly investigated, not promptly discarded by councilmembers who were either too scared or too complacent to look closer at one of their own."

Livella's smile dropped as her eyes narrowed slightly. For a moment, Ubadrii feared he had been too direct or insulting. It was a weakness of his, one that he would need to overcome should he have any hope of being chosen as Berenqar's successor. Such a feat would require a majority vote among the houses in Kefya, many of whom already had fond dealings with the king, and by proxy, his daughter. Ubadrii's difficulty understanding what could be construed as offensive at any given time would be a hindrance, but one he hoped was not insurmountable.

Thankfully, no offense appeared to have been taken, as Livella exhaled a soft chuckle through her nose. "Point taken," she said. "I'll keep the discussion alive, but it would be nice to have allies supporting me in this. Whether or not the accusation proves true, Elikar is still a bully, and I would prefer not to be on the receiving end of one of his tantrums."

"We're working on that," Ubadrii replied. "Once we know more, I'll send along the information."

Livella stood to walk him out, but yelped as she banged her wrist on her desk. "Edis's Eye!" she cursed, then blushed as she remembered her company. "I apologize for the colorful language. It's just this is the third time in as many weeks I've slammed my arm on this damn thing. Perhaps I need to have the height adjusted."

They said their goodbyes, and Ubadrii spared a thought for the councilwoman's clumsiness. Certain poisons could dull reflexes and make movements sluggish, but most would have left the victim severely ill over a three-week span. He held on to hope he was merely witnessing a string of bad luck rather than a wasting disease. If Elikar drew this process out, they couldn't afford losing a potential ally to an early death.

But as he stepped back into the depressing void of unoriginality that was the walkways of the Felonian Council Hall, he turned his mind back to hopeful thoughts, his mood bolstered by the opening he had created in the Council's defenses. After all, an advisor shifting the tide of a resistant foreign government would be a powerful introduction to his political aspirations in Qedrad. Ubadrii began contemplating the changes he would make to Vinsart Hold as he walked. Wasteful spending was one thing, but the eye deserved to look at *something* inspiring.

CHAPTER 22

FELONA

"Who was it?" Tetamii asked, pulling the veil tight around the perimeter of the hexant's head. The gaunt elf had already been sweating when Tetamii had cornered him in a side office, but now with heat venting out of the Wellspring and broiling his face, the man's hair was sopping and lank across his forehead.

"I . . . I don't know his name, sir," the man stammered. He plastered on a nervous smile that he probably hoped seemed helpful, but in reality, read as pure terror. "He was an elf, though. Tall and pale, and he was bald. Which is odd, right? Our kind typically do not lose their hair, so he must shave i—"

Tetamii raised his hand and clenched it, cutting off the man's blathering. He had heard enough. Habrum was right; baldness was not a trait common to their kind, but even without that descriptor, Tetamii could've guessed which of his prior captors was currently speaking with Livella Riber.

He still had nightmares about that man, his features distorted through the haze brought on by the hidden hand's own tinctures of severing. Tall and pale did not do justice to the lanky, skeletal figure that lived in the shadows of Tetamii's dreams, separating him from the power that had kept him warm and safe his entire life.

"And he's still in there now?" Tetamii asked.

The older elf nodded. "I just left her office not more than ten minutes ago. I've been keeping tabs on her and the other councilmembers as instructed, dosing them with a little misfortune each day in case we need a larger accident in the future. If the target is already primed, it makes a more powerful infusion easier to—"

"Go," Tetamii interrupted, pointing toward the door. Whatever angle the hexant was working to curry favor, he no longer seemed interested in trying if he was being offered the chance to leave. Tetamii watched the man stumble in his haste to reach the door, then right himself and march stiff-backed down the hall.

Tetamii was not concerned the man would speak of their encounter. Regardless of his obvious intimidation, the hexant did want to ingratiate himself further into the Clipped Gulls, and he wouldn't spoil all the work he had done with loose lips. But Tetamii was afraid of missing his own chance at retribution—and of letting down Magzii once again. Tetamii turned and stalked out of the room, making his way toward the first secretary of home's chambers.

Since his initial failing in Qedrad, Tetamii had not lived up to the standard Magzii held for him, and his mentor had not let it go unnoticed. Private and public chastisement had followed his race with Atusiin through the Trough—all to prove "who had the most crowded trousers," as Magzii had put it—not to mention the destruction Tetamii had unleashed on the poor residents below. It had stopped that particular contingent of guards in their tracks, but suspicions had only grown among the lower magistrates when no other patrol was taken out. Magzii believed his favored club was now lost to him with renewed guard presence around the SPOILED PUDDING, a predictable consequence of a single group being killed.

Tetamii should have known better, but he had lost himself in his desire to shut down Atusiin's arrogance. Rather than proving he was still Magzii's most valuable asset, all he had done was succeed in bringing attention to his bruised ego, which was only further blackened when Magzii dressed him down in front of the others, with Atusiin smirking just behind him.

Magzii had seemed more angered by the infighting within his crew than the devastation it had wrought, but that didn't matter—Tetamii was troubled enough by that disaster anyway. He had been responsible for so much devastation in his life, even burning entire villages off the map, but those instances had been purposeful and directed. He had taken those actions with mental clarity, understanding the consequences his power wrought upon the world. But this accidental destruction—of the only place that represented the innocence of his childhood, no less—was taking a new toll on him.

The mental chest the Clipped Gulls were taught to use for containment of errant emotions was failing, cracked open by the fresh wounds to his pride, his father figure making a mockery of him instead of building him up as he had done in the past. All the shame and hurt he felt for the damage he had caused to the beating heart of Felona lingered on his mind, unable to be forced back inside his emotional lockbox, and Tetamii knew the pressure was building to an eruption. The smoky wisps danced violently in his vision, and he didn't know if that outburst would be literal.

But those cracks in his control were not only the fault of his new dynamic with Magzii. They had also been widened by a budding friendship. Garla had been the only face in the crowd of his peers that demonstrated any sympathy during his tongue-lashing, and she had been the only one to offer a kind word once it was over. She didn't fit the mold of a typical Gull recruit, less callous and self-serving than amiable and easygoing. Whatever reason Magzii had brought her into the fold, Tetamii found himself grateful for the ally, which was a sensation so foreign to him that he felt conflicted.

His boots clicked on the tiles of labyrinthine halls, his feet finding the path less complex than the tangle in his mind. But he had walked these passages many times before, trailing behind the posh velvet coats Ilphas had worn when making his rounds. Tetamii remembered those days clearly, the short period of his life having left an indelible mark. He supposed that had been the point—Magzii wanted the initiation rite to be potent, to change the recruit forever, and it had. It had given Tetamii a family, and all it had cost was the life of a man who he was told was just like every other councilmember, greedy and pompous.

However, now that his mind was awash in unregulated emotional turmoil, he was beginning to realize that act had done more than click the final lock on his mental chest. Buried deep under all the disciplined repression was a doubt that had been rotting him from within. Doubt not only in his own actions at that time, but also in Magzii's judgment.

If Ilphas had not been the corrupting presence Magzii claimed, why had he been targeted? And hadn't Tetamii just considered the prototypical Gull callous and self-serving? How did that differ from the targets Magzii had set him on all these years, citing those very traits as justifications?

A sconce flared to his right, the previously gentle flame spilling over the brass lattice and scorching the wall. Tetamii shook his head and released his unwitting hold on the World Shroud, allowing the fire to flicker back into its container. This was becoming a pattern, and he could not afford to lose control again.

The echoes of screams sounding from the Trough played in his head, the people's cries of anguish as a mountainous slab descended toward their homes. And that was what he had unleashed with a temporary connection to an unfamiliar Wellspring. Imagine the conflagration he could summon into this place were he to open the tap to his own source. It seemed staying mired in his muddled anxieties and disappointments had turned him from an efficient assassin into a bomb with a short fuse.

Then there were the visions he still had to contend with. The lightblood plagued him day and night, appearing at random in the corners of his eyes, ducking around corners and open doorways. Even now, with his emotions heightened, he could just make out her mocking smirk from where she lay at the far end of the hall, broken and sprawled over a pile of rubble. Her arm was extended, as if at the end of a throw, and the scar tissue in his back raged.

He took a deep breath and forced the racing thoughts back into the recesses of his mind, banishing the hallucination along with them. They wouldn't stay there—his lockbox was broken and in disarray. But he had a job to do now, and he would keep them at bay until he could sort through them later. First, the hidden hand posed a risk to the Clipped Gulls' benefactor, and by extension the crew. He needed to be silenced.

This was not his captors' first foray into rallying support since their dismissal from the Council's hearing. The old women had met with the High Scholar and the first secretary of culture, and while he believed those two to be manageable opportunists, he was more concerned by the sighting of Tano Scrin in the Bindweed Conservatory.

The Clipped Gulls had agents watching the home the group was holed up in, their deaths only deferred by Thymes's wish to leave a gap between an accusation against him and the party's untimely disappearances, but it had provided useful information. Scrin was an idealist, holding the seat that Ilphas had been vying for and modeling himself after the elf's popularity. Whether he stood by those ideals was another matter, but if Tetamii was now entertaining the idea that Ilphas's morality was authentic, why not this man's as well? His targets couldn't be allowed to build an alliance like that by adding another councilmember to their ranks.

As he approached the home wing of the council hall, Tetamii could pick out the telltale cacophony of far-flung accents from across Anera. It was really the only way for a visitor to distinguish Livella Riber's offices from those of the other councilmembers. There wasn't much cause for visiting dignitaries in the defense wing, after all—not in times of peace, anyway.

Tetamii turned a corner, then ducked back just as quickly. The hidden hand, Ubadrii Tragala, was stepping out of Livella's chambers, and a chill gripped Tetamii's heart as if Magzii had been standing behind him. This was it, his chance to end the man who had made him small. It wouldn't take long; as furiously as the veil danced for him now, he could reduce the elf to char and ash in a matter of seconds.

It's a little man who chooses flash over family.

Magzii's words rang through his head, the second man to belittle him in as many months. But his mentor had been right, no matter how humiliating it had been. He had chosen to demonstrate his power because his reputation had been diminished, and as a result, he had not only proven himself reckless, but also ruined the lives of dozens in the Trough.

Sure, he could incinerate the elf right here, right now. But what would that accomplish? Ubadrii's partners would still be at work in the city, and Tetamii's involvement would be revealed. He relaxed the tension in his shoulders, allowing the scintillating wisps to do the same. Perhaps flash was not the right choice in this instance. Maybe there was an option that would strengthen his family's standing.

The lightblood would be proud, he thought, a wry smile gracing his face. *You taught me the value of connections. I'll be sure to thank you on our next encounter.*

Tetamii turned back the way he had come, eager to take one of the many other exits this palatial building had to offer. He had to speak with Magzii and fill him in on an opportunity that had just fallen into their laps. But he had learned his lesson; this time, Tetamii would not make a show of it. His success was the Gulls' success—and by extension Magzii's. His mentor would be thrilled.

Before he had that conversation though, he had another to make. If Garla was so close to their organization's new herb nurse, she might have a nose for the best hidden hand the Clipped Gulls had to offer.

Chapter 23

Felona

"Are you sure I'm going to be welcome here," Garla asked, not for the first time. Tetamii sighed and stared at her from his seat across the room. Considering how he typically dealt with repeated annoyances, this was progress on his path away from being a lone wolf.

"All right, I'll stop asking," she continued. "But if I end up dead, I'm going to come back and haunt you. You'll never know a moment's peace again."

The pair were sitting in two plush armchairs facing an impressive display of naval paraphernalia. A wall of shelves was filled with miniature ship replicas, old bottles of Draemooran vodka that had been stamped with a shipping decal predating the War of Arrival, and a handful of oil paintings depicting more species of fish than Tetamii knew existed. For a room that served primarily as Elikar Thymes's private study, the man did not want anyone who visited to forget his role as Kefya's port admiral.

It had only been a day since Tetamii witnessed the hidden hand leaving Livella Riber's office, but as he had suspected, Garla was well connected and worked quickly. Once he explained his plan, she immediately rattled off a list of the Gulls' own hidden hands. Together they honed them down, discarding all the run-of-the-mill poisoners that their organization slummed with on occasion. It didn't take a master infuser to kill someone if one didn't care too much about how it looked. However, one name on her list stood out as a true artisan, and to Tetamii's mind, she was the only hidden hand on the Clipped Gulls payroll who could pull this off.

"Shiina doesn't need to be here, too?" Garla asked. "Or are you keeping the crucial part of your scheme away from Magzii and his moods?"

"The hidden hand is not one of us," Tetamii said. "She is a freelancer, and therefore doesn't sit in on business discussions. She'll know what she needs to know, but she definitely does not need to know of the port admiral's involvement."

Tetamii's eyes flicked toward the door, which was still closed. Still, he softened his voice in case anyone was approaching. "It is already unfortunate that the hexant made that connection, though I suppose that was unavoidable. He certainly couldn't have infused Elikar's jacket with that fatestitcher ward without seeing the craftsmanship of the coat."

Garla nodded, seemingly content with the answer, but was only quiet for a moment before another question popped to mind. "Why does Berenqar have a hidden hand as an advisor anyway? I thought he was supposed to be the 'People's king,' all nice and supportive of his countrymen. Working so closely with a poisoner doesn't scream friendly to me."

Tetamii shrugged. "One doesn't have to be a bloodthirsty warlord to have enemies, and its likely better to have a man like that on your side than not. Besides, who better to be on the lookout for potential poisoning attempts than a master of the craft. He probably already has antidotes on hand for the nastier concoctions."

With no knock, the door swung open, allowing Magzii to saunter into the office with a grin that spoke volumes about the man. Tetamii knew his mentor loved the legitimacy he was building through his dealings with Elikar Thymes and wouldn't be surprised if he made the Clipped Gulls go straight in the years to come—only *official* rough-ups and legally sanctioned assassinations. But his daydreaming must have come to an end the moment Magzii saw Garla sitting in the room, as his mouth thinned into a tight line.

"I thought we had reached an understanding," Magzii said, staring at Tetamii so intently that the man didn't need to tap into the Wellspring for his iciness to be conveyed. "But here we are again, another opportunity for you to make a fool out of yourself, and me in the process. How exactly do you think he's going to react when he finds you've brought in a green member of our club to sit in on a meeting like this?"

Magzii sighed, then strode across the room to stand next to Garla's chair. He reached under her arm and started to pull her up. "Luckily for us, he's running late. There's still time to get her out of here so you can't screw up my reputation even more."

"She stays," Tetamii said.

His mentor stopped yanking on Garla's arm. To her credit, she had hardly budged despite Magzii's best efforts, though she now looked more concerned than Tetamii had ever seen her. The woman was the epitome of amiable nonchalance, but she had finally been shaken.

"What did you say to me?" Magzii asked. This time, Tetamii was sure the temperature actually had dropped in the room. He had been expecting this reaction, though, and was ready to make his leader see the benefit of his plan.

"I said," Tetamii said, crossing his legs and settling back farther into his seat, "she stays. She has much to add to this conversation." As he spoke, his breath started as a cold plume of air that quickly disappeared as it rewarmed. Magzii was not the only one who could alter the climate of a room, and Tetamii was tired of being walked on—he understood the mistakes he had made since returning to Felona and was capable of admonishing himself.

Bowing his head all this time had only led to mistake after mistake. Tetamii was through bowing.

Magzii dropped Garla's arm, then stood facing Tetamii as he worked the muscles of his jaw, making the long, ugly scar along the side of his face writhe in concert with his anger.

Garla let out a nervous laugh, then reached up and smoothed her hair down. "If you two are going to have a disagreement, can you do it without frizzing my hair before I meet the damn port admiral?"

The temperature in the room returned to normal as Tetamii loosened his grasp on the World Shroud, though he would not release it. In the last few weeks, he had been made to feel powerless and insignificant by too many people, Magzii included. Tetamii could still endure the man without allowing himself to be buried under the weight of his disapproval. He would no longer be his beaten lapdog, cowering in the corner after his master's tirade; an abused pet sometimes maintained a feral edge, and Tetamii could as well.

Magzii might relax and relinquish his siphon, likely fearful of ruining the room with moisture now that Garla had interrupted their pissing contest, but Tetamii felt the smoky tendrils of the veil snake along the outskirts of his mind, ready if needed.

"All right," Magzii said. "What's done is done. But someone needs to tell me what I'm walking into here. When you said you had an update for Elikar, I half expected to walk in and see one of the accusers dead on the carpet."

Garla shot a look at Tetamii that told him she wanted help walking out of this situation with not only her life, but all her fingers and toes. He exhaled sharply through his nose, then stood, striding over to face Magzii. Even after reaching adulthood, Tetamii always pictured looking up to meet Magzii's gaze in his mind, such was the impression his mentor had made on him growing up. Now, though, he felt every inch of height advantage he held over the older elf.

"I spotted Ubadrii Tragala meeting with Livella Riber yesterday," Tetamii said.

Magzii's eyes widened. "You know we can't have them sneaking around and making friends, boy. I told you as much." He made a show of looking around the room with his arms held out. "But I still can't help but notice there's no dead elf tucked away in here."

"That's because I let him walk," Tetamii continued, then raised a hand to stop Magzii's outburst. A vein on the man's forehead throbbed, but he held his tongue, perhaps more stunned than deferential.

"We have an opportunity here to strengthen Elikar's power over the rest of the Council," Tetamii continued, "which in turn benefits the Gulls. But beyond that, we could spark a war he stands to profit from in the same stroke."

"You mean the war you failed to kick off once already?" Magzii asked.

Tetamii felt the heat pulse through the veil, but he let the comment go. Further bickering would only demonstrate subservience. If Magzii didn't approve of his plan, Tetamii was certain Elikar would. With a direct line to the Clipped Gulls' primary benefactor, he would have no need to be placed below Magzii ever again.

"A delay is only a failure without another attempt," Tetamii said. "If we can implicate this Qedradan hidden hand in the death of a Kefyan councilmember, though, this conflict will be unavoidable. Elikar could easily maneuver the other members into supporting a retaliatory strike once it is widely believed that King Berenqar's personal advisor assassinated one of our leaders."

"It really is a good plan, boss," Garla said, flexing her arm where she had been grabbed. "I found this woman who can whip up any—"

"It sounds like a lot of chances to go tits up," Magzii interrupted. "Framing a man who is probably a master in his field with the work of a hidden hand who's willing to do business with a group like us? We get the job done, but no one would ever accuse us of doing it with finesse." He took a step toward Tetamii, then reached a finger out to jab it into his chest.

"This is why we stick to plans that are about as complicated as sticking something sharp into something soft," Magzii continued. "You always try to get fancy with things, and that's how you ended up bungling the job in Virdoba before you screwed up again up north." He scoffed and shook his head. "I mean, firebombs? Couldn't you have just run some people through and spouted off some nonsense about humans being filth? That would've gotten the job done just fine, but I've let you get too far off the leash."

"Unleashed pets make me nervous, Magzii," Elikar said from the doorway.

Tetamii turned to see the man standing casually with his hands in his trouser pockets, looking much too comfortable for a high-society type walking into a room of hardened criminals. He was dressed down relative to the other occasions Tetamii had seen the councilor, wearing no jacket but instead a simple, black silk vest over a white collared shirt.

Elikar's eyes traced over to Garla. "And I see you've brought along a stray. I do hope you intend to clean up after her if she's any trouble." The coded threat was not intended to be hidden, and judging by Garla's anxious shuffling in her seat, the message had been delivered.

Any hint of dourness dropped from Magzii's face in an instant, replaced immediately by his lopsided grin as he turned to address Elikar. "She won't be a problem, Councilman Thymes. In fact, Garla here has given us a chance to go for a bigger prize than you wanted. Why settle for trade tensions between your neighboring countries when you can line your pockets with coin from war contracts?"

For all his faults, Tetamii had to admit Magzii knew how to work an angle. Whether the man believed in it or not was irrelevant.

Elikar walked into the room, closing the door behind him, then continued on his path toward the collection on his shelves. He picked up a slightly curved scabbarded blade; Tetamii could picture it on the waist of a naval captain and wondered if Elikar had acquired it as a gift or as a peace offering. The port admiral turned the sword over in his hands, running a few fingers along the leather sheath as he turned around to face his guests.

"War is a messy business," Elikar said, "but one that can be profitable, I'll grant you that. What did you have in mind?"

Magzii's smile broadened, twisting his face further thanks to the stubbornness of his scar. "Picture it: the entire city in an uproar after one of our beloved councilmembers is discovered in their chambers, poisoned with spittle foaming out of their cracked lips. Rumors would spread like wildfire in all the neighborhoods, and who could blame them when we make it known that a foreign hidden hand had been spending time with our dear Livella Riber."

Elikar's face didn't move, but his eyes sharpened as he continued inspecting the blade. "Ubadrii Tragala has been meeting with Livella, then?" he asked.

"He has," Tetamii said before Magzii could respond. His mentor looked at him askance, but clicked his jaw shut. "I saw him leaving her offices just yesterday."

The port admiral drew his sword, then set the scabbard aside on the shelf behind him. "So it was you who decided on this plan of action instead of capturing one of the targets who threatens my position in this city?"

Tetamii nodded. "I made a judgment call. I could have picked off one of them in that moment, but then the others might have gone to ground. If we turn the whole city against this band of accusers, however, paint them as Berenqar's puppets in an attempt to weaken Kefya, then we discredit them all, and make you rich all at once."

Elikar paused, holding the sword out in front of him as he looked down its length. Tetamii tried to picture the councilor thrusting at him, furious at his disobedience after failing Elikar so recently. But he couldn't; the port admiral was not an idiot or suicidal. If he was trying to make a point with that blade, it was not meant to be a threat of physical harm. Elikar had to know that no matter his authority, Tetamii could snuff him out in an instant.

After an uncomfortable moment of silence, Elikar said, "I had a man in my employ once, a ship captain, when I was nothing more than the owner of a small fleet of shipping vessels. He liked to take decisions in his own hands, like adjusting shipping manifests based on weather patterns instead of customer orders, or hire on new hands from taverns when they beat him at a game of boatman's grasp. Sometimes those choices worked out, but sometimes they didn't.

"On one occasion, this captain decided it was best to disregard an entire order of wines for merchants in Seset, crates of the stuff that filled the entire hold, and replace it with rum." Elikar shook his head. "Cheap swill, too. Not the batches Kefya is proud to export. Needless to say, the value of my shipment dropped precipitously, particularly when you consider it was not even what had been requested.

"But this captain saw something I didn't. A detail I had overlooked. A fungus had run rampant through the Tangled Vines that summer, some of which had infested the vineyards or even spoiled the soil. While the wine the vineyards produced that year was drinkable, there was a certain unwashed foot taste that permeated the batches, and when the Achen merchants realized it, they turned my competitors and their shipments away without a coin for their efforts."

Elikar pulled the blade back and slipped it into the scabbard. "But there my captain was with a ship full of exotic island rum, and those merchants were happy to take what they could get. He had taken a gamble, but it was one that ended up making me a lot of libers." He returned the sword to its spot on the shelf, then added, "When I promoted him off that ship to an administrative role for his efforts, he gave me his sword to display and remember what boldness might bring.

"One day I might have your sword on my wall," Elikar said, meeting Tetamii's gaze with a paternal smile. "Though I will have to clear some space first. It's a bit unwieldy, isn't it?"

Tetamii returned the grin, appreciating that Elikar saw the value in his plan but also relishing how Magzii must be feeling. "I'm not ready to hang it up yet, Councilman Thymes. But I'm glad you see the merit in my plan," Tetamii said, and then with a sideways glance at Magzii, he added, "It must take one with vision to understand the opportunity here."

"Yes, we're all visionaries around here. Come on, then, Tetamii," Magzii said, as he walked over to slap a hand on his shoulder. He squeezed harder than his cocksure smile implied. "Now that Councilman Thymes has agreed to our plan, let's make sure we have everything lined up." Then, he ambled out of the room.

Garla stood, mumbling a goodbye to Elikar and bowing like a boor, though Tetamii couldn't fault her for that. She had likely never met someone in Elikar's station, and being so new to the Gulls, had not spent much time interacting with their occasional high society clientele. She shuffled backward out the door, and Tetamii followed suit after thanking Elikar for his time. Once out in the hall, he found Garla standing alone with a puzzled expression.

"You handled yourself fine," he said. "Next time, just remember there's no need to bow for a councilor. A firm handshake and eye contact is enough respect. He's not royalty."

"It's not that," she said, pointing down the hall. "I've just never seen Magzii walk like someone stuck a hot poker up his ass."

Tetamii followed her finger and saw the leader of the Clipped Gulls stalking away from them, moving at a pace that was a far cry from his typical confident stroll. Tetamii chuckled. "He didn't appreciate sharing the councilor's favor. Let him storm off and pout. Once he decides to grow up, he can join us in putting this plan together."

This meeting had been illuminating. Magzii had always been the picture of confidence to Tetamii's eyes, but he now had the opportunity to see it for the façade it was. When the man came face to face with true authority, he shifted into a craven toady, seeking approval in the same way he had forced Tetamii to all these years. And under Magzii's guidance, his organization fell far short of the power it supposedly strived for. Tetamii saw the Clipped Gulls for what they actually were: scared children lashing out at a world of happier people, searching for acknowledgment from those who used them as little more than a blade or a deft hand.

If Magzii wouldn't allow him to help right the ship, he might have to seize control himself.

Garla looked at him, her brow knitted. "If you say so, but the boss is a petty man who's had his ego stroked for decades now by his underlings, and you're the favorite. I don't want to imagine the punishment he's planning to put you back in your place."

"He can try whatever he wishes," Tetamii said. Glancing back at Elikar's door, he added, "Magzii's not the only one with the ear of authority now. He'll have to adjust to having me beside him at the table, rather than at his feet, begging for scraps."

Chapter 24

Felona

Kymil felt the breeze drift in off the Marrow Strait, the salty air complementing his cup of coffee as he and Mareq awaited their guest. It was an odd place for a meeting to take place: an open-air café situated near the front of the Horn and Planks district, near enough to the docks that plenty of passersby could take notice. But that was exactly why Kymil had chosen it—nothing put a soldier off balance like a public place.

Garend Hull, the first secretary of defense, had been chosen as Kymil's mark. Both Annika and Niri believed they would come off as abrasive to a military man who was used to the respect offered by chain of command rather than needing to earn it, and Ubadrii had thought his efforts would be better focused on a member of the Council who was already close to his king. But Kymil could play the sycophant if called upon to do so, and he could ingratiate himself with anyone, given enough time.

Time, though, was precisely what they were short of, as Annika was sure Elikar's forces would not be sitting idly by while they collected allies to put him away. If the process of swaying a stoic man's opinion could be sped up by unsettling him, Kymil would gladly take the opportunity. There was, of course, always the use of an infusion or two to tip the scales.

"I'm not sure why I'm here," Mareq said, twirling a spoon through his coffee after adding an Irasil-damned amount of milk and sugar into the cup. So much so, in fact, that Kymil was left wondering if the draqeshi should not have ordered milk with a splash of coffee instead.

Northerners, Kymil thought. *Wouldn't know flavor if they spent all night with it and woke up next to it in the morning.*

"You're here, my friend, because it helps to have a counterbalance against a man like Garend Hull," Kymil said. "I'm . . . not his typical conversation partner. It will be nice for him to have another man at the table who speaks plainly, to give him an escape from the anxiety of meeting in such a wide-open space.

"Plus," Kymil added with a wink, "we can't have the public see me meeting alone with a stone-faced brute like Hull. I don't want people to get the impression that I'm off the market."

Mareq laughed. "How did you get him to agree to meet here anyway? Everyone else had to meet with their councilmembers in the privacy of their own chambers."

"I didn't," Kymil said, before taking a slow sip from his cup.

His friend stopped stirring his dairy-based dessert drink. "What do you mean? We've been sitting here for over an hour waiting on him."

"Yes, and he should be arriving shortly. He just doesn't know he's meeting with us yet."

Mareq sighed, then took a long draught from his coffee. He still grimaced a little when he swallowed. "As much as I've come to appreciate your theatrics, how about you fill me in on the script for this one? I'm not the best at improvisation."

"There's not much to it, really," Kymil said. "Hull has a rose of an attendant named Beloma, who was rather affectionate for someone who works so closely with a closed-off sentry like him. After an evening of delicate convincing on my part, she agreed to arrange a special tasting for him at this very spot. Her sister is the pastry chef, and apparently the old war dog has a soft spot for turnovers."

"And what's to stop him from leaving after he gets his dessert?" Mareq asked. "He has no incentive to sit down with us."

Kymil smiled. "To be determined." When Mareq frowned, he added, "You have to leave me some room to extemporize. Besides, you know things have a way of working out for me."

"You mean like they did in our presentation to the Council?" Mareq asked.

Kymil's smile faded to a smirk, always resistant to completely dropping from his face. A hexant working against a fatestitcher could cancel each other out if they were equally skilled, but Kymil had not put all he had into that infusion. He would be ready for the meddling hexant next time.

"There's always a chance for blunders when not all the players are known," Kymil said. Then he nodded his head down the street, adding, "Today, though, it's just us and an ex-soldier gabbing over a cup of coffee and sweet bread. I like our odds."

Moving south through the city, Garend Hull walked swiftly from the direction of the Crest toward the Horns and Planks. He had a retinue of three guards, their black and cerulean Council tabards helping them cut a stark path through the crowd to give the secretary an unimpeded walkway. Much like the last time Kymil had seen the man, his gray curls were falling low to nearly hang over his deep-set eyes, and he walked with purpose, hands clasped behind his back as he neared the café.

Kymil adjusted his shortened right sleeve so the fabric was not pulled so tight against what was left of his arm. He found that leaving a little billow in the material was less distracting to others, and he couldn't have people's eyes drawn away from his own. Annika's words to him in the offices of the lower magistrates had been hard to hear—sometimes the din of a pity party could be deafening—but the old woman did have wisdom to go along with her years. He had been so focused on his losses, both physical and intangible, that he had assumed his worth had diminished along with them. With a missing arm and a reduced capacity to perform, who was he, after all?

Apparently, the answer was someone who Annika and Mareq continued to invest energy and care into. It was more support for him as an individual, not as a showman, than he had ever received, particularly from his own parents. Kymil held the two of them in high regard, so he now simply had to make sure he lived up to that effort.

Mareq eyed him. "It's not that noticeable, you know. As long as you don't keep fussing with it."

He let go of the fabric, sitting up a bit straighter. "I'm feeling up for a challenge today anyway," Kymil said. "Let them all stare at it, it won't trouble me. I can still pull attention with raw charm."

Before Kymil could think too long on his opening lines, a disturbance near Garend Hull drew his eye. The trio had made it just outside the sitting area for the café when a tall man with hunched shoulders attempted to walk past the two guards, his hair and bushy beard one contiguous tangle of dark hair. He wore a long brown leather coat and had seemed to be in a hurry before the trunk-like arms of Hull's protection barred his way.

"Secretary Hull, you have to turn around," the man said, still struggling against the barrier of men.

Mareq stood on his seat and leaned over their table, his eyes squinting. "Captain Tomau?"

The strange man snapped his head around, his eyes wide as they landed on Mareq. Kymil hadn't recognized the man without his hat, but his friend was right. This was the captain who had delivered them to Felona, albeit now with significantly more anxiety lining his face. Not to be outdone, Garend Hull's jaw clenched, and his eyes drifted back and forth between Tomau and the pair at the table.

"How fortunate you happened to be passing this way, First Secretary," Kymil said. "I was just telling my friend here how I would love another opportunity to speak with you. Our last encounter was a bit too muddled by the heightened emotions in the room, but I would guess a man such as yourself likes his conversations more straightforward."

Had all the noise of the café suddenly stopped, Kymil was certain he could've heard Hull's teeth grinding together. The older man spared a withering glance at Tomau before stalking over toward Kymil and Mareq's table, while the captain started shuffling away now that he had been released by the guards.

"No need to hurry off, Captain," Kymil called after him, smiling as the man froze in place. "You seem to know Secretary Hull well. Please, come and join us. The coffee is on me."

Garend walked over to join Kymil and Mareq, his face a practiced, unreadable slate. "I wish I could join you, Mr. Adii, but I'm afraid I only had time in my schedule to pick up an afternoon meal before returning to my work. The affairs of a nation cannot wait for a midday conversation," Garend said, then smiled in a way that proved the man did not do it often. "Not even one as pleasant as this might be."

"Nonsense," Kymil said with a dismissive wave, projecting his voice so that the other diners could not help but turn in their seats to take note of the councilor's arrival. "These are times of peace. What good is the first secretary of defense title if you can't relax a bit when the world is as it should be. You act as if a war is on the horizon."

The older man met his gaze with a dangerous glare, but Kymil turned and waved over a bronze-skinned young woman holding a tray of pastries. Her dark hair was shorter than her sister's, but she shared certain other familial assets with Beloma that had made her unmistakable upon their arrival to the café. When she saw his signal, the woman glided over sporting a sparkling smile.

She arrived at the same time as Tomau, whose shoulders remained hunched as he clasped his hands in front of him and kept flicking his eyes over to Garend.

"I only have the three twin tart turnovers right now," she said, placing one first in front of the seat Garend stood behind, luminescent trails that were only visible to Kymil's eyes drifting off the fork. "But give me one second and I'll return with one for you as well, sir."

"That's all right," Tomau managed to say, even ticking one corner of his mouth up into a nervous smile. "I won't be staying."

"Sit, please," Mareq said. He had maintained a politeness in his tone, but there was no denying the command. Kymil almost shed a tear of pride. "I'd like a chance to catch up."

The captain sat down wordlessly, keeping his eyes cast down and safely away from the older man who sat next to him. Hull scanned the other patrons like a seasoned general assessing a tactical map—most had returned to their meals, but a few were shameless in their gawking. He sighed, then unfolded the cloth napkin before him and laid it in his lap.

"You've twisted my arm," Hull said, still sporting his mirthless grin. "I wouldn't want to let this delicious pastry go to waste. But I truly can't stay long."

Or you simply can't be seen ruffled by a one-armed fancy elf, Kymil thought. *That wouldn't exactly inspire a legacy of unflappability.*

"Of course," Kymil said. "We understand your attention must be pulled all over, but I appreciate this opportunity to speak with you again about the danger posed by Elikar Thymes." Several cups paused at mouths around them, and forks were set aside. These nosey people were Kymil's tribe, and he would give them a show.

Unfortunately, Garend Hull was not interested in a collaborative performance, as the man took a slow, deliberate bite of the citrusy pastry and then scowled. "That matter is closed, Mr. Adii.

It would be best for everyone involved if you could find your way to that conclusion as well.

"Councilor Thymes is an ambitious man who has done great things, not only for Felona, but for all of Kefya. He's expanded our trade agreements to span the entire southern coast of Anera, so much so that it's not uncommon for even our citizens in the Trough to be able to find spices all the way from Ebkarii in their corner markets. And our smithies have certainly benefited from the rich ore we're now importing from Woross."

He paused for a casual sip of coffee, then continued. "Besides that, you had no evidence to support your slander. It's only by Elikar's ability to let matters lie that the lot of you aren't being detained at the moment. You should be grateful for that mercy. If I had been the target of your scheme, I might not have been so lenient."

Kymil laughed. You can promote the soldier from the front lines, but that bluster was always bone deep. "I would think not. You seem like a man who is not to be toyed with, Secretary Hull. I acknowledge that fully, which should tell you that my motives here are not hidden or deceitful. Every charge we discussed in our hearing—the profiteering, the terrorism, the assassination attempt—all of it is true." If he didn't have their attention before, the other diners were buzzing with hushed whispers now.

"As a man who wore this nation's colors in defense of its ideals, and now one who holds a position that directs others who do the same, do you not feel the weight of ensuring those principles are not being sullied? Kefya holds to Teacher Melan's teachings, the inherent value of connecting with others in good faith, no matter how many man-made borders are crossed. I presume you've sworn to uphold these notions as well, and one of your colleagues is currently smearing them under his heel."

Hull took another large bite from his pastry, then crumpled the napkin on his lap and dropped it onto his plate. "Kefyans hold closely to the Twins, Mr. Adii, and Teacher Melan's brother also has teachings we must maintain. Teacher Leros espouses the merit in expanding influence through favorable trade arrangements, but as you are merely a traveling minstrel, I suppose I shouldn't expect you to understand the finer points of negotiations. Needless to say, the goal is to leave the person on the other side of the table more unhappy with the deal than you are."

He leaned forward, placing his elbows on the table. Despite his age, the man's forearms still spoke to a lifetime of swinging a heavy blade. "And I don't need a Liiashan telling me about my own beliefs. Why don't you stick to your typical prattle about Teacher Irasil's charitable outreach? It's almost too pompous to stomach, but at least you would have a better grasp on the tenets."

That screed had been as bastardized an understanding of Teacher Leros's doctrine as Kymil had ever heard, but after hearing that bigoted tag at the end of Hull's speech, he knew there was no point in arguing about how fair dealings were always advocated by the Accountant. Unlike Elikar, who was an opportunist, Garend Hull appeared to be a full believer in the port admiral's claims. An elf stood little chance of swaying his opinion, no matter how charming he might be.

Waves of silent tension spread across the table, though Tomau's leg bouncing underneath and shaking the silverware diminished much of the ominous force. Mareq was still staring at their acquaintance, seemingly unperturbed by the secretary's words. His brow was furrowed, and when he spoke, Kymil knew that his friend's mind had been elsewhere during this short exchange.

"Why are you meeting with a councilor personally, Tomau?" Mareq asked. "As impressive as you make it seem, all you do is captain a merchant vessel."

"Well," Tomau said, "Secretary Hull and I have had dealings in the past, and whenever I make port, I like to touch base with anyone who might have a new contract on offer." The captain laughed with a higher lilt than Kymil was used to hearing from the man. "I can't simply fish coin from the sea, you know?"

"You might want to find a new business partner," Kymil said. "Apparently, the secretary isn't one to reach accords that benefit both sides."

Mareq ignored him, though, shaking his head and adding, "But shouldn't a man like Secretary Hull have people for that? An undersecretary or an aid. And when you approached him on the street, his guards stopped you like you were a stranger, then you said something about him needing to turn back. That doesn't sound like you were hoping to get a new job for your crew."

Tomau opened his mouth to respond but was interrupted when Hull slapped a heavy hand down on the man's shoulder. "The captain and I have met before, and I prefer to discuss my business without any intermediaries. My guard detail and I were not expecting to meet him on the street, though, and they did their protective duty admirably. But I believe I've had enough interrogation for one day, even if the dessert is this remarkable."

Hull stood and said, "Come, Captain. We can discuss your opportunities on my walk back to the Crest." The secretary hefted Tomau up from under the man's shoulder, causing the captain to stagger out of his chair.

"It was good to see you, Mareq," Tomau said, pulling his arm free from Hull's grip and rolling his shoulder. "You too, Kymil. Maybe we can catch up another time?" But the invitation rang hollow as the man hastily fell in behind Hull as the two departed, joined immediately by the cadre of guards.

"I'm sorry," Mareq said, leaning back into his chair with a sigh. "I guess I bungled that up."

Kymil shook his head as his eyes followed Hull and Tomau through the lunchtime crowd. "It was over before you spoke up, my friend. I suspect Garend Hull will stick to Elikar's story longer than even Elikar would."

He reached across the table to pick up the fork he had infused earlier that day. "And I suppose the veil saw no opening to help us out with that encounter. Personally, I was hoping to see the man miss his mouth a few times, but we can always save this for later." Kymil pocketed the utensil, then added, "You never know when an old infusion might come in handy."

Mareq picked up the twin tart turnover in his hand and took a bite. "So, what do we do now?"

"Now," Kymil said. "We eat, and tip this wonderful pastry chef well. And while we do so, we can talk about why we think the captain was acting so cagey. Good instincts on that, by the way. I might just shed the dairy farmer off you yet."

Mareq swallowed, then shrugged. "Cows aren't so different then people. Skittish is skittish, and it usually means something is worth looking into."

CHAPTER 25

— · —

FELONA

Tetamii stood from his crouch, forcing the small group of Clipped Gulls sitting near him on the edge of the rooftop to shift out of his way. They were grouped on the top of a five-story building in the Horns and Planks, one of only a few residential structures in the arts district, though it fit in well with the neighborhood's aesthetics. The limestone bricks that formed its walls had been painted with roiling waves and a radiant sunset that wrapped around all four corners, likely the work of the artists who lived inside. However beautiful the façade was, though, Tetamii had chosen the spot for a more practical purpose: It overlooked the café where that Irasil-damned fatestitcher sat.

Since his meeting with Elikar, Tetamii had taken it upon himself to ensure this bard wouldn't be bending luck away from them. He couldn't spend all this time organizing a perfectly framed assassination, only to have one of his men fumble over an untied shoelace and pour the poison on themselves. Having a hexant on their side was good insurance—and he had invited Habrum to join them for that very reason—but to Tetamii's mind, a personal close eye on the target was the best assurance.

He rubbed at the scar on his back, aching as it did each time he thought of the elf. Tetamii had been on the receiving end of this man's infusions once before—the lightblood could not have made that knife throw unaided—and he wouldn't allow it to happen again.

"Do you need another dose," Garla said, walking up behind him and placing a hand on his shoulder. He looked down at her other hand, where a bundle of brittle gray sticks that smelled of ginger was waiting for him. "My guy isn't always the most thorough with his infusions. They work great, as you heard, but sometimes they don't last as long as you want them to."

Tetamii shook his head. The infused grisha bark had indeed served its purpose—tapping into another foreign Wellspring to spy on a distant conversation—but he was not eager to get back to siphoning air. The veil was much more fluid than he was accustomed to when working with heat, and after his disastrous attempt at controlling earth, he didn't want to risk a sudden tornado whipping through the entertainment district. Creating a funnel of air to carry the sounds of the lunch party to his spot on the rooftop had been challenge enough for one day.

"Their conversation with Hull and Tomau is over anyway," Tetamii said. "And if I'm correct, that nervous fool of a ship captain will have just set them on edge. The bard has to be taken off the board."

Garla frowned. "Didn't we just talk about not spooking them? Otherwise, you let the hidden hand walk for nothing."

"We can't wait around and let the fatestitcher speak with that older woman of theirs," Tetamii said. "She's too intelligent, and if she picks out that Tomau is on Elikar's payroll, they'll go to ground anyway. We need them seen, making a fuss around the city, if anyone is going to believe they orchestrated the poisoning of a councilor."

Tetamii turned to address the four other Gulls sharing the rooftop with them. Each had scrambled to their feet after he did, showing as much deference to him as thieves and murderers could. Tetamii had regained the stature within his guild that he had lost now that Elikar Thymes had chosen to favor him over Magzii. If respect didn't come naturally to these types, they could certainly smell blood in the water.

"Wait here until those two leave," Tetamii said. "Tail them until they're in a secluded part of the city, and then do what you need to do. Make sure it looks like an accident. The draqesh isn't a fighter, but he'll be strong by nature. Don't get cocky around him."

Tetamii cast his gaze down on the bard he had maimed, remembering all the little needle-points of his daggered cloak as they pierced his flesh. "And don't discount the elf, either. I would guess he's better with his blades than any one of you are, and if you give him the opportunity, he'll twist fate against you."

Glancing at Habrum, Tetamii added, "Which is why you'll be joining them. Work your curses, hexant." The skeletal elf maintained his composure, stiff backed with his hands clasped behind him, but Tetamii noticed a slight tremble in the man. He was no combatant, but Tetamii simply needed him to even the odds.

One of the Gulls, a young man with a shaved head and a milky eye that Tetamii supposed had been injured in some street fight as a kid, chuckled. "I think we can handle a one-armed clown and his little hick buddy. I've scrapped with draqeshi three times meaner than that guy and came out on top every time. All you have to know is where to apply the pressure. They might be stronger than us, but their ligaments snap just the same."

Tetamii clenched his jaw, and Garla took a step back, holding her hands up and flashing a disarming smile at the other Gulls. "Might just want to trust his word on this one, guys. I don't think Scorchy makes a habit of talking out of his ass."

There was that nickname again, but strangely, it didn't seem to bother him as much as it had before he found himself in Elikar's good graces. Perhaps the name had come across as diminishing, but now that he had regained his status in the Gulls, Tetamii was less concerned with others adopting an epithet for him that would not be out of place on a dog's collar.

Without another word on his part, the four Gulls nodded, suddenly deciding to heed Garla's warning. These were relatively new recruits and had spent more time in Atusiin's shadow than Tetamii's, and consequently, had likely heard more than their fair share of reductive stories about him in his time away from Felona. But their stony expressions told him all he needed to know—Tetamii had reasserted himself, and while it might take a while to break some old habits of disrespectful behavior, word had already begun to spread.

"We'll get it taken care of," the Gull said. "No need to worry about us. That bard and his pal are gonna learn some parts of the city are a little rough to walk through."

"Just a few knocks to the head, mind you," another said, sensing her partner's overzealousness. "Like Tetamii said, we can't scare them into hiding. Nothing fatal, but maybe we just make things a little hazy for a while."

Tetamii nodded and gave them leave, then watched as the four Gulls leaped down one floor to a balcony on an adjacent building. He remembered the lightblood moving like that across the rooftops of Virdoba, and he flexed the muscles in his back, causing the scar tissue to throb. It didn't ache on its own when he thought of her, not like when he saw the bard or when stress-induced visions of her clouded his mind, but his relationship with the lightblood was more complicated.

She had been just as responsible for his failure, but Tetamii respected the lightblood in a way that he did not the fatestitcher. She had proven herself tenacious, surviving against all odds when she should have died several times over, even refusing to succumb to her own untrained siphoning. Tetamii saw something of himself in her, those same traits reflecting as if in a mirror. The fact that she could demonstrate such independence and strength while also benefiting from the allies that surrounded her was a lesson that had put him back in his rightful position within the Gulls.

Tetamii smirked as he watched his team scamper down to the street, while Habrum meekly took the stairs after one quick glance over the edge. If Tetamii continued on this path that the lightblood had taught him, perhaps he would end up even higher up the chain.

"Was it the best idea to trust those mouth breathers with something like that?" Garla asked, returning to his side. "They aren't known for subtlety when it comes to cracking skulls; they might just split them open. If it's so important that we stop them from talking to the rest of their crew without leaving them oozing their brains out onto the street, maybe we should've gone to handle it."

"Delegation is important," Tetamii responded, "and I believe they know what's coming to them should they fail. Besides, you and I have another encounter to make, and those brutes wouldn't be allowed within fifty feet of the secretary."

Garla whistled softly, running her hand back through her flaxen hair. "If you're going to keep introducing me to all these fancy types, please let me know ahead of time so I can wear a pair of boots that hasn't stepped in dog shit twice this week."

***

Tetamii and Garla were already waiting for Garend Hull and Captain Tomau as they reached the top of the Crest. It was astounding the time one could make through the city if one didn't need to push through crowded streets. Rooftops were convenient thoroughfares for those brave enough to take advantage of them.

When the trio of guards spotted Tetamii and Garla waiting expectantly near a row of hedges on council grounds, they each reached for the hilts of their swords, then moved into a protective chevron around Hull. To the secretary's credit, he appeared unfazed by their presence, though there was every possibility the man didn't know who Tetamii was—as far as he knew, Elikar preferred to keep his partners separated. However, Tomau's reaction contrasted the councilor's steely demeanor. Tetamii was surprised the captain's pants didn't drop to his ankles as much as his knees were quaking.

"There will be no need for all that," Tetamii said. "We're all friends of the port admiral here, after all. Councilor Thymes wouldn't want his colleagues coming to blows when a chat would suffice."

Garend Hull eyed the two of them, his gaze lingering longer on Garla as he took in her clean-as-could-be-expected attire for a woman who cared more about having a laugh than presenting a perfect version of herself. Tetamii always dressed well, his white tailcoat cleaned and repaired after its eventful journey along Anera's western coast, and he would not seem out of place as a man who had dealings with the Council. He hoped that would balance out his friend's more casual clothing—killing the guards would only sour the proceedings.

"Who are you?" Hull asked. He cast a sideways glance at Tomau, whose association with Elikar was not meant to be widely known. The fact that Tetamii possessed that knowledge should have bought him some credibility. "And how do you know our mutual friend?"

"Well, I have to say I've only recently become acquainted with the port admiral," Tetamii said, "though I believe if you ask him about me, you'll hear nothing but glowing accolades. However, the captain and I go way back, don't we, Tomau?" The captain stared at the ground as if he hoped it would swallow him up.

"We traveled together recently," Tetamii continued, "and while I appreciated the complimentary voyage home, I did find the accommodations a bit restrictive for my liking."

Hull's eyes widened almost imperceptibly before he returned to his stone-faced affect. Of course he knew about the failed Clipped Gull Tomau had brought to Felona; he was one of Elikar's closest allies on the Council. Now that identities had been established, Hull placed a hand on one guard's shoulder.

"At ease," he said. "I know who this man is. You three may report back to your stations." The guards shared quizzical glances with each other before releasing their hilts, then gathered as a unit and began to walk toward the council building. Much like Tetamii's Gulls, it seemed these men knew when it was best to listen to orders.

"You are putting us in a perilous situation, young man," Hull said. "Affiliation with Councilor Thymes or no, it wouldn't do for people to see me speaking with a pair of thieves and assassins. Not only do I have a reputation to uphold, but it might lead to questions that would eventually find their way back to Elikar. Nobody wants that."

"Now hold on," Garla said. "We're not dripping in blood and carrying slashed purses by the armful up here. I might not be dressed as fancy as Tetamii here, but I like to think if I caught someone's eye, their first thought wouldn't be 'murderer.'" She looked down at her simple cotton shirt and pants, then added, "Dockworker, maybe, but I can work with that."

"It's not us you should be concerned about revealing your involvement anyway, Secretary Hull," Tetamii said. "I had the misfortune of witnessing the captain's performance at your lunch meeting. He might as well have signed a confession right there at the table."

"I didn't say anything," Tomau stammered.

"You said enough."

Tetamii stepped forward, thinning the veil around the captain's face, and allowing heat from the Wellspring to leak out in waves. The man was already sweating from the confrontation, but there was so much more Tetamii had in mind. He was not to blame for Tetamii's imprisonment, but it was his vessel, and he could have at least provided a bedroll in his brig. Instead, Tetamii had been forced to kneel in place for weeks, his legs cramping and contorting for any semblance of relief in the moments he had not been drugged out of his senses. In contrast to that torture, at least Tetamii's flames would be quick.

Hull stepped to the side, clearly not inclined to involve himself in an effort to protect a replaceable asset. Ship captains could be bought, and for relatively cheap—there was no reason Elikar would need to stick with a buffoon like Tomau.

A pinprick hole tore in the veil, and a small gout of flame licked up the side of Tomau's face. The man's skin bubbled and split instantly as he screamed and staggered back into a hedge. The odor of burned flesh filled the space, and he saw the look of disgust on Hull's face before the secretary was able to subdue it to a mere crinkled nose.

"Wait," the captain shouted, gingerly holding his sleeve to his burned face as he stood. "You're right, I should've had a better story ready to go if someone asked why I was trying to talk to the secretary, but I was in a rush." He paused, pulling his arm away, but stopped as a string of raw flesh began to follow it. Tomau inhaled sharply through his teeth, then continued. "I didn't have time to think, so I just ran. I needed to make sure he wasn't near the Bindweed Conservatory this afternoon. Councilor Thymes told me to hurry."

This caught Tetamii off guard. He had presumed Tomau was simply a hired convenience by Elikar, but was the councilor actually meeting with the captain personally?

"Explain," Tetamii said, not offering any relief from the suffocating heat he had created around the captain.

"Apparently," Hull said, "your boss just sent a squad to the house where Councilor Thymes's accusers are staying. Elikar sent the captain to turn me back around to the Crest in case things became messy."

Tetamii's ears began to ring, and his vision tunneled. "Why would the Clipped Gulls send scouts to that house? This was supposed to remain quiet."

"Not scouts," Hull said. "A hit squad, if I'm not mistaken. Something about wanting to get back into Elikar's good graces, wasn't it?" Tomau nodded, and the secretary added, "It would seem Elikar wanted to ensure he didn't lose an ally on the Council if the Gulls were not as precise as Magzii intended, so he asked the captain to warn me away."

Magzii. The World Shroud trembled at Tetamii's fury, and Tomau gasped as the heat suddenly intensified. He knew the Clipped Gulls' leader was a petty, proud man, but to blatantly disregard Tetamii's plan—one that had been approved by Elikar, no less—was an unforeseen wrinkle. Tetamii had lived with the muttered comments, the sneers and jibes, since returning to Felona, all encouraged by Magzii as recompense for the worst performance in his career. But he had reestablished himself within his crew, returned to his place at his mentor's side, driven by what he now knew was a misguided need to impress his ersatz father.

Yet, when the inverse occurred, when Magzii was made to look the fool and brought down in stature, the man hesitated less than a week before he allowed his jealousy to consume him. He wanted to reduce Tetamii again, professional consequences be damned. Perhaps Tetamii should have recognized the lengths to which Magzii would go to preserve his place atop his empire, but a part of him had always been blinded by the memory of the man who offered him a warm, dry place to sleep and a guiding hand as he grew.

All those years ago, Magzii had offered Tetamii a choice between two men—himself, and Ilphas Trisarin. Tetamii had fought against his inkling that Ilphas was a legitimately good man; the loss of his parents thanks to wealthy men like him had still been too fresh, and Magzii's whispered words of encouragement had been too persuasive. He had chosen wrong as a child, and Magzii had created the man Tetamii was today. That man was now more than capable of delivering his undoing.

Tomau fell to his knees, wheezing through a parched airway until Tetamii released his grasp on the veil. "I appreciate the information," Tetamii said. "Your loose lips just spared your life, but I would advise staying clear of any further involvement in this world, Captain. It doesn't suit you."

The captain nodded, then fell back onto his rear, gulping down air as quickly as he could. Tetamii stalked past Tomau and the secretary, and Garla had to run to catch up with him as he made his way back to the winding path leading down to the Trough.

"Where are we going now?" she asked.

"To stop a spiteful idiot from ruining everything I've been working to achieve," Tetamii replied. "I've followed orders blindly for too long, been manipulated into seeking his approval. But I no longer have any need of Vulmar Magzii, and neither does this city."

Chapter 26

Felona

"Do you really think Tomau would sell us out like that?" Mareq asked, though when he glanced up at Kymil, he could tell his question had not been heard.

The elf had been barely listening on their walk from the café back toward Niri's home in the Bindweed Conservatory, offering only half-hearted responses to Mareq's inquiries and not slinging his typical pleasantries to any attractive person who walked by. Normally, Mareq wouldn't mind. Kymil was his friend, but sometimes he wondered if the number of words he had heard spoken in his life before meeting the bard had already been doubled.

Now, though, was not the time for quiet introspection. If Captain Tomau was in league with Elikar Thymes, then maybe Kymil was right; maybe they would all need to find another place to stay. He knew where they were hoping to find rooms when they docked in Felona, and they would all be in danger if the councilor thought it would save him time to simply eliminate the threat.

"Kymil!" Mareq shouted.

"Hmm?" he responded, blinking his eyes rapidly a few times as the bard appeared to come back to reality.

"If you're so concerned about danger," Mareq said, "it might be a good idea to wait until we're behind a locked door or two before you start daydreaming."

Kymil smiled. "Never discount the power of fantasy, my friend. It's how one discovers the most interesting things about oneself. But in this instance, I'm afraid my aloofness was far more practical." From his other side, Mareq saw Kymil release the edge of his cloak, and suddenly his distraction made sense.

"You were infusing your cloak," Mareq said. "You don't always have that ready to go?"

"It never hurts to top things off," Kymil said with a shrug. "Here's your book back, by the way."

Mareq gasped, then snatched his leather strap-wrapped journal back. Originally, he had used it as a ledger for his mercantile work in Alaboq, but since he had left that life behind and begun traveling with Annika's group, he had transitioned its purpose to more of a travelogue. He had described his constant battle with nausea at sea, but also the awe-inspiring beauty of days spent surrounded entirely by an expanse of blue.

Then, it had turned to his experiences in Felona and his feelings of inadequacy in such a massive city. Sure, Alaboq had also been a national capital, but he had lived as a merchant, which had been as humble an existence as his farm life in Brey. Now that he traveled in rich and connected circles, though, the world was opening up to him in ways that were both exciting and terrifying. No one was meant to read those thoughts, though, particularly not someone as loquacious as Kymil.

"How did you get this?" Mareq asked. He could feel his face flushing, equal parts embarrassment and anger.

"Calm yourself," Kymil replied. "I didn't sneak a peek. Give me a little more credit than that. A bard as well traveled as I doesn't need to read your words to understand your every emotion."

Mareq huffed, then stuffed the book back in his satchel. The sting of betrayal was still present, but he did believe him.

"But to answer your question," Kymil continued, "I picked it out of your bag before we left the café. You don't have a weapon on you—nor am I aware of you knowing how to wield one, anyway—so I thought, at least the heft of that tome could cause a little damage if I gave you some help."

Mareq glanced down at the journal in his bag. It didn't appear any different, but he had seen just how powerful Kymil's infusions could be, and while he hoped it wouldn't come to it, Mareq guessed that now his book might prove effective in a pinch.

"Don't forget and use it for something mundane, like writing down your favorite parts of our day together," Kymil said. "It would be the most comprehensive and descriptive list you ever compose, but it would be a shame if you got shivved right after when the book could've stopped the blade."

His infusions prepared, Kymil carried on like this as their walk continued, his chatter a welcome distraction from the anxiety his hypothetical scenario had induced. Mareq had known joining up with this band would come with its share of risks, but he had also seen no better way to spur forward his stalled wanderlust. Had he anticipated the possibility of assassination as a consequence, his calculus might have shifted.

It wasn't until the pair had turned off the coastal avenue and began to make their way into the wooded seclusion of the Bindweed Conservatory that Kymil's demeanor shifted once again. The elf kept the conversation flowing, but his easy smile had dropped from his face, and his eyes scanned the copses to either side of the cobblestone path.

"And thus ended my scandalous night out with the wealthiest lord and lady in Draemoor, bruised haunches and all," Kymil said, his voice devoid of mirth in a way that was so antithetical to his character that it set Mareq even more on edge.

"Now, on to other matters," he continued. "Take your journal from your bag as casually as you can, like you want to read me a sonnet or two."

"Why?" Mareq asked. He traced his gaze through the tree line but could see no reason Kymil had his hackles raised. "Do you see one of those sea cats? Annika said they wouldn't bother us."

"No, but we've picked up a tail of a different kind, and I don't think they'll be dissuaded by a fresh fish or two."

Underbrush rustled off the path in front of them, and a man with a shaved head stepped out of the trees. He wore simple clothing, a basic tunic, and a pair of linen pants with a cloth band wrapped around his head. The outfit was already out of place in an area of the city with this much concentrated wealth, but what stood out more were the scuffs and patches apparent throughout. This was a man who was accustomed to physical labor, and judging by his milky eye and cruel grin, it wasn't a harmless line of work.

"Good afternoon, fellas," he said. "Out for a little stroll? It looked like you might enjoy some company."

As he spoke, four more figures emerged from the trees. One, an elven woman with raven-black hair cut short to frame her face, joined him to block their path. Two other men, one human and one at least partially elven, stepped out to their rear. None wore clothing that spoke to a life of luxury, and they each carried a medium-length dagger at their sides.

The last individual was an elf dressed more presentably, though without the flourish that would be expected in the Bindweed Conservatory. He had sunken cheeks and a gaze that sent a chill down Mareq's spine, as if the man exuded a malevolent energy. Unlike the other four, this man held back. Judging by his lanky frame, he was not the type to involve himself in physical scrapes.

"Normally, I'm not one to turn away a group of strapping individuals looking for companionship," Kymil said, "but I think today I'll have to decline. My friend here isn't as worldly as me, and I wouldn't want to make him uncomfortable."

The four brutes laughed, and the bald man spoke again. "Well, how about I make you a deal then? You can break off with my three friends, and I'll carry on with yours. That way no one is overwhelmed, and we all get to have a little fun."

Mareq pulled his bag off his shoulder and dropped it on to the ground, but not before pulling his leather book free. He had spent enough time today steeped in anxious anticipation, and he saw no reason to prolong the inevitable. "Can we just stop with all the posturing and weird sexual energy? You're obviously here to try to kill us, so let's speak plainly."

Kymil shot him a look that was as much surprised as impressed, pursing his lips as a gesture for him to continue.

"As much as I'm against the prospect of you four attacking us, I'd still like to avoid anyone getting hurt if it can be avoided." Mareq pointed a thumb toward Kymil, then added, "I've heard from multiple sources that this man fought and killed a dragon in Qedrad. Do you really like your chances against a warrior like that?"

"Again, it wasn't a dragon," Kymil muttered, but then added louder, "It was indeed a bloody and ferocious encounter, yet here I stand, having vanquished that horrible reptilian foe."

The elven woman looked askance at the man with the shaved head, who shrugged. "That fairytale story must've been before someone chopped off one of your arms," he said. "Maybe if you still had both, I'd be pissing my pants right about now. But maimed like that? Nah, I like our chances."

A light tinkling of metal against stone drew Mareq's attention to his right, where he saw a series of thin blades had been released from inside the tail of Kymil's cloak. The bard looked down at him and winked. "Stay close to me and keep your head down. With a little luck, we just might make it out of this."

Mareq did as he was instructed, shifting to put his back to Kymil's and holding his book before him in both hands. Now facing the two men in the back, he saw they had both drawn their daggers and were approaching at a dash.

Mareq hunched his shoulders and ducked his head behind the book, then shouted, "Behind you!"

But his warning was unnecessary, as Kymil had already flicked his cloak out over Mareq's head and sent three of the thin blades on the hem into the half-elf's face, who had the misfortune of being faster than his human counterpart. The puncture wounds were not lethal—all having pierced into areas below the nose—but the man would never be able to get by on his elven good looks again without the aid of an herb nurse or witch.

A guttural choking sound came from behind him, and Mareq turned to see that Kymil had planted a boot square in the bald man's chest as he had twisted to whip his cloak at the threat to Mareq. The man's filmy eye bulged as he staggered backward, but Mareq could not focus on that side of the scuffle for long as the other human man was now bearing down on him.

Mareq swung the book at his assailant's hand, knocking the blade free and sending it spinning out into the trees. But before he could truly appreciate Kymil's assistance with that lucky blow, the man pulled a smaller knife from within his waistband and slashed down toward him. Mareq reared back, managing to get the book in the weapon's path so that it sliced through the leather strap rather than into his flesh. There was a loud snap as the band was severed, and the book tumbled toward the ground before it halted—the clasp having slipped itself over Mareq's forefinger knuckle.

The metal was wedged painfully over his thick draqesh finger, but it had prevented him from being disarmed, and while the attacker was momentarily stunned by the strange happenstance, Mareq swung the tome backhanded like a flail. The dense leather slammed into the man's temple, and he dropped to the cobblestone path, unmoving.

Kymil still lost an arm with power like this?

The thought was enough to make Mareq fear the reputation of that scorcher even more. Tetamii had fared well against a fatestitcher, a lightblood, and a well-trained soldier—even while drugged by one of Mrs. Luviire's concoctions. No matter how impressed Mareq was with the concussive blow he had just dealt, he held no grand illusions of success against a foe like that.

Maybe their luck was not simply a product of Kymil's infusions, and this ambush was unrelated to the Clipped Gulls. It was possible; a group of toughs could've followed a pair of well-dressed and unprotected individuals into a secluded part of Felona's wealthiest district. Mareq and Kymil didn't give off a threatening presence, and especially with his friend's amputation, the thugs might have believed they found an easy mark. But Mareq's optimism was cast aside as the half-elf with the punctured face steadied himself, pulling blood-matted dark hair away from his mouth to tie it behind his head and revealing a set of stubbed ears.

"Frosted scat," Mareq cursed under his breath, spooling the leather strap until he could grasp his journal by the spine. The scorcher was involved, but at least he wasn't here.

Where is he, then?

***

The half-elf spat blood onto the rocky path, his three facial wounds oozing into his mouth. "I'll skin your face off for that, pretty boy," he said, his eyes burning with hatred as he stalked toward Kymil, this time with much more caution.

"Jealousy is an ugly trait," Kymil said as he kept his two attackers at bay with cracking whips of his cloak. Both the bald man and the woman were covered in raking lacerations from the thin blades. "Then again, so is a few holes in your face, so maybe that's your new look. Everyone needs an aesthetic."

With a rage-filled cry, the half-elf leaped toward Kymil, dagger held high in his left hand while his right stretched out to catch any cloak strike that might come his way. However, with an impressive reaction time, Mareq threw his book at the man, and Kymil desperately hoped his friend had not already expended the infusion it contained. He held his breath, watching in horror as the throw arced higher into the air.

But just as Kymil was steeling himself to feel the blade bite into his flesh, he watched the flapping leather band snag the man's left wrist. The book's momentum suddenly halted and its trajectory plummeted, pulling the dagger down with it and sinking the blade into the man's right hip.

The half-elf screamed and began to delicately pull the blade out. It was likely the man was out of the fight, but Mareq appeared uninterested in taking that chance. He rushed forward, then swung his mallet-like fist into the man's already bloodied face, knocking him out cold like his partner.

Mareq shook his hand and glanced at Kymil, an interesting blend of fear and thrill on his face. "Punching hurts," he said.

Kymil chuckled and planted another kick into the bald man's sternum, this time sending him back onto his rear. "Use your boots, they have more padding. You might need to aim for the shins, though."

However, despite the tide of the battle shifting in their direction, Kymil's mirth quickly began to fade as he noticed the trailing luminescent wisps drifting off Mareq's journal being ripped to shreds. The half-elf's gloved hand rested on the leather binding, and suddenly Kymil could answer the mystery of the gaunt elven onlooker—a hexant, the one who had supplied this crew with cursed infusions to counteract his own. He scanned around, taking note of the gloves on each of his remaining assailants' hands.

"Oh, that's just not fair," Kymil shouted to the hexant, who was looking rather pleased with himself now that his curses had been noticed. "When I bend luck people find it endearing, but this is just annoying."

As the bald Gull gasped for breath, Kymil flicked his cloak down toward the legs of the woman who was charging toward him. A few blades sunk into her calf, and he yanked back, so that she plummeted to the ground to join her wheezing companion. She kept her wits about her, though, and reached down to grasp the cloak that still entangled her. More glowing trails were torn asunder as his infused cloak began to drain of its infusion. This hexant was skilled, but not enough to instantly reduce his infused garment to mundane fabric.

Still, he thought, *it might be best not to rely on chance to finish this up.*

With a grace that would be more at home on stage than in a street brawl, Kymil leaped between his two grounded opponents, catching the man in the face with his knee, then spinning around so that he was kneeling behind the woman trying to dislodge the knives from her leg.

Kymil wrapped his arm around her neck so that it wrested in the crook of his elbow and held tight. She started kicking at the ground, her boot heels scraping futilely against the cobblestones. Kymil tutted, scanning his eyes across her three unconscious allies, then leaned toward her ear and said, "Before you go to sleep, would any of you happened to be nicknamed 'the Dragon,' or something to that effect?"

The woman's face was scarlet as the saliva frothed out of her lips. Kymil continued, "Now that my friend brought that story up again, I quite like the sound of 'Kymil the Dragon Slayer.'"

She writhed, refusing to succumb to unconsciousness, and Kymil watched as the hexant began to slink off down the cobblestone path. He was no combatant and could see where this was heading. But Kymil couldn't have him reappear unannounced at a later date to ruin his day.

"Mareq," Kymil said over the woman's resounding heel strikes on the stone, "reach in my pocket." His friend hustled over and pulled out the fork from the café, then looked back at him, puzzled. Kymil gestured toward the escaping elf with his chin. "Give it a good toss, if you wouldn't mind."

Mareq's mouth opened as if to voice his confusion, but he must've thought better of it, because instead he flung the utensil down the street. It spun through the air, spinning past the elf's head before landing, wedged between two stones, tines up and at just the right angle to pierce the hexant's sole as he frantically ran away. The man howled, dropping to the path to cradle his injured foot.

After a few more moments of struggle, the woman's head fell forward, and Kymil released her gently onto the ground. "No?" Kymil said with a sigh. "Oh well. I suppose I'll have to be content with 'Slayer of Hearts.'"

Mareq jogged over to subdue the hexant, careful to step around the myriad splashes of blood that now stained the trail. "You were right," he shouted back to Kymil. "This was the Clipped Gulls coming after us. Do you think the scorcher will be next?"

Suddenly, the playfulness dropped from Kymil's face, his countenance turning dark as he stood. "I think there's no reason he might not already be on his way somewhere else. Help me tie these five up, then I need you to run to Niri's place and warn the rest of them. On my way back up the path, I'll flag down a city guard to haul them off."

The hexant groaned as Mareq hefted the thin man over his shoulder and walked him back to Kymil. "Where are you going to go?" Mareq asked.

"If Tetamii wasn't with this group, it might be he wanted to go after our heavy hitters himself. I need to go warn Ubadrii."

Mareq felt his chest tighten. "You can't stop him on your own."

Kymil smiled wanly. "Never underestimate the laws of storytelling. He took my arm in the first act of this tale, and now he owes me something in return. I can't allow this cliffhanger to dangle without resolution. What type of ending would that be?"

CHAPTER 27

—·—

FELONA

Tetamii looked out from the tree line at the rear of the estate, where the Gulls squad he was chasing had done a sloppy job of breaking and entering. A door was left hanging slightly ajar, the locking mechanism and handle smashed. One of the first skills taught to any initiate of the Clipped Gulls was how to pick a lock deftly and quickly, and this was often practiced on more advanced tumblers than one would find on a garden door. The fact that the team had opted for a more haphazard choice meant one thing: there was no intention of leaving any witnesses.

Garla had been sent around to scope the opposite wing of the manor home, ostensibly to cover the exits if Tetamii's sudden appearance led them to flee through the house. In reality, though, he simply wanted her out of the way. Tetamii had a sense of how this confrontation would play out, and he would not have his abilities constrained out of concern for harming her.

On his side of the house, there were no groves of twin tart trees, but instead an intricate array of flowering bushes. Any other time, Tetamii would have preferred more cover, but as he left the obscurity of the Bindweed copse, he felt no fear of discovery crossing the lawn. His thoughts were only of the stab of betrayal, and how he could stop the bleeding. If Magzii intended his kill

301

squad to be a wound on Tetamii's status, they would have to be cauterized.

Without knowing how long the other Clipped Gulls had been on site, Tetamii could not waste time being careful, so when he reached the cracked door, he flung it open wide. There was a loud crack as it slammed into the building's façade, and he was surprised to find that the study inside was filled with a crew of five Gulls milling about, turning out drawers, and leafing through books. Tetamii recognized a few faces, people who had run minor jobs with him before he had gone on to work alone, but there was only one name he knew: Atusiin, standing toward the back of the room where he leaned against a bookshelf.

The scrappy man was startled at Tetamii's appearance, but he quickly adopted his typical attitude, settling deeper into his lean as one corner of his mouth turned up. "It's a little unprofessional to barge in on someone else's job, Tetamii. Did you forget how to work as a group when you were chained up on a ship by an old woman and her traveling entertainer, or was it just your competence that fled your mind?"

The other four Gulls snickered, though it was apparent the reaction was more of a tension relief than actual amusement. Tetamii was no longer viewed as an inept failure with a reputation that had haunted his return home. His status was restored, his power no longer in question, and they knew he was not one to be angered. It was unfortunate for them that Magzii had already lit this fuse, and Atusiin was there to serve as an accelerant.

Tetamii pulled his bastard sword from the black leather sheath slung across his back, already thinning the veil along the length of the blade so the metal glowed a molten gold. Without taking his eyes off Atusiin, whose eyes reflected that bright light of Tetamii's rage, he addressed the others.

"Some of you I have worked with in the past, and some I have not. I understand what it means to follow the orders of the man above you, so I will allow the four of you one chance to leave now." The Gulls shared a look, their hands gripping the hilts of their weapons as they wordlessly attempted to decide the best course of action.

"Atusiin speaks for Magzii," Tetamii continued, "and Magzii no longer speaks in the interests of our family. He was once a great leader, even fatherly, in his own way. But he's grown into a bitter, jealous old man, who would spite an opportunity for our betterment only to see me put back where he feels I belong.

"I don't exist in the spaces below Magzii anymore," Tetamii continued. "I have surpassed him, not only in skill, but in temperament. The actions I take and the deals I strike are to enhance the Clipped Gulls' standing in this city. Elikar Thymes has already sided with me over Magzii, the power dynamic has shifted, and rather than bow out gracefully, Magzii felt it necessary to undermine our plan.

"So, go," Tetamii concluded, tilting his head over one shoulder toward the door. "Live and continue to work alongside your family as we reach new heights in the world. Or stay and burn. The choice is yours."

No one in the room moved, though a few of the Gulls could not seem to peel their eyes off the heated sword, until Atusiin began clapping slowly.

"Bravo, Tetamii," he said. "You clearly took advantage of all that time at sea with the bard. Did he also take the time to teach you about stage makeup and pretty costuming?"

Tetamii clenched his jaw until it ached. Atusiin was always an arrogant ass, but he was never a complete fool. When Tetamii's station had been diminished, he could understand Atusiin's sense of relative safety under Magzii's wing, but the man had no Wellspring connection of his own. He would know that when confronted by a scorcher intent on ending his existence, groveling would be the smartest play.

"That truly was quite the performance," Atusiin said, snapping the book he was holding closed, "but I've never really been much for fiction."

"What are you saying?" Tetamii asked. "You aren't here at Magzii's behest?"

Atusiin tutted. "Oh no, Magzii sent us here, you're right about that. But the idea that you're suddenly Thymes's right hand man?" The man laughed as he tossed the book onto the shelf behind him. "From what I hear, the councilor liked your idea, but a gutter rat is still a gutter rat. You belong in the dirt with us, no matter how much you clean yourself up.

"You were never going to be the new tactician, Scorchy," Atusiin continued. "You're the fall guy."

Tetamii's mind reeled, the mental chest that had once so diligently contained his emotions now overturned, its contents spilling out into a chaotic jumble. All the bitterness and jealousy, the fury and fear that had dominated his childhood following initiation into the Gulls intermingled with the security and sense of family he had fallen into throughout those years. The purpose and pride he had found in Magzii's eyes was now stained by mockery and shame.

He even felt his fondness for Garla surface amid the emotional maelstrom, her steadfastness during this tumultuous time the only positive sensation left unmarred by this internal storm. She had been his stalwart supporter since she had broken him out of Tomau's ship, and had been a steadying presence since his return to Felona.

She was not here now.

Without another thought, Tetamii tore open the World Shroud around him, paying no mind to any potential repercussions. Atusiin and the others had earned what was coming to them. An intense knot wrenched into the base of his skull with the sudden siphoning of immense power, so forceful that it took Tetamii's breath away, but that was probably for the best. Inhaling was not the wisest option when standing in the middle of a conflagration.

Dozens of jagged orange lines split the air before flames erupted from behind and below the four Gulls to the sides of the room, burning so hot that after the initial flash, little more than husks remained to fall forward onto the carpet. The bookshelves caught fire, red-yellow tendrils licking up the wood toward the ceiling as smoke began to fill the space. A dark, billowing plume drifted across the room, leaving Tetamii just enough time to see horror fill Atusiin's eyes before he was obscured.

Tetamii waited. He knew the scoundrel well enough to know he wouldn't flee. Atusiin wasn't a coward, and despite the obvious odds of defeat, the tiniest chance of success would force his hand. Tetamii trained his ears, listening for any creaking floorboard over the crackling inferno that would announce Atusiin's approach. But another familiar sound came first, the slight whistle of spinning steel flying toward him.

Not again.

Tetamii batted the whirled dagger aside with his bastard sword, then created a pocket in the veil in the direction from which it had been thrown. Building pressure within the veil bubble rose as Tetamii siphoned more and more heat into it, before he allowed it rupture, blowing a hole in the back wall of the room and sending splintered pieces of wood and flaming books asunder. More importantly, though, the explosion flung Atusiin through the air toward him.

Atusiin landed with a thud on his shoulder but tucked and rolled back into the obscuring smoke. Without a moment's hesitation, two more daggers darted through the air toward Tetamii, one blade managing to slice through his upper arm while he was able to twist away from the other. Blood began to trickle down his coat sleeve, somehow cooling against the ambient heat in the room.

"That was a lot of fire, Scorchy," Atusiin jeered. "I bet that took a lot out of you. How many more of my knives do you think you can dodge before I nick something important?" His voice was moving through the dark haze. He had learned his lesson and he wouldn't stay put for another explosion.

However, he was wrong about one thing: Tetamii was nowhere close to being spent. While the rapid siphoning of power had been intense and created an immense pressure at the base of his skull, he had unleashed far more flames than this before. Still, Atusiin was a skilled assassin, and he was right to think that Tetamii couldn't avoid his blades forever. It was best not to leave his opponent with the advantage of stealth. Striking from the shadows, Atusiin was deadly, but exposed, he would just be more kindling.

Tetamii created another veil bubble and let it rupture, blowing out a portion of the exterior wall. Billows of smoke were pulled out of the new opening in a rush, clearing the room and leaving him with greater visibility. A quick scan of the room revealed no sight of Atusiin, but quick footsteps from behind him announced the man's presence. Tetamii tried to twist around in time to impale him with his blade, but Atusiin had always been the faster of the two.

Atusiin arced through the air, a dagger in each hand ready to drive down into Tetamii's chest from behind. Fortunately, Tetamii had been able to turn just enough to put out an elbow between them, creating space so that when Atusiin brought his blades in, they instead punctured either side of his left shoulder joint. Searing pain racked Tetamii's body as steel sliced through muscle and sinew, and he felt his arm go lax. Atusiin seethed as he glared at him, spittle frothing at the man's mouth.

"This has been a long time coming, Tet," he said, ripping a blade free and sending more of Tetamii's blood out onto the wooden floor below. "And there won't be any pretty boy elves to swoop in and save you from me this time."

Flashes of Ilphas pierced through the agonizing pain gripping his mind. Not only the moment he had stepped in to stop Tetamii's brawl with Atusiin, but also the forever-ingrained association of Ilphas and a dagger dripping with blood. Tetamii screamed, tearing a hole in the World Shroud that sent a lance of flame up from the floor and across Atusiin's back. The man gasped, his own scream strangled in his throat as he collapsed, letting his knife clatter to the ground next to him.

Atusiin was scorched across his back, with raw, bubbling flesh exposed from his scalp down to his legs. His arms and legs spasmed, as he appeared to be trying desperately to fight off the shock of the burns. He managed to get an arm under him, but after a moment of straining, realized he couldn't muster the strength to flip himself over and collapsed back onto his face.

"Let me help you with that," Tetamii said, before driving a boot into the man's ribs with such force that Atusiin was lifted off the ground, flipping over to land on his back. He screamed in agony as his ruined skin scraped against the wood.

Despite what must have been immense pain, Atusiin managed a laugh that collapsed into a string of hacking coughs. "Killing me won't make you the favorite again, Scorchy," he wheezed. "Daddy doesn't love you anymore."

A high-pitched ringing filled Tetamii's ears as his adrenaline spiked. He'd had his choice of father figures once and had chosen poorly. Perhaps Magzii had loved him, in his own way, and Tetamii might have even felt the same. But that bond had been broken, shattered like the illusion that was Magzii's character.

The family that man had formed around him had been built on a rotted foundation, and Tetamii realized now there would be no salvaging it. They clung to their leader too tightly to see the fraud he either always was or had become. The Clipped Gulls had to end for Magzii to truly end as well.

Atusiin tried to say something more, but Tetamii silenced him with a boot across his windpipe. The man's mouth flopped open as he wheezed with desperation, and Tetamii pulled taut the membrane separating his Wellspring from the world. A thin, jagged crack of yellow-orange seared open through the air inside Atusiin's mouth before a spout of raging flames consumed his head.

Tetamii leaned back, shielding his face with an elbow, and then stepped off the man's remains. He walked forward, pulling the remaining knife from his shoulder and moving back toward the blown open entrance into an interior hallway. Magzii would be dealt with, but first, Elikar would as well. The people in this house would not be used as scapegoats to further enrich the bastard who planned to sell him out—Tetamii would remove them from the board before he gave him the chance. Thymes was yet another man above Tetamii's station who thought he could manipulate him, and Tetamii was becoming adept at snuffing them out.

Chapter 28

Felona

The explosion rocked the house down to the foundation, the walls creaking in protest as something detonated in a distant wing of the estate. Annika jumped to her feet, scattering the documents she had been reading across the table in the center of the sitting room. She knew Niri and Regi were in the opposite wing, and would have had to cross through this common area to reach the source of that sound. Additionally, as far as Annika knew, there was no one tending Niri's garden this day.

He's here, Annika thought, immediately jumping to the possibility that had been scratching at the back of her mind since the scorcher escaped Tomau's ship.

She had imagined the attack countless times, his lances of fire striking out at them from the sky or great, cleaving swings of his massive blade dismembering them one by one. Knowing he was out in Felona and free since their arrival had been a constant source of anxiety, but as each day had passed, she had felt the knot in her stomach loosen. If he were going to kill them, she remembered thinking, why would he bother waiting?

Clearly, I shouldn't apply logic to the mind of a murderer.

Annika knew she had precious few seconds before that psychopath burned a path through the house to her, and she wouldn't desert Niri and Regi—given the size of her estate, it was possible

Niri might not have felt the immensity of the explosion. But Annika also wouldn't traverse the house unarmed. If she was going to die today, it wouldn't be without making the scorcher work for it.

She hurried through the foyer, past the section where they had been caged in between Niri's iron portcullises, banishing any thought of capturing Tetamii within. He didn't need physical access to her to roast her alive, and he would have himself out of the trap in seconds. But another element from that day could save her if luck were on her side. As she reached the end of the hallway by the front door, she opened Regi's wooden locker and pulled out his crossbow. She hadn't seen Kymil infuse the butler's weapon, but the bard did have trouble sitting still; perhaps he had taken the liberty one day out of sheer boredom.

Annika cranked a bolt into place, then picked up a handful more and turned back toward the sitting room. But before she could take more than a few steps, she was nearly knocked over as the front door was flung open. Mareq skidded to a halt with wide eyes as he saw what he had done, then he placed a steadying hand on her elbow. Despite his heritage, his strength was always a surprise.

"I'm sorry, Annika," Mareq said, his voice frantic as he glanced past her. "But Kymil thinks we might not be safe here. We need to get everyone out . . ." He paused as his gaze fell to the crossbow in her hands.

"The Gulls are already here," he said, suddenly stone faced.

"One is, at least," Annika replied, then pointed toward the opposite end of the estate. "I need you to run, find Niri and Regi, and any of her other aids who might be inside, and get them out through the back garden."

Another explosion resounded from the direction of the first, though this one sounded closer and was followed by an ominous creaking that could only be the splintering of a support beam.

Despite his obvious terror, Mareq shook his head. "No, I'll stay here with you to help. Do you have another one of those?"

Annika scoffed, pulling her arm free and giving Mareq a hard shove toward Niri. "Don't argue with me, boy. Have you ever fired one of these before?" When she got no response, she continued, "As I thought. You'll do more good by getting everyone else out to safety. Now go!"

Mareq started to dart off, then stopped and turned back. "Have you fired one before?"

"Of course, I have," Annika snapped. "Stop stalling and run before I prove it to you!"

Mareq bounded off and out of sight, apparently believing her lie enough to find the bluff intimidating. It had been decades since her archery training as a girl, but she had always been a good shot back then. Her tutors were impressed a human who had spent most of her formative years outside of elven private study had picked the skill up so quickly, and she hoped the principles would come back to her as they were needed. She purposefully ignored the nagging thought that her training had always been with shortbows.

***

Smoke threatened to fill his lungs, but for the moment, Tetamii was beyond caring—there were other concerns on his mind. He had cauterized the bleeding on his upper arm and shoulder joint, though only after he had lost a concerning amount of blood. He could still barely move his left arm, but Garla's herb nurse was supposedly one of the best. They would have him back to full strength soon enough once he was done here.

His path through the estate was slow and deliberate as he took his time tearing into the veil, unleashing gouts of flames to scorch through walls and ceilings. Behind him, he detonated pockets of Wellspring energy to bring the house down bit by bit. Magzii had lost his way, scraping and bending to squeeze himself into society's upper echelons, but Tetamii could still appreciate the destruction of hoarded wealth.

However, much of the devastation was an afterthought—an autonomic function of a life spent bringing down the powerful. All Tetamii could focus on now was betrayal. His whole life had been marked by it. First, by the death of his parents, leaving him alone in the world. Then, by the city who had claimed them and couldn't bother to pull a boy it orphaned out of abject poverty. Magzii and Elikar were but the most recent examples, and perhaps Tetamii had been naïve not to expect it given betrayal's prominent place in his life.

An errant thought buzzed irritatingly through the haze of fury, fueled by one of his emotions he had kept buried so deep that he no longer recognized it: guilt. It was unrelenting, and a wave of nausea caused Tetamii to lose a step. He placed a hand on the wall, inured to its heat from a lifetime of exposure.

Betrayal is who you are, it said to him, and he felt a familiar wet warmth on his hand. As he looked down, for a moment, his fingers dripped crimson fluid on the carpet. Then he blinked and was surprised to see that his hand was not covered in the blood of Ilphas Trisarin.

He had laid this inferno, this scorched earth tactic, at the feet of those who betrayed him, but had he not done the same to a man who had offered nothing but support? Another pulse of nausea threatened to make him retch, but he clenched his eyes shut and punched a hole in the weakened wall, then continued forward once again, telling himself it had been nothing more than the acrid smoke.

Besides, the decadence of this place might have also been the cause of his unsettled stomach, as each step down the hall brought into view more luxuries than Tetamii had seen since his time in Vinsart Hold. While this estate was no royal palace, the dark stained wood and plush carpet oozed wealth, and the oil paintings he passed every dozen or so feet were all great works of talent and beauty that must have cost a fortune. Regardless of their value, it all became kindling as easily as any cheap throw rug or child's scribbled drawing.

Tetamii finally found himself stepping out of the collapsing hallway, cinders and ash swirling out from behind him as he entered an expansive sitting room. Crystalline timepieces sat atop mantels and tabletops, as if one clock was insufficient for people lazing their days away in the manor home, and each had a different swirling, fluted pattern shaped into their glass bodies that was reminiscent of Liiashan architecture. The display went well with the blue and green accented furniture, another common elven aesthetic, and Tetamii began to wonder which noble had housed this troupe. It wasn't unheard of for elves to reach this station in Kefya—Felona in particular—but it certainly was not common.

Before he could think on it more, though, a loud *twang* from his left sent his hackles rising. Without thinking, he tore apart the World Shroud at his feet, unleashing a wall of flame that spouted several feet above his head. A small object thudded against his chest with enough force to knock his shoulder back, but then clattered to the ground. Inches from his boots laid a smoldering crossbow bolt, the sharpened metal tip having snapped from the haft as the wood burned.

Tetamii folded the torn veil over itself to snuff the fiery barricade, and revealed Annika standing in the foyer, partially obscured by a corner while she cranked another bolt into place.

This was it, the first of many to fall this day. She had not been instrumental in his downfall, but Annika's connections were responsible for the thoroughness of his captivity. As simple as it would be to consume her body in flames or detonate a pocket of Wellspring energy near her, though, the others were not here, and Tetamii did not much feel like hunting them down without leads.

Today was a day for extermination, not puzzling out locations. If they weren't in the house with her, he would make Annika tell him where they were hiding.

***

Annika was surprised at how steady her hands were as she finished loading the second bolt into the crossbow. Facing down a scorcher alone was no enviable feat, but her body had not given in to the panic she knew should be making her fingers tremble. She had always been stubborn—perhaps that extended to a resolute calmness in the face of certain death.

But as she took aim at the scorcher once more, she couldn't help but wonder how it was she was still breathing. He stood where he had entered into the room, an inferno raging behind him as he stared her down. Gone was the arrogance the man had displayed in his battle with Rav and the others in Alaboq, where he had shown himself to be a proud man sure of his abilities even while outnumbered. That had been horrifying enough, but now when Annika met his gaze, she saw a hollowness that finally sent a shake into her hands.

This was a broken man, and in her experience, there was little in life that was more dangerous and unpredictable than a man with a wounded ego and nothing left to lose.

The crossbow wavered, but she took a breath and gripped tighter to still her hands. "I expected you sooner," Annika said. "Were we that difficult to find?"

Tetamii shook his head. The scorcher held his sword at his waist, the soft orange glow it cast creating eerie shadows that stretched up his face. "The Gulls have known where you were since you arrived in the city. The only thing that kept you alive this long was Elikar's penchant to avoid the chaos and questions your deaths would bring to his doorstep."

He took a step forward into the room, undeterred by the bolt aimed directly at his chest. "But I've had a falling out with my former leadership, and I'm looking to show them what it means to cross me. Fortunately, one of the best ways to damage them is to kill all of you. Your group makes less compelling scapegoats if you're dead, after all. Plus, the chance to eliminate my former captors at the same time? I'm sure you can understand how much that would mean to me."

"Do you think you'll be lucky enough to stop another bolt?" Annika said. Flames were now licking up the walls, spreading out of the hallway and into the sitting room. She was sweating, but she wouldn't dare risk taking a hand off the weapon to keep it out of her eyes.

"You might be fast with your siphoning, but I believe I can manage pulling a trigger a bit faster."

The scorcher smiled, though it didn't reach his eyes. "I wouldn't bet on that. With the way your hands are trembling, I doubt you could hit the wall behind me with any accuracy."

Now that he stood closer to her, she realized her initial assessment of his mental state was not quite correct. Annika couldn't explain it, despite priding herself on her ability to read others, but the scorcher seemed unwell. His eyes were not devoid of feeling, after all—rather, his amber-ringed eyes vibrated with emotion. They were focused by hatred one second, then flitting around in paranoia-fueled movements the next. At times, the sides even seemed to crinkle with genuine joy.

Annika released a slow breath, realizing her efforts at remaining calm had failed her. They had not been talking long, but her steely reserves were drained. He was likely correct—whatever aim she would've been able to muster with this unfamiliar weapon would now be impaired, and while she believed she could still hit him, she wasn't confident it would be a lethal shot.

But when she had opted to stay behind, she knew this would be the end. Mareq was fast, though, and she had to believe if she could give him a few more moments, he could get Niri and anyone else in the house out. Rav didn't deserve to lose a mother to this group, too. Insufferable as she might be, the girl deserved a chance to reconcile, and Annika would see it done.

I just hope that school taught her to recognize her own emotions, Annika thought. *Otherwise, she might take this silly grudge to her grave.*

"So, why the further delay, then?" Annika asked. "I'm right here, suffering in this heat. Why am I not being roasted alive? You don't seem to be in a mood to toy with your prey."

Tetamii spun his wrist, swinging his blade in a slow arc as he paced further into the room. "Where are the rest of your friends?" he asked. "You're correct that I'm not looking to prolong your death—seeing it done will be satisfaction enough. But if you withhold their locations from me, I'll be forced to keep you alive, no matter how much you plead for me to end it."

Annika swallowed and nearly choked, her mouth dry from more than the heat. "You know as well as I that Ravael isn't in the city, nor is Wymund, and I honestly couldn't tell you how to find them at this point. So, you'll have to settle for me, even though I had little to do with your resounding defeat."

"Don't sell yourself short," Tetamii replied, "and I happen to recall another young man who was prancing about, flicking his little knives into my flesh like a swarm of irritating insects. I remember that clown having two arms, though, and when I saw him recently, he seemed a bit lopsided. Maybe I'll even him out before I drop his final curtain."

The fire had covered much of the wall behind Tetamii, and Annika covered her mouth and nose with her sleeve to filter the air. If she had any chance at slaying him, it would have to be a surprise; pulling the trigger while talking or pretending to cough from the smoke might be enough to catch him off guard. But if she waited too long, he would either grow bored of her delays or the lack of fresh air would render her accuracy worthless.

Niri and the others had to be out of the house by now, so there was no point in putting it off any longer. Annika squinted through one eye and steadied the crossbow as much as she could, but before she could fire the bolt, a voice called out from her left.

"Annika!" Niri shouted. She had one arm up to shield her face from the blaze across the room, and was followed closely by Regi and Mareq. "I'm not leaving you alone in here to fend for yourself. We have to leave before—"

Her voice faltered as she dropped her hand, revealing Tetamii's presence in the room. The scorcher's face suddenly contorted, his unnerving cool crashing into a puzzled rage. "So, you did make your way to the city," he said. "I believe I owe you a blade in the back."

He really is unstable, Annika thought. Niri did look strikingly similar to her daughter, and the room had filled with smoke, but that didn't excuse a professional assassin like him misidentifying someone—particularly someone who had bested him. Rav's partial elven blood would be enough to make it obvious she was not the middle-aged human woman who had just entered the room, but as Annika had suspected, Tetamii now seemed to have only a tenuous grasp on reality.

Before Tetamii could take two steps toward Niri, Annika fired. Her bolt caught the scorcher in his left shoulder, right in what looked to be a recent wound. The impact caused him to twist in her direction and he screamed, seemingly more fueled by anger than pain. An instant later, a fiery explosion detonated in the foyer behind Annika, flinging her through the air. She crashed into the back of an upholstered loveseat and flipped over it, landing hard on her side. The seat toppled over with the collision and slid along the floor until it came to rest on top of her.

Annika's vision swam, and her back lit up with intense pain with any small movement. Her skin had been seared, and the crossbow had been blown out of her grasp by the fireball, but she wasn't dead. As long as that remained true, she would do everything in her power to keep her allies alive. She shoved the arm of the seat and felt the charred skin on her back tear in several places, but she succeeded in toppling the chair off her.

Across the room, Regi had placed himself between Tetamii and Niri. The butler held his hands up in a readied position, but the scorcher took his head off with a clean swoop of his blade.

Before he could reset, Mareq barreled into Tetamii's left leg, knocking it out from under him so that he slammed his right knee onto the floor. The draqeshi attempted to wrap a thick arm around Tetamii's neck while pinning his leg with the other, but his strength advantage couldn't compensate for the assassin's experience. Tetamii whipped an elbow behind him, catching Mareq in the temple and dropping him instantly.

Annika struggled to her feet as Tetamii did the same, albeit more gracefully. Niri had retrieved a poker from the fireplace and held it at the ready, but the woman was visibly trembling. Still, Tetamii was trained on her, with his back to Annika—she had an opening. She just needed to make it count. Placing one foot in front of the other was agony, and no matter how much she willed her steps to be faster, there was only so much her old body was capable of, particularly after being thrown across a room.

When Tetamii came within range, Niri lashed out with the iron poker, but he simply batted it away with the flat side of his blade. The tool flung from her grasp and spun down the hallway.

"Enough games," Tetamii seethed. "You won't even give me the courtesy of putting up a decent fight, lightblood? Fine. If you won't do me that honor, I'll settle for a satisfying kill."

Annika hefted a crystalline timepiece from an end table just as Tetamii clutched Niri's throat, lifting her along the wall. The scorcher brought his blade back for a thrust, but Annika clamped one hand on his shoulder for leverage and cracked the clock across the back of his skull. His head was knocked forward as blood splattered over her face, but she could still hear Niri drop to the floor.

Beaten by an old woman, Annika thought. *That should save us some trouble. He'll likely hide himself away forever rather than face that ridicule.*

Then, she felt a sudden pressure in her abdomen as she was lifted off the ground. Her legs felt cold as they dangled in the air, though she could feel a trickling wetness gushing over them. She blinked the scorcher's blood from her eyes and looked down to see half of his bastard sword sticking out of her belly as he stared up at her with unbridled hatred.

Annika tried to speak, but she only coughed up blood that dribbled out of her mouth to join the rest that was already pooling below her. Tetamii grinned, but then shook his head as his eyes focused on something behind her. He tossed his sword aside and fell to his knees, and Annika hardly felt the impact as she landed on her side.

Now facing the same direction, Annika saw the man was staring with slumped shoulders at the family portrait over the mantel. Flames had already reached that portion of the room, consuming the walls and the frame, but the three faces were still visible.

Annika had learned from her sister that trauma often plagued the mind; Alauvar had spent much of her time in the rebellion tending not only to physical wounds, but the emotional ones that came from seeing so much violence and death. Something about seeing a younger, happier Rav might have triggered a final break in the scorcher's already fragile state.

Alauvar. If the Dawn Ones were kind, perhaps Annika would see her sister again soon. She hoped she had made Alauvar proud, that she had made up for the complacency she had enjoyed as a young woman while her sister was out making a real difference for those who needed her aid. In the time since Alauvar's death, Annika had done much to live by her example, donating most of her wealth and working to lift others up. She had even taken a disagreeable young woman under her wing, and possibly saved her from her own power, in the same way she should have for her sister.

But Annika had not only taken on her sister's compassion. Alauvar was a fighter, and Annika had become one as well. Her last act in this life would not be daydreaming about what she had done. There was still a battle to be fought, and while Tetamii would win, an emotional knife had pierced his psyche. Annika wanted to twist it.

"You might make her an orphan today," Annika said, before spitting out a glob of dark blood on the floor. "But she still has more family than you can ever dream of having. More people who care about her well-being than even know you exist." Her vision pin-holed and blurred as her head slacked down to the floor. "She'll come for you, and you'll have no one to watch your back when she plunges another dagger into it."

***

The painted eyes of Ilphas Trisarin stared down at him as he knelt in the sweltering room. The old woman said something behind him, through burbled blood and rasping breaths, and perhaps somewhere in the back of his mind her final words had registered. But for now, all he heard were Ilphas's final words, spoken to him so long ago over similar death rattles: *You are a good person, Tetamii. No one has to be defined by the worst thing they've done. Not as long as they try to do better.*

Not only had he chosen the wrong man on that day, but he had repeatedly ignored Ilphas's parting lesson, offered to him over the knife Tetamii had stuck in his gut. He had always striven for excellence in his work, but that was not the self-improvement the man had meant.

And here he was, decades later, apparently standing in Ilphas's home after setting it ablaze and nearly killing the woman who must have been his wife because he had mistaken her for his daughter. Ilphas had never brought him here, only to his secondary orchard in the Tangled Vines, but it was undeniable. The young girl's face in the painting was the same one he had seen in taunting visions for weeks. Through the cinders dancing in the air, he could swear the corners of the girl's mouth ticked up.

Tetamii was constantly making the wrong choices, and Ilphas had finally decided it was time to look upon the failure his mentee had become.

"What if one doesn't try to do better, Ilphas?" he asked. The flickering flames offered the only response as they began to claim the portrait itself. "What if one makes a craven choice as a child and then spends the next twenty-odd years following that up with more of the same, securing power to fill a void that could've been filled by sincere support? Can one still be a good person then?"

A hand gripped him under his shoulder and hefted him onto his feet. Tetamii turned to see Garla, a sooty rag wrapped around her face and hair slicked down in sweat, looking a bit frantic as she gestured toward the front door.

"I don't know if now's the right time to be asking philosophical questions, Scorchy," she said, "but I like your company just fine. How about we get you out of here and find someplace you can kneel and monologue all you want, without an Irasil-damned inferno threatening to bring the whole place down?"

Just then, Kymil and Ubadrii burst through the front door, each man shielding their faces from the flames with an elbow. Tetamii vaguely recognized the figures in his state despite their history, and instead allowed himself to be pulled along by Garla.

"Don't leave so soon," Kymil announced. "An eye for an eye may be traditional, but an arm for arm would be a bit of poetic justice."

He heard a tinkle of knives unfurling from the bard's cloak as the elf dashed forward, but Garla pulled a pouch from her belt and loosened the drawstring before tossing it in their direction.

"Sorry, fellas," she called out to them as she ushered Tetamii away. "We don't have time for reunions at the moment. Try not to nap too long. It's a bit toasty in here."

Garla led the pair of them out of the house as a plume of powder exploded from her tossed pouch, then led the pair of them back out beyond the tree line. By the time they were out of sight, members of the city guard were rushing inside the estate to offer any help they could, but Tetamii could only sit on a bed of leaves as his head spun. He reached up and gingerly touched the back of his head, wincing as his finger grazed the gash created by the old woman.

Garla squatted beside him, reaching into a second pouch and pulling out a handful of dried lunok petals. She closed her other hand over the deep purple petals, and a sudden burst of garlic brought tears to Tetamii's eyes. He blinked them away to find

Garla pulverizing the petals between two stones until they became a fine powder.

"Inhale this," she said, holding the powder up to his face. "Not much time for a proper infusion, but it should at least slow the bleeding while I get you patched up." Garla eyed him, then shook her head with a smirk. "You keep things interesting, Scorchy."

"You're Magzii's new herb nurse?" Tetamii muttered before inhaling the lunok petals. The odor once again inflamed his sinuses, but he felt a cold tingling over the back of his scalp.

Garla brought a finger to her lips and shushed him with a smile. "Not even he knows that, so keep it to yourself. I like to keep a low-profile. Some people have made a pretty big deal about what I can do, and I get the feeling a guy like him gets threatened easily by other people's talents. I think you're learning that lesson as well."

INTERLUDE

BEFORE

The Buttoned-Up Lad. It was a simple note, innocuous, but Tetamii crumpled it in his hand just the same. If Ilphas had seen it, the man would have no cause to think anything of it, and Tetamii could've implied he had jotted it down as a reminder. But it felt good to destroy the note, to grind it under his heel after he dropped it onto the dirty street. Seeing the letters written in Magzii's hand made everything feel so calculated—so malicious. It might have started that way for Tetamii, too, but today wasn't going to be a day of victory for him. He walked down the street, leaving the shredded note on the pavement, all so he could bear the weight of his denial.

Of course, he hadn't needed to hold on to the note for as long as he had. Although Tetamii had not yet been invited into the Clipped Gulls' stronghold underneath the tailor shop, he had already surveilled the place on multiple occasions since learning of its dual purposes. He knew every entrance and exit, even the one tucked into the cramped alley on the building's right side—it was amazing the places a child could get to if no one cared to watch them. It had been so long since Magzii had slipped him the scrap of paper that the initiation was beginning to feel like a dream. But there was something about keeping the note over this past week, turning it over in his pockets and pulling it out to look at the scrawled writing every so often, that reminded him this was real.

He would soon have a family again.

Tetamii darted into a shaded recess between two storefronts and vomited. He wiped his mouth and gulped in as much fresh air as he could while standing among refuse and fetid puddles, then rose and resumed his journey. Ilphas was expecting him.

Sweaty and feeling as if each step drove his heart rate ever higher, Tetamii finally turned down the narrow street that led to the tailor shop. There, already waiting for him, was Ilphas. Not only was the man punctual, but he had taken it upon himself to use his extra time to improve the neighborhood.

Someone had knocked a sign down that once hung over the door of a barrister's office, and the rotund old lawyer had been unable to set it back in place. Instead, he had simply propped it up against the side of the building. It had remained there since Tetamii had begun scoping out the Clipped Gulls' front, collecting days' worth of refuse and likely serving as a makeshift lean-to for the city's vermin. But now, here was Ilphas, hefting the wooden sign over his head as the balding barrister stood behind him giving directions.

"That's it," the barrister said. "The latch on that hook can be a little tricky, but it should click in—ah, you've got it."

Ilphas lowered his arms, giving his shoulders a roll but smiling all the same. "The next time a passing cart knocks your sign down, you don't need to wait on someone to pass by with an offer to help. You have so many neighbors here who I'm sure would've been willing to lend a hand."

The barrister snorted and glanced down at his feet. "Begging your pardon, Mr. Trisarin, but folks around here try to steer clear of men who provide my services as much as possible. It's like they think I'm sniffing out any white lie they've told so I can slap some chains on them myself."

"The people in charge have seen fit to make distrust a natural state in this city, which makes it less likely those of us under their care will notice when they act against our interests." Ilphas paused, finally noticing Tetamii and waving him over. "But I hope that soon, we can change that mindset around here. Until then, find me if you need more assistance. I'll be around."

By the time Tetamii reached him with his leaden feet, Ilphas had already stepped away from the lawyer and was standing to face the BUTTONED-UP LAD. There in the window was a pristine white tailcoat, the kind that hardly anyone wore down below the Crest out of fear of muck and dust, but one that many aspired to don one day. It was sized for an adult, and if Tetamii put it on now, the tail would drag the ground behind him without extensive tailoring. But that hadn't stopped him from daydreaming about himself in it. He had imagined the authority of the flapping fabric behind him as he stepped with purpose through the city, no longer able to be overlooked. Now, though, the sight of the coat gave him no such thrill.

"I can see why you were so taken with this coat, Tetamii," Ilphas said. "I think with a few adjustments, it would suit you just fine. It might even turn a head or two with the young women up in the council hall," he added with a wink.

"Thank you, Mr. Trisarin," Tetamii said, his mouth drying like leather. He cleared his throat. "But I'm starting to think it's too expensive. Maybe I can keep saving my wages and come back another time."

"Nonsense," Ilphas said as he moved toward the shop and pulled the door open, gesturing for Tetamii to walk inside. "You've already proven yourself an asset, and more than that, I see a little of myself in you—determined, and with an eye for picking out what's wrong in the world. You might as well look the part."

This early in the day, the shop was still quiet, with most people in the district tending to their work, children, or both. But a few men milled about, looking at the shop's wares and paying no mind to them as they entered. Tetamii couldn't be sure, but he doubted the relatively empty storefront was an accident. Each of the three other customers in the store either had hair down to their chins or were wearing a flat cloth cap; both would easily conceal severed ear tips.

Behind the counter was a young man, likely a decade older than Tetamii if he had to guess, but humans did carry the burden of age faster than elves. For all he knew, he might have been the same age. The man had bushy dark eyebrows with short-cropped hair and was wearing a well-fitted vest and shirt to demonstrate the shop's products. When he smiled at them, though, his stained teeth detracted sharply from the image he was hoping to convey.

"Welcome," he said, his voice raspy but not unpleasant. "My name's Evin. I saw you two admiring that coat from the street, and if you don't mind me saying, I think it would fit you just right, sir."

Ilphas laughed, then glanced at Tetamii. "It seems everyone has a keen eye these days." Then, turning to the clerk, he said, "Not for me, I'm afraid, though it is a beautiful coat. No, I'm interested in purchasing it for my young friend here."

Evin turned toward Tetamii, looking him up and down as if he were actually taking mental measurements rather than playing a role. Finally, he nodded and said," I can make that work, though it will take some time. I'll need to take some measurements for you, boy." Then he snapped his fingers and beckoned them back to the counter, where he pulled out a length of rope with pre-measured marks along it.

As if on cue, a steam whistle sounded from the backroom. "Oh, that's the kettle," Evin said. "Can't start the day without a cup or two of tea—need it to steady the hands. Would either of you care for some?"

Tetamii held his breath. After spending this much time with him, he knew the man preferred coffee. Maybe he could avoid this fate thanks to a quirk of his palate. But the flicker of hope didn't last.

"I would love a cup," Ilphas said, polite to a fault. Tetamii nodded as well, and Evin slipped off through the door into the backroom.

"Are you sure about this, Ilphas?" Tetamii asked, using the man's given name for the first time. "It costs so much, and all I'm really doing is scribing for you—"

Ilphas clapped a hand on his shoulder and smiled. "Don't give it another thought. Clothes don't give a man his worth, but they can help the world pay attention to someone who hasn't had it for long enough. I can already see that you're going to make something of your life, Tetamii, and soon everyone out there in Felona will too.

"Besides," he added, "I always liked the idea of having an older sibling watching out for me. It never came to pass, but maybe you could fill that role for someone. You should stop by and meet my family soon. The coat will be sure to impress my wife and daughter."

Evin pushed back into the room, carrying a wooden tray set with three ceramic mugs and a scuffed old kettle. If Tetamii could've guessed which cup had already been laced with Smuggler's Hood, he might have grabbed for it first. Edis's Eye, even if he took one at random, there would be a one in three chance Ilphas's connection to the World Shroud might not be snuffed. But his arms hung like dead weights at his side as he watched Evin pass the first mug to Ilphas, then closed his eyes as the man drank from it.

After losing his parents to the ills of this city, two new families had been offered up to him. He just hated that he only felt he deserved this one.

PART IV

CHAPTER 29

The Illumined Scale

If it were not for the small punctures Nasargiel maintained in the World Shroud, allowing Tellahhr's Wellspring energy to seep out and warm his body, he would've died days ago. The Tesigan Peaks were desolate, with a wind sheer that tore through to the bone. When he had departed from the Achen mercenary squad, after his battle with Opysis, he had not considered packing for such extreme temperatures. Where he and his kind lived, weather was generally not a concern, so it was always a shock when Nasargiel appeared somewhere new, ill-equipped for the local climate.

But, bathed as he was in a shell of extraplanar heat, he had managed to survive, though he had not seen much success in finding the lightblood or this school. Occasionally he would draw from the Taisos Wellspring, shifting his vision to detect any life energy in his surroundings, but in the last week, all he had managed to discover was a small den of white foxes and a particularly curious ram that had taken to following his path along the peaks.

Nasargiel feared he had bypassed her, but he could not siphon continuously from two sources for long without facing complete exhaustion. Instead, he opted for life-sustaining heat with the occasional scan for golden silhouettes that would denote life in this frigid wasteland.

That had been only one of many choices Nasargiel had to make to optimize his search, sacrificing efficiency and speed for thoroughness and endurance. He could have siphoned wind energy and flown over the peaks, and had at times, but ran into the same issue with heat retention. Additionally, he could have traveled back to civilization at night for rest and renewal, but while it had been tempting, Nasargiel knew it would've ruined the quality of his search. He was not familiar enough with these mountains to pop in and out of them with any precision, and for all he knew, when he returned to the range, he might appear miles off from his intended destination, having skipped over the school without any knowledge.

He stopped as he reached the peak of yet another incline, his road boots crunching into fresh ice and snow before the bubble of warmth around him caused them to melt away. To the west was northern Achen, the expanse of land swathed in deep green conifers, many of which Nasargiel assumed were the famous heart-firs for which the nation had become known. The lumber was durable, yet easy to work with, and was a breathtaking crimson color that only intensified with age. He momentarily reached out with his senses and watched as the vast forest twinkled to life with small bursts of golden specks, an effect that was mirrored off to the east, where he was able to pick out the life energy present in fish swimming near the surface of the ocean. But there was still nothing of significance here in the mountains—

A red-orange glow caught his eye as he completed his turn behind him, surrounded by numerous golden forms. The sight was several days' worth of travel to his rear, on another peak that was relatively flat compared to the rest of the range's highest points. At this distance, Nasargiel couldn't make out features of the living creatures, but he was confident that the trailing ram he had picked up was not capable of starting a fire. The number of radiant shapes clumped together in this icy wasteland could only mean that the blade serpents and the rest of the mercenary band had made it to the mountains. Time was running out; while he was having trouble locating the school, they might have better luck.

Nasargiel hung his head, racking his brain for any other edge he might employ to locate the lightblood faster than her pursuers, when he noticed a handful of glowing silhouettes moving about within the mountain. They were far too large to be any small burrowing creatures, and he knew of no true subterranean people living on this plane—not since the draqesh had emerged from the safety of their tunnels following the Shroud Culling. Of course, this had all taken place after the sylidae had departed Slaeth during the Rupturing, so it was possible their records were incomplete. But it was also possible he had simply stumbled upon the school.

He leaped from the top of the curved peak, grasping at the cyclonic veilmarks that swirled around him as he siphoned wind from the Udynn Wellspring to buffet his fall. Nasargiel landed lightly amid snow drifts that had been piled to obscure the sight of a crevice cleaving deep into the heart of the mountain. The opening was narrow, but wide enough for an athletic individual to descend, if they were careful—and with a lightblood's ability, it might prove to be a fitting test of their mastery.

At another time, Nasargiel might have siphoned electricity through his own form, pretending to be a lightblood to ingratiate himself and learn more about why this girl had been granted such a deep connection to her Wellspring. It must mean something, as if the World Shroud was preparing an immune response for another Rupturing, but he didn't have the luxury of time to study if she were truly one of the Vanguard. He would have to reveal more of himself than he was comfortable—certainly more than the Assembly and the Archives Lost would allow—and hope that it lent him some measure of authority. But he could ease the shock of his sudden appearance with a touch of familiarity.

As he descended through the cramped dark space on a pocket of air, Nasargiel allowed his Achen body to be consumed by white-gold flames. This was the essence of traveling, the destruction of oneself to be born anew elsewhere, though in this instance, he chose to remain exactly where he was. Instead, he simply needed to avail himself of the regenerative properties of the talent, reconstituting the lanky man who the lightblood had encountered in Virdoba, complete with curly blond locks framing the sides of his face.

Nasargiel found himself in an icy cavern, with shadows cast over and around mounds of frozen rock from the only light source: a string of lanterns running around the space's perimeter and disappearing through a single exit. It didn't make the best first impression as what must essentially serve as a foyer, but the lights were a sign of civilization in this barren tundra, and he could hardly contain himself as he strode toward the tunnel. If people were living within this mountain, they must've been warm enough to stay here, and that would be welcoming enough.

Along the path deeper into the stone, short branching halls led into circular storage rooms. Beverages and dried foods were stored in barrels and crates in some, while others contained tools and supplies for upkeep, but each was decorated with etchings that featured the Dawn Ones prominently. It was rare to see all this plane's revered beings represented in the same place, as most had congregations that were spread across Slaeth, with factions bickering even on their best days.

Nasargiel chuckled—he supposed if one were going to worship those fools who played at godhood, why not go all in?

Rarer still, though, were the sets of verdant orbs inlaid within brass bands running around the tops of the rooms, as if peering down on the deities. A few on Slaeth recognized the significance of the green-eyed figures present in some of the Dawn Ones' ruins, though no theory Nasargiel had heard was even remotely true.

Some called them servants of the Dawn Ones, or even visitors from another world. The mystery of the sylidae remained intact, as the Archives Lost decreed, but it warmed Nasargiel a little to see his people placed in a position of reverence above the Dawn Ones and their squabbling.

Finally, he reached the end of the hallway and stepped into a much larger space, with icy rock shelves rising in disorganized layers up the cavern walls. Wooden structures had been constructed on some of these flattened areas at varying heights, with rope bridges and ladders strung about to connect them. The effect was an almost village-like atmosphere that had been created here in the heart of a mountain, with the role of a town square held by a central platform overlooked by two more enormous emeralds set in a brass-capped stalactite.

Before Nasargiel could determine which building to approach, he watched as a series of quivering, erratic veilmarks snapped into a straight line that ran from a lodge-like structure on the ground level to an iron plate affixed above his head. If he hadn't known he had entered a den of lightbloods, Nasargiel might have prepared himself to deal with an arcing electrical bolt from a stormforger. Instead, he watched with a slight smile as three figures lurched through the air toward him, flying directly along the path formed in the World Shroud.

Polarity riding, he thought as a slight smile graced his lips. *Advanced for lightbloods. Maybe they are more prepared than I thought.*

The first to reach him was a young elven man with dark auburn, shoulder-length hair who landed with a hand already at the hilt of his scabbarded blade. His face was hard, more cold than threatening, but Nasargiel had no doubt the man was capable of attacking without hesitation. Against nearly anyone else, he might have even had a chance at drawing blood.

Coming close behind were two women, one of whom clearly had both draqesh and elven blood coursing through her veins. She landed with a heavy thud, then stood to a height of close to six and a half feet tall. A muscular frame dispensed with any possibility of lankiness at that stature, but despite what her size might suggest, the woman appeared cautiously welcoming rather than openly hostile.

Finally, dropping down with the lightest touch was the woman he had been searching for all this time: the lightblood he had fished out of the Marrow Strait and saved from drowning as her body teetered on the edge of the Illuminated Death. Her hair was a bit longer, and she was now draped in heavy gray wool instead of the leather armor she had sported in Virdoba, but there was no mistaking those fiery blue-ringed eyes, both of which opened wide as she seemed to recognize his current form.

"You," she said. "What are you doing all the way out here? Still looking for someone and found your way back to me?"

The other two shot puzzled looks in her direction, but the young man's shoulders relaxed. Nasargiel smiled, keeping his hands visible to demonstrate that he wasn't a threat. Not that he would need his hands to defeat the three of them, but they had no way of knowing that.

"My search for that individual has paused," Nasargiel said. "I'll get back to it when I can, but I needed to find you this time. Your life is in danger."

The lightblood rolled her eyes. "When is it not? Look, I appreciate what you did for me in Virdoba. If you hadn't pulled me out of the water while I was seizing like that, well, I wouldn't be here now," she said, gesturing to the cavern around here. "I'm learning what I need to know to avoid reaching that point again, so I don't need people butting their concerned noses into my life anymore. I have enough anxious onlookers fretting over me as it is."

In the distance, two more figures were hurrying toward them from the main building, though they were walking rather than gliding across the space. One man was clearly of an elven lineage, though not entirely if Nasargiel had to guess—most full elves were far too vain to allow their hair to whiten to that degree. He walked with purpose but with ease, as if he knew the three who had preceded him had the situation under control. The other was human, impressively matching the half-elf's height and more than doubling his build, and though he walked at a pace matching the man to his right, a rested hand on his scabbarded blade told Nasargiel all he needed to know about his emotional state.

"I don't doubt that your abilities have grown," Nasargiel said. "That much is plain. But I do not speak of the Illuminated Death this time. Rather, my concern is for the small army of Achen mercenaries nearing this location, seeking to claim the bounty on your head."

That gave the lightblood pause, her mouth going slack. The elven man spoke up. "What have you brought down on us, Rav? I knew we were begging for trouble the moment we let you stay."

The taller woman placed a cautionary palm on the man's chest. "Cool off, Adiin. We don't even know what this man is talking about yet, and it looks like neither does she."

Finally, Rav's jaw clicked close before shaking her head. "Achen sellswords? That doesn't make any sense. I've never even been to Achen, much less pissed anyone off east of the Tesigan Peaks enough to want me dead."

"The contract on your life came from Kefya," Nasargiel said, and she gave him a knowing look as the two other men reached the group at the cavern entrance.

The human man spared a quick glance at Rav before returning his glare to Nasargiel, his hand never leaving the pommel of his blade. "Elikar's holding a grudge, is he?" the man asked. "I suppose we shouldn't have expected a rich man to be fine with a bruised ego. And he sent you?"

"Unclench, Wymund," Rav said. "This man isn't with Elikar, and I don't think he's out to hurt any of us. He could've killed me months ago and been done with it if that were the case."

"You know our guest, then?" the older half-elf asked.

Rav nodded grimly. "Yeah, and if he says a group of soldiers are on their way to the school, we should hear him out. I owe him that much."

Wymund's eyes flicked briefly over to the braided woman before he shuffled closer to Rav. "If they're after you," he said, speaking low as he leaned closer to her ear, "we should leave. Make our trail obvious for a mile or two, then try to lose them. We don't want to bring anything like this down on the school."

She looked ready to agree, but before she could say anything, the brawny woman gently pushed them apart. "You stand a better chance of surviving here with us," she said to Wymund, then quickly added, "You both do."

"Riqu is right," the white-haired half-elf said. "We'll make preparations for the school's defense while your training continues. I won't grant my blessing to the two of you wandering out on your own in the name of saving our necks." The man paused as he met Nasargiel's eyes, inhaling sharply before settling into a smirk. So, this was the one who recognized the significance of the sylidae.

"Besides," he continued. "I believe your friend is going to be a valuable source of protection for us all."

Chapter 30

— · —

The Illumined Scale

Rav watched her classmates pull themselves through the air, their arms outstretched toward the next iron plate before their gloves clanged against the surface. Riqu still lurched in her movements while Adiin's arcs were far more graceful, but that no longer impacted her speed, as she frequently matched Adiin's pace across the room. However, Rav had managed to maintain her edge over both of them, her experiences walking the border between life and Illuminated Death giving her a deeper understanding of just how much energy she could safely contain in her body.

She just had to remember not to fall back on old habits. Hopefully, the memory of the intense jolt she felt on the mountain would be enough to keep her in line. Rapidly pulling back from open siphoning to directed had nearly proved fatal—if she hadn't been able to stabilize her polarity folds, she would have plummeted to her death. It seemed she would have to choose for the upcoming battle, and she knew she needed to opt for her new disciplined siphoning rather than relying on the raw power of hurtling toward the Illuminated Death.

Besides, it wasn't as if Zylnala's instruction hadn't offered its own unique benefits. Nasargiel—or Nas, as she had taken to calling him—had called what they were doing polarity riding, though how he knew so much about the abilities of lightbloods remained unclear. In fact, much about the man was a mystery, and he was frustratingly guarded whenever he was pressed about personal information. Master Zylnala trusted him, though; he had given their guest the quarters directly adjacent to his own. Rav couldn't tell what exactly, but Zylnala knew something about the new arrival that had not only put the man at ease, but inspired confidence in their chances against a small army. His trust in Nas would have to be enough for now, because neither seemed willing to divulge their secret.

Besides, Rav had enough to worry about. A small battalion of Achen mercenaries was closing in on them day by day, specifically on orders to claim her head. She had faced overwhelming odds before, both in number of opponents and skill, but never both at once. These soldiers would be much more effective than the gangs of street toughs she had bested in the past, and while not the equal of a scorcher, the blade serpents they counted among them were supposed to be highly specialized fighters with a weapon she had never encountered.

If it weren't for the rest of the school's insistence that she remain within the icy halls, she thought she might have listened to Wymund's suggestion that they flee. But each time she almost gave into that fear-fueled instinct, she thought of her friend being run down by the mercenary band up above in the frozen wasteland that was the Tesigan Peaks. Like it or not, they both stood a better chance of survival remaining there, waiting for her pursuers to kick in the door.

As if her thoughts had summoned him, Wymund strode toward her, with Master Zylnala in tow. The half-elf had a curious look in his eye but seemed excited at whatever it was Wymund seemed intent on sharing with her. When he was within a few paces of her, he stopped and drew his shortsword.

"Hold out your hand, Rav," Wymund said. "We need to test a theory, and Master Zylnala seems to believe you would be the safest choice for a first attempt."

Rav looked down at her gloved hand, the heft of the iron plates on either side of her palm no longer a noticeable encumbrance. She recognized where this was heading, and she wasn't keen on being a test subject.

"You want me to catch your blade?" she asked. "And what happens when I'm not able to lock in a polarity fold in time? Do you have a witch or knitter I don't know about who can see that my fingers are reattached?"

"Mr. Sylnorin has promised to start slow," Zylnala said. "But I have every faith in you, Ravael—as does our new green-eyed friend. He speaks quite highly of your talents, you know."

"Does he?" Rav scoffed. "Because he always seems tight-lipped to me, particularly regarding anything that might be useful to us while a group of thugs is growing closer by the minute."

Zylnala tutted. "People are entitled to their secrets. I'm certain Nasargiel has his reasons for not being an open book with us, and I trust that it is for the best." The half-elf adopted his knowing grin that had become a common fixture on his face since Nas's arrival. "For now, though," he continued, "let's see if you are able to stop a blade with those gloves. It was Mr. Sylnorin's idea, and I would hate to see such a stroke of tactical genius go unused. We might have a future commander in our midst."

Wymund gave her an apologetic shrug and a half-smile. "If you prefer, we could start with Adiin."

Rav gritted her teeth. He knew her too well.

"Fine," she muttered, holding both hands out in front of her, palms forward—attempting to catch a blade in a clap would be even more foolhardy than this idea already was. "Just try not to let your hand sting too much when I stop your sword mid-hack."

Wymund did his best to hide concern behind a half-hearted grin, but despite any reservations, her friend seemed to have full faith in Rav's abilities. He brought his shortsword down in what was surely a lightning-fast arc, but to Rav's eye it suddenly appeared to be slicing through air as thick as molasses. She could feel the waves of electricity immediately pulse through her body as the Wellspring siphoned its automatic protective energy into her form. Unlike past battles, though, she was prepared for the strike and formed the coursing electrical current into looping folds around each hand.

As the blade struck the iron plate on her palm, she felt the familiar *thunk* as metal bound to metal. Rav followed the trajectory of Wymund's swing with her gloved hand, reducing the bone-shattering potential of the blow and allowing her to pull him off balance with his sword arm held out straight. With her free hand, she held a closed fist against his neck, mimicking how she might hold the hilt of a dagger.

"You're dead," she said, before releasing the polarity fold. Wymund's sword slid free from the iron plate, and he pulled himself back into a more stable posture. "That's a nice trick, though. Great idea."

"Yeah," Wymund replied, tugging his collar up closer to his neck. "Let's hope your peers catch on as quickly."

Over the next two days, the pupils of the Illumined Scale spent their time preparing the chambers for an imminent invasion. Iron plates were placed in strategic positions around the central cavern as directed by Wymund, with Zylnala and Nasargiel seeming keen to trust his insights on battle readiness. While those three worked on that project, Rav did what she could to bolster Riqu and Adiin's proficiency at looping the Wellspring's currents.

Unlike their experience with polarity riding, Riqu took to this new technique more quickly than her counterpart. It did not take many attempts before the woman was stopping Rav's daggers on impact, her brawny arms able to take the brunt force without moving such that shockwaves of pain shot through Rav's bones at the sudden deceleration. Adiin, though, took his fair share of glancing cuts as daggers slid off his plated gloves and nicked his skin.

"Agh!" he shouted before inhaling sharply through his teeth. Bandages wrapped around parts of his forearms from prior cuts, but those would be mended shortly—Zylnala had a stash of minor knitting serums for non-life-threatening injuries. Adiin would be back in fighting shape by the time the Achen mercenary group arrived; physically, at least.

The elf stood and massaged the base of his skull. They had been practicing for hours, and Rav knew that while maintaining a balance between determination and focus was not as skull-crushing an endeavor as racing headlong toward the Illuminated Death, prolonged siphoning of any kind would certainly produce one bastard of a headache. Still, they were getting nowhere fast, and she needed Adiin to be prepared—he would need to muscle through the pain.

"Let's try something else," Rav said, resetting her stance for the next strike. "You've been going at this Zylnala's way, and as much as I hate to admit it, your control over the polarity folds continues to outpace mine. But you have to admit that you're lacking a certain punchiness with what you can accomplish while drawing from the World Shroud."

Adiin grumbled, then rolled his neck back and forth a few times, stubbornly refusing to reset his stance himself. "Since when is losing control considered a good thing?" he asked. "Reckless fighters are frequently at a disadvantage when faced with a soldier who has spent years honing their craft, and they don't even have to worry about seizing as a deadly bonus for their efforts."

"Sometimes a frenzy throws your opponent off their game, no matter how disciplined they are," Rav replied. She sighed and shrugged, then stood and crossed to a natural stone step in the cavern where their waterskins sat. She tossed one over to him.

"But I guess you haven't had the chance to learn that life lesson. Growing up sheltered in the elven comforts of Choii Stier, you never had to navigate the complex web that is human motivation. A culture dedicated to Teacher Irasil and the charitable outreach of his followers must've been quite cozy."

She had expected the slight to get a rise out of the man, but instead, Adiin appeared more pensive than irked. He took a draught from his waterskin, then walked over to join her.

"A Choii Stieren life isn't as idyllic as you seem to believe," Adiin said. "Constant social pressure to always serve the community over yourself takes its own sort of toll. Then there's the culture clash of living in a colony away from our homeland and still trying to hold on to Liiashan ideals while integrating into Aneran society. But I take your point that I have been largely protected from the deception and greed of human cities."

"They aren't all so bad," Rav said with a laugh. "And the fact that their motivations are so varied keeps you on your toes. I didn't get so good at scrambling across rooftops out of a love of exhilaration—though that was part of it. But sometimes, I simply needed to get away from jeers of 'dagger-head' with haste."

"Is that what this is about?" Adiin asked. "The small army marching toward you, I mean. Do they hate our kind that much that they are willing to smoke you out like vermin?"

"No, this is more personal," Rav said. "After what Wymund and I went through before coming here, I forget that being tucked away in this mountain has kept you blissfully unaware about what's going on out in rest of Anera.

"Prior to our arrival, Wymund and I were part of a group who managed to foil a very important, very callous man's attempt at self-enrichment." Adiin's eyebrows shot up, but Rav continued before he could interject with any questions she was sure he had.

"He was practically willing to set the west coast of Anera ablaze to put Kefya and Qedrad at each other's throats again, all so he could funnel more and more trade through his own ports. Lust after your nation's gold, plus a veneer of old-fashioned bigotry, was almost enough to re-spark the conflict that the War of Arrival had supposedly concluded."

Adiin pursed his lips and appeared to study the icy ground at his feet. "All this time, I believed you were someone who breezed through life, fortune always smiling on you either by virtue of money or name. I know how to spot a rich brat when I see one," he said with a smirk. "And then watching you catch on so quickly to Master Zylnala's theories, well, it was enough to solidify my initial distaste.

"But I also know when I've been wrong, even if I take my time admitting it. I'm not devout myself, but my parents hold closely to the Advocate's teachings, and I appreciate all that he says we should strive to do for the world." Adiin looked up to meet her gaze. "Teacher Irasil would be impressed at how you've worked to keep peace in the world, at your own expense, no less. And if I can acknowledge you would meet the standards of a Dawn One, what kind of fool would I be if I continued dismissing you?"

Rav was stunned at the reversal but recovered quickly. "I'm no role model, so don't start volunteering me to hold seminars for your High Scholars back home. But if you admire me so much, maybe you'll be willing to loosen up a bit for this next round?" She stood and returned to their previous spot, beckoning for him to join her. "I might be able to teach you a thing or two about surviving against overwhelming odds."

Adiin walked over and resumed his ready stance, raising his plated gloves once more. "Fine, I'm open to any suggestion that won't result in more injuries. I'm grateful for the knitting serums, but having my arms sliced up repeatedly has not been a fun experience."

Rav shot him a mocking wince. "No promises. You'll never learn anything if I start going easy on you."

***

"Are you enjoying this?" Riqu asked, her smile lighting up the otherwise dour mood near the entrance of the central cavern. The impending conflict was weighing heavily on Wymund's mind, but her spirit had an almost infectiously calming effect on him whenever she was around, and he found himself returning her grin as he finished hammering a plate in place.

"I think I find it fulfilling, in its own way," he answered. "Using all I've learned about defensive tactics in the Virdoban Guard to protect this place makes me feel like I can at least contribute. When the fighting starts, I'm not sure exactly how much use I'll be." Wymund stepped off the ladder to join Riqu on the ground, where she was waiting with one massive arm wrapped around a stack of iron plates at her hip. "I don't want to be a liability."

Riqu laughed heartily. "You're the best fighter we have. Without you, I'm certain this place would be overrun. Where's this doubt coming from?"

Wymund took some of the plates from her out of courtesy but regretted it almost immediately. What seemed to be a light load for her was already straining the tendons in his arms. "Not doubts really, just a realization that I'm surrounded by individuals with talents that make me look like a targeting dummy. I'll do what I can to protect all of you, though."

"You're doing it again," Riqu said with a sigh.

"Doing what?"

"Predicting defeat as a reflex," she said. "You told me before about your father's life, how he gave up his dream so he could support you. Seeing that from him, you thought that practicality was the right choice in life, and you never pursued your own dream. But I think you learned the wrong lesson from him."

Wymund shifted his weight between his feet; he didn't like feeling exposed. But he had shared this aspect of himself with her after she relayed her own insecurities, after he had offered her fresh insight into what he felt she had been viewing incorrectly. He owed her this chance to call him on his ingrained beliefs.

"What was I meant to take from that choice, then?" Wymund asked.

"Maybe his dream wasn't to be a painter," Riqu said. "Or maybe it was, but then when you came along, that dream changed. What if he was showing you the lengths to which he would go to provide for his son?

"I've only known you for a brief time, Wymund Sylnorin," she continued, taking back the plates he was struggling to maintain, "but if there's one thing I'm sure your father passed on to you, it's a drive to put others before yourself. That doesn't have to come at great personal expense, though. Not when you have a support system that he lacked."

Wymund smiled. He had always been reserved growing up, never one for playing with the other children on his block when he could be getting lost in the majesty of the Faarasan Gardens and translating what he saw onto the canvas. It was as if the wall separating his childhood home from the vibrant plant life of the wealthier neighborhood had become a fixture of his personality, a natural barrier behind which he was accustomed to viewing the world.

He had never considered himself lonely, though—he had been happy indulging in that pass time, comparing his work to his father's as his skills grew with each stroke. Still, the relative isolation had led to a lack of openness with others, and most of his relationships never ventured past professional acquaintances.

But somehow, in adulthood, Wymund now found himself with a smattering of friends who seemed unperturbed by that same wall, some even able to scale it without issue. Rav never met a barrier she didn't see as just another path, and she had wormed her way into his life as effortlessly as she had slipped into many a window in her time. Riqu was different, though. There was an ease with her, no matter the interaction. Conversation or sparring, Wymund felt comfortable with her. Without knowing it, the woman had found a gate in his wall, and let herself in.

"So, whether you decide to continue this life of soldiering, or actually muster the bravery to try your hand at your true passion," Riqu said, "I hope you know that you have people who have your back."

"I'm starting to realize that," Wymund said. "And you're right, maybe I have been using my father's experience as an excuse to shield myself from the potential of failure. But if you can face the troubles of your own past and come to terms with that image your family forced upon you, I should be willing to accept a gentle nudge in the right direction when it is offered in return."

Riqu gave him a playful shove on his shoulder but trailed her fingers down the edge of his arm before dropping hers back to her side. "I'm glad to hear it," she said, beaming despite the danger looming. "If you don't mind though, before you pick up that paintbrush again, I think we could make better use of your shortsword in the immediate future."

Wymund chuckled. "I've held my artistic drive at bay this long. I think I can manage another day or two of swordplay, if needed."

CHAPTER 31

THE ILLUMINED SCALE

Nasargiel heard the invading force before he could see them. The only entrance into the Illumined Scale was the nearly vertical descent through the icy crag, so he could not keep an eye on their approach as he had days ago atop the mountains, beyond the occasional check-in on their life auras. Instead, he had periodically tapped into the Udynn Wellspring and shifted the air within the crevice, condensing it so that sounds above were amplified and carried to his ears. It wasn't perfect, but he had eventually detected the crunching of dozens of boots on the icy peak above and had been able to give warning so that final preparations could be made.

Rav had eyed him with suspicion when he announced the final approach of the Achen mercenaries, as he continued to hold close the secrets of his people. Although he was considered reckless—perhaps even a heretic by some of the more zealous sylidae—he maintained enough respect for the ideals of the Archives Lost not to expose too much of his power unless it was absolutely necessary. He would interfere in the lives of Slaeth's people if he believed it would stall or prevent the next Rupturing, and in fact, he felt not doing so would ensure the occurrence of that calamity. But the Assembly was right about one thing; revealing the true extent of his connection to the World Shroud to the wrong person would only hasten the disaster's arrival.

Luviila, Markis, and Fulja had been ushered into one of the back chambers in the network of caverns by Zylnala and Riqu, though the trio protested every step of the way. Concern for the young people Luviila looked after was plain across her face, but their logic had won out in the end—they were no combatants, and they would only be liabilities once the fighting began.

From his position near the back end of the central cavern, Nasargiel looked down over the soon-to-be battlefield. He had stationed himself on a ridge near the roof of the large chamber, bow in hand and a number of arrows bunched into a quiver on the ground beside him. They had belonged to a man named Trimon, apparently, one of the co-founders of the Illumined Scale, and had remained largely untouched since his passing some years ago. Zylnala had cared for the weapon diligently, as evidenced by its maintained quality despite its long period of disuse, and the elf had handed the bow over to him with wistful pride after Nasargiel promised to make good use of it.

He had neglected to mention he had never fired one of these contraptions before, but that felt immaterial at the time. Nasargiel did not need skill with the weapon when he could carry the arrow along a channel of wind to his targets straighter than any shot. He only needed the weapon as a smokescreen for his abilities.

At the center of the chamber, standing on the raised circular platform that served as a monument to the sylidae, Zylnala stood still under the symbolic emerald eyes inset above him. The elf held an iron bowstaff in front of him with both hands and had remained motionless for some time. Nasargiel assumed he was seeking a calm focus before their attackers' arrival, but there was little doubt in his mind that Zylnala would be ready once they did. The man had even donned a pair of his own iron-plated gloves, something Nasargiel had not yet seen from the instructor, and after watching the school's pupils excel at polarity riding in such a short time, he was certain Zylnala's prowess with the technique would be impressive to witness.

In front of the central monument, Wymund and Riqu waited, each with their weapons unsheathed and held at their sides. The human wielded a shortsword and buckler and was keeping himself ready by shifting his weight from leg to leg, periodically stretching to keep the cold from stiffening his joints. Comparatively, the woman standing next to him was still as stone, with the exception of an occasional roll of her wrist that flicked the head of her axe back and forth. Adding to her already stout frame were two larger iron plates that had been strapped around her upper arms like makeshift vertical pauldrons. Between the two of them, Nasargiel would keep a closer eye on Wymund during the conflict—as skilled as the soldier might be, the man might need an opportune arrow or two to survive.

Finally, Rav and Adiin waited to either side of the chamber, crouched on the edges of their respective elevated ridges. Once the Achen forces funneled into the central cavern, the idea was for both to pull toward the iron plate above the entrance, landing behind the mercenaries to surround them. Wymund had voiced his concerns that, with their opponents' superior numbers, the benefit of attacking from both sides would be minimal, but it hadn't taken much convincing to change his mind—his tactical acumen was laudable but didn't account for the sheer speed of lightbloods in total control of their abilities. Relative force size was always a factor, but a well-trained lightblood counted as more than one combatant.

As if to test that notion, just then the crunch of boots landing on ice and rock echoed down the tunnel that fed into this chamber from the crevice. First one pair, then a series of others as Nasargiel pictured the Achen soldiers descending in waves through the tight space before depositing out into the rocky foyer. Without his abilities, they were sure to be exhausted from the descent, but he had traveled with these men for some time—their stamina was not to be underestimated.

It wasn't only Nasargiel who had picked up on their arrival this time, though. The cracks and thuds of their landings were loud enough that his allies all notably tensed. Nasargiel plucked an arrow from the quiver and nocked it but did not draw. Instead, he found the Udynn veilmarks whisking freely throughout the chamber and tugged them into channels, readying pathways of wind through which he would launch the arrows faster and more accurately than any marksman could dream possible.

He inhaled, taking icy air into the foreign lungs of this human form, and settled his mind. In his journey to shield Slaeth, and thereby the entire Physicarium, from a second Rupturing, he knew deep down that protecting Rav was an integral step. Nasargiel just hated that he had been forced into a position where she had to do some of that task herself.

***

There was a sudden silencing of footsteps as the advancing mercenaries stopped within the darkness of the tunnel. Rav couldn't yet make out any of them from the shadows they lingered in, and she began to worry that Nas's assessment of their tactics had been incorrect. He had described them as ruthless brawlers; not wild or reckless, but rather brutally efficient in their approach to melee combat. The fact that they were hesitating in the tunnel instead of swarming out spoke to a change in strategy. Perhaps they wanted to lure their targets into the tight space with them, or simply unleash crossbow bolts in their direction. But it wasn't long before their opening strike disabused Rav of those concerns, replacing them with new ones.

Two snaking whips of segmented blades lashed out of the tunnel, extending fifteen feet from the pair of Achen soldiers who stalked out in their weapons' wakes. Wymund raised his left forearm to deflect the blade serpent's strike, but rather than glancing off his buckler, the strange, linked blade portions wrapped around his arm. Rav watched as deep crimson stained the sleeve of her friend's coat where the blade whip carved into his flesh, but while Wymund hissed in pain, his shield had at least created some space on one side of his arm—he was not completely at the weapon's mercy. He quickly maneuvered his shortsword between the buckler and the blade segments, then twisted against the wrap, causing the blade whip to unfurl.

Riku had fared better against the whip that had cracked in her direction, as she had shifted her left shoulder plate to intercept the steel. On impact, she locked the blade serpent's weapon in place with a polarity fold, then with all the draqeshi power flowing through her veins, yanked her shoulder back. The mercenary stumbled forward, nearly faceplanting as he refused to release the hilt of his weapon, but recovered in time to skirt away from the upswing of Riku's axe.

From Rav's position, the man appeared to move around Riku as if she were a violent maypole, his blade whip still held in place at her shoulder. But before she allowed her assailant to encircle her in the weapon, she released the fold, the linked segments clattering down to the icy rock at their feet. The blade serpent retracted his weapon and did not immediately unleash another crack, as it dawned on Rav that Riku had been set up for an attack to her rear. She readied a polarity fold herself, feeling the familiar tingling thrum of energy in her hands as she went to launch herself toward the iron plate above the tunnel entrance.

But before she gave away her position early, an arrow zipped along a preternaturally straight path and embedded its shaft halfway into the eye of an advancing Achen mercenary who had hoped to take advantage of the opening. Rav glanced up at Nas toward the back of the room, the distance too far to make out much detail, but she could swear the odd man did not have his bow drawn, despite the next arrow being nocked. There was no time to ponder his peculiarity, though, as their first fallen comrade had apparently been enough to unleash the full brunt of the Achen party's fury.

Close to two dozen soldiers poured out of the opening and into the central chamber, their shouts echoing off the icy walls as they moved in to surround Wymund and Riqu. With practiced precision, Wymund deflected the more ordinary blades of the first two mercenaries that closed on him before driving his shortsword into their abdomens, spilling their blood onto the ice below. Soldiers for hire appeared to be no match for his years of experience, and if the blade serpents had not numbered among them, Wymund might have been able to escape the onslaught unscathed.

However, once the elite soldiers took their positions behind the fodder, they rained their blade whips down on both Wymund and Riqu. *Cracks* resounded around the cavern as whip after whip darted toward the pair, and while Riqu was able to snag one or two of the blade whips at a time on her makeshift pauldrons, polarity folding was still new to her, so each successive strike she locked in place caused another to be released. Riqu did what she could, using her bulk to keep the worst of the onslaught away from Wymund, but the ranged weapons were quickly overwhelming them and leaving more than a few blossoming red streaks on their clothing.

Zylnala dashed forward and flipped through air, twirling his metallic staff under him so that it caught two blade whips mid-crack. Locking the steel segments in place on his own weapon, the elf leaped back toward the stage, pulling himself in a straight line to an iron plate they had affixed to the brass-capped stalactite, where he latched on with a plated glove.

The blade whips were yanked free from the grips of their wielders as the half-elf wrenched and twisted his staff in the opposite direction, then transferred their metallic segments to the iron plate as he dropped back to the platform, leaving the weapons dangling more than ten feet above the ground. Somehow, Zylnala had managed to maintain the polarity fold in the metals rather than his own body after he dropped back down, keeping the weapons tantalizingly out of reach.

That would've been a neat trick to share with the rest of us, Rav thought.

The disarmed blade serpents had been pulled toward the center of the chamber while attempting to maintain their grips on their weapons, and they defended themselves admirably for a few moments, but Zylnala was no novice to combat. Despite several impressive guards against the half-elf's swooping blows, the iron staff eventually found purchase on the sides of their skulls. Each mercenary slumped to the ground as if they were little more than meat wrapped in armor, which after those strikes, might have been accurate.

More and more soldiers teemed out of the tunnel entrance until finally their rear line solidified. Rav rocketed toward the back of the swarming Achen mercenaries, drawing her daggers in midair. Luviila had done a fine job repairing the one that had snapped during their arrival to the school—there was seemingly no task the woman was ill-equipped to handle, including metalworking.

Adiin had launched himself from his perch a bit earlier and was on the ground with his rapier drawn moments before Rav landed. In rapid succession, two more arrows plunged into a couple of the nearest blade serpents' chests before they could pull their longswords free. They crumpled beneath Rav and Adiin's feet as the pair launched themselves into the fray.

Between the two of them, Rav and Adiin dropped four of the mercenaries before the rest of the band took notice, her daggers slipping easily through the thinner portions of their leathers while his rapier punctured the side of one man's throat before slicing through another's. The sounds of their guttural cries drew the attention of the rest of the back row, however, and they soon fell in on the pair, leaving the rest of their group to surround the other three defenders of the Illumined Scale.

Despite Wellspring-enhanced reflexes, there was only so much a quickened pace could overcome, and Rav soon found herself with more than a few cuts from well-placed slashes and stabs. But the thrumming presence of electrical energy fueling her every move ensured she gave at least as much punishment back, and while none of her strikes were lethal, the three Achen mercenaries engaged with her slowed as their blood splattered to the ground, staining the white-blue ice.

None were the supposedly elite blade serpents though, all of whom seemed to be focused toward the front if the ringing *cracks* were any indication.

Adiin wasn't faring as well. Where Rav had only received cuts, Adiin had taken a puncture wound to the thigh and was now favoring his left leg. His rapier was simply not meant to defend against the heavier blades wielded by his opponents, and he was forced to pull himself up and away from his attackers multiple times using the iron plate to his rear as a magnetic tether. But no matter how strange his maneuvering must have looked to the invaders, they quickly learned that the elf was somehow drawing himself toward the metal, and adjusted themselves into positions that would limit its efficacy. Still, Adiin was not new to dueling, and a handful of quick rapier flicks tore open his opponent's eye with a clean slash, partially blinding the Achen soldier who had moved back into the tunnel to stay behind the plate.

More arrows volleyed down into the crush of battle, flying on straight paths rather than arcs and finding their targets with pinpoint accuracy, but the mercenaries had shifted their tactics to mitigate this strategy as well. They mostly stayed behind Riqu, Wymund, and Zylnala, preventing Nas from dealing any lethal strikes from above, and instead only clipping arms and legs. Her friends appeared to be holding back the wave of soldiers from advancing into the cavern, but Rav didn't like the way they were concentrating the bulk of their force toward Wymund's position.

Rav tried to focus on one goal at a time, but as seconds ticked away like the drops of her friends' blood spraying the ground, she felt herself losing that balance she had worked so hard to develop. She should not have allowed Wymund to expose himself like this. No matter his training, he didn't have the abilities the rest of their allies did, and he was being overwhelmed. And Adiin was proving to have the opposite problem—all the power without any of the combat experience to channel it appropriately.

Her polarity folds collapsed as more and more Wellspring energy poured through her—she would no longer be able to leap toward iron plates or halt enemy blades in their tracks, but the reckless siphoning had its advantages, and she was desperate. A small voice in the back of her head whispered something about the discipline she was supposed to have learned here, but it was drowned out by the pained cries of Wymund and the others as their bodies were being sliced and stabbed. Rav cut down two of the soldiers harrying her in quick succession, her daggers tearing through tendons and arteries before either had an opportunity to react. As she careened toward the threshold of the Illuminated Death, her speed increased exponentially.

Another of her opponents launched for her, but for all his skill, to Rav, he might as well have been moving through mud. She sunk a dagger into his back and spun around, launching her other toward the mercenary who was forcing Adiin to backpedal with broad swooping slashes of his shortsword. Her knife spiraled through the air until it found purchase in the man's shoulder, giving Adiin enough time to plunge his rapier through the man's screaming mouth and into a gap between his vertebrae.

Rav bounded back to the elf, bending to retrieve her blade from the soldier's body. "Thanks for that," Adiin muttered, his haggard breathing forming white plumes before him. "But you might want to reign it back. Your eyes . . ." he said, gesturing toward them.

She blinked at the flares that had already begun appearing in her vision, ignoring both them and the waves of crunching pain that had been building at the base of her skull. "No time. Move with me."

Adiin followed as Rav dashed straight toward the rest of her friends, though he chose to pull himself over the top of the crowd toward the iron plate fixed to the capped stalactite. A few of the mercenaries toward the back were quickly dispatched as Rav flitted her way through the mass of soldiers, severing the backs of knees and plunging a blade up under their arms. But before she was allowed to decimate the entire force, several of the blade serpents took notice of her movements and began cracking their segmented weapons in her direction. Despite her enhanced reflexes, the blade whips were fast enough to require her entire attention, so she was forced to pick her way through the rest of the throng without doing any more damage.

Rav broke through the front of their line to find Riqu and Zylnala standing defensively before Wymund, who was struggling to rise from a kneeling position, his face pale and jaw clenched. His defenders each had several blade whips locked in place, either on Riqu's shoulder plates or twisted around Zylnala's staff, and Adiin had joined their defensive posture to keep the other soldiers from advancing. Rav turned and crouched low, daggers held out to either side, and launched herself like a feral beast at the next mercenary to make a move toward them—her entire world was now streaks of steel, splatters of blood, and sparks of light.

CHAPTER 32

THE ILLUMINED SCALE

The members of the Illumined Scale had fought admirably, but the battle was not going as well as Nasargiel had hoped. The human guardsman appeared on the verge of collapse after suffering two deep gouges from blade whips, and even the light-bloods at the back had been forced to regroup with their allies before they could sufficiently thin the mass of bodies. Given their positioning, grouped as a barricade of flesh in front of the Achen mercenaries, he was finding it difficult to deal more than glancing blows with his propelled arrows for fear of damaging his allies.

Still, he was resistant to the idea of unleashing a torrent of Wellspring power and finishing the fight. The Archives Lost were clear—once the sylidae were revealed to be operating on Slaeth once more, power from other factions would begin to escalate, and a Rupturing would be unavoidable. It was the nature of power, after all, to seek more of itself.

Nasargiel's hesitation vanished, however, as a crackling bolt of lightning rocketed toward him from a split in the World Shroud to his left. The strange short hairs on his human form's arm had been his only warning of the attack, but it had given him enough time to shift earth and draw up a protective stone shield that absorbed most of the impact, though he had still been forced to stagger a few feet to the side. Glancing back down at the battle, a lone Achen mercenary had separated himself from the fray and was staring up at him, his head tilted to the side in mock curiosity.

Gone was the impish ginger man Nasargiel had left buried not far outside Ineset, but there was no mistaking Opysis's cruel aura, even from this distance. It was apparent in the way he stood, arms held at his sides and relaxed mere feet from clashing steel, that this man felt no concern for the potential of suffering a grievous wound. Nasargiel didn't need to rely on his life sense to see that the new human form was a disguise, albeit a better one in this instance—Opysis had adopted the look of a typical Achen soldier, braided hair pulled back into a knot at the back of his head, and a body that could have been chiseled from sandstone.

No, the man's identity was not a question. His intentions, though, needed to be interrogated.

Nasargiel sent a probing arrow in Opysis's direction, knowing the man would deflect or dodge it with little effort. It was a baiting tactic more than a true attack. He simply needed Opysis away from the non-sylidae warring below, before they saw—or were consumed by—power that would provoke too many questions.

Thankfully, Opysis seemed willing to bite the lure, leaping into the air and pushing himself up toward Nasargiel on a mighty current of wind, but not before he batted Nasargiel's arrow aside with another gust of energy from Udynn's Wellspring. The projectile soared directly toward Rav, but with a rapid adjustment of veilmarks by Nasargiel, it instead sunk into the neck of an Achen mercenary, who collapsed into a gurgling heap among his comrades. Rather than concern for their fallen ally, though, most of them spared a moment to watch one of their own fly off toward the back of the cavern before training their attention back on the fight.

Opysis's feet touched down in a running stop, and Nasargiel could feel hatred radiating off the man. The man's deflection of the arrow toward Rav had been no mistake—he had already threatened her before. It had been his first attempt at punishing Nasargiel for his embarrassing defeat. Veilmarks that appeared as jagged lines crashing and shifting against one another along the icy rock at the men's feet quivered with Opysis's every step. It was a dramatic choice, but Nasargiel supposed his foe felt the only thing that could convey the intensity of his rage would be an eruption of magma into the cavern.

"You've improved your disguise," Nasargiel said. "And I'm glad to see you made it out of the shallow grave I left you in."

"You're happy that I escaped your failed attempt at assassination?" Opysis said with a sneer.

"I've never wanted to fight you, Opysis. If I had wanted to kill you that night, you would not be standing here now. You know that as well as I."

"Hide your incompetence behind feigned mercy all you want," Opysis said, the tremor in the icy shelf on which they stood amplifying. "Deceit can be one more mark of filth on your already tarnished legacy."

Nasargiel tugged on veilmarks of his own, attempting to vent the pressure Opysis was building beneath the rock by creating fissures. Something was wrong, though. While creating enough force to erupt magma from otherwise stable earth did take time, Opysis seemed to be taking more of it than he needed. Nasargiel had known the man for decades, seen firsthand some of the more brutal and callous measures he employed to handle his concerns. Now, he was exhibiting a patience Nasargiel knew he did not possess. That could only mean the man had a more wicked blade waiting to be unsheathed.

"So, the Assembly has officially ruled for my execution, then?" Nasargiel asked as he expanded his awareness to the entirety of the World Shroud.

Behind the overt stirring of superheated earth rolling just below them, the dark, diaphanous veilmarks of Gesh's Wellspring pulsed slowly. They fluttered like a fading heartbeat as they crept closer to Nasargiel's form. The magma was indeed a feint—Opysis planned to siphon pure putrescence as had been done to him in their last encounter. It spoke to either the lengths the man was willing to go to bring Nasargiel down, or how ready the Assembly was for his particular brand of headache to be abated. In either case, the taboo power was being invoked, and Nasargiel suddenly knew this would only end with a dead sylid. Opysis was not known for his merciful disposition.

Nasargiel surrounded himself in the radiant glow of Taisos's energy, suffusing himself with the healing power of its Wellspring just as Opysis's rot tried to set in. Pustules rose and resorbed in quick succession, skin cracked and knitted back together, and Opysis's sneer deepened into a snarl.

"Always the golden soldier, Nasargiel," Opysis said. "Perfect in every way. Ready for anything. Is that why you've come to believe you know better than millennia of our collected knowledge?"

"It's not a deficit of knowledge I'm facing, but a failure to look beyond stale dogma," Nasargiel replied. "I'm sorry that I have been unable to open your eyes to the truth. Our people have been through enough, and I never wanted my actions to lead to this."

With a fury that could no longer be contained, Opysis pulled his shortsword free and leaped toward him, unleashing a flurry of thrusts and swipes so harrying that Nasargiel was forced to pull slabs of earth up in his defense. Steel struck stone time after time as Nasargiel slipped between his maze of rocky barriers, barely able to keep his pace ahead of Opysis's onslaught. Nasargiel had some training in martial combat, despite its rarity on Nyavelle, but even if he had a weapon to bear against Opysis, he knew he would've been outclassed. The man had taken to melee training like flames to kindling, and Nasargiel was already doing all he could to keep the rot of Gesh from taking hold.

The ice shelf shuddered, and thin rivulets of lava began to pop and hiss out of the gaps Nasargiel created in the ground each time he blocked a hacking slash with another stone slab. Opysis was continuing to build the pressure in the earth below them, and Nasargiel could feel he only had seconds to prevent its bursting. Ducking behind a frosty rock barrier, he went on the offensive, cracking his shortbow toward Opysis's face as the man skidded around the corner. Blood sprayed out from a split on his lip, coloring Opysis's breath plumes crimson as the man renewed his assault unabated. His attacks were reckless, but the pain seemed to invigorate rather than hinder him.

As Nasargiel stumbled back away from a lightning quick thrust, a violent release of volcanic energy poured in from beyond the World Shroud, finally overwhelming the strategic vents Nasargiel had crafted. An eruption of immense heat and concussive force sheared the icy shelf in two and shot out lava-coated debris. Great roaring rumbles filled the cavern as the wall collapsed, drowning out the sounds of battle below.

Nasargiel sheathed himself in a cocoon of ice as he tumbled down toward the chamber floor, opting to shield himself from the scalding fluid over buffering away the chunks of stone with gusts of air. While Opysis continued his assault on Nasargiel's health, he couldn't afford to split his attention in too many directions. Ice spit and hissed as it sublimated on contact with the lava, and on each collision with the tumbling rocks, his barrier softened and cracked more.

The world spun and churned around him as Nasargiel was knocked this way and that, until finally his frozen bubble burst and he was deposited onto a ruined wooden floor. Rent beams dangled precariously overhead and dust swirled, lit by flickering lantern light that had survived the rockslide into the school's main building, as well as the hellish glow emanating from globs of magma steaming around him. He staggered to his feet, tightening his grip on the veilmarks that would stave off Opysis's attempts at decay, but realized his well-being was no longer under assault.

Across the room—one of the pupils' bed chambers by the looks of it—Opysis was similarly trying to rise with an unsteady hand on a busted set of drawers, but a dense stream of blood was flowing from the back of his head and there was a glassiness to his gaze. At his feet was a large chunk of stone with a matching blood-stain. In the man's fury to maintain his multipronged attack on Nasargiel, he had neglected to protect himself from becoming his own collateral damage. But his dazed state wouldn't be permanent; once his senses returned, Opysis would be able to heal as readily as Nasargiel.

"For what it's worth, Opysis," Nasargiel said as he hobbled over to his foe, his gait steadying with each step as the life energy flowed through him, "I truly am sorry. But if I've been marked for death by the Assembly, I know you won't stop until you see that task done, and the consequences of that are too dire to permit."

Opysis opened his mouth, working his jaw as he tried to speak, but nothing more than garbled sounds passed his lips. However, he did manage to sharpen his stare once more and meet Nasargiel's eyes.

"May your experiences ink the Archives, so what once was lost might be recovered, and our home restored," Nasargiel said, before pulling taught the sickening Gesh veilmarks until a knotted, fetid fungus bloomed from within Opysis's head wound, its thick stalk cracking his human form's skull further until it slumped forward.

"Latheril is right, isn't he?" Luviila asked. Nasargiel turned to find the woman standing in what remained of the doorway, cradling an arm that bowed awkwardly. Beyond the obvious break, she was covered in scrapes, and her typical neatly pinned hair was a disheveled tangle of gray, but considering the devastation Opysis had caused, she had fared well.

"You're one of them," she continued. "The Witnesses."

The name was what some of Slaeth's people ascribed to his own simply from their representations in the Dawn Ones' works of art. If he had been as prideful as Opysis insinuated, Nasargiel might take offense to the name—sylidae were hardly observers during the events of that age. But given the knowledge with which these people were working, a mischaracterization was not inexcusable.

"Let me take a look at your arm," he said, ignoring her as he stepped over his dead cohort, but she pulled away from his touch to gesture back with a nod.

Over her shoulder was a clear view of the cavern, the front wall of the structure having been toppled by falling debris, and despite the distance, Nasargiel could see the tide of the battle had continued its shift against his allies. The lightbloods still held their own, though Adiin and Zylnala were nothing more than defenders at this point as they caught and deflected blades, unable to make parrying attacks before being forced to stop the next assault.

Riqu had fallen back on her sheer size, absorbing blade whip cracks on her plate pauldrons, and taking wide hacks with her hand axe at every opening, which kept most of the infantry at bay but did little damage; the mercenaries simply kept their distance from the woman while the blade serpents wore her down.

Behind her, Wymund's golden silhouette appeared to flicker in Nasargiel's life sense. Despite Riqu acting as his stalwart guardian, more than a few snaking whips had made their way past her defenses, and he was now unable to stand. Nasargiel could see the veilmarks around Riqu quieting, as the woman no longer held on to her polarity folds, freeing the officers' segmented blades for more unrestrained lashings.

But where the World Shroud drifted lazily around the half-draqeshi, it had become a violent vortex focused on Rav, who was lashing out with the ferocity of an uncaged animal. Even with his eyes accustomed to following such speeds, the woman bounced between targets at an impressive pace, sinking her daggers into openings in armor or slicing through tissue with ease. She was inflicting casualties on their force, but it wouldn't last. Not only were the blade serpents able to match her speed with their blade whips, but at the rate she was siphoning electrical energy, she would be consumed in minutes. Nasargiel had brought her back from that precipice once before, but he would need the time and space to accomplish that again, which meant a battlefield full of enemy combatants was not ideal. He couldn't reverse the flow of energy if someone simply slit her throat before he could reach her.

More importantly, though, was her life worth risking the exposure of his people?

"You have to do something to stop this," Luviila said.

"If I do," he replied, "it could mean the end of everything."

"If you don't," she said, "it *will be* the end of them. Wasn't stopping that your whole purpose?"

Nasargiel paused for a moment, then gently pushed past her. Seeing the amount of power Rav commanded reiterated to him just how important she might be in the years to come. No passive siphoner should be able to command this much Wellspring energy, unless the World Shroud had chosen her as an agent of its own defense.

Additionally, the secret of bestowing Wellspring connections to humans on Slaeth had already been uncovered, and now it would only be a matter of time before the sylidae were pulled back to this place anyway. He might as well have an ally that could help him in the conflict that would spiral out of this revelation.

"Not exactly," he said. "But close enough."

***

Rav pulled her dagger free from the thigh of the mercenary in front of her, sending a pulse of blood up and into the eyes of his partner before she cracked him across the jaw and sent that one tumbling back into the teeming mass of the remaining horde. She couldn't remember the number of Achen soldiers she had dropped; she wasn't counting. Details like that were lost behind the sensation of liquid fire racing over her flesh and the relentless pressure at the top of her neck, as if her skull might simply pop off and tumble forward at any second. But along with the number of enemies she had felled, any concerns for her well-being were also gone, those too consumed by lights and pain.

She sidestepped first one blade whip, then another, each having cracked toward her from opposite sides of the formation. The segmented blades pierced into the rocks where she had been standing before being yanked back, one of which caught her above the elbow on its return arc. Her arm involuntarily flexed, and the dagger grew heavy in that hand—the muscle at the back of her arm had been damaged, if not completely severed.

She screamed, fury and pain erupting in equal measure as the injury briefly overwhelmed the thrumming numbness that accompanied this level of siphoning. But before she could launch herself at the blade serpent who had maimed her, another two whips sunk their bladed tips into her from behind, piercing just above her left hip and nicking her right shoulder blade. She ducked and rolled free, narrowly dodging another cracking whip that chipped into the spot her feet had just been.

A shortsword spiraled through the air, flying past Rav's head before embedding itself into the cave wall. She turned to see Zylnala follow his disarming blow with a second to the mercenary's abdomen, and a third to the base of the man's neck that sent him flat to the floor. The teacher caught her eyes, his own narrowing as he recognized her glowing gaze. The man gave a faint shake of his head, then spun his iron staff in a looping flourish that ended in a strike on the combatant that had moved up to replace the other.

The Loop. Focus.

She had lost sight of the structure she had gained from Zylnala's teachings as soon as her friends' blood had begun hitting the ground, and had fallen back to what she knew best: raw determination—stubbornness, some might call it—to see the job done. But that unbalanced the scale, and riding the line of the Illuminated Death was not effective against foes with weapons who could match her speed. And while Zylnala, Adiin, and Riqu had sustained some damage as well, they were faring better than her without recklessly pushing themselves toward self-inflicted harm. She had already decided there was merit in his teachings of discipline beyond picking up a fancy new skill or two—it seemed she needed that lesson reinforced the hard way.

Rav took a breath. Surviving this battle was the goal, but one that could only be accomplished with a series of smaller steps.

Focus. One task at a time.

A second blade would be of no use to her for now, so she passed it to her other hand, recreating the looping polarity folds down each arm as she did. She gritted her teeth, and just as she expected, a searing jolt racked her body, the Wellspring punishing her for wrestling control of an open tap. But she had been prepared this time and managed to maintain her grip on her daggers while the muscles in her arms screamed at the effort to contain the energy.

Another blade whip shot toward her face, offering her no time to recover, but she used the advancing metal to tug on her iron-gloved hand, sending her mangled arm in an arc that intercepted the chained blade and locked it in place. With her good arm, she flung a dagger at the blade serpent who had severed her tendon, and watched as he dropped with the hilt protruding from his eye socket. Through the clearing haze of her mind, no longer intoxicated by oversiphoning, a part of her noted she had won that exchange: an arm for an eye was a deal in her favor.

A shout came from behind her, the sound of Wymund's voice clear despite the clashes of steel and grunts of exertion. Another blade whip had found its mark, and her friend was fading fast. But before she could regroup to join Riqu in his defense, the entire cavern shuddered and heaved as the rocky ice shelf at the far end toppled violently to floor. Boulders the size of wagons and covered in molten fire smashed through the roof of the school's main building, sending flaming debris spilling out toward the conflict. A few of the smaller pieces of wood actually spanned the distance, striking a couple of the Achen mercenaries and leaving fresh gashes in their arms.

With most of the crowd stunned by the rockslide, some nearly losing their footing, Rav took the opportunity to close the distance on a pair of troublesome blade serpents that had been harrying their flank from the beginning. She got her remaining dagger up and under the chin of the first before he noticed her approach, but his comrade reacted quickly, flicking a mechanism on the hilt of his blade whip that detached the majority of its length. He was left with a machete-like weapon, though thinner and with a sharper angled tip. It wouldn't be as swift or infuriating, but far more useful up close.

Rav had thought she might take the man down with ease and turn her attention back to protecting her allies, having dispatched two of the more lethal combatants. But it seemed the officers were not only trained with the strange, segmented blades—they were more skilled in general than their regular mercenary counterparts. While not nearly as fast as Rav, the blade serpent parried her strikes, ceding ground to her as he maneuvered them away from the front line of the conflict. If she had use of both of her arms, his martial technique would not have been able to compensate for her lightning-fueled attacks. In her current state, though, he was just talented enough to remain unscathed.

Luckily, now that she had returned to her more balanced state, she didn't have to rely on traditional fighting skills alone. Another magnetic tug of her limp hand dragged the blade serpent's sword off track, and she drove her dagger up under his exposed armpit. The man screamed, but was silenced as she brought her elbow up into his jaw, then shoved him back onto his rear. She was no longer quite as fast, but that did not mean she couldn't be effective.

A sharp, slicing pain screamed up from her ankle, and Rav looked down to find another blade serpent's whip had ensnared her. He had lured her into striking distance, and she was sent onto her back as he yanked the weapon forward, pulling her leg out from under her. Rav spun against the looped blade segments, trying to free herself but instead only allowing the edges to bite deeper into her tendons.

"Nothing personal, girlie," the blade serpent said, his sneer emphasized by a thin, black mustache. He rolled his shortened blade in his wrist as he approached. "Gold is gol—"

His voice caught as he coughed, spraying droplets of blood onto the jagged point of ice that had burst through his abdomen. Rav scrambled back, dragging the newly slackened blade whip along with her before reaching down to unwind it from her ankle with her good hand. Once free, she fought to regain her footing and readied herself for the next assault, only to find a morbid statuary of dead mercenaries, each impaled on their own ice spikes that had seemingly sprung from the ground like angled stalagmites.

She hobbled back to her friends, picking her way through the copse of bodies, many still twitching in their propped positions, and saw that beyond them, Nas was making his way toward them from the ruined building. His emerald eyes weren't focused, at least not on any of them. Instead, he appeared to be taking in more of the space around them. Had he done this?

Rav knew the man had healed her once before but had concluded he wasn't a witch or knitter at the time—after all, he was no elf. But maybe she had been wrong before; maybe he hadn't used the serums of others and instead was somehow capable of siphoning power from the World Shroud. And if he could heal others *and* do this with ice, what else was he capable of? More importantly, what was he?

Chapter 33

Felona

"Lowborn filth," Magzii said, spitting blood onto the floor of the Clipped Gulls' basement lair. "You've ruined everything. Placed all that I've done for you under the heel of your boot and trampled away. And for what? What has been promised to you that would make you turn your back on your brothers?"

"Lowborn?" Tetamii asked. "The frame of reference you used to build this organization up, to stand in the face of those at the top of the mountain who try to forget we exist down here in the Trough, now you use as an insult?

"You might not have been born with a silver spoon in your mouth," Tetamii continued, "but as soon as a councilor took you under his wing and offered one to you, it certainly found its way right up your ass."

Tetamii had some time to calm his mind since departing the Trisarin's manor. Ilphas's face staring down on him from the mantel as he ran through yet another innocent had been part of it, providing the initial break in his haze of rancor, and Garla had played her role, as well. Healing his wounds had certainly helped, but her steadfastness had been a more potent form of support. Still, it wasn't until he had plunged his bastard sword into the chest of Evin, the tailor, that he had felt his emotional storm begin to quell.

It had been the first death of many as Tetamii cleared the Clipped Gulls ranks, at least for this hideout, and the messiest, too. Once he was below ground, there had been no reason not to unleash spouts of flame and fiery explosions that would consume all inside—the basement was stone and would not burn like the building above. Tables and shelves were blown apart and toppled over, sending wooden shards to pierce the torsos and necks of his former allies, while iron supplies were propelled in all directions, dealing concussions or worse to many others. Never again would any Gull doubt the power that Tetamii commanded once they witnessed the carnage he brought down here.

This assault would not be the end of the organization; there were too many bolt holes throughout Felona for that to be the case. But it was a start, and most importantly, Magzii was there.

His former mentor stood, pushing the heavy iron pot off his chest. Magzii had been near the rear of the space when Tetamii began his attack, and had managed to avoid much of the damage. Frost covered the walls of the small room he had bunkered down in, providing some shield from the heat that permeated the rest of the basement. But it had not protected him from the flying debris, and had taken a serious blow from the projectile.

"So, this is your response, then?" Magzii sneered. "A plan doesn't break your way, and you throw a tantrum? It's how the game is played, Tetamii. You were bested. Elikar has chosen to continue his association with me, and you'll be hunted like the gutter runoff you are.

"A man like him cannot be seen associating with you, boy," he continued. "You must understand that, somewhere in that mind of yours. Or have you completely reverted back to that sniveling child I pulled off the street, so desperate for attention and affection that you would kill a man at my direction for nothing more than a pat on the back?"

Tetamii took a step closer to him, keeping a tight rein on the World Shroud, filling the space with tremendous amounts of heat. When a spire of ice erupted from the ground behind him, it did not come as a surprise, and it was sublimated nearly as fast as it formed. Icy mist sprayed around him, reflecting off Magzii's widening eyes.

More shards of ice shot forth, exploding from the floor, walls, and ceiling, but each was reduced to vapor before ever reaching him. The moisture inside Tetamii's mouth and throat began to crystallize, before suddenly warming once more. With each step Tetamii took, Magzii attempted another gambit, pulling energy from his own connection to the World Shroud, but nothing the man could muster matched the heat of Tetamii's righteous fury.

"Listen," Magzii said, the once booming, powerful voice that had instilled purpose in Tetamii's life suddenly cracking. "We've been your family, son. Families squabble, their members maneuver for their own self-interests—it's in the nature of the relationship. But at the end of the day, I'm all you have.

"You were alone and unwanted when I found you on the street, and I took you in, treated you as my own flesh and blood. And look at you now. I've never seen someone so empowered! We can get past this misunderstanding." Magzii's eyes were pleading as he extended a hand. "Don't throw away all we've built over the years."

It was insulting. Here was the man who had built Tetamii into the skilled, powerful monster he had become, reduced to groveling. This was the icy dealer of death who had instilled fear and demanded respect over all these years?

Even if Tetamii hadn't already decided to burn the Clipped Gulls away at the root, this display would have required it. The group was corrupt and manipulative, preying on wayward children to recruit grateful and obedient assassins who would one day dance at the whim of the city's powerbrokers. It deserved its fate. But even judged by its own twisted ideals, if its leader could so easily be brought low by a half-mad former pupil, its toppling was warranted.

Tetamii closed the gap between them and stopped, peering down at the man who looked so much older than he ever had before. Magzii's sleek, graying hair now appeared more brittle than distinguished, and the age lines on his skin that had once been disguised by battle scars had deepened in his state of fright. Even his normally sharp, silver-ringed eyes had lost their luster, reminiscent more of an old, tarnished utensil than a finely polished blade.

But there was something else there in that gaze, behind the shock and defeat, something Tetamii recognized because he had lived with it from the moment his parents had been ripped from him—a reckless thirst for vengeance.

Magzii's hand shot for Tetamii's throat, a frozen spike forming over his hand almost quicker than it could be perceived. But Tetamii didn't need to see it happening; he had been ready for it. Before the jagged tip came within a few inches of his neck, the ice melted away, hissing and sputtering as it entered Tetamii's ambient inferno. Magzii yelped as the steaming water scalded his hand, but Tetamii grasped onto the man's wrist before he could yank it away.

"You think you can just take over with me gone, boy?" Magzii seethed. "They'll never accept you after what you've done here today."

"The Clipped Gulls are finished," Tetamii said. "I'll see to that. But you should be more concerned for yourself than your legacy, Magzii.

"You've become old. Slow." Tetamii breathed in, stretching the World Shroud so taut throughout the basement that he could feel the Wellspring's power leaking through without him yet tearing the veil. There was a sudden wrenching pain at the base of his skull, but he only smirked.

"Irrelevant." A conflagration ignited, filling the entirety of the underground floor. Magzii's face opened into a soundless scream as the flames consumed the air in his lungs before latching on to the rest of his body. Tetamii's grip held firm while his former mentor writhed in the fire, twisting and kicking until finally his body gave out.

Tetamii released the charred remnants of a hand, his own red, charred skin cracking at the movement. While he had carefully controlled the release of heat energy to maintain a gap around his body, his hand had not been spared, but he wasn't concerned. Garla would be able to heal him, as he was healing Felona of a festering rot that had existed too long in its underbelly.

Tetamii turned, surveying what remained of the room, which was to say not much beyond ash and cracked metal, the tool or weapon the shards had once composed no longer identifiable. He crunched through the cinders and toward the stairs that would carry him back into the world above, and realized he did not have much waiting for him. But what he did have was more than he had possessed since childhood: freedom, and another person to share it with.

He would no longer be beholden to the wishes of magnates or madmen—he would decide his own fate, and Tetamii knew with an ally who had chosen to stick by his side for their own sake, he would not continue to be used as a means to an end.

Eventually, he would see Elikar Thymes and his cohort dance in the flames as well. Even charitable Irasil would see that he deserved such a fate. But first, he had to lance the remaining boils of Clipped Gull chapters throughout the city. He couldn't have some underboss rising to fill a vacuum and looking for revenge. They were symptoms of a greater disease affecting this city, but he would treat those first before excising the deeper infection.

When that day came, though, Elikar would wish he had assigned better men than Magzii and Atusiin to finish the job.

Chapter 34

Felona

Elikar sat alone in his office, the flickering lamplight casting an orange glow over the room's interior. Before him on the desk was the warrant for Tetamii Fiadar's arrest, signed by all seven members of the Council, including their newest councilor, Eular Bonid. That had been no surprise, though—Eular was one of Elikar's men, after all.

During the tumult that followed the discovery of Livella Riber's body in her office—her skin having taken on a hauntingly blue hue that complemented the dried, violet foam around her open mouth—it had been relatively easy to suggest someone loyal to him as the successor to her post. The first secretary of the home was responsible for Kefya's positioning and bonds with and against other nations. With the evident poisoning by a foreign ruler's hidden hand, it had been simple for a man like Eular, known for espousing stronger restrictions with Kefya's neighbors, to be welcomed into the fold.

Never mind that it had been Elikar's own hidden hand who had done the deed—a handful of witnesses had pointed out Ubadrii's comings and goings to Livella's chambers, and with a little help from prejudice and the elf's natural sullen disposition, the accusation had stuck with minimal effort on Elikar's part. Which had been a blessing, because he needed to look strong without being labeled domineering or manipulative. If he had been leading the calls for Ubadrii's arrest all along, then when he turned his attention to directing the Council toward his greater aim, it would've appeared more suspicious than righteous.

But as the blame had fallen on Qedrad without his intervention, many of his colleagues suspected nothing as he laid out what he had "discovered" in the aftermath of their fellow councilor's slaying: that Annika Iatorii and her band of emissaries from King Berenqar had actually been sent to sow discord against Elikar, as he had become privy to Qedrad's aims at cutting Kefya out of trade alliances with Choii Stier. Then, when her group failed to accomplish their slanderous task, the king had hired a scorcher to clear out the evidence against the crown. The fact that Tetamii had taken it upon himself to burn down the Trisarin estate and ram his blade through Iatorii's gut had been the perfect, fortuitous cap on Elikar's lies.

Tano Scrin had been the lone holdout, speaking against Elikar's story as being "too convenient" and "reactionary." At one time, Elikar had anticipated that Relus Vunii and Churi Bleone would stand against him as well, but he should have realized long ago that those two followed the prevailing winds. He knew they had been meeting with Annika and the others, and when they thought there was a chance Elikar would fall, they had been keeping their options open. But now that option was dead and burned away, so they had scurried back to Elikar's side like the good little sycophants they were. Without any additional support on the way, Tano folded, and there was unanimous agreement within the Council for the first time in ages.

An assassination ordered by a neighboring power could not be ignored—war was in the air, and Elikar would be channeling it as he saw fit.

He shuffled the remaining papers on his desk: arrest warrants for Ubadrii Tragala, Niri Trisarin, Mareq Iq'Urlset, and Kymil

Adii. They had scattered after the scorcher's assault on their home, and so far, none of Felona's forces had been able to locate the group. But Elikar wasn't concerned. They had already served their purpose, and their reputation within the city had been reduced to cinders, much like their hideaway. No one would listen to their protestations should they return, so they would either be caught or stay as far away as possible. Either would be fine with him.

A knock at his door caught his attention, and he glanced up to find Grively waiting patiently beyond the threshold. His attendant looked more apprehensive than usual, his grim expression only darkening when Elikar waved him into the room.

"Councilman Thymes," he said, "we've just received word from Achen. One of their coastal swallows arrived this morning, and the message was delivered by a Ghost."

Elikar had given Ias's faithful leave to report directly to Grively—he trusted the man with his life, and it was less risky than allowing himself to be seen with known thieves and cheats. "Out with it, then. I can see on your face that my hired help wasn't as successful in flushing out the rest of Iatorii's group as I had hoped."

"Indeed not, sir," he replied. "In fact, not a single man has returned or sent word ahead to their guild-masters. It is assumed that the entire force was lost."

Grively flinched as he spoke those last words, but it was an unnecessary response. While it was impressive that the lightbloods had apparently put down a pack of blade serpents, Elikar had already won. There was no stopping what was coming, troublesome lightblood or no.

"Shall I reply with a demand of a refund based on their performance, sir?"

"No," Elikar said. "But inquire about passing that credit along toward another job. I'll have need of entire battalions of blade serpents soon enough. The War of Arrival will be entering its second act."

Chapter 35

The Illumined Scale

"So, you're just going to run headlong toward the executioner's ax now?" Adiin asked. "Narrowly escaping this Elikar's hounds the first time wasn't enough of a thrill for you?"

There had been a brief period during the days after the fighting had concluded when the elf had been—well, pleasant wasn't the right word, but perhaps amicable. Rav had initially chalked it up to a battle bond—the two had fought side by side for most of the conflict, after all—but once she and Wymund had settled on traveling to Felona, Adiin's attitude toward her had soured once again.

"I thought I had already made this clear," Rav said, sinching her wool-lined coat tighter. "I have concerns beyond this school, if an idea like that can penetrate the thick air of importance that exists around your skull like a dense fog. If that man was willing to send a small army after me from half a continent away, I need to do what I can to protect my friends who are in the same city with him."

The pair stood near the entrance of the central chamber, where she had collected her and Wymund's things in their respective bags. Wymund and Zylnala were helping put the final touches on repairs to the school's main structure, though Riqu and Nas, with his seemingly endless variety of abilities, were doing much of the heavy lifting. Over the last few days, the landslide had been cleared, an insurmountable pile of rock that Nas literally made disappear beneath the earth, and the building's rough frame had been restored.

Adiin frowned. "And what will you do when your own recklessness kills you, then? You demonstrated quite clearly in the battle that you haven't rid yourself of your desire to flirt with the Illuminated Death. Like it or not, this school is the best place for you."

Rav's face flushed, and she felt the indignation begin to bubble up from her belly, but she caught herself and instead took a breath. Her face softened. Childish though it may be, she could recognize care disguised behind taunts.

"We'll make our way back here once I'm sure everyone is safe," she said. Then, punching Adiin lightly in the shoulder, she added, "Someone has to show you how to be a proper lightblood, anyway. Having to watch out for you against the mercenaries slowed me down. You haven't seen the last of me."

"I should hope not," Riqu shouted as she made her way across the circular platform, with Wymund and Zylnala trailing behind her and Livella and Nas bringing up the rear. "Adiin is almost unbearable when he doesn't have you as a focus for his angst. Like a little boy who doesn't know how to express his feelings."

It was still amazing to witness how easily everyone moved, when days ago Wymund could hardly stand, and everyone else had not been much better. Another mysterious boon granted by Nas, though it should not have been unexpected. He had done much the same for her before, after pulling her from the Marrow Strait in Virdoba. A knitter, orecaller, and rimespinner all in one—the man defied explanation.

Rav expected a barbed retort from Adiin as Riqu reached them, but instead only found a smirk had snaked its way onto his face. Maybe she hadn't had him pinned down from the start—the spoiled rich boy she thought he was wouldn't have allowed someone else to have the final word.

"Is this everything?" Wymund asked, gesturing to the bags at Rav's feet. "Those don't look large enough to have us fully stocked for a return trip. Especially now that there will be three of us." Wymund turned in time to see Nas and Livella join the rest of the group. "Though with everything I've seen this one do, it wouldn't surprise me to find that he could summon full roast dinner out of thin air."

The smallest hint of a smile crept onto Nas's face. "I am afraid that is not in my repertoire, Wymund. But nonetheless, rations will not be a concern."

Does he not eat?

But before Rav could linger too long on that disturbing notion, Zylnala placed a hand on Nas's shoulder and said, "Are you sure we can't convince you to rejoin us after you escort these two to Felona? There's so much you could teach us."

"Please come back," Livella said, her eyes nearly rolling out of her head. "If I have to hear Master Zylnala pine after your teachings, I would at least like to know there's an endpoint in sight."

"We will see where this journey takes me," Nas replied, before turning his gaze to Rav. "For now, I believe the most important place I can be is by her side."

"Yes, yes," Rav said, "your odd obsession with me continues. Can we at least talk about how misplaced that is while we're on the road? We're losing daylight, and while you might be used to the ice, Wymund and I aren't made for trekking across frozen expanses in the dark."

"Then let's be on our way," Nas said, clapping his hands together. His movements were still strange, as if too practiced to be natural.

Riqu gave Wymund an engulfing hug that made Rav's spine ache just to look at it. "Thank you for everything," the woman said. "You helped me find myself down here."

"I'm glad to have helped," he replied, a bit stiffly.

She released him, adding, "Sometimes it takes someone else to remind you what's important. Don't stop looking for yourself, or I'll have to come find you, too."

Wymund laughed. "I'll hold you to that."

As Wymund moved to stand at Nas's side, Zylnala approached Rav. "In many ways, you weren't the model student," he said, an impish smile gracing his face. "But in the way that is most important and enlightening for a teacher, you were invaluable—you taught me something in that battle. Sometimes a student's best instructor is themself."

Rav laughed. "I've been accused of only listening to myself before."

"That's not it," Zylnala replied. "I believe you heard everything that was mentioned to you here. But unlike some others, you needed to learn by experience that sometimes another way of doing things can be as effective as the one with which you are familiar."

"You're right," Rav said with a nod. "It's just difficult to resist the temptation when you know how much is possible by siphoning without a limit. I know of one woman who saved so many lives with her infusions, sacrificing herself to save her friends in the Rebellion of the Commons." Her mind once again drifted back to Annika's tale of her sister, and she felt guilty at invoking it for a contradictory message. "If the goal is that important, wouldn't it be unethical not to do all I could to accomplish it?"

Zylnala shook his head. "Don't you think this woman would have opted for another option if she knew of one? A path that allowed her to save her friends without dying in the process? Keep your mind open to the possibility that disciplined siphoning can accomplish just as much as burning yourself out.

"I don't know how much loss you've experienced in your life," he continued, "but take it from someone who has lost the one that mattered most: life is precious and tenuous enough. There's no need to rush anything along."

"All right, all right," Rav said, smiling despite her tone. "Enough lessons. I'll take the homework assignment, but I'm about to head out for winter break."

"And once you're done ensuring your family's safety, I expect you back here," Zylnala said. "Your education is incomplete, and it would be a waste of your potential to burn out due to a lack of discipline."

"It was pretty impressive how you managed to maintain the blade whips' fastening to the iron plate," Rav said. "That would be a handy trick to have in my back pocket. So if that's on the lesson plan, I'll find the time in my schedule."

"I'll see you then," Zylnala said, shaking her hand before stepping back to join Livella and his pupils.

"So what's next?" Rav asked. "You craft a pillar of ice to push us up through the crevice? I really don't feel up to a climb right now, and I doubt Wymund could make it halfway." Her friend grunted but made no objection.

"Nothing so pedestrian," Nas said. "Gather your things and place your hands on my shoulders."

Rav and Wymund shared a look, then Wymund swallowed hard and said, "If you mean to fly us out of here, I'll need more assurances than the strength of my grip."

"You'll be fine," Nas said. "Try not to panic, though. It makes the process more difficult, and I don't want to struggle more than is required to keep you intact."

"What th-" Rav started to ask before painless, white-gold flames erupted from the ground, licking up every inch of the three of them. The sight made her flinch despite the absence of pain—in fact, they had only resulted in a pleasant warmth—but a firm hand on her back kept her place. She took a deep breath, then exhaled slowly.

Sure, she thought. *Ice, rocks, why not golden flames, too?*

CHAPTER 36

— ◆ —

FELONA

Rav glanced down, only to find that her vision was entirely consumed by the roils and swirls of crackling, radiant fire. It was unlike what she had experienced as she neared the Illuminated Death, with flares of light superimposing themselves over her normal vision. No, this was as if all that existed was an expanse of gold-tinged, white flames—no view of her friends or their belongings, not even a view of her own body.

That proved troubling, for almost as soon as Rav noted the absence of herself from her sight, her sense of self started to unravel. A haze fell over her mind like a smothering blanket, time passed in what could have been measured in either seconds or eternities, and strange thoughts mingled with her own as if they belonged.

There was a fleeting sense of fear for herself, as if she were a separate entity, mixed, oddly with a concern for Riqu. Then, what felt like a struggle for concentration floated to the forefront of her consciousness, but it was distorted—like what was left of Rav's mind had tried to read a text written in Liiashan, and she could only interpret the emotional context of the material instead of its full meaning.

More and more disparate thoughts swirled together, with Rav fighting to maintain who she was against the torrent. Surprisingly, she found herself clinging to thoughts of Kymil, who had grown on her, from a grating nuisance to a friend, then to Annika, the only woman besides her mother who seemed to be able to get under her skin with precision, but who she also knew only wanted the best for her. The similarities to her mother were striking, and it was the settling of her tangled mind on Niri that snapped everything back to focus, silencing the alien thoughts encroaching on her own. She would be seeing her mother soon, and even with all the fraught history that entailed, Rav was looking forward to it.

A deep inhale filled her lungs with humid, salty sea air as the flames subsided, and Rav blinked away the bright midday sunlight. When she could finally take in her surroundings, it did not take long to recognize home. Somehow, the three of them were standing in the copse of seafoam bindweed trees that surrounded the Trisarin estate, their familiar spindly branches casting a cerulean shade over them.

"What just happened?" Wymund asked, staggering forward and patting himself down as if to convince himself his body was truly back.

But before Nas could answer, all curiosity about the wild experience fled from Rav's mind. However he had done it, Nas had deposited them at the rear of the neighborhood, near where she had described her mother's home was located. The same home that was now a blackened husk of its former glory.

She ran toward the ruins of her childhood home without a thought for the danger that might still be waiting for her there. Instead, her mind could only focus on the scorcher she had packed away and sent to this very island. Tetamii Fiadar had not directly been the source of the flames that tormented her recent past, the blaze that nearly claimed the life of an innocent boy, but he had known its effect over her. Had he somehow broken free, only to visit that same fate on Rav's family as retribution?

Rav moved into the ashy remains of a backroom—her bedroom, though she knew that only by her familiarity with the layout. There was no more four poster bed with its lavish canopy, no lush carpeting or finely carved heartfir furniture. There was only char. It filled her nose, bringing tears to her eyes that began to fall too easily. She thought she had time; time to spend sparring in a frozen cave, picking on a spoiled rich boy and learning to flip through the air a little better than she already could.

But that time was gone. Her mother was gone. And now any hope of rekindling the relationship she had cherished as a younger girl, before bullheadedness and hormones led to the fiercest clashes since the War of Arrival, was gone with her.

"Ravael," Wymund said from behind her, his voice soft but booming through the delicate silence all the same.

She turned, planting her face against his chest. Rav was sure he was startled—he had nearly stumbled to the floor—but she would be damned if Wymund was going to see her tears. She had protected him from so much in their time together, and he couldn't see his rock crumble. At least, that was the reason she told herself.

"Ravael," he said again, grabbing her shoulders and pushing her away gently. "They weren't here." As he pulled one of his hands free, Rav heard ruffling papers and looked to find five writs in her friend's gloved hand. They each had a tear at the top, as if they had been nailed in place and torn free.

"These were posted around the side of the house," he continued. "And glancing down the street, it looks like duplicates were made and plastered around."

Rav leafed through the pages: arrest warrants for Mareq, Kymil, and Ubadrii were first, then, oddly, Tetamii Fiadar. She puzzled at the implications of opposing forces being wanted for the same crime—in this instance, conspiracy and assassination of an elected official. But the final page made the breath catch in her throat. There was her mother's name, emblazoned as a criminal for all in Felona to see. It had been Niri's worst nightmare for the Trisarin name to be known with that label, yet she had always fretted it would be Rav's name on the wanted poster.

She dried her eyes on her sleeve. "Where is Annika's writ?" she asked.

Wymund frowned. "I'm not sure. Whatever happened here, I know she wouldn't have left them, especially if Elikar Thymes was targeting them with these lies."

Rav looked down and noticed the councilman's name for the first time. Of course he would attempt to frame them if their plan to bring him to justice failed, that was no surprise. It still made little sense why he would discard his own attack dog, but Rav was obviously missing some key details. Luckily, she had an idea where she might be able to get the answers.

"Come on," she said, moving past Wymund and heading back to the tree line, where Nas had remained. The odd man was crouched beside a tree, where he had found a tuft of shiny, short fur that was of a blue so deep it could be mistaken for black. He had a smile on his face, but Rav could see gears turning rapidly behind his emerald eyes.

"Born and raised so close to these Nyavellan immigrants," Nas said at their approach, never taking his eyes from the great cat's fur. "I wonder if proximity to an ancient fissure site might explain your particularly strong connection to the World Shroud."

"We don't have time for more of your cryptic musings," Rav said, before reaching down and pulling him up by the elbow. "Can you do that thing again? I think I know where our friends have gone."

"How would you know that?" Wymund asked.

"My mother has another estate," Rav said, "out beyond the Tangled Vines and closer to the northern tip of the island. It's an inheritance from her side of the family where we used to spend our summers, but because of some healthy paranoia on my great-uncle's part and an effort to avoid paying taxes to the Council, the ownership trail is more than a bit convoluted.

"She would have taken everyone there if they needed to get out of Felona. Its secret enough that they would be safe from Elikar's dogs, at least for some time."

Nas sighed, brushing the oily fur off his hands so that it drifted back to the ground. "If it's just the length of the island, I should be able to manage another trip."

As she had before, Rav took the time to describe the building's location to the man. It rested on top of limestone bluffs, overlooking the Marrow Strait and across to the mainland. The home was picturesque, and just speaking of it brought back the wonderful smell of sea air that whipped about on the winds buffeting their windows at that elevation. When she finished, she found herself smiling, but Wymund's jaw was clenched.

"Could you manage to make the trip less disconcerting?" Wymund asked, but Nas's only answer was to grip their shoulders before the brilliant white-gold flames consumed them once more.

Minutes or days passed in the conflagration for all Rav could determine, then finally, the trio were deposited at the bottom of an inclined path, lined to either side by waving expanses of light green grasses that stood nearly as high as their boots. Wymund bent forward, gripping his knees and stabilizing himself, ensuring that he was once again corporeal, but Rav was wasting no time—she could already see a silhouette at the top of the hill, standing alone in the garden on the house's eastern face.

Niri's hair whipped with the cliffside breeze, the few strands of dark hair she left unpinned buffeting her face as she turned toward Rav's breakneck footfalls. It felt good to have no need to use subtlety or stealth as she raced upward—regardless of their location, finally, she was home. Daughter crashed into mother, embracing her with both force and tenderness as years of tension and melted against intense relief.

"Ravael . . . ?" Niri said. Cathartic sniffles and laughter passed back and forth between the two of them. Words could be exchanged later, but right then, there could have been no better conversation if it had been penned by Kymil himself.

"I told you they would find us," Kymil said, as if the thought had summoned him. Rav pulled her head up from her mother's shoulder to find the bard stepping out of the house, followed shortly by both Mareq and Ubadrii. The lot of them looked healthy enough considering the state of her family home in Felona, but she knew Kymil would've kept a watchful eye on their draqeshi friend, and Rav thought Ubadrii might even be able to keep his composure while being burned alive.

"She can't stay away," Kymil continued. "I think she might be obsessed with me."

Rav laughed despite herself, blinking tears from her eyes as she tried to glance past them. If she couldn't manage a retort right now, she trusted Annika would have a witty barb in store.

Wymund and Nas finished trudging up the hill, all of their bags in tow, but when Rav glanced toward them to share in their excitement, all she found was concern on Wymund's face. He was looking grimly toward Kymil, and when she followed his gaze, she caught the mirth fading from the bard's face, replaced by pursed lips and a slight bow of the head.

A confusing array of emotions settled over her, the understanding of the old woman's absence finally breaking through the comfort of her mother's arms. She had managed to reunite with one mother after years spent apart and a heart-wrenching moment of assumed loss, only to have the woman who had become a perfect stand-in, steadfast and a pain-in-the-ass in a way she thought only Niri had mastered, ripped away without warning.

"She saved me," Mareq said, his voice heavy in his throat.

"She saved me, too," Kymil said, becoming wistful himself, "in a different way. I hadn't realized every decision in my life to this point had been a reaction, a refutation of a less-than-pleasant upbringing. But Annika helped me see who I am and understand that who I am is enough. I am forever in her debt."

Wymund strode forward, clasping Kymil's arm and then resting a comforting hand on Mareq's shoulder. He always emanated confidence, but something in the way he was carrying himself now felt different. He seemed to carry a sense of purpose that suited him well. A void had been created by Annika's absence, a steady hand on the reigns to provide direction and guidance, and Wymund appeared ready to fill it.

Tears began to fall more freely, growing heavier with the weight of grief. "She shouldn't have sent me away," Rav said. "If I had been there, she would be here with us."

Niri pressed her forehead against her daughter's. "She is here," she said, and turned aside to reveal a headstone, resting atop freshly turned dirt and nestled between deep purple irises spilling over from the garden. Rav crouched down and placed a hand on the cool stone, tracing her fingertips over the words "daughter" and "sister."

"Tell Alauvar, everything that comes next, I do because of the ripples her sacrifice left in its wake," Rav whispered through a tight throat to the grave. "You weren't able to save her, but what she did made damn sure you saved me. She should know that."

She took in a ragged breath, then sighed. "As for you, old woman. I'll give Elikar your regards."

EPILOGUE

ACHEN-KEFYA BORDER

Little lines formed across the steppe, the encampment delineating less and less by nationality as the officers began to sort through the newcomers and integrate them among their own troops. Yofie had spent the better part of a day watching the disparate banners of different Achen mercenary bands—each auburn in color but featuring the emblem of their respective guild-families—intermingle with the Kefyan forces, their long, cerulean and teal flags waving higher and welcoming them into the fold.

Even the blade serpents, who to her eyes seemed more willing to stand among their own kind than stand alongside their guild-family groupings, were separating at the request of Kefyan officers, moving to join this battalion or that within the camp. Yofie could recognize their prideful stances at this distance, but she had come to understand how Slaeth worked, and if enough coin was exchanged, pride was a mutable trait.

She turned, chin-length black hair whipping in the winds that were ever-present at this altitude in the Tesigan Peaks, to find Nasargiel had arrived, just as she had asked. He remained in the same human form in which she had seen him on the dusty expanse of Tellahhr, when he had come to deposit the chegatha's body after the poor creature had been slain for nothing more than defending a fresh water source. She didn't approve of how at ease Nasargiel had seemed in the form then, nor did she like his apparent growing affinity for it—when one could change their appearance on a whim, only fondness could explain a form's repeated use.

"I am here," Nasargiel said, his blond curls more resistant to the gusts but bouncing around his head all the same. "And while I appreciate your continued willingness to engage with me, I do grow tired of having the same conversation."

"Then you will be thrilled," she replied, "because the Assembly has formally called for your excommunication."

Nasargiel's face darkened, his body tensing. "News travels fast, it seems, even across Wellsprings. Though I am surprised at hearing *only* excommunication."

"The Assembly has marked you for death, though I suspect you already knew that. As disagreeable as Opysis was," Yofie said, her mouth curling into a sneer, "I don't believe you would have killed him if you thought there was another option. That's not who you are."

"How kind of you to notice a positive quality among my numerous apostatic traits," Nasargiel said. "But it does beg the question, why send you? I'm not implying you wouldn't be a formidable opponent, but you're no assassin. If the Assembly knows I've bested their most ruthless agent, I would have thought they would send a whole contingent of assailants the next time."

Yofie shook her head. "I'm here of my own accord, Nasargiel."

"Yofie dela Lyranos, going against the Archives Lost?" Nasargiel said, his smirk mirroring his cocked eyebrow. "Perhaps I have become a negative influence."

"I do not move against the Archives Lost," Yofie scoffed, then softened her voice. "But the Assembly is imperfect. Their interpretations do not always match the intention of the texts.

"The sylidae are few," she continued, "and must be protected, bound together so as not to be washed away by whatever forces might threaten us. That is the most important teaching of the

Archives. We cannot afford to sacrifice one of our own, no matter how intent he seems on driving us to ruin.

"Come back to us," she pleaded. "There will be a punishment for your actions, but I know I can talk the Assembly down from execution."

Nasargiel sighed. "Thank you, Yofie. You have remained a faithful friend, despite our differences of opinion. But I do not want you to become tarnished alongside me out of loyalty to a cause I no longer revere."

Those words stung to hear, but she had already expected it to be true. One could only bend the teachings of the Archives Lost so much before they had to acknowledge the truth: He was no longer on their path. Nasargiel had diverged long ago.

"The most important thing is not preserving the sylidae, but existence itself, and everything I do will be in service to that ideal. Otherwise, the Archives, the Assembly—none of it matters." Nasargiel turned away from her, summoning the white-gold flames of rebirth that began to consume his form.

"I've already discovered one woman I believe to a member of the Vanguard—possibly two, if I can ever locate that herb nurse again. She certainly took to our advanced infusions with little difficulty. More are sure to follow, but it is your prerogative to deny the actions of the World Shroud if you so choose. Continue to keep your head below the comforting waters of Nyavelle with the Assembly for as long as you can. Just don't be surprised if the Rupturing boils them away.

"If you change your mind, though," he said, "I will always welcome your company. Treason looks good on you."

Then he was gone, and Yofie was left alone on the butte overlooking the early stirrings of war. A war that could lead to an escalation in World Shroud siphoning, and consequently, the Rupturing. A war that Yofie had already argued to the Assembly would claim Nasargiel's life, convincing them to risk no more of their own people on shortsighted assassination attempts.

But wars could also cleanse, and if events broke in her favor, perhaps the problem of Nasargiel could resolve itself. He was one man¬—powerful, without a doubt—but even he could not stand alone against an army. She just needed to ensure he survived.

The girl he was protecting, the one who had captured his interest so strongly, had aligned powerful forces against her. Yofie didn't believe Nasargiel would be enough to prevent what was coming her way. Once she was crushed beneath the consequences of her actions, maybe Nasargiel would become disabused of his fascination with non-sylidae affairs and return home, where he belonged.

Acknowledgements

Many would think finishing a second book should be easier than the first. I had already proven to myself that I could reach the end of a first draft, which is often the most difficult part, and I had also already successfully navigated *The Light of Shadows* through the editing process and out into the world. But somehow, *A Reckoning of Cinders* was more of a struggle for me, and without the tremendous help of the people below, it might never have been completed. At least, not in a shape worth sharing with readers!

I always have to begin by thanking my wife, Morgan, who not only encouraged and supported me through the process of writing this book, but simultaneously exemplified the best partner and co-parent I could ever ask for. Grayson and I are so fortunate that you continue to put up with us and our obliviousness to the running of a home. It's cute when he does it, but the "being a toddler" excuse stopped working for me a long time ago. Thank you for the continued love and support, and I hope you always feel it is reciprocated.

Next, my parents have continued to be a major source of motivation and assistance on this publishing journey, not the least of which is by their role as babysitters! I know they enjoy it, but I also know how much work toddler-duty can be, and it has been a massive help over the last year in providing time and space to work on this book.

Chase was joined by Michael this year on beta-reading duty, and I want to take a moment here to thank them for their suggestions and insights. Reading a draft is not always as enjoyable as reading a finished product, no matter how much I believe I've polished the manuscript beforehand, and I appreciate the time they spent helping me out.

My editing team shifted a bit for this novel, with Michelle moving up to developmental edits and Clara joining me for the line editing phase. Michelle truly helped me find the emotional core of this story and drove me to breathe more life into the characters, while Clara tightened up my prose and fought back against my at times unnecessarily long sentences. As always, this book would not be what it is without their guidance, and they deserve a round of applause.

Finally, I was lucky to again work with John and Dewi on the artwork in this novel. John once again created a beautiful cover that really turns heads, and Dewi created a new, gorgeous map from an even cruder sample image than I had provided him last time. I look forward to working with them again on Book 3!

Thank You for Reading

As a fantasy author in the self-publishing space, it means the world to me that you've made it this far into the book and haven't wantonly discarded it or buried it at the bottom of your To-Be-Read pile. Without the backing of a major publisher and their marketing team, it makes me happy that you've even found this book among the numerous that are released into the wild every day.

If I could ask a simple favor: it would have a massive impact if you took a minute or two to leave a review online where you purchased your copy. The only way self-published authors can be picked up by the algorithm is by becoming visible with higher review counts, and letting others know that you enjoyed the book might help them discover it as well!

Finally, if you want to keep up with Rav and where her journey goes from here, sign up for my mailing list at blueaxispress.com

I promise not to blow up your inbox, but as the next book nears release in (hopefully) 2025, you can expect a title and cover reveal, as well as a pre-order announcement.

Thank you again, and I hope to see you in the back matter of the sequel!

ABOUT THE AUTHOR

Ryan Elledge is an epic fantasy, science fiction and horror author who has been crafting stories in his mind since he was a child. He has been actively working toward publishing since graduate school, starting with The Light of Shadows, the first novel in the Balance of Shade and Radiance trilogy. He lives with his wife, son, and their dog, Smaug, who is far less ferocious than her namesake. She spends her days in tireless combat with their robotic vacuum, Bilbo.